Ko i

)

I hope you enjoy
the story — I took
the plot from the
Gospels!
God Bless

Dave

Moon's Mercy

a novel

by
David J. Claassen

Copyright 2012
by
David J. Claassen

Cover Photo Courtesy of NASA

ISBN: 9781477598528 (paperback)

Author's web site:
www.daveclaassen.com

Author's e-mail:
djclaassen@gmail.com

Chapter 1

Josh's stomach felt like it was digesting concrete and his pulse hammered painfully in his head. He knew why. He was trying to keep his anger under control, bracing himself for the coming meeting, and it took its toll.

The orange ball of the sun was slowly rising over the horizon behind him. A blue jay was scolding a cat that had strayed into its territory. A maintenance man was adjusting a sprinkler head on the lawn. Josh was oblivious to it all, his eyes locked on the building ahead. He walked by the sign on the manicured lawn that stated in gold letters

ERR Center
2025-2075
50 Years of the Pioneering Spirit

He had an 8 a.m. appointment with the Admiral. The e-mail request late yesterday afternoon hadn't indicated the reason for the meeting. Another e-mail that came through about the same time from an old friend and co-worker had given him the shocking news: the Admiral was going to inform him of the decommissioning of the Dolphdroids on the lunar surface. Decommissioning sounded so innocent, but it wasn't. It was murder, annihilation of a unique species.

The gold-tinted glass pyramid, home to the Extraterrestrial Research and Resources Center, shimmered in the morning light like a giant jewel. Josh glanced at the pinnacle as he approached the main entrance. The Admiral was in his office at the very top, the point of the pyramid providing a clear 360 degree view of the sky from where he sat at his desk. He had always possessed a voracious appetite for making it to the top. Josh recalled the news web site headline at the time of the building's recent dedication, pun obviously intended: "Admiral Imus Hartung at Pinnacle of Success."

The Admiral had certainly chuckled at that one.

Josh knew the Admiral's decision to decommission the Dolphdroids was politically motivated. There would be no changing the Admiral's mind. Still, he was going to try; he had to.

Josh passed the large reflecting pool and its fountain. The massive front door opened automatically. Josh glanced up. The door had to be at least 12 feet tall. As he entered the building he saw the large circular information center straight ahead, an imposing structure of alternating wood, glass, and metal.

"Dr. Christopher!" the receptionist exclaimed in pleasant surprise.

"Good morning, Becky." Josh was certain his forced smile and the artificial tone of his greeting hadn't worked. It had surprised him to see a familiar face, especially Becky. He thought she had been long retired. Her red hair was cut shorter, exposing her ears from which dangled large turquoise earrings. Her makeup fought a losing battle trying to cover the ample supply of wrinkles around her eyes and mouth and a few tributary lines on each cheek trying to connect them. Glancing around the opulent décor and at the several story-high ceiling, Josh added, "Too bad we didn't have a building like this 10 years ago."

"That's for sure," Becky responded as she gave the area a cursory glance. "Isn't it something?"

"How's Jeremy?"

"He's fifteen now. No one ever told me it would be such a challenge raising a teenage grandson." She gave Josh a studied look. "So, what brings you here? I know this isn't a social call."

"I have an appointment with Admiral Hartung."

She punched a key, glanced at her information screen, gave an unconscious nod of acknowledgment and looked at Josh. "You know the way?"

Josh sighed, "No, I'm afraid I don't."

"Silly me, of course you couldn't know the way, this being your first time in the pyramid." She pointed to her left. "There's the circular lift. Insert your I.D. card. It's been programmed to give you entrance and take you to the Admiral's office." Looking at Josh again she added, "It sure is good to see you, Dr. Christopher."

"Good to see you, too, Beck," Josh said as headed down the hallway.

Josh made his way to the lift, a glass cylinder that reached from the floor through the three story ceiling of the atrium, like a giant tubular stalactite and stalagmite come together. When he inserted his I.D. part of the glass rotated, creating an opening. He stepped in and the glass rotated closed. Josh felt himself pressed into his shoes as the lift moved quickly through the ceiling of the atrium. The floors flickered past, the pulsating strobe giving him momentary glimpses at each floor that captured people in mid step and gesture. Soon the cylinder slowed, coming through the final floor into a magnificent office with four giant triangular glass walls that slanted inward and came to a point 30 or so feet above the center of the room.

The cylinder rotated open; Josh stepped out and it closed behind him. The room was filled with the blue haze and the all too familiar odor of cigar smoke. The Admiral was at his desk, his bulk seeming to spread across a majority of the back of the huge oak piece of furniture. As Josh made his way toward the Admiral the man lifted his weight with some effort from his chair, tapped his cigar on the edge of the ashtray, switched it to his left hand, and extended his right hand across the desk. Josh hesitated a moment, then extended his own hand. It was a brief handshake by mutual, unspoken agreement.

"How was your flight?" Imus asked.

"OK," Josh said.

While the Admiral took his time settling back into his chair he said, "Well, Josh, it's been a few years, hasn't it?"

"About 10," Josh said. Then he added, "I believe the last time we were together was when you signed the authorization for the Lunar Dolphdroid Project to be fully implemented."

The Admiral leaned over to tap his cigar on the edge of the ashtray, though Josh noticed there was no ash on the end of the cigar. "Ahhuuumm, you know, I think you're right, Josh." He swept his cigar holding hand in a large gesture to the right and added, "Won't you have a seat?" as he eased his own large frame into the expansive black executive chair.

Josh hesitated and then sat down, his eyes fixed on the Admiral. The man had gained considerable weight in 10 years. The hair had turned white. The years had eroded the facial lines deeper and the chin had a double and was working on a triple manifestation, rolling over the Admiral's collar. Josh remained on the edge of the chair, his back straight, his elbows resting on his knees and his right hand fisted, nestled into the palm of the left. "I understand you've signed the papers to terminate all of the Dolphdroids," he said.

Imus glanced at Josh, cleared his throat with a deep, raspy sound, and focused his attention on the cigar again, tapping it on the edge of the ashtray with the same lack of results as before. He adjusted himself in his chair, took a drag on his cigar and blew the smoke upward. Josh's eyes were beginning to sting. They had recently reversed some long standing smoking laws in the county, obviously to the delight of the Admiral and to the added misery of everyone who had to work with the man. Josh was enjoying watching the Admiral squirm. He waited for him to say something. Finally the Admiral looked at Josh, cleared his throat again, and said, "That's right. As the commissioners see it there's no other way, Josh. I understand what the project has meant to you. The fact is, the project has gotten out of control." Imus shifted his weight forward, the chair creaking in protest. He put both elbows on the desk, folded his hands with the cigar between his thick fingers, and looked at Josh. The Admiral appeared to regain his composure. He had put the ball back into Josh's court.

Josh got up from his chair and walked through the haze to the west window. He could see the old gray three story structure that had been the birthplace of the Dolphdroid project. The sight of it rekindled old memories that fed Josh's anger. Still staring out the window, he said with coldness in his voice, "Imus, you can't simply terminate the entire population of Dolphdroids!"

Imus swiveled in his chair toward the window. "Oh, come on, Josh. They're only robots. Look at it as pulling the plug on an old household appliance that has outlived its usefulness."

Josh turned and looked at the Admiral. People often let slip words they would later regret, words that represent thoughts long harbored. Josh could see by the expression on the Admiral's face that he was nervous. He was really uptight about this meeting. "You know as well as I do, Imus, that they're more than glorified household appliances. Those so-called robots are living beings! They may have a computer for assistance in the thought process, but it's interfaced with a living brain – a dolphin's brain, remember? They're more than a bucket of bolts with a super-sized processing chip. They have living, thinking flesh in them. They're conscious, sentient, feeling beings. You know that!"

"Josh, the matter has already been decided." Imus rocked back in his chair, the cigar between the first two fingers. He had regained his composure; his voice was calm. Rocking unconsciously back and forth he said, "I've called for a press conference to announce the conclusion of LDP. It's set to start in just a few minutes." Glancing at his watch, he added, "I'm going to announce that the project will be terminated in nine months. That's when we'll be initiating our new mining operation on the lunar surface. Grade F workers will be used, although that part is classified. It's estimated by our people that 300 grade F workers should be able to provide lunar resources equivalent to the colony of 150 Dolphdroids, and without all of the problems."

Josh gazed out the window, looking at nothing in particular, and turned to look at the Admiral again. "You're going to throw in the towel on a full line of so-called robots and instead use grade F workers in a work environment that is so inhospitable to humans that grade A wages wouldn't be half enough. You're just preying on their inability to get jobs and you're recreating the sweat shops of centuries ago! The Dolphdroids were created for that kind of environment and can do the heavy work without discomfort. It was the whole reason the program was approved in the first place. You know that as well as I do, Imus." Josh felt a tinge of guilt for arguing from such a mercenary point of view. He had always been motivated by a desire to create the Dolphdroids so that they could delight in simply having been created. Still, Josh was a realist and knew that Imus and others in decision-making positions took a far more pragmatic view.

The Admiral was silent. Josh knew his mind was made up. He heard his own voice turn conciliatory. "We were both part of the great creative process, and no one was more excited about the project than you were. Sure, there's apparently some kind of conflict within the colony, but that's no reason to terminate them. We put brains in those so-called robots, Imus. They're intelligent beings who have lives of their own. They're self-aware, they're free moral agents."

"Don't get philosophical on me," Imus interrupted.

Josh ignored the comment. "They've successfully colonized

the moon, exporting valuable mineral resources and electrical power, just as the project was designed for them to do, and until recently, had meaningful lives." The Admiral sat motionless, just looking at him. Josh turned his gaze from the Admiral and looked out the window again. He knew he was getting nowhere.

Rising from his chair, the Admiral said, "We have a press conference to attend. Please go along with the decision of the commissioners. It will be better for all concerned."

"Correction: You have a press conference to attend. I don't. And it won't be better for all concerned, certainly not for the Dolphdroids. I won't give the impression of endorsing this mass murder." Josh shook his head as he started for the cylinder lift. "I can't believe you expected me to go along with you on this."

The lift opened and Josh stepped in and turned, looking at the big man puffing on his cigar until the lift began its descent. Within a few minutes Josh was walking from the ERR Center and onto the landing port. Fortunately, Becky had been busy with someone else at the information desk, sparing him the need to exchange further pleasantries. He wasn't in the mood. Imus would eventually inform the other commissioners of how uncooperative he had been, polarizing the all-too-powerful group against him – Imus the manipulator.

Josh reached his personal air vehicle, called a PAV, and spoke his name to deactivate the security system. The canopy opened and he climbed in. As the canopy closed he activated the engine and punched in his destination. He waited impatiently for the engine operation gauge to move from red to green, a process that took less than five seconds; then he slammed the throttle forward, lifting the PAV with a shudder and roar that turned the heads of a few employees walking toward the pyramid to begin their day's work. He banked sharply to the right and headed in the direction of his office some twenty miles away. The sun was well above the horizon and flooded the earth with a glow of yellow-orange light, but Josh failed to notice the splendor of the morning. His mind was absorbed in considering the ramifications of what was being announced to the world at Imus' press conference.

Josh shook his head and sighed. This was happening too fast. He hadn't even been notified by Imus' secretary of this morning's appointment until yesterday afternoon at four o'clock. If it hadn't been for a tip-off by Bill Zucker, who worked under Imus, he wouldn't have known the subject of the appointment until he walked into the Admiral's office this morning.

Things simply didn't add up. Normally Imus was more cautious about making major decisions. Five years ago he had agonized for weeks about putting a penal colony in high orbit. In this case he hadn't even asked for any facts, input, or suggestions from Josh or anyone who was connected with the Dolphdroid project. The Admiral knew that no one possessed more knowledge about the Dolphdroids than Josh did, because he was the creator of the Dolphdroids. Why hadn't the Admiral consulted him?

Josh wished that he had stayed for the news conference. What kind of excuse would Imus offer for terminating such a well known, expensive, long-term project? He punched on the televiewer. The image filled the right half of the smoked glass canopy. Imus apparently had given only a short statement; the reporter was already doing a summary.

"...so Dr. Imus Hartung announced the termination of a unique, innovative, and controversial program: the Lunar Dolphdroid Project. Dr. Hartung reported that the production of such raw materials as helium-3 from the lunar colony, a key element in fusion-generated power, as well as the transmission of electrical power, has dropped dramatically and will eventually cease because of what he terms 'the moral malfunction of the Dolphdroid units.' When pressed for details, Dr. Hartung admitted that the problems are essentially behavioral in nature, but that it's placed the decision-making functions of many of the units outside acceptable parameters."

Josh was astonished: a dramatic drop in production? Why hadn't he been notified? He had heard rumors of some problems, but he hadn't been told any details, through the rumor mill or from official channels. He had intended to talk to Imus about it, but his present job assignment left no time during regular hours and he hadn't been able to reach the Admiral after hours, though he had tried several times. If things were this bad, however, Imus should have taken the initiative to inform him.

Josh heard his name coming from the televiewer. "Conspicuous by his absence was the man considered to be the father of the Lunar Dolphdroid Project, often abbreviated LDP, and the original project head, Dr. Joshua Christopher. We'll be working to locate Dr. Christopher to get his take on the decommissioning of the Dolphdroids. Until then, this is Jack Webber for NTS News. Have a good day."

Josh punched off the viewer. He flexed his fingers on the throttle, his jaw tightened, and his face flushed. He took a deep breath. His years as a fighter pilot and then as a research and development head had taught him that an initial knee jerk response prompted by anger usually caused more problems than it solved. The landing port was just ahead. As Josh gently set the craft down on the roof of the office building, a calm determination had come over him. The LDP wasn't over yet, the Dolphdroids' fate was far from sealed, and Imus' troubles had only just begun.

Chapter 2

Josh couldn't remember where he had laid the file he had been studying. He had been having trouble concentrating all morning, unusual for him because he found his current responsibility as head of the Saltwater Reclamation Project interesting and challenging. The team at the Saltwater Reclamation Project – SRP for short – hadn't heard the news about the Dolphdroid project when Josh arrived for work. However, word quickly spread among the workers that their boss was unusually quiet and distracted.

A delivery boy told a researcher about the news conference. Word quickly spread, and soon everyone knew what was occupying their boss's thoughts.

Josh glanced at the time. It was 10:46, and he had done nothing of any consequence so far that morning. He had no idea where he had laid that file. He closed the door to his office, called up his communications file on the computer, highlighted the number he wanted, and clicked on it. Becky came on screen with the usual smile and the expected cheery litany: "Good morning, you've reached the Extraterrestrial Research Cen," then interrupted herself. "Dr. Christopher!"

"Hi, Beck."

Becky became serious. "I'm sorry to hear about the Dolphdroids. I think it's terrible what they're planning to do, just terrible." She bit her lip and asked, "Would you like to speak with Dr. Hartung?"

"No, Beck, I need to talk to Bill Zucker."

"Sure, Dr. Christopher."

"Beck, I'd appreciate it if you wouldn't mention to anyone that I called Bill."

"Of course not." There was loyalty in her voice; then it softened when she added, "I hope things work out for you and the

13

Dolphdroids. Bill's televiewer is notifying him. You should see him in a second."

"Thanks, Beck," Josh said as he leaned back in his chair. It had been a couple of years since he had seen Bill, and that was purely by chance at a researcher's New Year's Eve party.

"Bill Zucker here." When his image came on screen Bill was looking at some paperwork on his desk. Glancing up, he smiled, then his brow furrowed. "Just a minute, Josh."

Bill moved from his desk, leaving a still life of the back of his worn chair for Josh to view. In a moment he returned. "Decided I'd better close the door to the lab; ears are always listening, you know. I saw the news conference. Obviously you didn't have much influence over the Admiral, assuming he gave you the time of day."

"The time of day is about all he gave me, Bill. All he wanted was for me to be a prop at his news conference. Listen, I know I might be putting your job in jeopardy by calling you, but I need more information. I have to start someplace, and you were the logical choice. By the way, thanks for the heads up about the decommissioning."

"No problem, Josh. I don't know anything other than what I e-mailed you. Late yesterday I got a secure e-mail from Imus stating he was going to announce the termination of the project. I fired off the e-mail to you as soon as I heard. It's unbelievable."

"Bill, I know your people keep tabs on all the projects, and that includes the Dolphdroids, so you must have known about the deterioration that's supposed to have led to the decision to kill them off."

Bill ran his fingers through his black hair, a habit that always had clued Josh in that his friend was upset or frustrated. "Josh, I wish I could have kept you assessed of the developments. In fact, we needed your input. No one here's forgotten that the whole project was your baby from the start. The problem is that Hartung came down with this order that the LDP was going classified. We all thought it strange. He even paid a personal visit to impress upon us the seriousness of the decision. Then he specifically mentioned you, 'the original creator of the project,' is the way he referred to you. You weren't on the 'Need to Know' list. When I questioned keeping you out of the information loop in front of a dozen or so of us here he got visibly upset and raised his voice. He said that people should adhere to the new classification of the project or they'd lose their jobs."

Bill took a deep breath and looked intensely into the camera on his monitor. "Josh, you know I would have risked the job and told you if I had known this was all going to lead to the termination of the project and to the killing of the Dolphdroids." Bill shook his head in disbelief. "I just can't believe it," he said, staring off at no particular point in the lab. Then he turned back to the camera and said, "You know I'm behind you one hundred percent on this. I'd never turn my back on you, or on the Dolphdroids, Josh."

"You probably have already jeopardized your job," Josh replied with concern. "Imus has to know you informed me."

"I'm sure he does, but at this point he doesn't want to cause any more of a stir than he already has. Firing me wouldn't be in his best interest. For the time being I think my job's secure. It just doesn't make sense."

Josh shook his head. "No sense whatsoever." Josh leaned forward. "Maybe there's something more to it, but for now what can you tell me about the problem with the Dolphdroids?" He clicked on an icon on his computer and a small window popped up. He clicked "search" and turned his attention back to Bill.

Bill took a deep breath. "Josh, I don't know how much I can tell you. There are a lot of missing pieces to this whole thing. I do know that the Dolphdroids…"

"Bill!"

"What?"

"Are you aware that our conversation is being monitored?"

"No. How do you know? By who?"

"A research assistant gave me this program as a gift. It detects the presence of an eavesdropping worm in my computer or in any computer my computer is linked to. It's sending our conversation to a third party as we speak and they're getting it in real time. The program's indicating that the worm's at your end."

"Who would do that?"

"I'm not sure. I'd better be going. It's good to see you again, Bill. As far as the problem with the Dolphdroids goes, I'll handle it. Tell your wife I said hi. And to whoever is out there listening, I hope you're having a better day than I am." With that Josh abruptly broke the communication and leaned back in his chair.

He hoped he hadn't jeopardized Bill's job.

Josh thought about people who might want to put a spy worm in Bill's computer. He realized that it might not have anything to do with the Lunar Dolphdroid Project, but he also had a strong sense the LDP was the reason for the spy worm. Attempting to focus on his current work was going to be futile. He needed to have another conversation with Hartung. He punched in the numbers on his wrist phone as he walked out of his office. Becky informed him that the Admiral was in his office. "Tell him I want to see him in fifteen minutes," Josh said, then terminated the connection and headed for the elevator that would take him to the landing pad on the roof.

Josh reflected on the benefit of having a personal air vehicle as he streaked across the sky where the only other traffic in the vicinity were two other PAVs, a private helicopter and clouds. Below, traffic traveled like thick blood along the narrow artery of a freeway. The high speed rail cars were becoming more popular, but they didn't take you every place you wanted to go, only where there were tracks. Josh's love of flying made the perk of being given the authorization to purchase a PAV a high point of a year that had been mediocre at best. He had been plodding through several years of mediocrity. Those who knew him called it depression. Whatever it was, he had been this way since his wife's death. Josh gave some thought to the possibility that his being authorized to purchase the PAV might have been a manipulative move to keep this over-the-hill researcher in line.

It seemed to take forever, but Josh eventually found himself back at the ERR Center, standing in front of the receptionist's desk. "He left just minutes ago, Dr. Christopher," Becky said in an apologetic tone. "The Admiral didn't have any appointment on his schedule, so I don't know where he is. He gave no indication where he was going. I could tell he was in a hurry, though. Sorry you had to make the trip for nothing."

"It's OK, Becky. I took a chance flying back here to see him without making an appointment."

"If there's some way I can help, I will," Becky said. "Unfortunately, I can't tell you much. All I know is what the Admiral said at the news conference. After all, I'm just a lowly receptionist."

"What's the rumor mill churning out at the center since the

press conference?" Josh asked, glancing around the glass foyer.

Becky shook her head. "Nothing specific. First, this has come as a big surprise to everyone, as far as I can see. Of course, those working directly on the LDP – and I know a few of them at least on a first name basis – aren't saying much, but I can tell this caught them by surprise, too. They look to me as if they're grieving. Some are saying that the Admiral is caught in some kind of a squeeze, that pressure's being put on him by someone. The ones who are going to pay the price are the Dolphdroids, aren't they? I can't imagine who would want to wipe out the entire colony! I just don't understand."

Josh noticed that her eyes were brimming with tears. He put his hand on hers. "It's a tragedy, there's no doubt about that, but it's a tragedy that hasn't happened yet, Beck. I'm going to take a walk around the center to see if I can get a better sense of what's going on. If the Admiral or anyone else gives you a difficult time about my meandering around, just tell them I didn't ask you for permission." Josh smiled. "Because I didn't." He patted her hand and walked away.

It was a homecoming. Tracy, Tim, and Betty were at the drinking fountain. Sam and Jordan were walking down the hall and spotted Josh at a distance. The warm greetings quickly changed into expressions of surprise and anger over what was happening with the Dolphdroids. Josh was disappointed that no one had any information. Josh discovered that all of the long-time employees had been transferred out of the main control center, away from the most recent and revealing information, with their clearance levels dropped by at least one level. Both the water cooler and hallway conversations were peppered with references to tense relations between the new, more highly classified employees and Josh's old co-workers.

Josh spent about an hour making his way through the office complex, but he avoided the control center where the new employees worked. His conversations bore little fruit in terms of helpful information. Everyone was effectively kept from the day-to-day communication with the Dolphdroids and the telemetry from the colony.

As Josh passed the last intersecting corridor on his way back to the lobby, he saw a familiar stooped form methodically moving a

17

floor polisher back and forth. Josh reached down and unplugged the polisher's cord from the wall socket. The old man fiddled with the switch as his gaze followed the cord with frustration. Suddenly his white eyebrows lifted and smile wrinkles formed around his eyes. "Doc Chris!"

Josh walked up to him, extending his hand. "Oscar, how are you doing?"

The old man shook Josh's hand vigorously. "I'm doing fine, just fine, Doc. I'll tell you, though, it hasn't been the same around here since you left and we moved into this pyramid. I've always believed that cleanliness is next to godliness, but I'm not considered a saint of the mop and bucket. Except for some of your old team, people generally ignore an old cleaning man like me. I'm just an extension of this polisher and the mop and vacuum, sort of a human attachment that makes it all run, the low-powered brain at the end of the handle. You should have made a custodial robot while you were putting together the Dolphdroids, Doc. It would have put me out of a job and out of my misery."

Some things never change, Josh thought, and Oscar was one of those things. It always amazed him that Oscar had more verbal skills than many a public relations person, and more philosophical insight than his old college philosophy professor.

Oscar continued, "This pyramid needs to be populated by more people like you, Doc." He paused, glancing down both ends of the hallway. "It's absolutely ridiculous, and it's criminal what they're doing to your Dolphdroid friends." Oscar's bushy eyebrows lowered as he glanced around to see if there was anyone within earshot. He added in a voice barely above a whisper, "If there's any way an old codger like me can help you out, just let me know, Doc." His eyebrows lifted. He smiled slightly and added, "Knowing you, I suspect you aren't going to be taking all of this lying down. I suspect the Admiral has seen just the beginning of his troubles."

"Thanks a lot for your offer to help, Oscar, but I'm not certain what I'll do. You're right about the Admiral and his coming troubles. I'd better be going."

"You take care of yourself, Doc, and don't wait so long to stop back again. Come when I get off work and we'll go out for a sandwich, just like old times."

Josh nodded, plugged in the polisher, and waved. "See you,

Oscar."

He had only gone a few steps when something Oscar had said prompted an idea. Josh never ceased to be amazed by the human mind and its ability to bring together seemingly unrelated factors that didn't make sense at first but suddenly coalesced into a plan. This was one of those instances. He needed access to the control room if he was going to get any helpful information, and Oscar was his key to gaining that access.

Josh made his way back to the wall outlet and pulled the plug on Oscar's cord again. Oscar's polisher went silent, and he immediately turned toward the outlet. Not surprised to see who the culprit was, he said, "You know, I'm never going to get my work done if you keep doing that."

"Oscar!" Josh said.

The old man smiled broadly and leaned on the handle of his polisher. "I can tell by the tone of your voice that you have a plan and that it involves me. It sure doesn't take you long to come up with an idea. Some things never change. What is it, Doc? How can I be of help?"

Josh drew close to Oscar. Now it was his turn to glance around to see if there was anyone near before he spoke in a low voice. "You always worked second shift. Are you on days now?"

"Nope. I'm still on the second shift, generally speaking. Get most of the cleaning done when there's no one around to get in my way. I came in early today to do some catching up. Usually I'm not in for a few more hours."

Josh nodded. "I really need to see the project logs on the Dolphdroids. Of course they're classified. Technically, I could go to court and get an injunction to gain access to them, but I can't afford the time. Plus, the Admiral would do everything in his power to delay that – probably indefinitely." Josh glanced up and down the corridor. A man and woman were talking at the end Josh had come from. Josh moved closer to Oscar and spoke softly. "Oscar, is there any way that I might be able to get in to see those tapes tonight? Obviously this is highly irregular, the kind of irregularity that could cost you your job."

Oscar's stooped shoulders straightened and his eyes twinkled beneath their bushy brows. He gave a broad smile and replied in a voice barely above a whisper, "Sounds to me we're talking about a little industrial espionage here. Well, it's about time this old codger had some excitement in his life." Oscar paused, glancing at the couple at the other end of the hall, and then pointed his finger at Josh's chest. "Tell you what, you be here about 9:30 tonight at the shipping and receiving door out back. It's kind of a nice evening, and I might just leave that door open for some fresh air while I work nearby. The LDP control center is just down the corridor, and I most likely will be in the middle of cleaning out the wastebaskets so the door will be open. Now, if someone were to come in through the shipping and receiving door and make their way to the control center, they could be in there and out again without my seeing a thing."

Josh smiled and gave Oscar a pat on the shoulder. "I'll be there. Thanks, old friend."

"You know," Oscar said, "I've had top level clearance for years. You need it to clean wastebaskets and toilets in secure areas – isn't that a hoot? But I've never used that clearance for anything other than its intended purpose. I can't think of a better reason to expand my career experience than to save our friends the Dolphdroids. Why, I think of them almost as cousins."

Josh nodded and gave Oscar a couple of pats on the shoulder. "See you tonight."

Chapter 3

When Josh left his house that evening he didn't take his PAV. It was parked in the middle of his backyard by a clump of irises, a temporary solution until he could have a landing pad constructed. He had also decided against ground travel using his gray and black 2068 Plutar that was parked in the garage. Either vehicle might be spotted and identified as his at the Extraterrestrial Research and Resources Center. Instead, Josh made the 10 minute walk to the nearest subtrain station. Only two other people were in the station when he arrived, and no one else came during the 15 minutes until the train arrived and they boarded. It was the last express run until morning to the other side of the city where the ERR Center was located.

Josh had no sooner settled in his seat than the train began to move. He leaned back and tried to sort out his swirling thoughts and feelings. It wasn't at all like him to do what he was about to do. Although he never enjoyed filling out forms and following procedures, he had always tried to work within the system, but this was different. The system wouldn't work for him this time. This was a desperate situation and required desperate measures. He knew that if he didn't do something, the Dolphdroids would be killed.

As the train streaked along his mind drifted back to the first time the idea for the Dolphdroids had come into focus. He had been at his late brother Jim's house playing with his young nephew Tommy, whose favorite toy was a robot that could be programmed to do amazing tasks. Tommy's pet dog Scout would run around the buzzing, whirring robot, barking excitedly. You never knew if the dog was irked by the intrusion of the machine or whether he simply found it entertaining in his own way.

An offhanded remark by Tommy had started Josh thinking those many years ago. "Uncle Josh, I wish we could put Scout's brain into my robot. Then my robot could really love me, because Scout sure does."

It had been one of those "aha!" moments for Josh. The insight had come quickly, but turning it into reality had taken many years, many dollars, and many people. Josh reflected on some of the people who had become like family. There was Les Mesner, a neurosurgeon; robotics specialist Risner Billingston; cybernetics expert Phil Kirkpatrick; computer designer Tony Williams; Jim Roeper, who developed the super magna joint; and Roger Masters, the world's foremost artificial optics expert. There had been many more, but Josh didn't feel like completing the list.

As the subtrain moved swiftly and silently through its dark tunnel with nothing but an occasional tunnel light streaking by in a blur to indicate the train's high speed, Josh smiled. He was thinking about Fido, their first attempt at what was called a "nearly complete" configuration of a computer and brain in a working robot. Fido, the world's first robot canine with the transplanted brain of a fatally-injured dog, had made news when he was created, and again when he was accidentally killed. Fido had functioned so much like a real dog that he was hit by a car while he was chasing it. The incident had provided the concluding comic relief for many a newscast. Josh and his team didn't see the humor in it at the time. Later, at the research group's Christmas party, they had managed to laugh at the irony of what had happened. They hadn't known the original host dog of the brain. They had opted not to use a brain from an elderly pet that needed to be put down because they didn't want any unnecessary emotional attachment, given the odds that the experiment wouldn't work. The host dog had been a street mutt that had also been killed by a car. They had given the robotic dog the name Fido. Fido had been killed within days after the surgery, so little bonding between them and Fido had taken place. Poor Fido had been killed by a car twice.

Josh's thoughts turned to Adam, the team's prototype of all future Dolphdroids. A variety of feelings welled up from somewhere deep in Josh. Adam represented the start of a new life form.

Josh's feelings for Adam were like that of a parent's pride, joy, and love for a child. Josh had done the major work of testing and training Adam, much of it in his own home. The images flashed back clearly: Adam walking around, trying to navigate his six hundred pound, six-foot-five-inch frame safely through the domestic maze of furniture, a sleeping cat, scattered newspapers, and who knows what else. Adam developed a fondness for one particular chair, Josh's favorite. In his attempt to learn as much as possible, Adam had accessed the entertainment archives which stored programs that had been on television a hundred or so years ago. His favorites had been a show about a dolphin named Flipper and one about a robot. That show had been called "Lost in Space."

With sadness Josh reflected on the day Adam shut down because his dolphin brain had died. Production had already started on the 150 Dolphdroids destined for colonization on the moon. To Josh, Adam had been more than a prototype; he had been the patriarch of those Dolphdroids to come. Toward the end Adam even referred to the others as "my children." Now Adam stood silently on display in the Smithsonian West in California, his final resting place, a permanent lying in state with thousands of people parading by each day to view him, not grieving but curious. Josh had never felt good about the final arrangements for Adam, but that's what the powers that be had wanted, and they had gotten their way.

The subtrain slowed, interrupting Josh's nostalgia. This first stop would put him nearest to the Extraterrestrial Research and Resources Center. His throat and stomach muscles tightened, and the palms of his hands became sweaty. Dr. Joshua Christopher was very uncomfortable with the activity he was about to embark upon. Going through proper channels, having his I.D. checked, writing reports on all of his activities: that was how he normally operated. This clandestine visit to obtain highly-classified information was unnerving.

Most of the triangular windows of the ERR Center pyramid were illuminated by the soft glow of security lighting with only a few here and there at full illumination, undoubtedly the rooms where custodial work was taking place. Josh noted that Imus's office, at the pinnacle, was dark. He made his way to the west side of the building, taking a winding sidewalk lined with shrubs, small ponds, and large stones. Walking behind a privacy wall that hid the unseemly side of the building – the air conditioning units, the recycling processor and trash containers – Josh found the door that Oscar had described propped open with a waste can. Entering, Josh spotted Oscar down the corridor, whistling while he methodically moved a mop back and forth. He had undoubtedly cleaned the area a hundred times while he was waiting for Josh to arrive.

"Good evening, Dr. Christopher," Oscar said as he leaned his mop handle outward, removing his tattered gray hat with a grand sweeping motion as he bowed. Replacing the hat, he continued, "Welcome to the Extra Terrestrial Research and Resources Center, the pyramid of the 21st century. Unlike its Egyptian counterparts, this pharaoh dwells here alive. I am one of his slaves." Oscar chuckled at his own attempt at humor, and Josh forced a smile. Oscar had always tried to inject a little comic relief when things got tense back in the old days, but tonight Josh was in no mood for humor.

"Thanks, Oscar, for letting me in. Is there anybody else around?"

"I haven't seen anyone for a couple of hours. There's the usual couple of guards and the other custodians working. You shouldn't be running into any of them."

Josh took a deep breath. "Good. You know, Oscar, I could have won a court injunction to see the data, but I don't have the time to waste. I also don't want to raise suspicions at this point that I'm going to fight the termination of the Dolphdroids."

Oscar waved off the comment, shaking his head. "Doc, you don't have to defend yourself with me. I'm in your corner on this."

"I know, Oscar."

"Now, Doc, in case I see somebody coming, I'll buzz you on your wrist phone. Just interface with my phone so I got your number." Both men coded their wrist phones to exchange the number, placed their wrists near each other, and heard the confirmation beep on Josh's phone.

Josh left Oscar standing in the hall as he headed to the control center. The door to the center was easy to find because Oscar had placed two trash cans in the hall and one was propping the door open.

Josh took a deep breath, glanced both ways, saw no one in the hall, and entered the center. He had never worked on the Dolphdroid project in the new pyramid facility so nothing was familiar. The center of the room had a cluster of desks, each with a monitor that displayed telemetry from the various projects. The screens flickered as the data was updated, and several of the printers were spewing out hard copies of the data. He made his way around the desks, looking for the computers handling the Dolphdroid project. He knew the projects currently under management at the ERR Center: the Life Wheels in near and far orbit, the Mars initiative, and the lunar project that at this point was focused on the Dolphdroid colony.

Josh found a couple of computers that were displaying telemetry from the colony. His heart sank. Much of it was impossible for him to interpret. The layout of the data, some of the abbreviated terms, and the program itself were unfamiliar to him.

When Josh turned his attention to the logging equipment located against the far wall he was relieved. For once he was thankful for cost-cutting measures. The equipment hadn't seen any major upgrades since he had last worked on the project.

Josh sat down at the console and rubbed his hands together as he glanced at the various screens. He put his fingers on the keyboard and held his breath as he typed in his old access code, exhaling in relief when he saw the message, "ACCESS GRANTED."

"Might as well start at the beginning," Josh mumbled to himself, giving a furtive glance over his shoulder as he inputted the first command taking the data back 10 years to when he had left the project. The log consisted of oral reports that Josh bypassed for the written version in the interest of time. Occasionally there were short video clips of the Dolphdroids, usually an outdoor construction project on the lunar surface. Time was precious, but Josh couldn't resist sitting back and watching one of the clips. It felt as if he were watching old video clips of his son when he was small. Feelings of nostalgia bordering on sadness came over him as he looked at a past that was irretrievable. There were scenes of the Dolphdroids digging a foundation hole for a building, blowing up a big rock, and playing catch with what would have been a 300 pound boulder on earth. Josh hit another key. He had to move on.

The log entries for the first couple of years held few surprises because Josh had kept in touch with the people working on the project. He noted with pleasure that the Dolphdroids were able to adjust to their environment by assessing their own needs, the objectives of the project, and the resources their environment provided. Unlike previous robotic applications, the Dolphdroids didn't need installation in their workspace. They were self-determining creatures. The word "colonization" was an apt description for what the Dolphdroids had accomplished. Like their human pioneer counterparts, they could adapt.

The data slowly painted a picture of a collection of 150 bio-mechanical creatures that had developed a fully-functioning society and had established their own unique culture. He felt deep satisfaction because what the Dolphdroids were enjoying had been his dream for them from the beginning.

The material from the last five years was less familiar. His whole world had come apart at the seams when Anne died. They had loved each other deeply, and a part of him had died with her, like an amputation of his heart. The part of him that remained had wanted to go off somewhere and stop living. The demands of the Saltwater Reclamation Project had helped give something of a focus to his life, or perhaps it was more a distraction from thinking about not wanting to live. Watching the data from the last five years, Josh realized that the Salt Water Reclamation Project could never be as large a part of his life as the Dolphdroids had been, and still were.

Another entry came up on the screen and Josh had to smile. The Dolphdroids had developed and installed tiny air tubes by their optical apparatuses, their eyes. An occasional slight blast of compressed gas kept the lunar dust from accumulating on the lenses and obscuring their vision; it was their version of a tear duct. What creativity, he thought, and he delighted in it.

As Josh moved through the log entries he had a sense of growing satisfaction. The production goals for mining lunar minerals, especially the helium-3, were usually exceeded and it became clear that the Dolphdroids needed less support from earth as they became more self-sufficient.

One of the last projects of ERR had been the successful installation of a solar disk array farm that not only supplied electricity for the Dolphdroid colony but allowed them to transmit substantial amounts of energy back to earth. Josh had been aware of the project, but he was intrigued by some of the details in the reports. He finally had to discipline himself to review the data more quickly.

As the log entries continued to scroll by and as he flashed through accompanying images, Josh was delighted again and again at what the Dolphdroids had accomplished. He even chuckled out loud when he saw that they had created furniture, including chairs. They had no physical need to sit down because their brains could go to sleep while their mechanical bodies remained in a standing position, so sitting in chairs was obviously an effort to mimic human society. Art had become a part of their lives as well, with a variety of drawings and paintings appearing on their walls. Zooming in on several of the pieces of art, Josh noted that most were a blend of lunarscapes and seascapes, with the Dolphdroids featured almost always in groups. They were giving expression to long ago memories of a previous life in the sea.

Josh checked the time. He had been reading the data for two hours and he still had two years to go in the data logs to bring him up to the present. Those entries would tell him the most about what had gone wrong. He would find that out in the next hour.

Josh's thoughts were interrupted by the sound of somebody walking down the hallway, just around the corner. It wasn't Oscar's shuffle, Josh knew. It had to be one of the security guards. Josh's heart pounded. He couldn't be found here. He had to hide, but where? The steps echoed more and more loudly as the person came closer. Any moment now the figure would turn the corner.

Chapter 4

The computer screen! The glowing screen would alert the guard! Josh quickly punched the power button on the monitor. Where to hide? The little illumination from the hall kept the room dark enough that he might bump into something and alert the guard. Now the footsteps had turned the corner. His hand was on the corner of a desk. He pushed back the chair and quickly crawled underneath, kneeling, his head low and shoulders hunched so that he would fit. A beam of light danced around the room. Josh held his breath.

"Officer Jim, you checking to see if my garbage cans are behavin' themselves?"

It was Oscar's voice. He was attempting to distract the guard and let Josh know who was interrupting his clandestine activity.

"Oscar, you ol' codger, I'm just doin' my job. You wouldn't want to find me in one of your broom closets taking a nap, now would ya? Besides, you really oughta have this door closed; it's got classified information, you know."

"Don't get your feathers all ruffled. I was in the middle of cleaning the trash out of there. I'll get it closed soon enough. It seems we have more classified information around here than we know what to do with. Hey, my wife sent along a piece of apple pie in my lunch. Want to try it? I can always sneak a piece for myself when I get home."

"Naw, I gotta get up to the next floor and have a look 'round. Maybe some other time. Just try to keep these doors closed, OK?" The man's steps grew fainter, a door closed, and it was quiet.

Josh was aware of someone by the desk! He worked to turn his head in the small confined space and saw that the figure bending over and looking at him was Oscar.

The custodian chuckled. "That is indeed a humbling position for someone of your stature, Dr. Chris."

Josh grunted as he crawled out from under the desk. "Thanks for the rescue," Josh said as he stood.

"No problem. Officer Jim is about as swift as a bean soup sandwich. It doesn't take much to distract the likes of him. He would have taken me up on the pie offer but he was wearing a tracing device. It records wherever he goes throughout his night on the job and keeps a running record on the time. His boss has the custodians wear it every so often to help them maintain healthy work habits. Truth is, Jim stopped looking for work the day he found this job. In fact, he loves work so much he could sit and look at it all day. And I *did* catch him taking a snooze in one of my broom closets a couple of months ago. That little device will help him stay hard at work tonight. He'll be back in an hour or so."

"Thanks, Oscar. That should give me just enough time to do a quick review of the rest of the data. So far I haven't found any substantial reason why they should want to terminate the colony."

"Politics, that's the only reason they need, Doc, just politics. It might have very little to do with the facts of the situation. I smell a skunk in the woodpile, if you want my opinion. Well, I better get back to work and let you get back to playing spy."

"I wish you wouldn't put it that way, Oscar. My stress level is already in the stratosphere."

Oscar patted Josh's shoulder, then slowly headed down the hall. Josh made his way back to the computer, powered up the monitor, and settled back into the chair.

Within a couple of minutes Josh found a video file and activated it. The Dolphdroids were kicking a spherical object back and forth on a marked playing field on the dusty surface of the moon. They were playing a version of soccer!

Another video file that soon followed showed the Dolphdroids seated in various rooms having conversations. The absence of air meant that Josh and his developers had to come up with a means of communication other than simple audio sounds. They settled on low power FM signals; each Dolphdroid possessed a transmitter and receiver. Interfacing the devices with the portion of the dolphin brain that processed the animal's sonar-like capability for object recognition and communication had worked well. The language they used was English.

It pleased Josh that the Dolphdroids were using communication in such a highly developed social manner. It was a level far beyond the initial objective of the program, which was to enable them to have basic exchanges for the purpose of working efficiently together and for group problem-solving. They were using communication to enhance their leisure time. Often, they appeared to be immersed in animated conversation, their faces shifting to different shades of color.

Their faces had been designed with the latest electronic display material, with over a thousand pixels per square inch. These would change color according to the Dolphdroids' emotional responses. The colors on their faces in the video seemed more vivid than when they were first activated. Obviously they were learning to express themselves more effectively.

As Josh moved on through the files he noted hints of power struggles among the Dolphdroids. This was a curious development, because all of them were mechanically created equal. One of the units had been picked at random to be Unit One. Josh had insisted on assigning leadership because, as he had argued with the development team, every society needs order and that comes from a hierarchy of authority. But this was an obvious anomaly. Although Josh and the team had allowed for the development of unique characteristics, the units had also been programmed to work together in equality, with Unit One in charge. It was obvious that some were seeking leadership for the purpose of domination.

The reports of the leadership issues appeared just before another development that shocked Josh. The Dolphdroids had begun to wear clothing!

It appeared in the last video report, which was six months ago. The report revealed a variety of clothing being worn, including hats, capes, long open coats, and robes. All of it appeared to be made of metallic cloth of different colors. The dolphin brains that had been harvested were from male and female terminally ill dolphins and those on life support after an accident, usually with a boat at sea, but the Dolphdroids themselves had been designed without sexual parts. Why the clothing?

As the dates of the entries approached the present, Josh noted the increasing deterioration of the Dolphdroid society. The production from the lunar colony also showed a steady decline. Earth was seeing less and less of the materials that were desperately needed by several defense contractors and by top-priority research and development programs. The last log entries showed a very limited, erratic shipment of raw and processed materials sent to Earth. Of greatest concern was the substantial drop in helium-3 production. In a system where production quotas and dollars called the shots – a system which Josh had fought hard to defeat – this spelled trouble for the Dolphdroids.

Josh leaned forward as he read an entry toward the end of the logs that referred to some kind of religious observances. The focus of this activity seemed to be someone or something called LEM, but beyond that there were no details. It came as a complete surprise to Josh, and was disappointing. The Dolphdroids had been designed for their primary allegiance to be for their human creators.

Having skimmed the last log entry, Josh clicked on the program that had been running when he came into the room. He was overwhelmed by all the developments among the Dolphdroids that he hadn't been aware of: their interest in art, the leadership struggles, the clothing, and the worship of something called LEM. He was also confused about why none of this had been reported to him, or why none of it had made the news. Anthropologists, psychologists, sociologists, and androidologists would all jump at the chance to study the developments he had just reviewed. This was headline material for all kinds of professional journals and magazines, but not a word of it had been released.

There had to be a reason why all of this had been kept under wraps. Had there been a plan to terminate the Dolphdroids for months? The colony had been doing well for over nine years. What had suddenly caused the Eden-like colony to go bad within a few months' time? It would take some effort to sort it all out, but sort it out he would.

Josh stood, his back sore from leaning toward the monitor for so long. He glanced at the computer he had been using to be sure that he was leaving things as he found them, and then he stepped out into the hall. It seemed to take forever to exit the building, the fear of being caught stretching out the seconds. Finally he was at the door Oscar had propped open for him and he took deep breaths of fresh air as he walked briskly to the subtrain station. The ride home provided him with time to review all he had seen in the logs and to come to the same conclusion he had arrived at while still at the computer console: things just didn't add up.

Two days later at 10 in the morning Josh stepped off the lift into the hazy world of Imus Hartung's office. It had been difficult getting this appointment. When he had called yesterday afternoon the Admiral's secretary grumbled that the Admiral was extremely busy, but Josh had insisted. She had put him on hold for what must have been five minutes, long enough for Imus to consider his options. When she came back on the viewer she had grudgingly told Josh he could have 15 minutes of the Admiral's time this morning.

Imus was standing by the east wall gazing out the window with his ever-present cigar in his right hand, poised to take another drag. He turned, saw Josh, put the cigar into his mouth, and pulled another mouthful of polluting smoke which he then proceeded to exhale into the room for Josh to enjoy. Sweeping his hand through the air, causing the smoke to swirl like mini storm clouds, Imus motioned for Josh to take a seat in one of the chairs across from his desk. "Morning, Josh," he mumbled as he slumped down into his desk chair.

As Josh sat he asked, "Admiral, I'd like some clarification on several points. First, exactly what has gone so wrong with the project that it can't be salvaged? Second, why was the LDP classified to the point where the public couldn't be informed of the socio-economic developments among the Dolphdroids including the wearing of clothes, the development of art, and the worship of something called LEM? And in particular, why wasn't I informed of these unfolding events? And third, are all five commissioners really convinced the project needs to be terminated?"

The Admiral leaned forward, elbows on his desk, cigar grasped between his fingers, and asked, "Where did you get this information?"

"That's irrelevant at this point," Josh snapped back.

The Admiral stared at Josh, his face expressionless, then he finally spoke. "Josh, as I said before, the project is, for whatever reasons, classified and I am not at liberty to release any classified information, including why it was classified, nor am I at liberty to discuss classified information." Josh couldn't help but observe that the Admiral's statement was the epitome of high-level bureaucratic double-talk. The Admiral tapped his cigar into the nearly full ashtray on his desk and continued. "The commissioners determined that the anomalies being observed among the Dolphdroids were a serious threat. If the general public knew there was even the possibility of a revolution developing on the lunar surface with the Dolphdroids, panic might result."

"You mean that you informed the commissioners that there was a real danger to the general public with the Dolphdroids?" Josh knew that any information the five commissioners had concerning the Dolphdroid project would have been fed to them by Imus. Each of the five represented a major area of scientific research and development. They possessed significant policy making power as a group. They were all scientists, so the theory was that there would be a spirit of camaraderie while at the same time there was competition for a significant portion of the pot of government funding. It was meant to be a system of checks and balances. In part the system worked: they did keep each other in check. However, there was also the tendency to be a secret, elitist club operating under the informal policy of "I'll scratch your back if you scratch mine, and I'll guard your back if you guard mine." When one commissioner wanted to make a major funding change, it required a majority vote.

"Yes, Josh, of course it was I who informed the other commissioners of the potential threat of the Dolphdroid lunar colony. Things are quite tense right now, both worldwide and here at home. No one – not our own people, our allies, or our potential enemies – needs to see us dealing with a threat from a race of robots gone haywire. You, of all people, know the tremendous threat the Dolphdroids could pose if they were to really turn against us. Plus, we can't afford the loss of lunar productivity. The robots could easily sabotage the whole operation, and have, in fact, already done so."

"Then why did you decide to go public with the termination?" Josh asked, leaning back in his chair.

The Admiral took another pull on his cigar, tilted his head back, and exhaled, watching the smoke form a cloud above their heads. "The commissioners felt the lid was about to come off this thing, so we decided it would be best to let the public know what might have to happen, let them know we maintain the upper hand when it comes to robots in our society." The Admiral leaned back in his chair. "And don't try to do any arm twisting with the other commissioners, including your own boss on the water reclamation project. I remind you it's a criminal offense to put pressure on a federally-appointed commissioner, which you're getting mighty close to doing with me, Josh. The only reason I was willing to see you this morning is that we've traveled many a mile together over the years and I thought I owed you this much."

Ignoring the Admiral's effort to threaten and patronize him, Josh asked, "So there was a vote by the commissioners to approve this whole thing. Was it unanimous?"

The Admiral shook his head. "I'm not at liberty to say. That's privileged information." His evasive response led Josh to believe that maybe one or two had voted against termination, including perhaps his own boss.

Getting up from his chair, Josh shoved his hands into his pockets as he walked over to the northern wall. Without looking at the Admiral, he asked, "What kind of effort has gone into correcting these so-called anomalies of the Dolphdroids?"

The Admiral coughed and cleared his throat. "As you know, Josh, we haven't had much of a human contingent on the lunar surface for quite some time. In fact, the only active human colony was the Earthshine Resort Center, and we quietly shut that down a couple of months ago; we thought it would be too dangerous, what with the Dolphdroids acting up and all. We wouldn't have been able to keep the lid on that much longer because several of the congressmen go there for vacations. As of now there are no humans on the lunar surface, and until this gets cleared up none will be authorized to travel there. We just don't know what the Dolphdroids are capable of. We could end up with a hostage situation, or worse."

Josh spun around. "That's all pure conjecture based on fear or, more likely, based on a hidden agenda to get rid of the Dolphdroids. Have you tried communicating with them? Have you sent anyone to the lunar surface to meet with them and negotiate, if necessary? Did you do anything at all to try to solve this supposed problem?"

Imus got up from his chair, moved to a corner of his desk, and leaned against it with his arms crossed and a look of resignation on his face. Maybe Josh had worn the man down enough to get something of a straight answer. Imus looked at Josh and said, "About three months ago we sent Ross Bodanis along on one of the auto-pilot freight ships that regularly goes to pick up the production materials. He was instructed to determine the problem and try to work things out. Then about a month ago we sent…"

"Wait a minute," Josh interrupted, "what was Bodanis able to do?" Josh knew Bodanis; he was a good man. He should have had some kind of positive impact on the situation.

With a look of annoyance at the interruption, Imus sighed. "Bodanis reported a growing awareness among the Dolphdroids of being autonomous, far beyond the smart machines we intended them to be. The reports Bodanis was sending back indicated that he might negotiate too much away, giving the Dolphdroids the freedom and flexibility to make choices that went well beyond the performance guidelines we set up for them. We pulled Bodanis off the assignment and brought him back on the next freight vessel."

"Performance guidelines? I don't recall any performance guidelines. When we activated the Dolphdroids they were given what we called a 'Contract of Life' but nothing about specific performance guidelines. And this business of the Dolphdroids being 'smart machines' is ridiculous. Where did you get a term like that? They're living creatures, sentient beings. We gave them real life, a self-conscious awareness. They're a unique life form, the likes of which the world has never seen before." Josh paused and tried to regain control over his emotions. The best thing he could do now was to glean some new information from the man, and blowing up in anger was not the way to get it. Josh took a deep breath. "So, who did you send after Ross Bodanis?"

"Jake Stawson. We sent Jake Stawson on the next freighter."

Josh didn't recognize the name. Stawson wasn't one of the original design team members or anyone remotely connected with the team; Josh knew them all.

"Who's Jake Stawson?"

"He's had some training in neutralizing underground movements and straightening out situations that have resisted previous efforts. But just to show you how bad things have gotten…" Imus paused. "He had to terminate one of the Dolphdroids."

Chapter 5

Josh stared at the Admiral in disbelief. Imus avoided Josh's gaze, busying himself with relighting his cigar and sending a fresh puff of smoke billowing toward the ceiling.

Josh managed to keep his voice calm. "You mean to say that you found it necessary to kill a Dolphdroid?"

"If you insist on using the term 'kill' I guess that's your prerogative. Yes, the unit had to be terminated. It's just one of the many indicators of how serious the whole issue has become. The project is no longer viable for producing lunar resources."

Josh decided any additional conversation with the Admiral would be unproductive, and he turned toward the circular lift. Then he remembered he'd have to ask the Admiral to bring the lift up, another way the Admiral retained control. You couldn't even leave his office in a huff without his allowing you to do so. Josh stood in front of the spot where the lift would rise through the floor. Without turning around, Josh said, "Call for the lift, Admiral. I need to be going." Imus activated a control under the edge of his desk. Within seconds the lift came up through the floor.

Josh turned and said, "I brought the Dolphdroids into existence. I won't let go of this as easily as you had hoped, Imus."

"Don't jeopardize the rest of your career and your retirement by trying to beat the system. You can't do it. No one ever does. Go with the flow on this one, Josh. I mean it: back off."

Josh stepped into the lift and kept his eyes locked on the Admiral as the lift took him down through the floor and out of Imus' sight.

Josh left the pyramid without talking to anyone and within minutes was deep in thought as his PAV cut through the sky above the city. A plan was forming in his mind. He had a year's sabbatical coming to him; he would take it now and devote full time to saving the Dolphdroids. Richard Ellis was capable of heading the Saltwater Reclamation Project. The final decision would be up to Dr. Randolf Maxim, commonly referred to as Dr. Max, the commissioner under whose jurisdiction the SRP fell. The request for the sabbatical could be on Dr. Max's desk in the morning. Josh wasn't worried. It was clear in his contract that he was long overdue for a sabbatical and could take it at his discretion.

Banking his craft sharply to the right, Josh changed the computer's heading to his office. The mechanics of changing course only intruded on his thoughts for a moment. He would get together with former co-workers Bill Zucker and Ross Bodanis to get a clearer, less prejudiced perspective on the situation. A talk with Jake Stawson was also in order. He wanted to meet the man who found it necessary to kill one of the Dolphdroids. Grief and anger welled up within Josh. He considered whether he could handle a meeting with Stawson in an appropriate manner, without doing something to the man that he would later regret.

Josh knew that there were many missing pieces and that Imus was only giving the press and him part of the picture. What was clear to Josh was that events were unfolding in such a way that the Admiral would have the Dolphdroids terminated on schedule. Josh's heart was pounding and his face was flushed. He hadn't been this angry in years. He realized that he hadn't felt any emotion strongly in years, not since the death of Anne. Now another part of his life was being threatened. He had felt powerless when she died, but this was different. He would not stand by and let the Dolphdroids be destroyed!

Two days passed before Josh could line up a meeting with Bill Zucker and Ross Bodanis at a restaurant 50 miles from the Extraterrestrial Research and Resources Center. Bill and Ross walked in together; Josh was already on his second cup of coffee, having arrived 15 minutes earlier. He stood when the two men reached his table. Bill had a worried look that a forced smile couldn't conceal as he shook Josh's hand and said, "This must be a great restaurant, if it's worth the long trip." The man's black hair was thinning and the lines around his mouth were deeply etched. His glasses had thick lenses which he pushed up further on his nose with an index finger as he glanced over at Ross, giving his partner a chance to greet their old friend.

Ross extended his hand to Josh and quipped, "I'll tell you, he wouldn't be so quick to suggest lunch way out in the middle of nowhere if he had to drive a car like the rest of us mere mortals. How long did it take you in your new PAV, Josh, all of 15 minutes?" Ross was a big man, about six feet four inches tall and weighing somewhere around 300 pounds. Josh had often kidded him in the early years about being his bodyguard. Shirts always seemed to be one size too small on him, the buttons straining to hold things together. He had a gruff exterior but a heart of gold. He also had a way with people once he got to know them and they could see more than just his size. Still, he was a man with an independent streak. That's why it hadn't surprised Josh that Bodanis had been selected to ride a pilotless freighter ship to check out the Dolphdroids' situation. Not many people can stand several days in space without a view or any human company, all the time knowing you're shooting thousands of miles an hour away from earth. Bodanis was probably the only upper management person at the ERR Center willing to take a freighter to the moon.

Josh replied, "I'm not certain it was worth a 50 mile trip, but I suspect it's preferable to the commissary food at the research center, though it's been ages since I've eaten there." Josh motioned for the men to take a seat. Bill slid into the booth beside Josh. Ross took additional time to squeeze his bulk into the seat on the other side of the booth.

"The food might be better here than at the commissary," Ross said, "but all we'd risk there would be indigestion. Coming here, to see you, we risk losing our jobs."

"Unfortunately, he's got it figured about right, Josh," Bill stated as he glanced at the specials displayed on the bright orange menu screen being shown on the wall at the end of their table. Looking back at Josh, Bill added, "You're not very popular at the ERR Center these days."

"Hence the 50 mile ride to enjoy lunch with me," Josh added.

The waiter arrived and took their orders. When he left Josh shoved the salt and pepper shakers against the wall beneath the menu display. He glanced to his left at Bill, then across the table at Ross. Both men were silent; they were done with the pleasantries of conversation and ready to hear what their friend had to say.

"Ross, you were with the Dolphdroids. What happened?" Josh leaned forward, anxious to hear his old friend's reply.

Ross took a deep breath, expanding his already expansive chest, and then slowly exhaled. He shifted his water glass, shaking his head. "It was something to see, Josh. I mean, their society had developed way beyond what I would ever have imagined." His eyes locked with Josh's and he continued. "Your dream of creating a new intelligent species of life that could work and play together has happened. They're doing a lot more than mining lunar minerals and sending energy to earth. They're creating social traditions, have a sense of history, are developing plans for the future, enjoy art, and seem to really get a lot out of relating to each other."

The waiter returned with their beverages. Bill left his tea where the waiter had placed it. Josh repositioned his cup of coffee on the table but didn't take a sip. Ross grasped his milkshake, and began to drink, gulping about half of it before putting the large glass down. He said, "I guess what amazed me the most, though, was how they adapted human characteristics that we didn't necessarily program into them."

"For instance?" Josh asked.

Ross smiled at Josh's impatience. "For instance, the rooms in their modules. We figured they would live in a minimum environment because their biological needs were so few. After all, we're talking about a few pounds of living dolphin brain tissue with the rest made of steel, hoses, hydraulics, brain chips, etc. At any rate, they have rooms with furniture and pictures on the walls. They take refreshment breaks during work, like our coffee breaks, and, get this, they wear clothes! Now, doesn't that beat all?"

"They've done a remarkable job of colonizing the lunar surface, Josh," Bill interjected. "They've made far more than the necessary adjustments needed to get work done effectively and efficiently. They've expressed themselves in many non-essential ways. Art, philosophy, and even some hint of religion seem to be part of what's happening up there."

During Ross' description Josh's expression had changed from concern to curiosity. Now it showed concern again as he asked, "What about the slowdown in production?"

Bill shook his head. "There certainly has been a decline in production and an increase in trouble, no doubt about that. But it doesn't add up. The team has been meeting more times than I can count and going over the data again and again. We've sought dialogue with the Dolphdroids. Ross's input has been helpful since he made a personal inspection. All in all I'd say we felt we had a handle on it, but…"

"Then out of the blue, wham!" Ross interrupted. "The Admiral comes down with the decision to terminate the project. Can you believe it? I just wish he had gone to the lunar surface himself to see the way things are. It was bad enough that he slapped the high security rating on the project so we couldn't even inform you, let alone consult with you, but then there was his announcement about terminating the Dolphdroids. It will mean the annihilation of an entire race of an intelligent life-form, all 150 of them! Take it from me, it's impossible to be in their colony very long before you realize that these creatures are more than machines doing a job."

"One hundred and forty-nine," Josh corrected.

"Yeah, 149," Ross said.

"What trouble did you observe that would lead to Imus' order to terminate?" Josh asked.

Ross was starting to reply when the waiter returned with the condiments and Ross's double sandwich. He left and Ross took another long drink from his shake. He continued as he eyed the sandwich. "There's trouble, no doubt about that. Up until about a year ago everything was going smoothly, according to all the reports we got from actual visitors, as well as from the telemetry. The Dolphdroids had a tremendous spirit of cooperation. Everyone had a job to do and did it, and they enjoyed life in the process."

Ross grasped his sandwich with both hands and took a large bite out of it. The two men waited. Ross washed it down with a swig from his shake and then continued. "When I observed the colony in person I was pleased to see that we had an accurate assessment of the situation. But being there gave me a better handle on the personalities, power plays, and the politicking going on. Things were deteriorating, there's no doubt about that. Every Dolphdroid I got to see had a distinct tendency to be self-centered with a 'what's in it for me?' attitude. The spirit of cooperation had been replaced by competition. The focus was on their own individual feelings instead of the feelings of others. I know I sound like some kind of psychologist, but I just couldn't help noticing stuff like that. I mean, they're acting like my three brothers and I did while we were growing up, and that's not good, let me tell you!"

"Anything else?" Josh asked..

Ross shook his head, "That pretty well sums it up. It's scary. Too bad we didn't program them so they couldn't be selfish or do any of the other things we don't like ourselves doing."

Bill responded. "You know as well as anybody, Ross. We didn't want to limit the Dolphdroids' power of choice. Putting limitations on them would have created a mental prison for them. The computer interface was only to enhance the IQ of their dolphin brains, not limit how they thought and what they decided to do. They needed the same kind of freedom they originally had at sea, as dolphins. My own guess, Josh, is that they possess some latent negative characteristics from their lives as dolphins that are a part of who they are as Dolphdroids. We discussed it before, when we were developing the project, that the Dolphdroids would be capable of both moral and immoral behavior because of their power to choose."

"And that's where I think we goofed up," Ross said. "Computers do what they're programmed to do, unless of course the programmer messes up, and then the old adage comes into play: 'Garbage in, garbage out.' But now you're talking about the imperfect human factor."

The waiter arrived with the rest of their food. After he left, Ross continued. "Computers use zeros and ones, miniature on/off switches, black and white, yes or no. There's no gray area. It's the perfect world of math. Now we've got ourselves all kinds of gray areas, and worse, because we put some gray matter in the Dolphdroids. In hindsight maybe we should have at least built in a sub-routine to keep their thinking in line."

Josh smiled slightly. "You're repeating conversations we had years ago, when we were developing the Dolphdroid concept. But what has happened is precisely the result of the risk we knew we were taking when we created the Dolphdroids with the power to make choices. We had to make them free moral agents if we were to give them the ability to give and receive love."

"But love and hate seem to be throwing a monkey wrench into their ability to do their work," Ross said.

"It's never been just about the work they could do," Bill reminded Ross.

Ross sighed. "I know, I know." He picked up his sandwich for another bite.

The waiter came back and refilled Josh's cup. When the waiter moved to another table Josh leaned forward with his elbows on the table and folded his hands. His voice was soft and reflective. "From the very beginning I wanted the Dolphdroids to experience life to the fullest, and that meant giving them the ability to love and be loved. I was thrilled at the idea of being able to give them that gift. Yes, the risk was great. Love, by its very definition, means that the one doing the loving can choose not to love and the one receiving the love can choose not to receive being loved. That's what makes love so valuable a commodity. By giving them the ability to be good to each other, we also gave them the ability to be bad to each other. But without that ultimate choice there is no real meaning to life. I wanted the Dolphdroids' lives to have meaning." Josh looked at both men and then gave his attention to his plate of food.

Bill put down his fork. Taking a sip of his tea, he said, "I remember how you explained to the team one day that you can program your computer to say, 'I love you,' but it's completely meaningless because you programmed it to say the words."

Ross put up his hand and said, "OK, OK. I recall a similar conversation in the early days, when Adam was still a pile of nuts and bolts on the machinist's work table. Yeah, you're right. It's got to be this way so let's get on with it."

"What about the clothes?" Josh asked. "The Dolphdroids didn't need them when they were performing within the parameters of their created purpose. Their individual identities were secure and each had a sense of unique completeness and purpose. Now they wear clothes?"

"Yeah," Ross replied, "when they started doing their own thing, they started playing dress-up."

"But why?" Josh asked.

"Beats me," Ross added.

"I've been thinking about that," Bill said. "Ross is right, they started wearing clothes about the time we noted the first problems with their performance. It's occurred to me that when they began making personal choices they knew they were in conflict with their initially designed purpose. They moved beyond being self-aware to being self-conscious."

Josh looked at Ross, staring at him for a few moments before speaking. "You might be on to something. Little children aren't afraid of being naked. They'll parade around nude, not giving it a second thought and actually delighting in being free from the confinement of clothes. They have no shame."

"But then children also play dress-up, pretending they're someone they're not," added Bill.

"True," Josh responded. "It seems the Dolphdroids have lost their innocence. Wearing clothes may be a way for them to hide themselves from each other, out of a sense of shame. It could also be a way for them to project an image, pretending like a child does when playing dress-up."

"Is this getting too deep for you, Ross?" Bill chided.

Ross put down his glass after draining the last of the shake. "I was just going to say something to bring this conversation back down to earth. Let me get this straight. Josh, you don't believe we could have prevented what has happened to the Dolphdroids, no neat little sub-routine to keep them innocent and perfect?"

"That's right."

Ross sighed, then said, "Well, just so you don't think everything's bleak, I had a chance to talk with several of the Dolphdroids on my little excursion, and some are pretty much OK characters. Sure, there's several who have lost their focus of why they were created, but most of them still have a good grasp of who they are and what they're supposed to be doing. Of course, from what I could gather none of them are perfect anymore. Most, I would say, are sort of in the middle on the good-to-bad scale. There's an unpredictability about the behavior of even the so-called good ones."

Josh asked, "You apparently got to know the Dolphdroids on more or less an individual basis. Do you know anything about the one Jake Stawson killed?"

"Eric was the one he killed, and I can't, for the life of me, figure out what could have put Stawson in a position to do such a thing. Eric was a good unit, pretty much a saint, if Dolphdroids can be saints. He'd been one of the prime movers and shakers in the pro-earth group, as they call themselves."

"Pro-earth group?" Josh looked at both the men.

Bill nodded toward Ross. "It's the term he came up with after his trip to the lunar surface. There's a number of Dolphdroids who appear to be very dedicated to their place of origin. I think it's an apt phrase. Unfortunately we don't have any details about Eric's death. Stawson filed his report directly to Imus, and Imus instructed him to leave it out of his written report, so it's their little secret."

"It would seem," observed Josh, "that the more we dig for answers the more questions we unearth."

Ross slowly shook his head. "I just can't believe that there could be any situation that would have justified killing Eric. I have a feeling Stawson knew there was going to be at least one dead Dolphdroid by the time his visit was over. Imus probably used this to seal the Dolphdroids' fate."

All three were quiet as they picked at their food; even Ross's appetite was gone. Josh finally spoke. "I believe there's an unknown player in this whole scenario who's orchestrating a lot of what has happened and will happen. Someone has a vested interest in seeing the Dolphdroid colony terminated, and I'm going to find out who it is."

Chapter 6

Jake Stawson appeared on Josh's computer screen. It was now 3:30 p.m., the day after Josh's luncheon with Ross and Bill. He had tried several times to connect with Stawson without result. His wife had told Josh this morning that he had been up half the night on a project and that she would not wake him for any reason. Now, halfway through the afternoon, Josh had called back. Finally he had the man on screen, a large man bulked up with muscle, not fat. His head, topped with thinning gray hair, seemed to sit directly on his shoulders without benefit of any visible neck. He did not look rested, and his manners matched his tough look. "Yeah, what do you want?"

"This is Josh Christopher."

"I know that. If it's about the LDP, you're barking up the wrong tree."

"Let me bark, OK? I think I have the right tree," Josh said. "I'd really like to see you and ask a few questions about what happened when you tried to correct the problems on the lunar surface."

An impatient look came over Stawson's face. "Look, Doc, you know that all this stuff with the LDP is classified. Go talk to ol' Admiral Imus if you need to know more. All I can say is I was told to try and straighten things out and I did my job. Sometimes a little force is the only way to communicate, like hitting the proverbial mule over the head with a board to get its attention. Unfortunately your Dolphdroids were a little thick-headed and pushed me too far."

"How do you mean, pushed you too far? How exactly did that happen? I understand it was one of the pro-earth Dolphdroids

47

you killed. Being forced to kill a Dolphdroid that was anti-earth would make some sense, but killing a pro-earth Dolphdroid? That doesn't make any sense whatsoever." Josh felt his face flush with anger. He had to keep his cool. He knew his tone was becoming accusatory, but he couldn't help himself. "Why would you have a run-in with a Dolphdroid who was in favor of maintaining the current working relationship with earth?"

"Pro-earth? That's a new term to me," Stawson said with a huff. He took a deep breath. "Listen, Doc, I don't think this conversation is going anyplace worthwhile. I did my job. Things happen. I'm not associated with the Admiral anymore. If you want more answers, you'll have to see him." Josh sensed Stawson was about to break the connection, but then the man apparently changed his mind. He leaned forward and said in just above a whisper, "Let me give you some free advice, Doc. Drop it. Just let the project die. You can't fight this. You'll get ground up as fine as talcum powder. The only thing you'll gain by poking around on this is trouble, lots of trouble, for you and for anyone associated with you. Back off, just back off." Stawson's image disappeared. The conversation was over.

Josh got up and walked over to the window. The sun was going behind a cloud; a robin was searching for a worm under a tree. The images failed to register; his thoughts occupied his full attention. Now he knew why Jake Stawson had failed so miserably at working things out with the Dolphdroids. Imus had sent a man who solved everything by force. Imus was an astute judge of character; it was one of his few redeeming qualities. You don't get to the pinnacle of the ERR Center without putting the right people in the right places to do a job the right way, or at least the way you want it done. Imus knew exactly what he was doing when he chose Stawson for the mission to the lunar colony.

Josh found it difficult to believe that Imus would do something like that, after having overseen the Dolphdroid Project for so many years. There really wasn't any other explanation, however. There was little doubt that Imus knew what the outcome would be when he sent Stawson to the moon. Stawson was anything but a mediator. Sending him to the colony was like sending a pyromaniac to explore a gasoline spill in a tinder-dry forest. Someone must be putting pressure on Imus, a great deal of pressure. Josh shook his head in bewilderment. The more he learned, the more confusing things became. He would have to check into the background of Jake Stawson to find out who employed him before the Admiral and who he was working for now. Apparently Stawson's involvement in the Dolphdroid Project had been short-term, just long enough to do some real damage. Josh's thoughts were interrupted by someone at the front door.

"Rob!" Josh exclaimed when he opened the door.

"Hi, Dad." Josh stood, his hand still grasping the edge of the open door, looking at his son. Rob's eyes glanced about the room behind his father, and then said with a hint of awkwardness, "Can I come in?"

"Oh, yes, of course, come in." Josh opened the door wider, stepping aside to let Rob enter. The alienation between the two had grown deeper when Rob's mother had died five years earlier. Their relationship, however, had not been good even before her death. Rob had taken an anti-establishment, pro-universal life, pro-environment stance. Josh's Dolphdroid Project was at the heart of the debate. The politically correct view was that it was wrong to harvest the brains of dolphins, even critically injured dolphins, and put them into robots. The view of the ERR Center, argued persuasively by Admiral Hartung, was that only brains from dolphins that were certain to die were used in the project. It had been Josh's concept from the beginning and it was he who had shepherded the project through the research and development stages to its being fully implemented. Imus, however, had taken much of the heat, doing most of the interviews, appearing at the protest marches to give the other point of view.

Josh was able to stay in the background of the controversy, but he still had taken his share of the criticism. Rob had been caught in the middle, wanting to be part of the "Renew Our Earth" movement but also wanting to stand by his father. In the end he realized he couldn't do both, and the distance between father and son grew.

Seeing news reports of Rob participating in the demonstrations against the Dolphdroid Project had hurt Josh deeply, although he never stopped loving his son. After Rob's marriage to Heather and the birth of their son Randy, Josh attempted to rebuild their relationship, but Rob had resisted. Josh was at least grateful that Rob allowed him to spend some time with his grandson. However, Josh usually avoided stopping by the house when Rob was around; it was an unspoken agreement between the two.

Rob sat down on the edge of the couch, leaning forward with his elbows on his knees, looking at the carpet as he began to speak. "Dad, I know I've been a royal pain to you over the past years, especially after Mom's death." He glanced at his dad, then focused on the carpet again. "I guess maybe I've mellowed a little bit as I've grown older. Things that used to be black and white now have changed to shades of gray."

"It's so good to see you again, Rob," Josh interrupted, wanting to save his son the embarrassment of an apology. He was just glad to have his son in the same room with him.

"Please, Dad, just let me finish my little speech," Rob said, turning his attention from the carpet to his father again. "I've been following the news reports about the Dolphdroid situation. At some point, some time ago, actually, I began to see the Dolphdroids as living beings, creatures with inherent value and rights. Maybe it was when I saw those first reports of their settlement on the moon, I don't know. I couldn't admit it to you then, because I wasn't able to admit it to myself."

Josh had been standing but now he took a seat in the large chair across from the sofa. Rob shifted his weight, settling into a more comfortable position. "I guess things began to come into focus for me when I was out in California on a week's assignment. I had some free time so I toured the Smithsonian West. I knew Adam was on display there, so I walked by the display just to take a look at him. I was surprised by my reaction. Coming around the corner and seeing him behind those ropes like some department store mannequin prompted feelings I can't even really put into words. I know they removed the dolphin brain after it died, but when I saw him standing there with a couple of flashing LEDs, he still seemed alive."

"Well, in a sense he still is. The computer portion of his mental processing was never fully deactivated. In fact, he walked on his own power into that display booth. Once he was in place, I gave him the command to go into an extended shutdown mode. He can remain in that suspended state indefinitely." Josh stopped talking. He had to let Rob finish.

Rob continued, "I still don't know if I believe that the creation of the Dolphdroids was wise, or even moral. The fact is they now exist, and I think they have a right to continue to exist. I know you've believed that from the beginning. When Admiral Hartung held that news conference, I realized how I really feel. It made me incredibly angry when I heard what he said. I could only imagine how you felt. Dad, I've come to believe that the Dolphdroids are a new life form and need protecting. Besides..." Rob paused, glanced off into the distance, and then locked eyes with his father. "I think it's time I stopped acting like a real jerk and started acting like a son again."

Josh felt a happiness that he hadn't experienced for years. He had lost his wife through death and his son through alienation. Now he had his son back again. For the next hour Josh filled his son in on all that had happened since the early morning appointment at the Admiral's office. The negative events and experiences that he related were balanced by the thrill of sharing them with his son from whom he had been alienated so long.

Before he left, Rob informed his father that he had already checked with Heather and that he was invited over for dinner that evening. Josh didn't have to think twice about the invitation and immediately accepted.

Within an hour Josh was on his way to Rob's place. It filled him with anticipation, a feeling he realized he hadn't experienced in any significant way for years.

"Hi Grandpa!" Randy exclaimed as he ran to give Josh a hug. "I sure like us all together like this."

"I think it's great, too," said Josh, hugging Randy tightly.

Heather came up to Josh and gave him a hug. "Thanks for coming," she said.

"I wouldn't have missed this for the world," Josh replied.

"Dinner's ready," Heather said. Randy took his grandfather's hand and pulled him toward the table. While they ate there was non-stop conversation that covered a multitude of subjects and events of the past years that had remained unshared until now. Any lull in the conversation was quickly filled by some story enthusiastically told by Randy. After the meal Heather insisted on cleaning up by herself, suggesting that Josh, Rob, and Randy move to the living room and continue their conversation.

"Grandpa, come to my room and see my ant farm, OK?"

"An ant farm! I wonder whose idea it was to get an ant farm?" Josh said, with a wink to Rob. "Your dad always talked about getting an ant farm."

"I guess I probably encouraged him to get it," Rob admitted as they moved down the hallway toward Randy's room. "Having a son allows you to enjoy some of the experiences you missed out on as a kid and not feel foolish about it. After all, what adult would be seen flying a kite in a park all by himself? Not many. But as long as a child's standing alongside him he doesn't feel foolish."

Josh chuckled as they made their way into Randy's room. "It's over here," Randy said. "The two of you can sit on the edge of my bed, OK?"

Randy carefully retrieved the ant farm from a bookshelf and sat down in front of his father and grandfather, placing the ant farm carefully on the floor in front of his folded legs. He slid off the screen that covered one side of the glass enclosure. Leaning forward and looking carefully, both men could see dozens of brown ants running back and forth through the tunnels.

"They certainly are busy little creatures, aren't they?" Josh said.

"They sure are, Grandpa. I guess they get a lot of work done, because I never catch them goofing off. They're always working so hard."

"You know, Dad," Rob interjected, "we had a dickens of a time catching those little beasties. It's easy to dig up an ant hill and get a few ants, but to get the queen ant, that's another story. We finally did it, though, and Randy's been real good about taking care of his little charges."

"Yeah," Randy added, "and if we hadn't rescued them they'd be dead for sure. Their ant hill was by a new house being built, right where they were going to put in a sidewalk. We got them just in time."

All three of them were quiet for several moments as they watched the ants scurry back and forth, apparently alarmed that their dark tunnels now had a wall of light. Randy finally broke the silence. "You know, Grandpa, it would have been a lot easier catching these ants if I could have turned into one."

"Why's that?" Josh asked.

"Because I would have explained to them that their ant hill was going to be destroyed and that they'd be OK if they'd let me put them in my ant farm, that I would take real good care of them." Randy reflected a moment. "Of course I might have gotten squished by somebody walking by."

"True enough," Josh said.

The three eventually made their way back into the living room after Randy showed his grandpa what must have been every toy he owned.

As Josh and Rob talked, Josh stole an occasional glance at Randy playing nearby. It was wonderful having the three generations together again. Still, Josh sensed an unsettled, even sad feeling within. He finally realized he was missing Anne. She would so loved to have been with them all. She would be so pleased to see how Randy was growing up to be such a great kid.

There was a lull in the conversation and Josh reflected, "You know, I never realized how much the Dolphdroids meant to me until things turned sour for them. I mean, as long as things were going well with them I could let it be and move on to other things."

"Like the water reclamation project?" Rob added.

"Yes. But now that the Dolphdroids' existence is threatened I find it hard to focus on anything else, including my current responsibilities." Josh paused, leaning back further in the living room chair, and then continued. "I remember how fond I was of Adam when he lived with us during training and orientation time." Then Josh turned and looked at Rob. "On my way over here I had an insight that caught me by surprise. I think I see why that wasn't always a positive experience for you. After all, it was like instantly having a big brother around, a several-hundred-pound, metal-bodied brother that went from kindergarten status to college graduate in a few weeks."

Josh could see by the look on Rob's face that he had identified a painful area in his son's past. "And for that I am truly sorry," Josh added.

Rob's demeanor changed again, the apology apparently hitting its mark. It was enough for now, and Rob felt good about changing the subject. "You know, Dad, I had all kinds of feelings when I saw Adam at the Smithsonian West. I felt some of the past little brother jealousies bubbling up. But I also felt sadness, seeing

Adam standing there like some encased Egyptian mummy. There are some good memories; we had some fun times together. I realized that I had even looked up to him in a way."

"And now the entire race is going to be no better off than Adam. That's simply unacceptable," Josh said.

Rob looked at his dad. "You really want to do something to stop the termination process, don't you, Dad?"

Josh nodded. "I'd like to be there, on the lunar surface, though it would probably do little good. The reports are clear, the antihuman feeling runs strong and deep among them. They probably wouldn't appreciate my presence. Then there's the fact that the order to terminate is irreversible."

An hour later as Josh flew home he watched the lights of the city flickering below, the moon backlighting a cloud. It had been a good evening with Rob, Heather, and Randy. His mind reviewed the conversations, the images, the feelings of the evening. The reflections, however, were clouded by a persistent feeling of deep sadness; the Dolphdroids were to be annihilated.

The image of Randy looking at his ant colony kept coming back to Josh, with the words they exchanged while viewing the little busy black creatures.

Piloting his PAV through the night sky, Josh's thoughts began to coalesce, forming a vague plan. As he prepared to land the PAV he marveled at the miracle of how ideas are conceived. His work with the Dolphdroids had involved a significant amount of research in the area of artificial intelligence and the mysterious process of thinking. He had been captivated by the concepts of consciousness, problem-solving, the formation of ideas, and planning. He banked his craft for the final approach to his home. Where had this idea come from, the plan that had coalesced in his mind just minutes earlier while flying above the city? His mind had utilized his concern for the Dolphdroids and the recollection of the conversation about the ant colony. Images, words, the problem at hand, and who knows what else were all used by the sub-conscious to present the gift of an idea to the conscious mind.

For now the plan was vague. It had to be fleshed out in major ways. Josh knew not to push the process. It would happen, a clear plan would come together. All he knew now was that something had to be done to save the Dolphdroids, that something would be done, and that he would implement and carry out such a plan. Josh landed the PAV gently onto his back lawn. The Dolphdroids had to be saved, and there was a way!

Chapter 7

Josh had never taken a sabbatical, but now was the time. His PAV sliced through some low altitude moisture and he glanced to reassure himself that the anti-collision warning system was operating. He was confident that his request would be granted; the guidelines clearly confirmed that he qualified for a year's sabbatical. Dr. Max would grumble, of course; that was to be expected. As the commissioner overseeing the Saltwater Reclamation Project it would be in Dr. Max's best interest to keep Josh on the job. Josh could understand; projects run more smoothly when consistent key leadership is at the helm.

Commissioners were a necessary evil; Josh knew this and had always tried to play by the rules, going along with the system. He had never had a serious run-in with Hartung or Maxim, until now. There was, of course, the usual tension between people like Josh who were primarily concerned with the creative process and the administrators like Imus and Randolph who were fixated with following procedures. What didn't help was that the commissioners had too much to oversee and often had to make uninformed decisions. Imus was responsible for not only all activity on the lunar surface but also the coming colonization of Mars, the space stations scattered about, and the life wheels in earth orbit. No one person could keep well enough informed about all of these projects to manage them well. Randolph Maxim had an equally diverse collection of responsibilities, of which the Saltwater Reclamation Project was only one part.

It often frustrated Josh and the other heads of research and development projects that the commissioners were overextended, preventing them from giving adequate time and effort to any one project. Added to this were the political concerns that always had to be factored in with almost all decisions; it was amazing that any progress was made at all.

At least Maxim seemed to care less about personal empire building than Imus and some of the others. Most likely Dr. Max would hesitate but then give him the sabbatical, because he liked him and, more importantly, because he had earned it. Soon the center was in view on the horizon. Josh banked the PAV slightly to the right and descended to a lower altitude but maintained his speed. Josh enjoyed flying his new toy faster than most that flew a PAV, just for old time's sake. His flying skill was still sharp, a skill he was unaware would soon be needed to save his life. He brought the craft in for a perfect three-point landing on the research center's roof.

Compared to the pinnacle office of Imus, the ambiance of Dr. Max's office was decidedly utilitarian, outfitted with basic metal and glass furniture, and located near the lab. The only nod to personal indulgence was the presence of several large saltwater aquariums that filled the office with a cacophony of gurgling sounds.

Pointing to a chair, the short, slightly built Dr. Maxim, immaculately dressed in suit and tie, expressed his excitement in his characteristic high-pitched voice over a new kind of pumping system Josh and his team had recently developed; then he abruptly changed the subject and his tone. "Sorry about the negative turn of events with the Dolphdroids, Josh. I've been down that road, seeing years of work hit a dead end."

Josh nodded. "More painful than its being a dead end is that it leaves the Dolphdroids dead; that's what's painful."

Maxim, clearly uncomfortable with Josh's response, cleared his throat. "You certainly took robotics a quantum leap forward, Josh. I happened to see the prototype, Adam, a couple of years ago. I was very impressed. Of course, everyone has seen news reports over the years on the Dolphdroids, but observing Adam, even in his shutdown state, leaves an impact. I know that after so many years on a project you really become personally involved, more so when the main component is so humanlike."

"Dr. Max, my perception of the Dolphdroids as being 'humanlike' isn't a personal effort at anthropomorphism, like some children's book that has animals walking on two legs and talking and acting like people. This is real life. The Dolphdroids are intelligent, thinking, feeling, self-aware creatures who have been given life and now deserve to keep it." Josh stopped himself from saying any more, trying to maintain control of his feelings.

Maxim was visibly relieved to hear his secretary interrupt their conversation, informing him over the televiewer that the mayor of New York would be arriving shortly.

"I'm making an official request for a year's sabbatical," Josh stated as soon as the conversation with the secretary was finished. "I believe Dick Ellis would be an ideal replacement for me. He has a sixth sense about the direction a piece of research should go, and he gets along well with people. I've talked to him and he's willing. I reassured him I would be available for consultation, for at least part of the duration of my sabbatical, if needed. I don't foresee any problems, however, that would be beyond Dick's capabilities. He's the best. The paper work's done; your secretary has it."

Maxim placed his elbows on his desk and leaned forward, glanced at one of his aquariums in the room, then looked back at Josh. "A sabbatical is something you have coming. You know that, I know that. For your sake, however, I'm half tempted to turn you down anyway, though I know you'd just raise a legal stink and end up with your sabbatical anyway. I know you, Josh. You're going to try to do something about the Dolphdroid situation. Don't! Just for your information, I tried to talk Imus out of terminating the project. I know what the project means to you, but Imus is going to shut it down, no matter what. He's under a great deal of pressure, a great deal." Maxim leaned back in his chair, putting his hands behind his head. "As for me, my own life is simpler. I stick to science and making it work. I play politics as little as I can. I had to be coerced into being a commissioner. It wasn't my idea and frankly I'd give it up at the drop of a hat. Imus, now, he's different. He thrives on a blend of science and politics, a deadly combination as far as I'm concerned. That's why Imus is in the mess he's in." Suddenly Maxim looked uncomfortable, moving his hands from behind his head and placing them back on the desk again. He glanced at a different aquarium this time, then at Josh, then at the top of his desk and some undefined point just beyond his hands. "That's all I can say about that. In fact, I've said too much already."

The commissioner adjusted his glasses and looked at Josh. "I'm not much for words, everybody knows that. I should have told you a long time ago that you're the best. You're doing absolutely amazing work here. I'm in your corner. But, Josh, though I don't try to play politics, like Imus I know when to fold the cards – and this, Josh, is one of those times. There are forces at work that would do anything to see the Dolphdroid Project terminated. The termination will happen no matter what you try to do to stop it, so don't try." Maxim leaned back in his chair in an attempt to regain his composure, and added, "I want you alive and back here a year from now."

Within the hour Josh was leaving the facility with the signed papers for the sabbatical and the new information that Dr. Max had unwittingly given him. There was no doubt about it; someone was pulling Imus' strings, somebody big and dangerous.

The next several days Josh kept busy transferring the leadership of the Saltwater Reclamation Project to Dick Ellis. People were cooperative, anxious to show full support for Josh. They understood that Josh had no choice but to spend full time attempting to stop the termination of the Dolphdroid Colony. Although he had given himself completely to the Saltwater Reclamation Project, the consensus was that Josh saw the creation of the Dolphdroids as the greatest achievement of his career and that nothing he ever did would match it.

Rob called and wanted to have lunch with his father. Josh agreed to meet at noon the next day at Kinsey's Restaurant near the Reclamation Center. Josh couldn't pass up another chance to see his son after such a long period of being alienated from him. His enthusiasm cooled considerably, however, when Rob informed him that he was bringing along a friend of his who was a reporter with a local paper. Rob reassured him that Vince could help tell Josh's side of the story.

The next day Josh was already seated at a table at Kinsey's when the two young men walked in. Rob spotted his dad, waved, and the two walked over to the table. "Dad, this is Vince Johnson. Vince, this is my Dad." Josh rose from his chair and extended his hand to Vince.

"It's a pleasure to meet you, Dr. Christopher."

"Please, have a seat," Josh said, motioning for him to sit down.

"Thank you for giving me some time, Dr. Christopher."

"Well, as you undoubtedly already know, I'm not enthusiastic about interviews. You found my Achilles' heel, however, and that's my son. Connections count."

After their beverages arrived and they ordered, Vince removed an audioprinter from his knapsack. "I don't want to rush you, Dr. Christopher, but can we get started?"

"Certainly." Rob glanced from his father to Vince and back to his father again. Concern showed on his face; he wondered if his father noticed. He wondered if this was such a good idea after all. He really wanted his father to have the chance to tell his side of the story, to get some conversation going about who the Dolphdroids really were and the great tragedy that awaited them. Rob was painfully aware that his father had not been portrayed in a very good light since the news had broken of the termination. He also hoped Vince would treat his father fairly. Vince was a good friend, but he could also be unpredictable.

Vince cleared his throat, turned on the audioprinter, and began. "As you are well aware, Dr. Christopher, there has always been a great deal of controversy over the procedure of removing the brains of dolphins for use as a biological base in your robots. Do you feel any remorse about having headed the project now that things have taken a turn for the worse on the lunar surface with the Dolphdroids?"

Rob felt his face flush. This was not good. What was Vince doing? Rob glanced at his father, whose face appeared taut. Rob averted any possible eye contact with his father by gazing down at his glass of cola.

Josh arranged his napkin and silverware, methodically putting the fork, knife, and spoon on the napkin, then folding the napkin once, covering the three utensils with half of the napkin. Both of the young men watched the process. Finally he spoke. "Vince, to suggest that I feel some kind of remorse now that something is supposedly going wrong with the Dolphdroid Colony, but that I apparently didn't feel such remorse before, suggests that the validity of the whole project is contingent on whether or not it's successful. It does not. I have always believed that the concept is sound and moral. I still believe in what I've done, regardless of the results. An old saying states that the end doesn't justify the means, which is true, but neither do the results condemn the means."

Josh paused to sip his coffee. Vince started to open his mouth to ask another question, but Josh continued. "You see, Vince, we identified only those dolphins that had been critically injured by watercraft, underwater construction, or other accidents as potential candidates for the transplants. With people utilizing the sea more than ever, the dolphins' safety is often jeopardized and accidents happen all too frequently. It was those critically injured dolphins, dolphins who would have died, who were used in the project – really, given a second chance, a new life."

"Dr. Christopher, some would argue now more than ever that the entire enterprise was a mistake. Reports indicate that the Dolphdroids are in a great deal of conflict among themselves and that they may even be a threat to us. Many people are asking if you really did those dolphins a favor by transplanting their brains into robots."

Josh shook his head slowly. These were the same issues he addressed at the time the project was implemented. The press wasn't coming up with new questions, but he would try to be patient with his son's friend. "When we set the parameters for this project we made the decision to limit the role that the personal computing module of each Dolphdroid would play. We didn't want the module to dictate all of the actions and reactions of the Dolphdroids, but simply to raise their I.Q., increase their thinking capacity. It was important that there be freedom of choice. We gave them the gift of freedom. This gift of free moral choice allows one to respond to a situation rather than simply react. The power of choice gives meaning to life. We wanted the Dolphdroids to have the opportunity for a meaningful life. The power to choose comes with a price. It means there is the option to choose wrongly. Giving a creature the freedom to do good means you also have given the creature the freedom to do evil. The problem of evil exists because of the gift of freedom."

"But was it fair to these injured dolphins to turn them into something else instead of simply letting them die a natural death?" The thought occurred to Josh that perhaps Rob had set his father up, that maybe Rob really hadn't changed, but the uncomfortable, almost pained look on his son's face told him otherwise. No, his friend's questioning was obviously a surprise to Rob. Josh felt a flush of shame at even thinking such a thought about his son.

Their food came. Eyeing Vince, Josh nodded at the young man's plate. "I see you're eating chicken, Vince. Just remember, a chicken had to lose its life so that you could have this meal. At some point a few days ago a chicken, content with pecking, scratching and roosting, was unceremoniously dispatched from existence as a living creature so it could be your lunch. The same with the cow that contributed to the steak I'm eating."

"Yes, but most agree that a dolphin is a great deal more intelligent than a chicken or a cow."

Josh nodded agreement. "As you know, once we were successful with the first Dolphdroid we were able to communicate with him and test him. It solved the great mystery of just how intelligent dolphins are. They're smart animals, but not as intelligent as people had thought. For years there was the hope that these mysterious and wonderful creatures might be our equals in the sea. We didn't like the idea of being the only intelligent creatures in the universe. And when our best studies of distant space still left unanswered the question of the existence of intelligent extraterrestrial life, we turned with renewed vigor to looking beneath our own waters in the hope that we might yet discover that we're not alone, that we're not the only self-aware, goal-setting, conceptualizing species in existence." Josh paused to take a bite of steak and then continued. "The dolphins are graceful and very intelligent animals. They deserve to be respected. But just where do we draw the line? We want to preserve the dolphin, but we go out and hunt for tuna for our sandwiches. What about the tuna's life?"

"But, Dr. Christopher, most would agree that the dolphin is a higher life form than the tuna; it certainly has a higher life-value rating than the tuna, as I'm sure you're aware."

"Why, Vince? Simply because the dolphin can perform at Sea World and the tuna can't? Maybe we just don't understand the tuna as well as we do the dolphin. Life-value measurements have always greatly concerned me. We're making judgment after judgment based on a species' life-value quotient. It has become ridiculous, to the point where a specimen of the new breed of two-tailed mice at Lenderson's Research Labs is rated of higher value than an unlicensed lost dog that may be the pet of some child who's at home crying because Spot is lost."

"So you don't care much for the life-value system, Dr.

Christopher. I suspect, though, you were delighted when they assigned a rather high life-value quotient to the Dolphdroid."

Rob could remain silent no longer. Vince had no right to talk to his father this way! He couldn't help the edge his voice carried when he interrupted. "Vince, the Dolphdroid's life-value quotient isn't as high as the condor or even the dolphin itself. Yet the Dolphdroid is a unique life form closer to us than anything else that exists."

Josh glanced at Rob, unable to hold back a look of pleasure. His son was defending him. He turned to Vince, the hard lines returning to his face. "I find it curious that there seems to be no consistency when it comes to assigning a life-value quotient to a creature. Labs will go to great lengths to insure that the lab mice they use in experiments are properly fed and cared for, but let one get out and a trap is set for him that'll snuff out his furry little life when he takes to the bait, just like any common mouse. His escape to freedom not only polluted him by lab standards, his life-value quotient dropped off the charts." Josh turned his attention back to his steak. No one said anything. Vince glanced at Rob but then continued to eat his own meal.

After a few bites Josh broke the silence. "Science often uses lab animals as a means to an end. I'm afraid that to Dr. Imus Hartung and others, the Dolphdroids have always been just that: a means to an end, not even a scientific end but their own political ends. I gave each one a name. They may be mismanaging their freedom, failing to live up to the standards I had for them, but they're creatures I brought into existence. They're more than a means to an end; their existence is an end itself!"

Vince decided to back off, asking questions that carried far less emotional punch, about Josh's current work and interests. Josh sensed what he was doing and was polite but brief with his answers. It seemed to Rob that it took forever for the meal to be finished. No one asked for dessert. They finally left the table, Vince offering to pay the bill.

Vince shook Josh's hand. "Thank you, Dr. Christopher, for your time." He paused, searching for the right words. "I appreciated your candor."

"You're welcome. Thanks for buying lunch," Josh said.

Rob and Vince said good-bye to each other and Vince left

father and son standing by the front door of the restaurant.

Rob turned to his father. "Dad, I'm sorry. I didn't have a clue that Vince was going to get on your case like that. I would have never lined up this luncheon if I knew he was going to treat you like that!"

Josh waved off the comment and then said with a smile, "Did you notice? He didn't finish his chicken!"

Chapter 8

Rob was surprised to see his father on the televiewer. "Morning, Dad."

"I hope I didn't call you too early," Josh said.

"No, not at all. I would have been up in another hour or two anyway," Rob said, grinning.

"Good," his dad replied, ignoring the humor. Rob could tell his father's mood was serious. "Rob, I've been working on an idea. You said you wanted to help in some way. I could really use that help now. Do you think you could get a few days of vacation time on this short notice?"

Rob paused. His father's request had caught him off guard. It pleased him, however. "I don't see a problem with it, Dad. I'm finishing up a feature story today and there's not much else in the pipeline that can't be reassigned or wait a few days. Why? What's up?"

"I don't think we should talk on the viewer. Let's get together for breakfast. You name the place."

"How about Fieldlander's Restaurant? It's on the corner of 12th and Langston. You can land your PAV there. It's sort of a truck stop, so there's plenty of room."

"Good. In a half an hour?"

"Don't forget, Dad, I don't have a PAV. I'll have to crawl through traffic along with all of the other lowly sorts on their way to work."

His dad laughed. "OK, just get there as soon as you can." They both broke connection.

Twenty minutes later Josh was at Fieldlander's sipping his first cup of coffee as he took in the ambiance. His son always had a knack for picking unique places to hang out and this was no

67

exception. The manager was behind the counter, leaning against the pie cabinet and talking with a man who was hunched over his morning cup of coffee at the counter. The nearest waitress sported a soiled blouse that likely carried a sampling of every item on the menu. Perhaps this was the kind of place where Rob met those unnamed sources that made him an award-winning journalist.

Josh's thoughts were interrupted by Rob's arrival. The waitress wearing the samples from the menu greeted Rob by name and handed him a mug of coffee as he sat down at the table. "How's the weather up there?" Rob asked, glancing upward, an obvious dig at his father's ownership of a PAV.

"Great. You should have seen the sunrise. From a couple of thousand feet it was brilliant," Josh said, returning the dig. Then he added as he glanced around the room, "I take it from the waitress's greeting that you frequent this esteemed establishment."

"It's a good place to meet contacts. I was meeting regularly with a guy here who was feeding me good information – that is, until someone who didn't appreciate his dispensing such information made sure he never did it again." Rob's face turned grim, then lightened as he added, "I like the farmer's omelet here. Four cheeses and four eggs, a real heart clogger, but it can't be beat."

The waitress with the smorgasbord blouse ambled slowly up to their table with electronic pad and stylus in hand. "What d'ya want, Robby, baby?" she asked.

Rob ordered the heart clogger and Josh had the early bird special. When the waitress left Josh began filling Rob in on his idea. "I believe that there's some organized effort to terminate the colony, that someone has a lot to gain if the Dolphdroids were off the scene. I don't think I'm giving in to paranoia. I have a strong intuitive sense about this, Rob. Somebody is sabotaging the project, but I have no idea who. Actually, the Dolphdroids have been in place so long that I wouldn't have expected trouble of this magnitude at this point." Josh took another sip of coffee and continued. "It's usually in the development stage where you're always competing with other projects, or a better way or more economical way to carry out the same project. This whole field of humaniform robotics was about as competitive as I've seen anything get a dozen or so years ago. Everyone was trying to come up with a plan using robotics to reap the resources on the lunar surface because the environment is so hostile to humans. But I thought that was long past, that the Dolphdroids had earned their place. Now I'm not so sure."

"Who were the people involved in that competition? That wasn't really my area of interest back then. My interest was general opposition to the whole project, if you recall." The smile on Rob's face reassured Josh again that Rob had come a long way since his days of protesting.

"I recall," Josh replied, returning the smile. Then his face turned serious. "Who was involved in the competition back then? Quite a few. Let's see, there was I.Q. Inc., Boyd McMasters and his outfit. Tasmer Radcliff and his research group, BRAIN Enterprises, Artificial Thought Labs, The Merkel Mind Group, J. & R. Robotics; they were all major players, and then there were a few minor league participants, most of whom I can't remember offhand."

"You want me to check into them to see if any of them might be getting their hands dirty with this?" Rob asked.

Josh looked at Rob and nodded. "That's right. The list is a little shorter than the one I just gave you. A couple of players are no longer around. The Merkel Mind Group went belly-up when we were about halfway toward development of the Dolphdroids. Then there's Tasmer Radcliff. His is quite a tragic story. You may remember, he committed suicide a few years ago. Several people saw him swim out to sea but he never came back. They found a note in his pocket when he finally washed up on the beach. Actually, it didn't surprise me that he took his own life."

"Oh? Why not?"

"Well, he was one of the most intense men I've ever met. He was like a dog with a bone: just would never give up on something. He was taking the usual approach to developing a humaniform robot, working purely with computers to achieve a new level of artificial intelligence. He was doing well, coming close to even having a computer emulate human intuition. A number of people thought his robot concept would have been better than my Dolphdroid Project." Josh paused, then added with a knowing smile, "I suspect you and your friends back then would have much preferred Radcliff's approach. It was pure computer, no living creature involved. I still don't believe that what he was planning to come up with would have been self-aware, but it certainly would have given the appearance of possessing that quality."

69

Rob was listening but also reflecting on how things had changed, how he had changed over the years that he and his father had been alienated. Rob had told Heather yesterday that his father had become a lot smarter during their years apart. Both had laughed, knowing that the change was more with Rob than with his father.

Sensing Rob's receptive mood, Josh went on. "You know, Rob, the problem with computer programs is that they're rule-based. They must operate within logical parameters. They can only process creatively to the degree that the programmer was creative. Intuition doesn't figure in at all. Artificial Intelligence work hits a brick wall at this point. To simulate the neurons and their work in the human brain, or even a brain of far less complexity and capacity, would take thousands of computers, and then they'd still be crunching numbers. Radcliff came close to simulating intuition, according to my sources at the time, but close wasn't good enough. We got the contract."

"So that's what drove Radcliff over the edge?"

"I suspect so. I remember talking with him a week before his one-way swim. He admitted to me that he had chosen a direction for his research that he now realized would never generate the results he'd worked so hard to achieve. He really seemed depressed." Josh sighed. "I've often wished that I'd been a little more sensitive to his frustration; maybe I could have been instrumental in preventing what he did. You just never know."

"It was his choice, Dad."

Josh nodded and was quiet for a moment, then let the self-incriminating feelings go. "The reality is that Radcliff and all the others chose the wrong approach in their research and development from the very beginning. It's like the start of the space program during the middle of the last century. The U. S. space industry depended on the work of German scientists who had been involved in the rocket technology of World War II. They looked to expendable rockets that shoot up to get payloads into space. A lot of people believe they should have used airplane technology from the very beginning. Flying into space is a lot cheaper and less dangerous than blasting into space. The first choice was wrong, and first choices are critical to the success of any long-term development project. I heard about a handmade road sign in the wilderness of Alaska that read, "Choose your rut wisely, you'll be in it for miles." That's the kind of mistake the others, including Radcliff, made: they settled into the wrong rut. I accepted, as a scientific given, the mystery of the mind. Instead of duplicating its process I decided to piggyback on it. The dolphin's brain provided the intuition, emotions, and consciousness while the interfaced computer simply increased the thinking capacity of that brain – the IQ, if you will."

Josh could see an old, familiar expression coming over Rob's face: that of borderline boredom, taking Josh back to when Rob was a boy and had a low tolerance for his father's enthusiastic and long-winded scientific explanations of things. Josh also realized that though their relationship was going well, there might be some residual feelings that a prolonged dissertation might stir up in his son. "But none of that is relevant to things now," Josh concluded.

They concentrated on their breakfast and Josh asked Rob about Randy. Josh sensed his son's relief at the turning of the conversation toward a mutually enjoyable subject. Josh really did want to hear more about Randy. He had missed much of his grandson's early years.

They finished their breakfast, and after another cup of coffee Josh paid the bill. The waitress gave Rob and Josh a hearty "See ya" and waved as they left the restaurant. Josh handed Rob an envelope.

"You're going to have expenses, so here's something to take care of those. I'm not giving you this, or the job, because you're my son." Josh looked Rob in the eyes. "I need your help on this thing. I need a good reporter to help me get to the bottom of this, of who's making things happen. I know you have the contacts. If anybody can get to the truth, you can. Just be careful. I don't want you failing to show up at this greasy spoon place for our next breakfast like your previous contact. I suspect that whoever is behind the sabotaging of the Dolphdroid Project is going to play for keeps. Just be careful, son."

Josh's wrist communicator went off. "Josh here."

"Josh, this is Bill Zucker. We've had a couple of major negative developments. We need to talk, as soon as I get off work. Where can we meet?"

"My place," Josh replied. He knew it was serious; Bill was no alarmist but Josh sensed tension in his voice.

The day was long. Josh couldn't keep his mind on anything but Bill's coming visit. He tried doing some additional research via the internet, but learned nothing of consequence about the problems on the lunar surface or who might be trying to put the Dolphdroids away. Finally Josh heard the words he had been waiting for from the house computer: "You have a visitor at the door. He indicates his name is Bill Zucker. Should I allow him to enter?"

"Yes," Josh quickly replied.

"So, what's up?" Josh asked as he let Bill in.

"First, we received a confirmed report that three Dolphdroids have been killed and two wounded, one seriously, in a skirmish." Bill paused, seeing that Josh was visibly shaken by the news. Then he continued, "As far as we know this is the first incident of physical assault in the colony. Of course, it was between the pro-earth and pro-lunar factions. Apparently they used their laser rock picks as weapons. I was surprised we got as full a report as we did. I think the deaths shook up both sides considerably. As you can well imagine, tensions are reported to be high and we see a high probability for things to escalate. Both sides claim the incident was the fault of the other, of course."

Josh stared blankly at the floor. "I find it hard to believe that things have turned so bad that there are deaths."

Bill looked at his forlorn friend, wanting him to have time to absorb the news but knowing he also had to tell him all he knew. "There's a few other things too, Josh."

"Oh?" Josh asked, looking at his friend.

"Well, along with the information about this clash, we've been getting bits and pieces of data concerning other difficulties."

"Like what?"

"For instance, there's a monopoly on the oxygen pods. Before all of this started the Dolphdroids could easily purchase the necessary oxygen supply needed for brain function, but now it goes to the highest bidder. It appears that one of the pro-lunar Dolphdroids saw an opportunity to make some extra income and started buying more than what he needed in the way of oxygen. When a shortage started to develop he sold his extra at a mark-up. Oxyphobia seems to be rampant among the Dolphdroids now."

Josh shook his head in amazement and disappointment. "Oxyphobia? The fear of not having enough oxygen? Amazing. You said, 'other difficulties' as if there were more than this one issue. What else?"

"There's virtual reality abuse. They've adapted the 3-D

mapping computer used for designing future tunnels and buildings. Now it's interfaced with several specially designed terminals that they call 'pleasure machines.' They're being used to create images and senses that are highly pleasurable and exciting. Some of the Dolphdroids regularly 'plug in and tune out,' as they describe it. Several of the Dolphdroids are interfacing with the pleasure machines to the extent that they're habitual users, are getting little work done, and have nearly stopped socializing with others. They're called 'chip addicts.' Apparently the problem is getting worse with more Dolphdroids becoming victims of the addiction."

    Josh had a difficult time comprehending all that Bill was telling him. He had envisioned creating a form of life that could find a meaningful, full existence colonizing a new and productive society on the moon's surface, but that dream was turning into a nightmare. Finally Josh became aware of the silence, of Bill standing in front of him with his hands in his pockets. Josh put his hand on Bill's shoulder. "Thanks for coming over here and getting me up to speed."

    Bill said nothing, just nodded. Soon, after a brief exchange, Bill excused himself. An hour later Josh was walking in Spencer Park. The breeze rustled the leaves and the swans glided effortlessly on the glassy surface of the lake that now reflected the orange glow of a setting sun. Josh walked and thought. His hopes and dreams for the Dolphdroids were shattered. Imus was determined to decommission them, kill them off by the initiation of a simple termination program on the project's mainframe computer. They would die where they stood at the predetermined moment of termination. Now, as if all of this wasn't bad enough, the nightmare had grown even bigger. Josh wondered if it would have been better if he had never created the Dolphdroids in the first place.

    He recalled the early days when the project had been launched. After the colony had been established on the lunar surface he had been invited to appear on all of the talk shows, and it was a cover story for all the major news magazines and web sites. But people lost interest in an amazingly short time. He had actually been glad about that. Oh, there had been an occasional expedition to the lunar surface by the very rich to see the moon and the Dolphdroids, but that had slowly declined over the years.

    There had been little financial gain from the project. He

worked for the government, so the perks were few and small. The PAV was a surprise, probably a way to appease him before they dropped the bombshell about the project being terminated. No, there had been no financial windfall from the project, and he hadn't expected one. He simply had felt that it was in his power to create this life form. The usefulness of such a creation for utilizing the resources on the harsh lunar surface had only been the means to his end. His real vision had always been to give the Dolphdroids the pleasure of existing, the delight of being something like their creator, getting a glimpse of what it means to be human.

Now he felt compelled to do something to rescue them, not that they deserved it. He had given them the freedom of choice and they had used that freedom to turn from their created purpose. But there was no doubt in Josh's mind that the tragedy unfolding among the Dolphdroids had some outside help. It didn't excuse their recent behavior, but it certainly helped to explain it. He could take the advice he had received and just leave it all alone, let things play out, but that would certainly mean the death of the Dolphdroids, every single last one of them. He couldn't let that happen. He wouldn't let that happen. A plan was beginning to form, a way to rescue the Dolphdroids inspired by his grandson's ant farm. It was an extreme measure, and it would be life-altering for him. It was a plan that would be difficult to explain to others, yet he would have to do that, because he would need a great deal of help.

Who would be the first to contact? Who would he first try to explain his wild and crazy plan to? It had to be someone involved in the project from its inception and who would at least listen. Two people came to mind: Risner Billingston and Tony Williams. He would tell them about his plan. They'd be honest with him about whether it was at all feasible.

Josh stopped walking, looked up, and spotted the first star beginning to flicker in the darkening sky. Tomorrow he would meet with Risner and Tony and tell them about his plan. He stood near the water's edge, staring into the dark surface. Yes, tomorrow he would tell them. It was going to begin.

Chapter 9

Risner and Tony had never flown in a personal air vehicle. They were cruising at 5,000 feet, the long distance-designated altitude or "freeway of the sky" for PAVs. The three looked down on a few scattered low clouds casting shadows on the quilt-like fields below them. Josh loved flying; the sky was almost a second home to him. His years as a pilot in the Air/Space Force had given him a taste for flight that seemed never to be satisfied. Although the PAV was a far cry from the fighter A/S planes he had flown in the service, it was still a thrill to get up and "slice through the blue" as the pilots called it.

Risner sat to the right of Josh. A large man with thick gray hair and a matching mustache, he was a no-nonsense kind of guy with a tough exterior. In Josh's opinion he was the best roboticist in the world; that's why Josh had hired him to be part of the Dolphdroid development team. That era seemed ages ago now. It amused Josh that Risner always found flying to be white knuckle time, grasping anything he could curl his large fingers around as if his personal grip was responsible for keeping body and craft airborne. It was a tribute to his allegiance to Josh that he was even riding in a PAV.

Tony sat in the back. He was a man of slight, short build and a matching high voice. His physical presence often failed to inspire respect, but Josh was in awe of the man's brilliance when it came to computers. He was always ahead of his time, envisioning well beyond what was, or what most people ever thought might be. It was his unique interface design that allowed the dolphin brain and the Dolphdroid's computer to work as a single unit, merging nerve and chip. Others had written papers on several theories about how it might be done, but Tony put theory to practice and accomplished the feat. Because no one had taken his ideas seriously, he had joined Josh's team. He was not the recognized authority on neuro-assisted computer processing. His loyalty to Josh still ran deep, after all the man had believed in him when no one else did, and so it was without hesitation that Tony took the day off from work at Josh's invitation to go to Florida.

Josh had invited them both to his house two days earlier and brought them up to date with all the information he had gathered about the Dolphdroids' status. Then he had told them his plan. Their first response was disbelief. Josh persisted, encouraging them to give it serious consideration. He had been open to their concerns and tried to answer their questions, but he always brought the discussion back to the fact that there was no other way. It had to be done if the Dolphdroids were to be saved. In spite of great personal risk, they knew Josh was committed to the plan. In the end both men agreed to at least investigate the idea.

Their destination was New Atlantis, the first official city-sized metropolitan area designated as an underwater city. Josh had visited many times with the Saltwater Reclamation Project and knew his way around. New Atlantis was home to Dr. Gunnard Kippler, a retired neurosurgeon. Tony Williams and Kippler were friends, having pioneered a technique which allowed a patient to be unconscious during surgery but still able to communicate with a monitoring computer to help guide and place probes properly. Josh didn't know Kippler. He agreed with many who said Kippler had been the greatest surgeon in his field but that he never received the recognition due him because of his personal style, which could be described as flamboyant and aggressive. Some of his techniques were brilliant and innovative; Josh believed that they were ahead of their time.

Tony entertained Josh and Risner with stories of the great Dr. Gunnard Kippler as Josh's PAV flew over the Florida landscape. The laughter helped ease the tension that had developed during their discussion of Josh's plan.

"I'll say this for Kippler," Tony stated. "He's probably the finest example I know of a person who walks the fine line between brilliance and insanity. His decision-making process, for instance, is unique – to say the least. If he feels confused about an issue he'll insist on going swimming. I don't care if it's a meeting with seven presidents of leading university hospitals, he'll leave to go swimming right in the middle of the meeting. He puts on a wetsuit and swims around outside his office building complex. When he comes back the issues are clear, his position firmly established, and there's no sense wasting your time trying to change his mind; it never happens."

"Sounds like an interesting character, but I'm not sure I'd trust him to operate on my brain," Risner observed, glancing at Josh.

Tony chuckled and continued, "Then there's his jokes. He loves to tell them, and often at what would be considered inappropriate times. I often thought he was working on the issue being discussed when suddenly he diverted everyone's attention with a funny story. I finally figured out that he does it to give himself more time to think about the issue at hand."

"Maybe he operates on brains because he's trying to figure out why his is so messed up," Risner interjected with a shake of his head. Josh only smiled as he scanned the sky for other traffic.

"Well," Tony continued, "the fact is, he's a great neurosurgeon. You just have to cut through all of the outlandish and quirky personality traits. Most people give up on him before they get to know him. He's not only brilliant, he's compassionate and caring, in his own way."

"I'm counting on that compassionate side," Josh said quietly, as if speaking to himself.

With several refueling stops, the trip took most of the day. Finally, they could see the shore in the distance and the tops of the half dozen tallest seascrapers that actually extended out of the shimmering water, marking the location of New Atlantis. The landing platform soon became visible with its flashing runway lights. Neither the platform nor the city of New Atlantis was their immediate destination, however. Just before the PAV crossed over the shore Josh banked it sharply to the right and started to descend, calling in a request to land on the roof of Sea Labs Inc.

"Aren't we going to New Atlantis?" Tony asked.

"I thought we'd enter the city a slightly less obvious way," Josh replied. "Have you heard about the Sky and Sea vehicle?"

"Sure," Tony offered. "I heard you developed the basic design when you first started work on the Saltwater Reclamation

Project. As I heard it via the grapevine you dreamed up the idea one day on the back of an envelope over lunch with some young engineer who ended up developing the vehicle and becoming president of the company."

"The grapevine has it surprisingly correct for once," Josh responded as he began a final approach for the roof landing pad. "Actually, it was on the back of a place mat, but, yes, it was over lunch. The engineer was William Fersdon. He had always admired how I pulled together a team for the Dolphdroid Project." Josh laughed. "Willy said that if I could orchestrate a research team and development project and get the kind of results I did with the Dolphdroid Project, with little or no knowledge in any given area but just depending on organization and leadership skills, then he could do the same. In a way, it was a backhanded compliment. My sole talent, according to Willy, is pulling together brilliant people to get a task done. I guess I can live with that."

"I feel honored," Tony joked.

"Don't take it personally," Risner fired back.

The windsock on the roof blew strongly from a westerly direction, so Josh compensated, flying his PAV in at a slight angle. Interrupting the bantering between his two passengers, Josh said, "Willy just wanted an idea from me – any idea, he didn't care what it was. He wanted an idea for something that hadn't been done so he could organize a research and development team, put them to the task, and do it. I had been flying frequently to New Atlantis. Skimming along just a few feet above the water, I often wondered why no one had developed a craft that could fly in the air, then dive into the water and enter the city from one of the underwater ports. At present, you either take an air vehicle and use the landing platform or you take a boat or a seaplane and use a surface dock. The third option is to take a subtransport from the mainland and use the underwater ports. The underwater ports are ideal because they function in all weather. Why not a sky and sea vehicle, something that could make the transition from sky to underwater, sort of like some birds who spot fish from the air, then dive into the water to pick up their lunch? I jotted down a few of the major problems that would need to be solved, such as the wing stress at entry into the water, then slid the place mat across the table to Willy. To make a long story short, Willy's company is called Techno Air, and their

Horizon craft is in the final testing stages and should be in production within two years. We're taking a Horizon craft to visit Dr. Kippler."

"We are?" Risner exclaimed with unmistakable concern in his voice. "We're riding in an experimental craft, taking it intentionally into the sea? This wasn't part of the invitation, my friend."

Josh just laughed.

"Then why are we landing on the roof of Sea Labs instead of wherever Techno Air is located?" Tony asked.

The PAV settled softly on the roof and Josh shut down the engine. He undid his seat harness, shifted his body weight to be more comfortable, and glanced across at Risner and back at Tony. "Because I don't want someone tracking us to Dr. Kippler. There's a tunnel from the Sea Lab office complex to their dock in the bay. Next to Sea Lab's dock is Techno Air's dock and hangar where they have a couple of their Horizon craft."

"Won't flying to New Atlantis on an experimental craft actually call more attention to us?" Tony asked.

"On the contrary," replied Josh. "The landing platform at New Atlantis records the coming and going of all craft and passengers on those craft. The underwater port for Techno Air's Horizon craft is private. They only have to report the arrival and departure of their craft and how many people are on board, but no names. Willy owes me a favor. He also guarantees me that his test pilot can keep our visit hush-hush – and I haven't had a chance to ride a Horizon yet." He had landed the PAV and the doors opened with their customary "wooosh" sound. As they climbed out Josh added, "I'd love to pilot the Horizon myself, but that would take a couple of days of orientation so we're letting Zach, the test pilot, do the honors and take us down under."

"Oh, great," Risner exclaimed as he hefted his weight slowly out of the craft. "I'm just getting slightly comfortable flying in your fancy PAV and now we move on to something even more exciting like diving a craft into the ocean. I can hardly wait."

Josh and Tony only smiled as the three of them made their way to the elevator that took them from the roof to the basement. Once at basement level they found the tunnel and hopped onto one of the electric transport carts parked near the entrance. Josh punched in the activation code Willy had given him and drove the three of them through the tunnel to the dock. A dozen or so seagulls, startled when the cart left the tunnel, fluttered into the sky. A loud group of people, most appearing slightly inebriated, had just disembarked from a nearby yacht and were laughing and staggering down the pier, heading to the Lobsterfest Restaurant nearby.

"This way," Josh directed.

It was no more than a hundred feet to a small metal-roofed hangar. Willy Fersdon was there to greet them, energetically shaking the hands of all three men but keeping his eyes primarily on Josh. It was obvious that he was excited about the opportunity to offer Josh and his friends a ride in one of his Horizons. He expressed sincere concern for the Dolphdroid's situation but made no attempt to probe as to why Josh wanted to make a clandestine visit to New Atlantis. Willy introduced the three men to Zach, the test pilot who had just come out of the hangar. Zach was tall and young and had blond hair with a faint mustache.

Leaning close to Tony, Risner whispered, "Young enough to be my son and he's taking us for a plunge in the ocean."

Zach pushed the hangar doors open, giving the three men their first view of a Horizon craft. Painted dark blue on the top half and light blue underneath, the craft had a sharp needle-like nose and two small stabilizer wings just below where the canopy began. From this point the body quickly flared to delta-shaped wings that appeared to be hinged. "The wings retract 78% just before you do the transition from air to sea," Willy explained as he caressed one of the wings. He pointed to one large and one small inlet just where the delta wing began behind the stabilizer wing. "The big one is the intake for the jet engine, the small one the intake for the water propulsion turbine. During flight the water intake is closed for aerodynamic purposes and the air intake is closed during submarine travel."

Josh praised Willy for a wonderfully designed craft, then gently hinted that they were a little behind schedule and needed to get going. Willy seemed disappointed that he couldn't give a more detailed explanation of the Horizon, but he instructed Zach to show them how to board the craft.

Risner looked around the highly congested bay area and was about to ask where the runway was located; it was obvious that the

Horizon wasn't a vertical-take-off craft like the PAV. Then he glanced at the nearby pier and realized that it was longer than the others.

Willy noticed where Risner's attention was focused. "Yes, that's the runway."

"Doesn't look very long," Risner commented.

"Long enough," Willy replied. "Don't worry, if it's not enough and you go in the drink you simply submerge and do a water launch into the air, exactly what you'll be doing after leaving New Atlantis."

"I hadn't thought that far ahead," Risner said with obvious concern in his voice. "You mean we're going to jump out of the water into the air? Great; first we have to do something worse than a long walk off a short pier, and then we've got to bob up out of the water before we can get safely back here. I can hardly wait."

No one was listening to Risner. Zach had opened the doors of the craft and Josh and Tony were leaning into the craft, taking a first look at its interior.

Within minutes all were strapped into their seats and Zach had taxied the Horizon from the hangar to the pier. Zach put the engine at full throttle, shoving them back in their seats. The nearby sailing boats docked along the piers parallel to the Horizon's went by in a blur. Then the Horizon's nose thrust upward and blue sky filled their view from the canopy. Risner groaned but said nothing.

Circling New Atlantis, Zach tipped the left wing of the craft sharply to give his passengers a better view. The towers glistened in the sun. Several structures just underneath the surface were visible, the light from the small waves refracting in ever-changing splotches of light and dark on the subterranean structures. Coming out of the turn and quickly dropping altitude, Zach said, "We're going in."

"Oh boy! I'm not particularly wild about the idea of ditching this thing in the ocean," Risner exclaimed.

Josh just chuckled. Risner would get no sympathy from him; he was thrilled with the prospect of riding the Horizon from sky to ocean.

Zach punched several controls in rapid succession and the computer voice filled the cabin: "Prepare for water entry."

"Gentlemen," Zach said, trying to deepen his youthful voice, "I don't care how much you've flown; this will be a unique

81

experience." Looking at Josh he added, "Sir, you came up with one exciting concept."

Josh waved him off as he stared at the quickly-approaching water's surface. "It was just a drawing on the back of a place mat."

"Watch this," Zach said, with an edge of pride in his voice. He punched another control and moved his hands to his lap. "The computer does the transition. Human response simply isn't quick enough."

The craft was skimming along the water at no more than a hundred feet, Josh estimated. Suddenly the engine went into reverse, throwing all four of them forward, hard against their shoulder restraints, stalling the craft. They started to drop. The engine kicked in with full forward thrust, vectoring the thrust so that it pitched the tail of the craft upward. They were in a nose-down position with the ocean filling their view. Glancing out the side of the canopy, Josh noted the wings quickly folding back and inward toward the tail. The engine went silent.

"Oh, great!" Risner exclaimed.

Just before they hit the water Josh noted a peculiar whirring sound coming from the underside of the craft. They entered the water with a jolt and the canopy turned dark blue; the whirring sound immediately increased in volume, vibrating the craft.

"We're now under water turbine power, Dr. Christopher," Zach explained as he took control of the craft again. A small fish darted in front of the canopy, trying to get out of the way of this strange metallic invader. Rows of light glowed in the distance. "The Hasford Tower," Zach said, as if anticipating their question. "We'll head for the docking port in the tower."

Before long they found themselves entering a narrow passageway illuminated on both sides with powerful lights. The craft tilted upward and a moment later it bobbed out of the water into a large room. Zach explained that they were in the entry bell.

"I heard about this system of entry into New Atlantis, but it's still strange when you experience it," Tony commented as he turned his head, taking in the view beyond the canopy.

Looking at his watch, Josh thanked Zach for the interesting ride and told him when he could expect them back at the entry bell for the return trip.

"I'll take care of the paperwork, gentlemen. I don't need any names," Zach said, giving Josh a knowing look. Willy had a good man in Zach, Josh thought.

Tony and Risner followed Josh as he stepped through the door of the entry bell room into the reception area of Techno Air and then out into a main concourse. "This way," Josh instructed, as he picked up the pace.

Large ornate entrances to offices graced both sides of the wide concourse. Soon after passing a sign that indicated they had left the Hasford Tower and were entering the Foster Tower, Josh led them to an elevator where he punched in a code. The elevator's door soon opened; they entered, it closed, and they were alone. "In New Atlantis the floors to the towers are numbered opposite the usual way: they go from the top down. Everything is measured in distance from the surface to the ocean floor rather than from the ground up," Josh explained. "Dr. Kippler has a place near the surface, on the third floor, so he can exit through a special dock and do his swimming. Fortunately, Dr. Kippler's place is in the same pod as Techno Air, just a different tower. If we're lucky we won't see anyone we know but Dr. Kippler."

They exited the elevator into a long, wide corridor. "This is both office and home for the doctor," Josh explained as he came to a massive oak door with the words "The G. Kippler Practice" stenciled on a smoked glass window to the right of the door. Entering, they found a small reception area with a couch and three matching chairs. A large round saltwater aquarium was built into the end of the reception counter and towered to the ceiling. Behind the counter a man glanced up from reading a book. "Doctors Christopher, Billingston, and Williams, I presume."

Josh was nearest the reception counter, with Risner and Tony still by the door. "You'd think we were in the deepest part of Africa and one of us was Dr. Livingston," Risner whispered to Tony.

"You presume correctly," Josh responded to the receptionist.

"You may go back to Dr. Kippler's living quarters this way," the receptionist said, pointing to an open door to his left. "Once inside Dr. Kippler's office, take the door to your right, activate the sentry computer, and he'll greet you. You'll be in his private quarters." Then, as if an afterthought, the receptionist added, "You must be close friends; the doctor rarely invites guests into his private quarters."

"We are. Thank you," was all Josh said as he started through the door with Risner and Tony following. The office was large. Another saltwater aquarium dominated the space. Feeling awkward about being in Kippler's office without Kippler present, Josh quickly moved to the door to his right and pushed the button. Perhaps a sentry computer operated it as part of a larger system, but it appeared to be an ordinary doorbell button. The door opened and they were greeted by a short man with a barrel-shaped body and thinning white hair. A smile erupted on the doctor's face. He swept his arm back toward his residence in a warm gesture. "Gentleman, please come in. Good to see you, Tony, and you two must be Dr. Christopher and Dr. Billingston. I am Gunnard Kippler."

After Josh and Risner exchanged greetings with Kippler, Tony asked, "When did you move to New Atlantis?"

"About three years ago. You know how much I like the water, Tony, especially large bodies of water with salt in them."

When Kippler had shown everyone to a seat and poured each a cup of coffee, he asked, "Now, tell me the reason which brings me the honor of your presence."

Josh glanced at his friends, then began with the recent news stories about the decommissioning of the Dolphdroids. He explained his own confusion about the true motive or motives behind the decommissioning. He went on to describe visiting his grandson's room and the conversation about the ant farm that ensued. Josh leaned forward in his chair, placed his elbows on his knees, folded his hands together and locked his eyes on Kippler. "Dr. Kippler, the Dolphdroids are my creation. They're like children to me, my children. I brought them into existence. Now their existence is being threatened. I've done other work that's been meaningful to me before and since the creation of the Dolphdroids, but they're the best thing I've ever done."

"I can understand that," Kippler said as he put down his cup of coffee and leaned back in his chair, his round stomach a comfortable place where he rested his hands.

Josh nodded and continued. "It was word association that planted the seed of the plan. 'Colony' was the word. My grandson's ant colony, the Dolphdroid colony. He imagined the benefits to the ants if he could have become one of them and told them they were about to lose their lives. He imagined showing them a better way to live: in his ant farm."

"What exactly are you proposing, Dr. Christopher?" Kippler asked, with a mixture of impatience and curiosity.

"The colony on the lunar surface is polluted," Josh said. "The Dolphdroids have lost a sense of their prime objective, which is to export key mineral products and energy to earth. But it goes much, much deeper than that. They've lost a sense of who they are. They've forgotten where they came from. They need a model of what it means to be a Dolphdroid. They need to see one at his best. Most of all, they need to be rescued from certain death."

Kippler interrupted. "There are a couple of problems for which I can see no solution. First, I understand that the wheels of the system are already in motion to terminate them, and a change of heart on the Dolphdroid's part isn't going to alter that fact. Second, you've been out of production for years. I'm sure the entire network of specialists that helped you create the Dolphdroids are scattered far and wide. It would be impossible to build another Dolphdroid in the time-frame that's required. As far as I know, you don't have a spare Dolphdroid waiting in the wings."

"Adam," Tony said. "We have Adam, the prototype."

"But he's in the Smithsonian West. I saw him two or three years ago while I was out there. You'd have to find a dolphin brain you could harvest, do the transplant, retrain Adam..." Kippler's voice trailed off and he was shaking his head.

"You haven't heard the half of it, Doc," Risner interjected. "There's no need to harvest a brain from a dolphin." Kippler looked at Risner with a raised eyebrow, then looked at Josh.

"Perhaps, Dr. Christopher, you'd better fill me in on the rest of the details, the 'half of it' that your partner is referring to."

Josh stood and went over to the sea window. A small school of fish passed by, light from the room reflecting off their scales like shimmering sequins. He turned around and looked at his two friends, then at Kippler. "I'm going to become Adam."

Chapter 10

"A brain transplant? Your brain interfaced with Adam's?" Kippler asked. "Is that what you have in mind?"

"Bingo!" Risner responded.

Josh glared at Risner, then turned to Kippler. "I realize, Dr. Kippler, that there are a great many issues involved here…"

"Not the least of which," Kippler interrupted, "is the fact that no human brain transplant has ever been done, and that until it's approved by the Medical Ethics Committee it would be illegal."

Tony leaned forward. "Dr. Kippler, we understand that there are a great many issues to be resolved in what we're suggesting, but we've begun to address them. As to the legality of our plans, the surgery will be done in a leased portable medical operations unit on a small ship in international waters. International law has no jurisdiction over such medical procedures. We would be breaking no law."

Kippler was quiet for a moment; then he changed the direction of the conversation. "How exactly is this termination process going to work?"

"Each Dolphdroid," Risner explained, "is outfitted with a self-destruct mechanism. It fries the motherboard in their personal computing module. They drop in their tracks. Life support for the biological brain ceases, and the brain dies of oxygen starvation. Legal death occurs, however, when the motherboard is destroyed."

"Who does this?" Kippler asked. "Who pushes the button?"

Risner continued, "No one. A computer-generated signal from the control center here on earth actually does it. The wheels have already been set in motion and now it's out of anyone's control."

Tony added, "The termination process was started by Admiral Hartung, head of the Extraterrestrial Research and Resources Center. Hartung can only act to terminate the project with approval of the Committee of Commissioners. That's happened, the termination countdown has begun, and it's irreversible. Josh has tried. There's no putting the horse back into the barn."

Risner interjected, "The approval by the Committee of Commissioners is designed to be a fail-safe system so that no one person, aggravated at the Dolphdroids for looking ugly or walking funny, can zap them out of existence. Inexplicably, the procedure has their approval. The wheels are in motion."

Kippler took a deep breath, glanced at Risner and Tony, and then focused on Josh. "I'm still not clear as to how you propose to save the Dolphdroids, Dr. Christopher. First of all, from what I've gathered, things have gotten quite nasty in the colony. It's doubtful that you could really turn things around. Second, you've just informed me that the termination process is irreversible. Even if every Dolphdroid started to live an angelic lifestyle, the order would still stand. Am I not right?"

"There still may be a way, Dr. Kippler, and that's why we're here," Josh replied.

"Perhaps you better explain."

"Thank you, Doc," Risner said. "Tony and I've been waiting for the rest of the details ourselves. You see, up to this point, Josh hasn't clued us in on the details. We're interested in hearing more ourselves." Risner gave Josh a wry smile.

Josh returned the smile. "I wish I could give you the complete picture, but I'm following the policy of not giving out more information than any given person needs to know. I can tell you that it has to do with their life-value rating."

"What is it?" Kippler asked.

"Only three," Risner said with distinct hostility in his voice. "The same as the house sparrow."

"I find that hard to believe," Kippler responded. "After all, the bald eagle has a life-value of somewhere around three hundred, doesn't it? The dolphin itself has a life-value of four hundred and eighty, only twenty life-value points below humans. I know that because of my obvious interest in oceans and ocean life. Why the great disparity between the dolphin and the Dolphdroid that possesses a dolphin's brain?"

"It's the anti-robotics attitude that exists," Risner stated with the conviction of someone who had thought through the subject long ago. "People are scared silly that robots will overtake us some day."

Tony continued, "Dr. Hartung himself crusaded to have the Dolphdroids rated above the primates, closer to the five hundred figure for humans, when they were first developed. His argument was that they possessed a dolphin's brain. Of course, harvesting dolphin's brains was a controversial procedure. Many people rejected the whole project out of hand because of that."

"The debate made the top of the news many times," Kippler added. "As I recall, Dr. Christopher, your own son led some of the demonstrations against the harvesting of dolphin brains for the project."

"He's come around on that whole issue," Risner said in a defensive tone. "I just wish some other people would wise up to the unique kind of creature we have in the Dolphdroids. The fact is, they have a measly rating of three because people don't like robots. There's little doubt that their real popularity took a nose dive when Tasmer Radcliff's test model of his robot design went berserk while working as a store clerk, remember? He killed a half dozen people with his bare hands, just because a customer thought he had priced an item wrong."

"At any rate," Tony interjected, "the Dolphdroids ended up with a life-value rating lower than new biologically-engineered bacteria. The entire colony of one hundred and fifty Dolphdroids have a life-value rating of only four hundred and fifty! With the deaths it's even less now."

Josh appeared calm, his legs crossed, and his arms resting limply on the chair's armrests, as he added, "Their low life-value rating will work to their advantage."

No one spoke. "Explain," Kippler asked.

"That's what I can't go into right now. When the mission's complete, it'll be clear."

"There he goes again, playing Dr. Mysterious," Risner exclaimed.

Kippler shifted his weight in his chair. "Let me get this straight. You want me to perform a mind transplant, your mind into Adam, a feat that has never been attempted before and is highly risky at best. You want to permanently change your form of existence from human to Dolphdroid just for the outside chance that you might be able to save them?"

Josh smiled and nodded. "In essence, that's correct, although I was hoping you'd have the courtesy to reverse the operation if the mission is successful."

Kippler threw his hands up in the air and brought them down to the arm rests of his chair again. "Take it out, put it back, sure, no problem." He paused, studying Josh carefully. "It would be a tough enough task to do a transplant to Adam, but keeping your body in suspended animation for the duration until the reversal could be attempted is entirely another matter."

"If anyone can do it, you can, Dr. Kippler," Josh said.

Kippler was silent for a few moments, appearing to study a spot on the floor. He looked at Josh. "You really think this can be pulled off, don't you?"

"Yes," Josh said.

"You'll need someone who knows suspended animation forward and backward. It's an iffy science at best. You could be stuck as a Dolphdroid if your body's not tucked in properly for a long sleep."

"I've considered all the ramifications many times, Dr. Kippler. I know the risks."

"Is the doctor who did the mind transplants to the Dolphroids available to assist on this?" Kippler asked.

Tony responded, "That would be Dr. Richard Gray, and yes, he's available. His emotional involvement with the Dolphdroids runs deep, as you can imagine."

Josh was encouraged. Kippler's questions indicated that he was taking the proposal seriously.

"Tony, do you feel the wetware used to interface the dolphin mind with the Dolphdroid computer can be adapted to work with human tissue and neurons?" Kippler asked.

"I see no insurmountable problems. If we get your cooperation, one of the next steps is to take a sample of Dr. Chris' nerve cells as soon as possible and start growing a culture on an interface chip."

Kippler walked over to his sea-view window and stared at the fish that swam slowly in and out of view. After what seemed an eternity to the three men, Kippler walked back to his desk and pressed the call button for his secretary. He ordered a meal for his three guests. "I won't be joining you, gentlemen; I'll be taking a swim. I think best when I'm wet."

Within twenty minutes the food arrived. They were eating in silence when Risner said, pointing to the window on the sea, "There he is." Kippler wore an orange and yellow wet suit. He seemed to be intentionally swimming in and out of a school of large fish. Risner continued, "Some people pace back and forth when they're thinking through an issue; Kippler swims back and forth. He's a very strange man. Are you sure you want to put your mind in his hands?"

"I'm sure," Josh said.

When the food trays had been removed by Kippler's secretary, the three men occupied their time waiting for Kippler to return by studying his paintings of the sea and watching out the sea window. Finally Kippler walked in, drying his hair with a towel. He flung the towel over the back of a chair by the door, and as he made his way to his desk he said, "I've decided I can use a little excitement in my old age. This retirement is driving me crazy. Consider me part of the team." His three visitors smiled.

Kippler invited them to stay another day to work out some of the details. Risner and Tony worked with Kippler, going over data on the dolphin's neuro systems and studying the characteristics of human dendrites, the synaptic inputs and outputs, and how they differed from those of a dolphin. Josh busied himself with fleshing out the schedule and came up with a specific date for the inrobation. At one point he allowed himself a few moments to reflect on what he had been planning. He was to become a robot, like those he had created. He would become one of them. They had no idea what he had planned, what their creator was about to do for them.

That evening Kippler treated them to dinner at what they later decided had to be the most expensive restaurant in the undersea city. The tables were placed along a wall of glass through which they could watch fish swim beside men and women outfitted in wet suits. Soft waltz music played and it seemed as if the fish and divers swam to its beat. Over dessert Josh shared his plans for a meeting with all the principal players. Then he looked at the gathered team and said, "We need a code name for the project."

"I suspect you already have one in mind," Risner said.

"I do."

"Well?" Risner prompted.

"The colony has been judged and condemned," Josh explained. "Do they deserve to be terminated? Some say they do. I agree that their world is a fallen world. They may not deserve a second chance according to many people, but they're going to get it. It's mercy we're talking about; that's what we're going to show them. I'd like to code-name the project 'Moon's Mercy.'"

By noon the next day the three men were ready to leave New Atlantis. Zach was waiting for them, the Horizon prepped and ready to go. He promised that the transition from water to air would be just as exciting as the transition from air to water had been.

"I can hardly wait," Risner said as he climbed into the craft after Tony.

They made their way slowly away from the walls of the underground city and began ascending at an increasing speed. Just before breaking the surface Zach pushed the throttle ahead. The craft leaped out of the water like a dolphin. There was the blast of the aircraft engine exploding to life and the men found themselves pushed back into their seats. Seawater on the windshield streaked upward and was gone. Zach leveled off and throttled back, banking the craft.

"That does it!" Risner explained. "I'm never riding in one of these contraptions again! I don't care if it was a brilliant idea conceived on the back of a restaurant place mat. Give me an aircraft or a watercraft and I can cope, but don't give me both in one."

Once they were in the PAV it took Josh only a moment to set the travel coordinates and be airborne. Someone parked in a van nearby, unseen to Josh and his companions, noted the time of their departure and relayed the message to a bearded man drinking a cola in a small café in the Smoky Mountains. The observer gave him the PAV's travel coordinates.

"Don't miss. Failure is unacceptable," the observer said.

"I won't," the man in the café assured him, and broke the connection on his wrist communicator.

He asked for another cola and checked the time every few sips. The cola finished, he tossed a bill on the counter and walked out to his sky bike. Looking around to make certain no one was coming or going, he pushed the bike behind the small restaurant. It was no easy task on the gravel, because of the sky bike's small wheels. It was meant for flying, not for road use. Sweating, he parked the bike near an overflowing dumpster, glanced around to reassure himself that he wasn't being watched, and unzipped his bike bag. He pulled out several tubular pieces and some other parts, quickly snapping them together with the speed and precision of someone who had done it many times before. Soon he had two weapons mounted on his bike, one on each side.

He put on a dark helmet and tight-fitting gloves, mounted the bike, and activated the canopy. It came forward and down, and as it did he leaned forward, laying his chest on the foam-covered rest and gripping the steering shafts. The twin engines roared to life, spewing flames behind the bike. Seconds later the man and his bike were at treetop level. The sound of the lift-off gave the waitress pause as she cleaned the table where the man had sat. It wasn't often they had a sky biker stop by. The thin walls of the café vibrated, shaking the framed health certificate above the cash register.

Straightening the bike's trajectory, he gave it full power and was soon out of sight of a customer who had just arrived at the café and had paused at the door to watch the bike rise above the restaurant. Ten minutes later he saw his target. He prided himself on a quick, clean job. His proficiency put him in high demand with those who needed people removed. A quick kill was his standard procedure, but he felt playful today. "Let the cat play with the mouse before he eats it," he whispered, his words loud inside his helmet.

"I still say the man is a little wacko," Risner said. "Do you really want to put your brain in the hands of a man who has to take a swim in order to make a decision?"

"He's the best man there is, and I'm certain…" Josh was interrupted by the sudden appearance of a sky bike that came from above, diving at a steep angle, nearly clipping the nose of the PAV.

"What in tarnation was that?" Risner exclaimed.

"A sky bike," Tony answered.

"He nearly clobbered us," Risner said.

"It was intentional." Josh's voice was calm. His years of experience flying in battle situations made him trust his instincts. He glanced through the canopy, then at the monitor showing a rear view. "He's coming up from behind. I think he has a couple of missiles."

"Missiles? You mean he's going to fire them at us?" Risner asked.

Tony looked at Josh. "Why?"

Josh didn't answer. Watching the rear monitor, he saw a flash of light from the side of the sky bike. Josh jerked the PAV to the right, slamming Risner and Tony into the left side of their safety harnesses. They all saw a streak of light just outside the left of the canopy speed off into the horizon and disappear.

"He's got one more missile," Josh said, still watching his rear monitor.

"He tried to kill us!" Risner exclaimed.

"Where is he?" Tony asked, as he glanced to the left, then to the right.

Josh looked out the canopy and tightened his safety harness. "He'll be moving in for the kill, and this time he won't shoot until he's close. He won't miss. We can't outrun him; the bike's faster than the PAV. My maneuver clued him in that I've been in this kind of situation before. Next time he won't take any chances."

"What are we going to do?" Risner asked, adding, "I don't like flying in the first place and now we're in a dogfight for our lives. This is not good!"

"Quiet!" Tony snapped. "Let Josh think."

Scanning earth and sky, Josh mumbled more to himself than to the others, "I need to gain some advantage." Just then he noticed the monorail train, moving like a gray snake near the base of a mountain. It appeared to be a freight train, and that meant it was unmanned. Where was that tunnel? He recalled seeing one on the flight down. There it was! After the train took another curve it would be heading through the tunnel. Josh glanced ahead. The size of the mountain told him the tunnel had to be about a mile long. He glanced at the entrance. It had a single monorail, and appeared to have no room to spare. Josh glanced in his rearview screen; the sky bike was gaining on him. He had to do something, and he had to do it now.

"Hold on," he ordered. He jerked the nose of the PAV up sharply, went into a tight half-loop, and came out flying upside down toward the sky bike. He paused momentarily as the two vehicles streaked toward each other, then sent his craft into a dive, filling the front of the canopy with a view of the earth. A moment later Josh pulled out of the dive, leveling off the craft in an upright position, then sent it into a steep climb, giving a forward view of nothing but clouds. Then he rolled to the left and leveled out again.

The terror that made Risner mute abated enough for him to cry out, "We're going to die, I know we're going to die."

"It's just like the good ol' days," Josh mumbled to himself. "I wish I had a fighter craft with something to throw back at him. But maybe this will work."

"What will work?" Tony asked anxiously.

Josh glanced at the train, then the tunnel, then his rearview screen. The sky bike wasn't in sight – there it was! It was about a quarter of a mile behind and would gain on them fast.

"You said 'maybe' something would work. I don't like that word 'maybe.' What are you going to try?" Risner asked.

"This." He pitched the PAV to the right and into a dive.

"Whooooa!" Risner exclaimed. Josh pulled up at the last moment, flying the PAV at treetop level, a blur of foliage streaking by. Then the trees were gone and they were skimming over a small pond, whipping past a fisherman who, for them, was freeze framed in mid-cast. The lake was behind them and the blur of trees was back. Josh jerked the PAV to the left, then straightened it. They were flying inches above the monorail.

Tony saw the tunnel first. He glanced at Josh. "You're taking the tunnel?"

Josh nodded.

"Will we fit?" Tony asked.

"I think so," Josh said.

"Oh, great, he 'thinks so!'" Risner exclaimed.

"Keep an eye on the rearview monitor. See if he follows us in," Josh said.

"What if a train comes?" Risner asked.

"Not if – when," Josh responded. "The question is, how good is my timing?" He decreased his speed slightly.

The small black hole that was the opening of the tunnel quickly grew larger as they approached, seeming to open up like a giant monster anxious to swallow its prey. Then the canopy went

95

dark. The illumination of the instruments increased automatically, though Josh didn't notice. He resisted making even the slightest change in his flight path, leaning forward as he tried to force his eyes to adjust more quickly to the dark. He strained to gauge his position by the faint tunnel lights as they streaked past on both sides at a dizzying, nearly disorienting speed. The exit in the distance was just a pin prick of light.

"I think the biker followed us into the tunnel," Tony reported.

The light at the end of the tunnel was quickly growing larger. Trees could now be seen outlining the opening.

"Good, we're almost…" Risner said but was interrupted by Tony shouting.

"A train!"

The lighted opening now had an even brighter, piercing light in its center, the headlight of the train.

Josh pushed the throttle all the way forward and the PAV lurched ahead at its top speed. "Come on, baby," Josh whispered to his PAV.

Risner closed his eyes and Tony moaned. The headlight of the train was nearly blinding. Then light filled the canopy and Josh jerked the PAV into a steep climb, the antenna on the train making a whipping sound as it slapped against the underside of the PAV. Josh brought the PAV out of its near-vertical climb, banked, and came around for a view of the tunnel opening. The train was slowing, coming to a stop. Smoke began to billow from the tunnel.

"He didn't make it," Tony said with relief.

"Let's head home," Josh said as he banked the craft again, leveled it, and took a course between two mountains.

Chapter 11

Josh wasn't surprised by the order from National Airspace Control to stop in Dayton and file a complete report of the incident with the sky bike. Risner had tried to talk him out of reporting the incident, certain that it would cause just such a delay. Josh had insisted, however, arguing that the mid-tunnel collision of a sky bike and train, and the record of Josh's PAV flying through the airspace at the time, would be enough to pull him into the investigation. While they went from interview to interview and filled out a tower of reports, Josh caught himself wishing that he had gone along with Risner's suggestion. Tony reminded them that even if the paperwork were expedited the process would take some time, because the authorities had removed the PAV's black box and were analyzing the data.

Three hours after walking into the offices of the National Airspace Control they were finally finished, but the NAC director wanted to see them before they left. The area director, a short, thin man with white curly hair who was wearing a shirt one size too big for him, met them at his office door and invited them in. He closed the door behind them and motioned them to take seats in the chairs clustered about the front of his messy desk. He sat down behind the desk, shoving a sheaf of papers to the side.

"Dr. Christopher, I have studied many a flight tape from many a black box, but I have rarely seen flying like that which I reviewed on your tape. I ran the data through our flight simulator just a few minutes ago. It was truly amazing. Your records show that you earned a variety of medals for your flying during the last war; I can see why."

Josh nodded.

The director cleared his throat, changing his tone from admiring to authoritative. "Chances are good that when the investigation is complete you won't be charged with anything, other than perhaps reckless flying, which will result in some kind of fine. Considering your overall record, military and private, I suspect the review board will likely believe your statement that you were certain the train approaching the tunnel was an unmanned freighter and that you did not willfully endanger human life."

"The whole event was intended to endanger only the life of the attacking sky biker, which is exactly what it did," Risner interjected.

Josh shot Risner a look that kept him from saying anything more.

"Thank you," Josh said, as he began to rise from his chair. His traveling companions did the same.

"There's one more thing," the director said with caution in his voice. The three stopped and turned toward him. He paused, glancing at each of them, his eyes settling on Josh. "I shouldn't be telling you this. It has to be off the record." He paused. They finally realized that he was looking for assurance that what he was about to say would go no further. All three nodded. The director continued. "Just moments ago we received a report on the sky bike that attacked you. It belongs to a known hit man who, according to our sources, was under the employ of the Warwick Crime Syndicate."

"Oh, great!" Risner exclaimed, rolling his eyes. "Now we've got one of the biggest crime syndicates in the world on our tail."

Tony shook his head in dismay. Josh glanced at his friends, then back at the director.

"That's right," the director said. Looking at Josh, he said, "You're the Dolphdroid creator, I know. I don't know what you're working on now, but whatever it is, the Warwick Syndicate must not like it. They play rough, Doctor Christopher, real rough."

The remainder of the flight home was uneventful, cloud cover obscuring their view of the earth below. "I never thought I could enjoy a boring flight as much as I have since leaving the NAC," Tony said.

That night, after fixing himself a sandwich, Josh headed to

bed and quickly fell asleep, completely exhausted from the trip to New Atlantis and the encounter with the sky bike. He would have slept into the morning, but his computer intruded on his sleep, announcing, "Rob is at the front door."

Sitting up and swinging his feet off the edge of the bed, Josh stated, "Computer, let Rob in."

Ten minutes later Josh and his son were seated at the kitchen table drinking coffee. Rob had offered to brew some while his dad took a shower.

"I heard about the attack on the news this morning," Rob said, a smile on his face that ineffectively masked his deep concern. "Quite a trick, using the train tunnel like that."

"Fortunately, the old reflexes were still there. Nothing like adrenalin pumping through your body as you stare death in the face to bring them out," Josh said. He took a sip. "Good coffee," he said.

Rob's face turned serious as he caressed his own cup of coffee. "Dad, are you sure you want to pursue this? The news said it was a random attack by a crazy sky biker but that doesn't ring true."

Josh took another sip of his coffee. "You're probably right," he said, deciding against telling his son what the director of the NAC had said. "So, what did you find out?"

"Well, I think I uncovered a few pieces of the puzzle, but you won't like the way they fit together. I know I sure don't. First of all, a man by the name of Emmerson Brunner seems to be the one behind the move to get rid of the Dolphdroids. He runs his own company in the L.A. area."

"He worked with Radcliff, didn't he?" Josh asked.

Rob nodded. "He was his right hand man, then took over when Radcliff made his long one way swim. It was difficult getting any current information about their operations, but I managed to find out a few things. Emmerson always felt that Radcliff wasn't moving fast enough, investing enough, taking enough risks to make things work. Radcliff was brilliant – I guess I don't need to tell you that – but he was also methodical. Emmerson became really frustrated. It was no secret around the company that he wanted to see Radcliff go, because he wanted to take over the company. I got this information from a disgruntled former employee, so I'm not certain how accurate it is, but she said it was way too convenient for Radcliff to have drowned when he did. She said the artificial intelligence program they were working on was at a crucial stage. It had something to do with moving into what she called 'fuzzy logic,' but Radcliff wasn't as convinced as Emmerson that it was the way to go."

"Fuzzy logic has to do with all the gray areas of thought," Josh interjected. "It sounds as if Emmerson might have made more headway in the field than others had. He undoubtedly wanted to create a computer program with real intuitive senses, maybe even emotions, or at least pseudo-emotions. That's been the big prize all along. Interesting." Then, realizing he was digressing, Josh added, "Sorry, Rob. Go on."

"My source seems to feel that Emmerson may have had a part in Radcliff's death."

"So his death may not have been a suicide?"

"Oh, it was a suicide, all right. It's just that Emmerson may have psychologically manipulated him to feel he had failed so miserably that there was no reason for him to continue, that his work had hit a dead end."

"Could Emmerson really have done that? Radcliff was brilliant."

"But not exactly mentally stable, according to my sources. There had been growing concerns that Radcliff was being manipulated by Emmerson. Every so often Radcliff recognized it, got really upset, and would storm off for hours, even days on occasion. He may have possessed superior intelligence, but his emotional development left something to be desired."

"So when Radcliff committed suicide, Emmerson took over," Josh said.

Rob nodded. "Right."

Josh got up to refill his coffee cup. "What's the status of Emmerson's research now?"

"This is where it gets interesting, Dad. Emmerson and company apparently have a humaniform robot ready to go that can really think much like a human, but they're keeping it hush-hush. You ought to see their facilities. No big corporate sign, waterfalls or gold-trimmed lobby. It's nothing but an old warehouse. Public relations is non-existent. If anything, they have an anti-public relations policy. That's why nobody knows how far along they are on this project. I'm led to believe they're in actual production and a dozen or more humaniforms are operational. A couple of test sheets that accidentally got tossed out with the remains of someone's sack lunch, which I dutifully retrieved from near their garbage incinerator, suggest they're stronger and perhaps more agile than the Dolphdroids. I have the papers; you can have someone go over them."

"And you think that Emmerson has something to do with Hartung's insistence to kill off the Dolphdroids, maybe to make way for Emmerson's humaniforms?"

"It seems very possible. But Dad, that's not the worst of it. Emmerson developed a cash flow problem a few years back. He ended up borrowing heavily from a loan company that's reputed to be connected to a crime syndicate."

"The Warwick Crime Syndicate," Josh interjected.

Rob stared at his father in disbelief, then nodded. "How did you know?" No sooner had he asked the question then a look of comprehension came across his face, followed by a look of concern. "You have more to tell me about your dogfight yesterday involving the sky bike, don't you, Dad?" Rob didn't wait for a response. He wanted to finish giving his father all the information he had uncovered. "Well, as I understand it, the loan company was getting anxious to collect. Emmerson had convinced them his humaniforms would be in high demand, but with the anti-robot sentiment he wasn't finding much of a market for them."

"You mean," Josh interrupted, "he's been trying to market his humaniforms? I can't believe that's not public knowledge."

"You have to remember, Dad, that unemployment is high in this country, and even higher in other places. It's the old story of the unions being dead set against robots doing jobs that people can do. Emmerson was smart enough to approach company heads privately, but he still never got to first base. No company wanted any part of using humaniforms, or have it leaked that they were even seriously considering it."

Leaning back in his chair and pushing his empty coffee cup aside, Josh added, "So Emmerson figured the only way he could sell his humaniforms, get back his massive investment, and pay off his massive debt was for them to be purchased by the government for lunar mining."

Rob nodded.

"It makes sense," Josh continued. "But Emmerson needed the Dolphdroids to become unproductive and to be seen as a threat to human life."

"But something troubles me, Dad. I thought Imus said he was going to put some low-level human workers on the lunar surface."

"He did say that. But I have a strong suspicion that he really knows differently. Of course he's aware that public opinion wouldn't be in favor of replacing the Dolphdroids with humaniforms at this point, but the fact is that humans need expensive life support systems, at a substantial cost. It's beginning to make sense. Eventually Imus is going to suggest using humaniforms as the only logical solution."

Rob brought the conversation back to his father's encounter with the sky bike. Josh explained the police's theory about the Warwick Crime Syndicate. He realized that his son was now deeply involved in his wild and crazy plan and that he had a right to know all the details. By the end of Josh's retelling of the events, he could see that Rob was worried.

Josh tried to change the subject. "Rob, there's something I still don't understand. Why does Imus seem to be cooperating with Emmerson's plan? He's risking his entire career by the decisions he's making. If it's ever proven that he's cooperating with someone with mob connections, his career as a commissioner is over."

"I happen to have a little piece of information relating to that subject. It seems that Emmerson has something on Dr. Imus Hartung. A friend of mine, Darren Baker, was commissioned to write and do the photography for a book on the commissioners, a huge coffee table-sized book. I decided to meet with Darren and see what he could tell me about Dr. Hartung."

"And?"

"It seems that Imus cheated on his civil exam when he was in his early twenties. Dad, if that ever came to light Imus would be through. There are plenty of people waiting in the wings to take his plush job who would make certain that the information was leaked to the press."

"How do you know that Emmerson's aware of it?"

"Simple: the crime syndicate keeps a file for emergency purposes. They call it information leverage. My source tells me they've been aware of this for a long time. Of course we can't be absolutely positive that Emmerson knows about this and told Hartung, but it's likely."

Josh's televiewer intruded on their conversation. Bill Zucker at the Research and Resources Center appeared on screen. His frown forewarned Josh of bad news. "Josh, I've been fired. Imus is replacing me tomorrow morning."

Chapter 12

Rob had left and Bill Zucker hadn't yet arrived, so Josh spent the time viewing computer file images of the Dolphdroids. As he moved from one image to the next, memories and feelings came flooding back. An image came up of the first 50 production models of the Dolphdroids. It had been taken at an orientation and training camp.

Much had been programmed into the software, but these were living, thinking, feeling creatures, and they required a different approach. Day-to-day living at the camp had uncovered a variety of small glitches that were corrected by a mass wireless download of new programming data to all 50 Dolphdroids before they graduated. After graduation the wireless connection was permanently terminated, making them fully-independent beings.

Another image was of Adam standing by the Christmas tree. His face had a warm yellow color, the Dolphdroids' way of smiling.

Josh's heart seemed to jump from his chest at the next image: Anne standing by him in front of the Christmas tree. How he missed her! He felt a deep yearning for the image to become real, for that scene to be lived again, but then reminded himself that a pity party of one was of no benefit to anyone. He had spent more time than he could measure grieving over Anne. Now the Dolphdroids needed him. He advanced to the next picture, another image of Adam. It was just as well, he thought. He couldn't bring Anne back, but he could Adam.

Yes, he could and would bring Adam back. The prototype was in a form of suspended animation. Of course he no longer had a dolphin's mind, but he could be given a new mind. Josh tried to

105

comprehend what it would mean to no longer be Dr. Joshua Christopher but to be Adam, to have a body, not of flesh but of metal. After a moment he abandoned the effort and thought about more fundamental issues. The procedure would be planned as reversible, but he had to make a decision based on its being one way: he might be Adam forever, a man locked in a robotic body. The other possible outcome was that he would die in the attempt to reverse the process. There were other issues, too. What about transportation to the moon? Once there, could he integrate himself sufficiently into the lives of the Dolphdroids to help them see a better way? And there were Imus, Emmerson, and the Warwick Syndicate; could Moon's Mercy succeed with so many wanting it to fail? There was the ultimate question: would he be able to save them? Josh's thoughts were interrupted by the computer announcing, "Bill Zucker is at the door."

"Let him enter," Josh commanded.

As he walked toward the door he knew that another piece of the complex plan was falling into place. Bill's organizational skills were what he needed to have the mission succeed.

"You have any work for an unemployed person?" Bill asked in jest.

"Imus really let you go, after all these years?" Josh asked, still in disbelief as he let Bill in.

"I guess he figured that I was too close to you. They need to guarantee that the decommissioning of the Dolphdroids will move ahead with as few complications as possible, and I'm a complication as long as I'm in charge of the center. I expected this to happen."

"The answer is 'yes'," Josh said.

Bill looked puzzled. "Yes?"

"Yes, I have work for an unemployed person." Josh motioned to a chair. "Have a seat."

Bill listened intently. He was a man who appreciated details, and Josh knew that not a word of what he told his friend would be forgotten. After hearing the plan, Bill expressed the same concern that Rob, Risner and Tony had: the personal risk was enormous. Once again Josh tried to explain that since Anne's death, nothing held a true and deep fascination for him. He added that his only hesitancy was the possibility that he might not be able to grow old enjoying his renewed relationship with Rob and his grandson. Josh explained that saving the Dolphdroids was something he had to attempt; he couldn't go on living if he knew he hadn't tried. Bill asked how Rob had reacted to the plan. Josh explained that after Rob's initial shock at the boldness of the plan and the risk involved, he realized that his father couldn't be talked out of the plan, and gave his blessing. In fact, Josh explained with pride that Rob was actively involved in the project, ferreting out needed information. Josh went on to explain how Risner and Tony were already working on the project and detailed their visit with Dr. Kippler.

Bill bombarded Josh with questions. An hour later, satisfied, Bill pulled out a tablet-type from his pocket, unfolded the paper-thin keyboard on the coffee table, and began to make notes. They worked out a preliminary schedule of what needed to be done.

Josh suggested his Uncle Ben's farm outside the small town of Parkersburg, Iowa, as an ideal headquarters for the mission. It would be a great place to store and work on the space plane they would need for the mission.

"The farm has an old barn that could be used as a hangar," Josh explained. "My uncle and aunt don't get out much, and can keep a secret when they do go to town."

Bill nodded. "We'll need someone to help us locate and outfit a space plane."

"I already have that taken care of," Josh said. "Max Henderson has agreed to do the work. He and I go way back."

"To the war?"

"To the war. He was my ground support chief on the craft I flew. When you fly under wartime conditions you put your life into the hands of the ground support chief who has the responsibility to make sure your craft won't fail you and turn into your ultimate enemy. Max was the best there was."

"How about Jamison Faberson?"

Josh thought for a moment, then nodded. Jamison Faberson was a multimillionaire who had always shown great interest in the Dolphdroid project. "Good idea. I know what you're thinking and, yes, I think there's a good chance he'll help fund the project. I'll contact him myself."

"And how do we acquire Adam?" Bill asked.

"We still need someone to lead a midnight raid on the Smithsonian West to free Adam. Rob's got some contacts. I'll

107

check with him," Josh said.

After a couple of hours of work the initial plan seemed to be roughed out to their mutual satisfaction. "We need a meeting of all the principal players," Josh said as he walked Bill to the door. "Loyalty, trust, cooperation, and confidence in each other are essential for the project to work, and it only can happen if everyone feels a part of the team."

"Where?" Bill asked.

"My old friend Nathan Pickering's cabin in the Upper Peninsula of Michigan," Josh said.

Bill glanced back at Josh as he left the house. Both men's faces registered the sobering reality of the amazing challenges and obstacles they faced with Moon's Mercy.

"Bobo McClarin is his name," Rob said.

Josh glanced out the canopy of his PAV to the left and to the right, checking for air traffic, before looking at his son who was seated beside him. "Bobo McClarin? With a name like 'Bobo' are you sure you didn't get someone who wants to storm the Smithsonian West instead of making a quiet midnight requisition?"

Rob chuckled. "Since when did we start making judgments about people's character and ability on the basis of their names?"

"But Bobo?" Josh shook his head. "So you think he can do the job."

"I'm certain. He comes with very high recommendations, although I'm not at liberty to give his list of references."

"And you wonder why I'm concerned," Josh said, rolling his eyes.

"Ten thousand feet," the PAV computer announced. It was the highest flight path a PAV was allowed to take. Josh enjoyed the view from this altitude and appreciated the better mileage and faster speed that the thinner air offered.

"Well, I can tell you that he has no outstanding warrants," Rob continued. "He's just served three years for a break-in, so he's clear with the law. Bobo's the best at getting into places you aren't supposed to get into."

"But apparently not always the best at not getting caught," Josh said.

Rob shrugged. "No one's perfect."

Josh took a deep breath and glanced out both sides of the cockpit. "I don't like this kind of cloak and dagger stuff. I wish I could just walk in and reclaim Adam."

"You could, Dad."

"I know, but it would make the news and draw too much attention to me and what we're planning to do. This way it will be reported that Adam was stolen and our plan stays under wraps." Josh touched a button, prompting the computer to give the time of arrival.

"Ten minutes and thirty seconds," the computer responded.

Suddenly the craft went silent. "Engine failure, engine failure," the computer announced, its lack of emotion belying the seriousness of the situation.

"What's wrong?" Rob asked, leaning forward and gripping both armrests.

"I don't know," Josh said as his eyes darted from instrument to instrument. They both felt their stomachs rise as the craft started plummeting toward earth.

Rob remained silent, knowing that his dad needed to give full attention to the silent craft. A strange calmness came over him, a deep trust and confidence in his father. He felt like a little boy again, helpless as his dad solved the problem at hand.

"Eight thousand feet," the computer announced. Josh reached under the instrument panel in front of him, flipped open a protective cover, and punched the restart sequence control, but nothing happened. "Seven thousand five hundred feet," the computer stated. The craft began to shudder and slowly turn clockwise, the earth below rotating counter-clockwise. They were no longer moving forward, just downward at an ever-greater speed. A strange whistling sound began which Josh had never heard before, the result of the unique air flow on the craft as it continued its vertical plunge.

Rob and Josh glanced at each other; then Josh looked back at the instruments. "I don't think we're going to get things up and running."

"Seven thousand feet," the computer stated.

Josh continued to work deftly with the controls, trying to coax life back into the silent vehicle. "Six thousand feet," the computer said. The computer had skipped the five hundred mark and was only using increments of thousands, a response to their increasing speed.

Josh changed the setting on the thrust-vectored engine nozzle and the craft pitched sharply to the right. He worked with it and the wing flaps and was able to coax the nose of the craft nearly straight down. The front view through the canopy was filled with the earth coming toward them quickly.

"There!" Josh exclaimed. He had managed to use the adjustable engine nozzle as an additional control surface to get the craft to do what he wanted. "Five thousand feet," the computer announced. Rob's fingers dug into the upholstery of his armrests. His body felt weightless. Gravity was pulling them down to a quick death. "Four thousand feet," the computer said.

"Computer, stop altitude checks," Josh commanded. He didn't want the distraction of its incessant reporting. He didn't need the computer to tell him how fast the ground was coming up. He glanced out the canopy and saw Lake Huron as the PAV continued to plummet. "If this thing is falling like a rock, we'll see if it can skip like one," he mumbled loud enough for Rob to hear.

"Do something, Dad," Rob moaned, his eyes fixed on the quickly approaching lake where the glimmer of small waves was now visible.

Josh held the controls steady for another few seconds. "Here we go," he whispered, pulling back on the steering column. The G forces pushed them hard into their seats. In the next moment Rob realized they were flying nearly parallel to the water, the lake a blur just outside the cockpit.

Two fishermen were in a small outboard, fishing poles leaning against the edge of their boat as they pulled beverages from a cooler. They heard a rush of wind and saw a silver streak only yards above their heads. Reacting in fright, they nearly upset the small boat. "What the..." one of them began to say, but whatever it had been was now a small dot in the distance, heading toward shore.

Josh banked the PAV slightly, turning it back toward the shore and slowing it dramatically. "Hold on, Rob!"

He pulled up the nose just as the craft slammed down on the water's surface, driving their spines into their seats. There was the sound of the exterior metal crumpling, then silence. They were temporarily airborne again. Then another spine-jolting hit on the water, though not as intense as the first, silence, another slam onto the water's surface, silence again, another slam onto the water's surface. The shore was coming up fast. Again and again they hit the water.

The nose pierced the surface, and the craft flipped, tail over nose. Both men lost consciousness.

When he regained consciousness Josh tried to push the mental fog away so he could think. He felt cool water. He suddenly remembered hitting the water. They were in the lake and the craft was upside down and taking on water. He heard Rob moan, slowly turned his head, and saw his son hanging from his seat harness, his body limp. Rob moaned again. "Rob! Rob! Wake up, Rob!" Josh pleaded.

Josh struggled to unbuckle his seat harness; then he fell to the top of the canopy. Reaching up, he struggled with Rob's harness. Rob was slowly waking up. "Rob!" Josh shouted. He needed his son's cooperation to get him out of his harness. Rob finally realized what his father was attempting to do. Together, they worked on his harness and finally he fell to the top of the canopy, joining his father. Josh reached for a control; the canopy began to slide open and water rushed in. Holding their breath, they struggled out of the cockpit and swam to the surface.

Three fishermen in a large boat had seen them hit the water and immediately headed in their direction. Pulling alongside the bobbing, upside-down PAV, they reached over the side of their boat and pulled the two men to the safety of their boat.

"Thanks," Josh said. "Can you save my PAV? Is there some way you can tow it to shore?"

The fishermen studied the situation and moved their boat alongside the PAV. Within minutes they had a line attached to the PAV and were pulling it to shore.

A small crowd had gathered on the beach and several of them helped pull the craft onto dry ground. Josh and Rob, soaked and becoming chilled, walked around the PAV. It had sustained major damage to its underbelly where it had taken the full force of the impact of the water.

By the time the police arrived, made their report, and impounded the craft for the National Airspace Control investigation, two hours had elapsed. A kind retired couple offered Josh and Rob some towels they had retrieved from their cabin. By the time Josh and Rob climbed into a rented car that was delivered to the beach they were reasonably dry. Rob drove, and in an hour's time they arrived at the cabin for the meeting.

The sight of the cabin brought back a flood of memories for Josh. It seemed the same as he had remembered it. The cabin was not small, having three bedrooms downstairs and two upstairs as well as a large living room and kitchen. As they approached, someone rose from one of the rocking chairs on the porch that ran the width of the cabin's front. He was a slightly overweight man with graying hair and beard, wearing green pants and a bright yellow shirt. The extra weight and beard temporarily concealed his identity, but Josh finally recognized his walk. It was Phil Kirkpatrick. The Dolphdroids' bodies were his design, and he had always claimed they were his best work. Josh was concerned that Adam had been incapacitated a long time during his display at the Smithsonian West and that Phil's expertise might be needed to put Adam back in prime shape. On a personal level, Josh wanted as much of the original team back together as possible.

With the rest of the team slated to arrive over the next few hours, Josh had time before the next team member's arrival to sit on the porch and reconnect with Phil, but Phil wanted to hear all of the details of their accident. Josh found it difficult to keep his attention on the conversation. Although he said nothing to Rob or Phil, Josh already knew what the outcome of the National Airspace Control's investigation of the PAV would report. It had been sabotage.

Chapter 13

The team arrived throughout late afternoon and dinner. The young man from the restaurant who had catered the meal came back at 7:30 to retrieve the remainder of the food, containers, and utensils. It was close to 8:00 when Josh walked to the center of the living room to start the meeting.

Seated on the aged couch, threadbare loveseat, and squeaky wooden chairs from the kitchen table, the team members were chatting, waiting for Josh to begin. Josh thought about the diversity of the group. Several of them had been a part of the original Dolphdroid development team, and this was a reunion for them. The new members would have to be incorporated – even Bobo McClarin, who sat silently in the corner with his large arms crossed on his great shelf of a stomach. The room slowly grew silent. All eyes were on Josh.

"Thanks for coming. It's good to see all of you," Josh said, glancing around the room. "As they say at funerals, too bad we had to meet under these circumstances. We're here to implement a plan to prevent the deaths of the Dolphdroids. The powers that be have decided, for reasons not entirely clear at this point, that the Dolphdroids need to be terminated. It's increasingly obvious that some people stand to gain a great deal from the failure of the Dolphdroid community, and they apparently stand to lose a great deal if the community continues to exist."

"Everyone needs to understand that involvement in this project carries a high level of personal risk," Risner interjected. "I'm sure you've heard about the episode with the sky bike and the train tunnel. Then there's the episode with Josh's PAV while he and

Rob were flying to this meeting. They're lucky to be alive. We're playing a dangerous game here."

"Risner's right," Josh responded. "It's clear that organized crime is involved. We believe that they've given extensive loans to a man named Emmerson Brunner. Brunner's working on an android project and will have his units waiting in the wings to take over the lunar mining operations at the right time. The government's purchase of the androids will mean that Emmerson can pay back his loans and live to see another day."

"But aren't they going to replace the Dolphdroids with low-grade workers?" The question came from Nancy Saunders a sociologist with doctoral work in android relationships and behavior. Josh had hired the petite woman with short blond hair when the project had been established 10 years earlier. She had done the preliminary studies and projections on potential problems that the Dolphdroids might face working as a colony on the lunar surface. Her expertise would be needed to plan Adam's entry into the colony.

"It appears that the idea of using low-level workers is just a smokescreen. We believe the ultimate goal is the utilization of Brunner's androids," Bill Zucker replied. Glancing around the room, he continued, "What we need to realize is that each one of us could become a possible target when we commit to this project."

Nancy Saunders tucked her pen into her notebook. Looking around the circle, she said, "Moon's Mercy is a crazy plan. There's a significant chance it won't work. We knew the personal risks when we signed up, and what's happened so far only confirms that fact. But here we all are. So give us the details."

Josh nodded, activated his hand-held electronic notepad, and the video display wall over the fireplace brightened. Under the title "Moon's Mercy" the board displayed 10 phases of the project: (1) acquisition of Adam, (2) refurbishing of Adam, (3) preparation of air/space craft, (4) surgical transfer procedure, (5) therapy and training for Josh/Adam, (6) the trip to the lunar surface, (7) the mission, (8) the return of Josh/Adam to earth, (9) reversal of the procedure, (10) therapy for Josh.

A lengthy planning session followed concerning the scheduling of the various phases of the project. Much of this time Josh found himself watching and listening. He reflected on how much he was depending on each of them and how much they would need to depend on each other in order for Moon's Mercy to succeed.

The acquisition team met in the kitchen. Gathered around the table were Josh, Bill Zucker, Phil Kirkpatrick, Risner Billingston, and Bobo McClarin.

"Fill us in on what we face getting Adam out of the Smithsonian West, Bobo," Bill Zucker asked.

Bobo leaned forward, his large forearms on the table. He looked at Phil, paused, and said, "First, are we sure that the robot, this Adam, is charged up enough and his computer is computing so that he can follow us out under his own power? I sure ain't gonna' carry that big pile of bolts."

"No problem," Phil replied. "The museum staff has a maintenance schedule for displays to keep lights, bells, and whistles going. Our reports indicate that Adam's fuel cells have been given the recommended maintenance charges. He should be good to go."

Turning to Josh, Bobo asked, "Doc, I've been told he needs to be activated by your voice command, and yours alone; is that true?"

"That's right. Once he recognizes my voice it should only take about 10 seconds for him to power up and do a systems check. He'll be fully operational at that point. Of course he's only a shell of what he was before his interfaced dolphin brain died, but he can still follow basic commands and function in a rudimentary way."

"How rudimentary? Can he run?" Bobo asked.

"He can run," Risner said. Then, looking concerned, he asked, "Why would he have to run?"

Bobo ignored the question, asking Josh, "Won't the authorities know that you're the one who removed Adam from the museum, since yours is the only voice he responds to?"

Phil answered for Josh. "We've covered that problem. We plan to leave a small transport cart outside the museum. The authorities will assume we used it to carry Adam out. We could actually do it that way, but he weighs a great deal and that method would slow us down. Like Risner said, he can run."

Satisfied for the moment, Bobo reached into his hip pocket and unfolded a wrinkled tourist's map of the Smithsonian West, flattening it out on the kitchen table with his big hands. "All right, then, this is where your Adam character is located, in the west quadrant toward the back," he said, thumping the map with his thick

115

index finger. Glancing around the table, he added, "I assume you all know that the complex is made up of four pyramid-shaped quadrants clustered around a square center area containing the information desk, main restrooms, eating area, and gift shop."

He didn't wait for a response. "There's no easy way of gaining access to the facility at night; the alarms are the latest in high tech and I don't have the code that will roll out the welcome mat for us."

"Then how are we going to gain access?" Risner asked.

"I was just getting to that, if you'd stop interrupting me. We're going to walk in just like everyone else during visiting hours, just not leave after visiting hours are over. We'll use a team of three: Doc, me, and one other of your choice, Doc. That's all we need. Any more and we'll be stumbling over ourselves. Near closing time we'll hide out over here in the historical farm display area," Bobo said, pointing to a location on the map next to the lunar display. "In this farm display is a facade of an old barn and a silo. When people are leaving we'll find an opportue moment, slip into the barn and up into the small hay loft, and hide under the hay. That's why I don't want half an army on this project. Doc, don't choose anyone with hay fever! Anyway, when the museum is closed for the night and things get quiet, we'll climb out and do our dastardly deed."

"How about leaving? Won't an alarm go off when we open a door from the inside?" Bill asked.

"It sure will. The night guard in that quadrant usually sits in an 18th century chair that's part of one of the displays. He removes the 'Do not sit on the furniture' sign and makes himself comfortable with his magazines. I guess it's his way of rebelling against a system that pays him peanuts. That chair is here," Bobo said, tapping the map with his finger. "I'll come around this corner and waft a little sleeping gas his direction and he'll doze off like a baby. We'll use the code box on his belt to open the door. You can hold the door open for me while I replace the code box; he'll wake up and think that he dozed off, none the wiser as to what just took place."

"Sounds simple enough," Risner said, though the tension in his voice revealed his skepticism.

"I'm not done yet," Bobo snapped, giving Risner a piercing glare. "There's a little detail that may be a problem: the HT bees."

116

"The HT bees?" Josh asked.

"The HT bees. The 'HT' stands for 'high tech.' They're miniature robotic flying machines the size of a bumblebee, but they pack a punch much greater than any bumblebee. The bees are the result of some recent government defense project in nano technology. Somebody got the idea to put them on active display at the Smithsonian West as part of the security system."

"How in the world can mechanical bees provide security?" Risner asked, failing to be put off by Bobo's attitude.

"Your questions are interrupting my explanation. Just let me finish, OK? These mechanical beastles are collected together in groups, called hives, at eight locations around the museum. Two hives are located in each of the four pyramids. They're attracted by heat, not flowers. The hives are activated each night as part of the security system. Sensors in the hive pick up any movement after hours and the bees spring into action. Each is a tiny heat-seeking missile. Unlike their biological counter-parts, their stingers, small hypodermic needles, are located in the front of each bee, not the rear. They fly right into their target. The needle pierces the skin, even through heavy clothing, and the impact releases a strong sedative. The sting from one HT won't put a person down, it'll just make you a little woozy, but if you get zapped by four or five you're down for the count, in lala land until the police show up."

"So what do we do about these bees?" Bill asked.

"Same thing the guard does when he enters a quadrant to make his rounds. I've got a gizmo that can hit all the possible frequencies that might deactivate the bees. We'll watch through binoculars. When the little light on the hive turns from red to green we know it's been deactivated."

Bobo pushed back from the table. "Well, that's about all I have for you. I'll get you in and out. All you have to do is get your pile of bolts to wake up and follow us out the door. I put my stuff in the far upstairs bedroom. I'm going to bed."

Bobo glanced back just before leaving the kitchen "Doc, I've done a lot of different jobs over the years, but this is the craziest thing I've ever been a part of. Lots of luck." With that, he waddled slowly toward the stairs.

When he was out of sight Risner huffed, "He's the only one getting paid and he acts like he's doing us a favor. He's got the

117

personality of an overripe tomato."

Josh chuckled. "I'm going to take a walk and then turn in myself. I've had a tiring flight up here and I could use some sleep." The comment drew smiles from Bill, Risner, and Phil.

Risner replied, "I know I'll never ride with you again. I don't enjoy flying through train tunnels." Josh walked into the living room and said good night to the group there before heading outside for a walk.

The next morning, mist lay like a white, moist blanket over the lake. The sunrise was a light show that only the early-rising Josh observed on his walk. When Josh returned to the cabin after following a winding trail that took an hour to hike, he found everyone up. Breakfast was being laid out by the caterer from the local restaurant. The server put out a spread of scrambled eggs, French toast, bacon, sausage, oatmeal, toast, and bagels. Bobo was first in line and took some of everything. A few people grabbed only a cup of coffee and a piece of toast or a bagel, breakfast clearly not their favorite meal of the day. By 8:30 the caterer had things cleaned up and was gone. The group divided into smaller groups of two or three and settled down in various locations in the cabin to continue the planning.

Josh met with Phil and Risner. He considered Phil Kirkpatrick to be the world's expert when it came to cybernetics, while Risner Billingston had his vote for the best robotics specialist alive. He had complete confidence and trust in both men. They had done the major physical design of Adam and the upgrades used on the production model of Dolphdroids. Adam would need their deft touch for renewal after his years of inactivity.

Tony Williams joined the group about half an hour later. He had designed the computer interface for Adam and his descendants and would be instrumental in doing the diagnostics and upgrade on Adam. Jim Roeper, designer of the super magna joints, was asked to join them. He had done some major innovative design work on the hands and feet of the Dolphdroids, research that had since been applied to human artificial limbs. Seated around the fireplace, they discussed Adam's reactivation and rejuvenation.

At 10:30 Josh had a meeting with Bill Zucker and Max Henderson on the front porch. Bill was one of the most organized people Josh knew, and trustworthy. He was glad he had put him in charge of the project. Max had been assigned the job of acquiring and outfitting an appropriate air/space vehicle. He was brisk and forward, personality traits that prompted most people to give him a low score on social skills. His 200 plus pounds of weight should have been distributed over a taller frame than his five feet, five inches.

Max knew air/space craft like few others. He had helped design the Stratus and Stratus II air/space crafts as well as the Sunstar light transport vehicle. Max had also built several racing craft that placed well in the semi-annual Cloud Nine event held in low earth orbit. If there ever was a king of air/space mechanics, Josh was convinced it was Max.

"What you need, Josh, is a McCord 983 Defender," Max stated. "It should have never been taken out of the armed services fleet in the first place. What a dumb, political move! Sorry, I'm being redundant: dumb and political mean the same thing. But the government's loss is our gain. I can get us a good deal on one. Of course, we'll be making some minor alterations," he said with a smile.

Josh knew air/space craft and his intuitive reaction was that Max had made a wise choice in the McCord 983. He couldn't help but ask what "minor alterations" Max had in mind.

"We'll replace the Spencer engines with bigger Heidstars. They have a simpler design, are more reliable, and can burn a more common fuel, none of that exotic stuff."

"Aren't the Heidstars designed for a much larger craft than a McCord 983?" Bill asked.

Max smiled again. "They certainly are. That's another reason we're using them. The McCord's structural integrity is good enough to handle the extra punch and Josh may need the extra kick the engines can provide if he gets himself into a tight situation, which is likely to happen. His episode with the sky bike and train tunnel told me we'd better plan for some unfriendly and unwanted participation in this project. The sabotage of the PAV confirms my decision."

Bill worked on a host of details with Max. Their conversation became a murmur of indistinct words to Josh as his eyes glazed over. Details bored him, and his thoughts were on other facets of the project. He eventually excused himself and checked on the progress of some other groups until lunch time.

Several people commented that the roast beef sandwiches tasted good, but Risner complained that the potato salad was a far cry from what he remembered his mother making. It was a different young man serving the meal than had served breakfast. He had forgotten the coffee and seemed to have his mind elsewhere than on his work. "A beginner," Bill commented. The server had gone out to his truck for some additional supplies.

Nancy commented, "He's really not with it."

"I know," Bill said, reaching for a glass of iced tea and wishing it were coffee. "Forgetting coffee is an unpardonable sin for a caterer."

"No," Nancy corrected, "I mean that I asked him about some of the sights to see around here, just to make conversation, and he didn't know a thing. He had just told me a few minutes earlier that he grew up in the area. It doesn't make sense. He makes me uncomfortable, though I'm not sure why."

"Woman's intuition?" Bill asked. Nancy frowned at the suggestion but said nothing.

Max leaned forward and said in a soft voice, "Maybe catering's not his real line of work. Maybe we've got ourselves a real problem here."

Chapter 14

The caterer appeared to be concentrating on packing up the leftover food and utensils. The focus of his thoughts, however, was elsewhere. He had been surprised at how easy it had been to wave down the caterer on the little-traveled gravel road that led to the cabin. People in this rural area were so trusting, so willing to lend a helping hand to a stranger, so naive. The caterer had thought he needed assistance when he saw him frantically waving his hands, standing along the road. The caterer-turned-Good Samaritan now lay in a weed-infested ditch, tied and drugged into unconsciousness.

The imposter was still thinking about the man in the ditch when he walked back into the house, but he sensed that the atmosphere of the cabin had changed slightly. The forced conversation and unnatural silence set off an internal warning. He had the uneasy and distinct sense that he had been the topic of the conversation while he was out at the catering truck. Trying not to draw attention to himself, he slowly walked back out the door, then jumped off the porch, forgoing the steps completely. It was time to make a quick exit.

"Get him!" he heard Tony shout.

Running to his truck, he glanced back and saw that he was being pursued by Tony and Max. He took a few more strides toward the truck and stopped, reaching under his jacket. The movement of his hand left his pursuers with little doubt as to what was going to happen next.

"He's got a gun!" Risner shouted.

Everyone scattered, ducking behind nearby vehicles and

trees. Three shots rang out, the sound echoing off the trees. All three shots went wild, one shattering the cabin's front living room window, another destroying a hanging flower pot, and the third zinging harmlessly into the woods.

The driver's door on the truck slammed shut, the engine roared to life, and the wheels spun on gravel. "He's getting away!" Bill shouted. "We've got to stop him!"

Several of the team members ran to their cars. Soon the vehicles were speeding down the gravel road, eating the dust that was still settling from the half-minute advantage the would-be caterer possessed. The ruts and rocks forced their lighter vehicles to travel more slowly than the catering truck.

Rounding a bend in the road, they found the truck with its driver's door flung open. The cars skidded to a halt and the drivers all jumped out but remained low behind their open doors for protection. Then a roar from a nearby gully drew their attention. A moment later they watched a PAV climb straight up to treetop level, bank sharply, accelerate, and disappear beyond the immediate treetops, its sound fading fast.

A police cruiser with two officers arrived at the cabin half an hour later to investigate. Waiting their turn with one of the officers, the team members talked among themselves, reviewing their conversations, wondering how much the imposter had heard.

Another cruiser pulled up. One of the officers doing the interviews walked over to Josh and whispered, "It's the chief."

Josh nodded, realizing that if the chief was joining the investigation he must consider the matter serious. The chief slowly climbed out of his car and started walking toward the group scattered about the front lawn. Josh judged him to be in his late 60s. Age spots showed through his thinning gray hair; his long narrow face matched his tall, thin body.

The officer who had just whispered to Josh nodded to the chief, then to Josh by his side. The chief started walking their way. "You Doctor Joshua Christopher?"

"Yes."

Motioning Josh away from the crowd and turning toward the woods, the chief said, "Can we talk privately?"

They moved to the shade of a large oak tree on the east side of the cabin. The chief glanced around to assure himself of privacy. "You've probably gathered by now that the man who served you lunch wasn't an employee of the Busy Bee Restaurant."

"It had occurred to us."

A smile flickered across the chief's face. He was expecting a "brainy," as he called Josh's type, to be uncontrollably upset. He turned serious again. "We found the real caterer, a boy named Jeremy, tied up with strapping tape and lying in a ditch not too far from here. He was heavily drugged, but he's coming out of it. He'll be OK, and for that I'm relieved. My wife and I play cards with his parents every Thursday evening, and it would have broken their hearts if something had happened to the kid." The chief realized he was rambling. He cleared his throat and continued. "At any rate, we consider ourselves fortunate that the assailant only drugged him. We did a trace on the PAV and got an ID on the guy. He's connected with a crime syndicate, a nationwide big-time crime syndicate."

"The Warwick Crime Syndicate," Josh interjected.

The chief's eyebrows arched; then he recovered his professional demeanor. "We've also got a preliminary report back on your PAV. It seems that you had a little more than the usual mechanical or electrical failure up there in the wild blue yonder. They tell me someone wired in a circuit disruptor that was designed to be activated at a certain altitude, which you obviously reached. They knew just where to wire it so you had total engine failure. To put it bluntly, your craft was sabotaged by someone who wanted you dead."

The chief paused, looking for a reaction from Josh, but when he saw none, he continued. "Evidence of the sabotage would most likely have been destroyed in a crash, because it was a sophisticated but simple design meant to blend in with the charred or mangled circuitry after a crash. Actually, it was nothing but a fuel flow chip in the on-board computer. They replaced the real one with this altitude-sensitive one. It also disabled your backup system. The experts at the Michigan State Lab got right on this case, which surprises me. Usually it takes days, maybe weeks, for me to get any info back from them. I guess the computers red-flagged the investigation when your name popped up in connection with some train and tunnel incident. Anyway, the boys at the lab were really impressed with whoever did this. Here's the bad news: this little chip isn't something you can buy at your local computer store. Its development and use is tied virtually one hundred percent to organized crime. I know, I'm beginning to repeat myself." The chief leaned toward Josh. "I don't know what your meeting is all about here. You and your friends check out OK, but I want you to know that some really powerful and nasty people are out to stop whatever you're planning. I just hope you do the rest of your business someplace else other than in my district. If not, I'll never get any rest until your bodies are found and hauled off. They won't give up, that much I know. They're going to keep it up until they stop whatever you're planning to do."

The remaining meetings included the surgical transfer team of Drs. Kippler, Mesner, and Gray. A rehabilitation team including Dr. Stuart McKay, Tony Williams, Jim Roeper, Roger Masters, Phil Kirkpatrick, Risner Billingston, and Bill Zucker met. Tracy Mason joined them, having done extensive studies on dolphin behavior compared with Dolphdroid behavior. Partway through the meeting Risner expressed thoughts to which the rest nodded in agreement. "Josh, I can't for the life of me imagine what it would be like to have my mind put in a robot's body, having wires instead of nerves, metal for flesh, and a computer interfacing you to your metal body. You have a good life going for you. There's so much working against you on this project. On a purely logical level this is lunacy. I know, I know, the Dolphdroids are the apple of your eye. I know they need saving and I know you think you gotta be the savior, but it's still crazy in my estimation. Don't get me wrong: I'm with you on this, but I still think it's crazy." Josh just shrugged and asked his next question.

A late afternoon meeting was held with Max in charge concerning the phase that involved getting Josh to the moon and back. Tony gave his input on the feasibility of the air/space craft's on-board computer being interfaced with a "no-hands" control system through Adam's support computer and Josh's brain.

Nancy Saunders made reservations for the entire group at a large, upscale restaurant for a late dinner. The Busy Bee, they had been told, was closed for the remainder of the day after the assault on their caterer. Following dinner and the return to the cabin, Stuart McKay invited Josh to walk along the lake shore.

The sky was clear except for a few scattered clouds illuminated by the full moon, making them glow softly against the black sky. The reflection of the moon danced in silvery, ever-changing patterns on the lake. The waves made a soft lapping sound against the rocks that edged the shore. The two men walked, heads down in thought and conversation, failing to observe much of the night's beauty.

Josh changed the subject from their exchange of observations about the meetings. "Some of the team members put you up to this little walk along the lake with me, didn't they?"

Stuart chuckled and glanced at Josh, then at the full moon. Looking back at Josh he said, "Your powers of observation and analysis never turn off, do they?" He stopped walking, and so did Josh. "I want to be honest with you, Josh. Several of the team, your friends, thought it would be a good idea to get an expert's opinion as to how you're handling this whole project. Admittedly, Moon's Mercy is a dangerous and certainly bizarre plan. I told the others I wasn't sure I could do an objective analysis of you. After all, I'm into this project up to the gills myself."

Josh took a deep breath, shoving his hands deep into his pockets and glancing at the few stars not obscured by the bright moon and scattered clouds. "Well, I sometimes have wondered about the whole project myself. The transfer of my gray matter to Adam certainly is a medically dangerous procedure. No one is more aware than I am that we're in uncharted waters."

"It could have a psychological impact on you far greater and more harmful than we can imagine," Stuart interjected.

"I know."

Stuart continued, "Even if it succeeds, even if the whole project succeeds, there's no guarantee that the procedure can be reversed. Many things could go wrong, including the loss of your physical body while it's being held in suspended animation. You might be stuck as Adam for the rest of your brain's life."

"Believe me, I'm aware of that more than anyone, Stuart. The truth is, I haven't had much to live for since Anne died. For years I've felt like a boat adrift. Admittedly, my renewed relationship with my son and his family has tempered the isolation significantly. They're the only reason for any hesitation on my part. But Rob understands that the Dolphdroids are like family. In fact,

Adam was part of the family when Rob was still a boy. He recognizes the risks, but he also understands that I wouldn't be able to live with myself if I didn't make an effort to save the Dolphdroids. I know there's a very good chance things will go wrong, and I'll admit to being apprehensive about the whole project."

"Josh, I'm glad to hear you express concern and some anxiety. These feelings are a natural protective mechanism. I'd have some real concern if you were going into this without some fear and apprehension. I'd have to question whether you had a clear grasp on reality."

Josh absentmindedly kicked a small piece of driftwood as they continued to walk. "You know the old observation, Stuart, that people do courageous things not because they lack fear, but in spite of their fears."

Stuart nodded, then asked, "Do you ever seriously think of aborting the project?"

"Less and less. This episode with the caterer reminded me of the danger everyone on the project is exposing themselves to, and that concerns me. I'd feel a lot more comfortable about the mission if the risk factor was something only I had to deal with. As for the personal risk, I've discovered over the years that the further I move along in a project, the deeper my commitment becomes. I call it the 'It's too late to turn back now' principle. But the risk factor for everyone else seems to be increasing, and that has me concerned."

"Josh, we're all in this project because we want to be. We each have made our own choices. You shouldn't hold yourself responsible for our choices."

They walked in silence most of the remainder of their time along the shore. As they climbed the steps from the beach to the cabin, Josh asked, "Do I pass, Doctor?"

Stuart smiled. "With flying colors, Dr. Christopher, with flying colors."

Several meetings the following morning and two more in the early afternoon took care of most of the remaining details. For Josh, the time seemed to pass quickly. He enjoyed the reunion with old friends, though the pleasure was tempered by the immensity and complexity of what they were planning. Moon's Mercy was at best a long shot, he knew. He also knew there was no alternative if the Dolphdroids were to be saved.

One by one the members of the team left. Risner and Tony stayed one more night with Josh and Rob. The insurance company had promised to fly in a new PAV for Josh by 9 a.m. The replacement would be the latest updated model with an improved flight control system and a larger engine because they didn't have a replacement available that matched Josh's damaged PAV. Josh was glad; the way things were going there was a good chance that he might need all the advantages in the air that he could get. He couldn't know that the opposition was planning an entirely different approach to sabotaging Moon's Mercy.

Chapter 15

Why do tuxedos have to be so uncomfortable? Josh wondered, as he adjusted his bow tie in the mirror. He mused that the clothes matched the event: both were formal, stiff and uncomfortable. The event was hosted by a worthy charity, though he was certain that the high overhead costs of putting on the affair couldn't leave much more than a 20 or 30 percent profit for the cause. There had been no way he could get out of attending. Various research and development corporations and government agencies had supplied the charity with names of worthy scientists to be honored. The corporations and agencies were also taking care of the per-plate cost of their respective scientists. Josh tried to comfort himself with the thought that at least he might renew friendships with colleagues who had been hovering over mold-infested petri dishes for the last several years.

It had been two weeks since the meeting at the Upper Peninsula cabin, and Josh was getting more anxious each day for the plan to unfold. A formal dinner wasn't part of that plan. He still hadn't gotten over the news that another Dolphdroid had been killed a week ago. Details were sketchy, but apparently it was a direct hit in the back with a laser weapon. The lunar colony reported that there had been no witnesses or evidence to incriminate any Dolphdroid. Imus had played it up big with the press. Josh had done the math and came to the conclusion that Imus had delayed the announcement of the death until there was a slow news day when it would get more coverage.

Josh took his ground car to the Alexandria Country Club, deciding that it would draw less attention. As he drove through the gate, a knot formed in his stomach. The facility was even more imposing than he had imagined. A long string of water fountains lined the middle of the boulevard. He pulled his car around to the entrance and a valet immediately opened his door for him, gave a greeting, and slipped into the driver's seat. Josh made his way to the cathedral-like glass archway at the entrance. A greeter who seemed very comfortable in his tux, smiled and pointed him in the right direction. Walking with some other arriving guests, none of whom he recognized but who looked as uncomfortable as Josh felt, he made his way slowly down a long, wide corridor with a thick purple carpet. The dull rumble of conversation emanated from huge, open double doors at the end of the corridor.

The ballroom was large, with thick drapes and large paintings. A waiter with a tray of drinks quickly walked up to the cluster of people Josh was with. Josh took a soda from the tray and, feeling self-conscious, started across the room to no place in particular.

"Dr. Christopher! Could I ask you some questions about your recent close calls while flying your personal air vehicle?" It was Jack Webber from NTS News accompanied by a cameraman. Josh sighed. He could have figured the media would be covering an event like this. Jack was a good newsman by most standards; it was just that he could be annoyingly persistent when you had information he wanted but you didn't want to give. A tall, slim figure with his hair and tie always in place, he was ready at a moment's notice to jump in front of the camera and do a national broadcast.

"Hello, Jack. How's the news business going?" Josh asked.

"I'm supposed to be the one asking the questions, Dr. Christopher," Webber said with his made-for-the-media smile.

Josh smiled back, though he sensed his smile seemed forced. "Oh, I didn't know there were some unwritten rules about who could ask questions and who couldn't."

Webber ignored the comment and began asking a question. The cameraman had the dark, unblinking eye of a camera aimed at him. "Dr. Christopher, do you believe the sky bike attack over Kentucky and the engine failure over the Upper Peninsula were orchestrated by organized crime, and would this have any connection to the Lunar Dolphdroid project?"

Josh started to walk away. He glanced back at Jack Webber and the cameraman and, looking into the dark lens of the camera, said, "Stay away from the hors d'oeuvres – they're fattening." He knew they'd never use his tidbit of dietary advice for a sound bite. He wouldn't have to worry about being on tomorrow's news.

Josh looked around the room, sipping his soda. There was a grand piano in the far left corner. The table of hors d'oeuvres and the bar were against the wall to his right. Clusters of people, most holding a napkin and beverage, were involved in conversation. People eating unhealthy food, drinking beverages that kill brain cells, and making small talk about nothing worthwhile: that's how Josh summed it up.

He made his way to the table of hors d'oeuvres, and in spite of the advice he had just given, selected several and placed them on a small plate. It was something to do. Glancing around, he decided to make his way to the other side of the room where he spotted an empty chair partially obscured by a large artificial plant. Perhaps he could sit there and observe without being observed.

As Josh made his way to the chair by the plant, his eyes met hers. She seemed flustered at being caught looking at him; she glanced at the punch bowl and made work out of refilling her glass which wasn't empty. Putting down the dipper, she hesitated a moment, then started walking toward him, a slight embarrassed smile on her face that she momentarily hid by taking a sip of her punch.

Josh stopped walking and took a bite out of some indefinable little round thing on his plate. He didn't know her, and he was surprised by his reaction to her presence. He was confused by his feelings, but then it came to him: it was uncanny, how much she reminded him of Anne. The facial features, the length, color, and style of her hair, the way she swung her head to put the hair out of her eyes, and now the walk; it all reminded him of Anne. He was thrilled but also felt a sense of sadness, almost grief. The rest of the room faded to gray as she came up to him, extending her hand.

"Dr. Christopher, right?" she inquired.

Her eyes were hazel, like Anne's, and then there was the familiar scent, the same perfume Anne always wore. He had often commented in conversation and lectures about how amazing it is that scent is often the most powerful opener of doors to locked-away memories. Another footnote had just been added to the list of anecdotal experiences he often used to illustrate his point. He forced himself back to reality and searched for a normal response. "Yes, I'm Joshua Christopher, but I don't believe I know you."

Her slight build complemented a light blue dress that cascaded from her shoulders in loose, flowing folds, dipping just below a necklace of pearls. Anne had always worn pearls. Josh held her hand momentarily after she extended it for a handshake. She had long, gentle fingers and a palm as soft as a pillow. It felt good. "My name's Ashley Spencer. I work for Dr. Hopkins." Realizing that he might wonder why an associate of an acclaimed scientist would attend such a gathering, she quickly added, "He's divorced and didn't get around to asking one of his lady friends, so I'm his last-minute partner." She nodded toward the far end of the room. "He's the man with the reddish hair talking to that blonde. It seems they go way back. He told me that I should feel free to mingle, and that if I found someone else to sit with at dinner it would be fine with him. He even gave me cab money to get home. I can take a hint. All in a day's work." In an effort to change the subject she added, "It's a real pleasure to meet you. I've heard a lot about you."

She was 15 years his junior, at least. He didn't care. He liked the attention, and it surprised him. "Listen, I don't have anyone to sit with at dinner, so if you think the good Dr. Hopkins is going to be concentrating on that blond , how about joining me?"

There was no hesitation on her part. "Why, yes, I will, Dr. Christopher."

The evening surprised Josh by being far more pleasant than he had anticipated, thanks to his encounter with Ashley Spencer. He kept his acceptance speech for the award relatively short; he conjectured that his moment of fame had been intentionally placed near the end of the program when everyone was tired and bored from all the speeches. He was certain that the strong applause for him after his short speech was as much out of gratitude for the brevity of his comments as it was for anything he said.

Josh made polite conversation with a few of the other scientists that he knew, but nothing more. They annoyed him; most probed for non-published details of the LDP situation. In all fairness, he realized that their curiosity also contained an element of empathy: none of them wanted to see a major project of theirs go down the tube like they saw the LDP heading. Josh didn't want to talk about the Dolphdroids, afraid he might say more than he wanted to. At this stage, secrecy was a major advantage for Moon's Mercy.

The evening went quickly, and Josh was disappointed when he saw it coming to an end; that was due to Ashley, he realized. He also observed that his word count for conversation had to have been triple or quadruple what it usually was at such events. Ashley was a good conversationalist. It also occurred to him that he had even forgotten to do battle with his tie. Ties on tuxes always proved too constrictive, but this evening he nearly forgot he was wearing one.

Ashley was remarkable. In so many ways she reminded him of Anne, and that concerned him: was he attracted to Ashley, or was he simply attracted to a living reminder of Anne? He didn't know for sure, but for the moment he decided to resist psychoanalyzing himself. The feelings for Ashley were a welcome relief from the constant emotional drain that the Dolphdroid situation had placed him under.

"Can I see you again?" Josh found himself asking her as he prepared to leave.

"Certainly, Josh. This evening was far more interesting and enjoyable than I had anticipated. Our conversation had a lot to do with that."

Josh nodded, not sure what to say next. "Then I'll give you a call sometime, soon, sometime soon." Good grief! He was stumbling over his words. He felt his face flush. If Ashley noticed, she didn't let on.

"That would be wonderful," she said. She smiled and walked back into the crowd.

Would he really call Ashley? He had to admit that he probably would, though now back in his house, away from the intoxicating young woman, he was uncomfortable with the idea. He didn't need any complications or distractions when it came to Moon's Mercy. Then there were his feelings for Anne, his respect for her memory. He felt bad about having any type of feelings for anyone else. He stopped on his way to the bedroom at the video viewer cabinet and the file of stored programs. He opened the

133

drawer that contained the home video cards of Anne. It had been months since he had looked at any of them; it was a conscious effort to try to break himself of the habit of having a private pity party. Josh searched for the video card of Anne and himself at the beach. It usually was the first one in the file, because he viewed it most often. There it was, several cards back. He removed the card and was about to place it in the viewer when he stopped himself. This was no time to start another pity party. It was late, and he had plans to fly out to meet Max Henderson in the morning. Max wanted his input on some of the decisions concerning the kind of craft needed for the mission. Max exuded confidence concerning his own views and opinions, but when another person's welfare was involved he always wanted someone else to make the final decision and take the responsibility.

Josh went to bed, but sleep didn't come easily for him; the memories of the evening with Ashley replayed again and again. Eventually he drifted off. The alarm jarred him out of a deep sleep.

Within the hour Josh was flying through a crystal blue sky with the sun flooding the earth below in a golden sunrise. It was good to be alive. Josh caught himself enjoying his mild state of euphoria and knew that Ashley was a major contributor to his new emotional state. He had to get ahold of himself. Focus on Max; yes, think about Max. Thoughts of Max would certainly distract him from any thoughts of romance!

Max's place wasn't hard to spot from the air. He was always in the process of rebuilding two or three flying vehicles, and he had the habit of starting another project before completing one already in progress. Three hangars, one large and two small, were in a clearing. It looked like an aeronautical graveyard with the skeletal remains of several craft lying around, their parts cannibalized so that other craft could fly again. Many of the aircraft body parts had weeds and small trees growing through them, claiming the same space as the vehicles. Several were covered with tarps, like the dead in a morgue. Josh took all of this in as he circled for a final approach near Max's mobile home between the large hangar and one of the small ones.

He spotted Max just as he landed his PAV. He was moving a piece of equipment from one pile of junk to another, a seemingly senseless activity that Josh suspected consumed a big part of Max's work day.

"Hi, Doc," Max shouted, tossing the nondescript item onto a pile of other nondescript objects. "Well, did you make it out here without incident? It seems flying has become hazardous to your health."

"No problem, Max. Looks like you're keeping busy as ever working on who knows what."

Max wiped his hands with a greasy rag that he pulled from his back pocket. "I know, I always seem to have too many projects going at the same time, but since the meeting up at the cabin I've spent most of my time working on the craft you're going to be using on the mission."

Josh was relieved. It had concerned him that Max might not stay focused on the project. Max led him over to one of the two smaller hangars and slid the door open. They stepped inside.

It was a McCord 983 Defender. "This must have cost plenty," Josh mumbled as he began walking around the craft.

Max chuckled with delight. "Not to worry, my friend. I got this at a fraction of what you'd expect. I didn't want you flying in some pile of junk, which I have plenty of around here. Actually, it's being refurbished from the parts of about five, maybe six, 983s."

Josh walked slowly around the vehicle. He was pleased, always having a high regard for the 983. Classified as a fighter craft, it had been one of the standard air/space craft during the last earth orbit dispute with the South American alliance. That was long enough ago that not too many of the 983s were still flying. Most of them had been replaced by the smaller, faster Tessmore XL. The XL carried only two heat-seeking missiles; it boasted a new weapon, an energy ball called an eneredo. The XL had three eneredos, but the aim had to be perfect: being essentially balls of high energy, they lacked a guidance system. Still, they were great weapons and another reason why the 983s were retired.

The McCord 983 appeared to be in reasonably good shape, though that was difficult to tell because it was in partial tear-down. It had a near-hit carbon stain on the starboard side. All things considered, Josh was pleased with Max's choice. He had flown one the last year of his military service, but never in battle. His combat craft had been one of the old Jasper 2000s.

How things change, Josh reflected. At the time, the Jasper

135

2000 was state-of-the-art, but then came the much bigger and faster McCord, and now the military vehicle of choice was the smaller Tessmore XL, which many considered to be the ultimate fighting machine.

"A good choice," Josh said. The short wing design was nearly as wide as the craft was long and swept forward resembling a backward flying wing. The end of each wing held a fuel pod. Each fuel pod had a small stabilizer fin that swept back and up about two feet. The wings and pods drooped downward so that the horizontal view from the cockpit wasn't obscured. The cockpit was a mild hump in the middle that narrowed as it moved toward the back of the vehicle until it faded into a trailing edge.

"I'd like to make some modifications," Max said as he rubbed the starboard fuel pod with the greasy cloth. He turned toward Josh and put his hand on his shoulder. "What you need is some extra punch in case you get into a tight situation. It seems to me the chances of that happening are pretty good. You're going to be vulnerable during the time between ground launch and your entry into the lunar trajectory."

"What do you have in mind?"

"Well, Doc, I'd like to attach a couple of extra booster engines on this baby: two Ramsey Boosters."

"Ramsey Boosters?"

"Yeah, they were used to boost small payloads from low to high orbit until last year."

"I know. But can the McCord take the extra stress those boosters will put on it?"

"When I get done with it, the McCord could have a couple of Mega Load Lifter engines attached and not fall apart. I'll be doing some frame reinforcing and some other modifications, don't you worry. I was planning to check out a place that has a couple of the Ramsey Boosters. Why don't you come along? After all, it'll be you riding that thing to the moon and back."

"Thanks for the vote of confidence that it'll be a round trip. I'm not nearly as certain about that as you seem to be. As for going along to check out those engines, I don't know."

"Aw, come on, Doc. Besides, it'll give me a chance to ride in that PAV of yours. It looks like a real beaut."

"You want me to go with you, but you want to ride in my

PAV? Who's taking who on this little jaunt? OK, Max, I'll 'go with you' in my PAV."

"Great. Just give me a couple of minutes to tidy up around here."

"While you're doing that I have a call to make."

When Max was out of earshot, Josh called Ashley. There was no answer. He was about to disconnect when the video screen flickered. "Hello," Ashley said with some exasperation as the viewer came into focus. She had a towel wrapped around her head and another under her arms, covering her body. He had interrupted her shower.

"I'm sorry for the poor timing," he said.

A smile replaced her look of annoyance when she recognized him. "Dr. Christopher! That's OK. Sorry I was so short. It always seems that salespeople call when you're in the worst position to come to the televiewer." Rolling her eyes toward the towel wrapped around her hair, she added, "Like in this particular situation." A blush showed on her moist face. "Come to think of it, I'd rather have a salesperson see me like this than you."

He couldn't help but interpret her comment as flirtatious, but he was at a loss as to how to respond. He chose to ignore the comment. "Ashley, I just wanted to call and ask if perhaps I could take you out to dinner, say, about seven?"

"I'd love that," she said with no hesitation.

They exchanged a few words of small talk and then said goodbye. Josh breathed a sigh of relief. He couldn't believe that he had the same feelings of anxiety and excitement about asking someone out on a date as he had when he was young. Uncomfortable with where his thoughts were taking him, Josh decided to access his home computer from his phone.

The computer informed him that three calls had come in. One was from a salesperson asking about the opportunity to give a quote for insurance coverage on his new PAV. Another was from work; they would call someone else to get the information they needed. The third was from Imus Hartung. He wanted a meeting with Josh first thing in the morning.

Josh's heart pounded. He was beginning to have strong negative reactions every time he thought of Imus. What in the world could the man want now? He wished he hadn't checked for

137

messages. Anticipating a meeting with Imus was something that could ruin your day.

Chapter 16

Max enjoyed the ride in the PAV, continually glancing around the cockpit, studying one gauge and control after another, intrigued by the latest improvements and surprised by the little extras that he never thought would find their way into a personal air vehicle. "They've made it as comfortable as a doggone living room," he said.

Within minutes they had landed. As Josh shut down the engine he noticed a sign hanging at an angle on the chain link fence: BILL'S USED AIR & SPACE PARTS.

Walking through a door that complained with a loud squeak as Max pushed it open, they made their way to a grimy counter. To the right was an old truck bench seat with several major lacerations through which stuffing protruded; it was the seating area for waiting customers. A large dog of nondescript breed slept curled up on one end of the bench. Behind the counter sat two overweight men in grease-stained T-shirts that strained to cover their bulging bellies, but failed to do so. One of the men was smoking a cigar and the other had a big lump of chewing tobacco expanding his left cheek, the contents of which threatened to ooze out at any moment. Their skin was dark with years of grease and grime.

The man with the wad of tobacco spoke. "What can I do for ya?" He made no effort to get up.

"We're interested in buying a couple of Ramsey Boosters," Max said. Josh saw that Max was far more comfortable in this particular social environment than he was.

Turning his head, the man hit a rusty can on the floor with deadly accuracy, then rose to his feet with a groan and a sigh. "Well, I happen to have three out back. Two are on a craft that skidded off a runway; one of the Ramseys is good. I also got one more that came with a whole load of stuff a few weeks back. Kind of an unusual item. What do ya want 'em for anyway?"

"We're putting together sort of an experimental aircraft," Max replied evasively. "I knew you had at least a couple on hand. I dialed a printout of your parts list yesterday."

"Oh, yeah, I keep forgetting about that. My nephew, he's the one who's into all that kind of fancy stuff." He glanced at a desk where a computer console was protected under a dusty plastic cover, surrounded by piles of paper, scattered coffee cups, and candy bar wrappers.

"Can we see the engines?" Josh asked. He had a deepening concern about using any parts from a place like this.

"Sure, just follow me," the man replied. Then, as if reading Josh's thoughts, he added, "You know, even if you buy new parts and use them, even for a minute, you're running with used parts. Might as well buy used parts and save yourself a heap o' money, that's what I always say." Josh had the sense he had just heard the commercial given to every customer while being escorted to the junkyard out back. They walked past scores of ruined vehicles lined up on both sides of the dirt drive. He led them through some short weeds and on to another dirt drive, walked a few more feet, stopped, and pointed. Breathing hard from the exertion of their walk, he said, "There they are."

Max carefully looked over the engines, opening the service doors, and then went over each engine again. Max assured Josh that two of the engines were in good shape. Within an hour a price was negotiated, papers signed, a delivery order filled out, and Josh and Max were back in the air.

"How will those extra engines affect the aerodynamics of the McCord?" Josh asked as he leveled off at five thousand feet.

"Not a whole lot. Your on-board computer will compensate for their weight, thrust, the aerodynamic changes they cause, and everything else. You might notice a slight sluggishness in response at lower power. The Ramseys will only burn enough to compensate for their own weight and air resistance up to 50 per cent thrust.

After that, watch out! When the 983's engine goes into afterburner mode and the Ramsey engines go to full throttle, you'll have one mighty thrust that'll shove that mechanical body of Adam's into its seat and you'll think you're a bullet being fired from the barrel of a gun."

"Where's the additional fuel coming from to power the Ramseys?"

"I'll be stashing extra fuel in the small cargo bay, but that won't make up for all that they'll burn. I'll also be connecting them to your regular fuel pods. Remember, these engines are your ace up the sleeve. Use them only if and when it's necessary to save your skin." Max smiled, then added, "I mean, when it's necessary to save Adam's metal surface." Josh ignored the attempt at humor and made a slight correction in their flight path at the computer's suggestion.

"At any rate, Doc, you'll need 23 per cent of your fuel remaining once you're in earth orbit to reach orbital escape velocity, maintain a flight to the moon, make your landing, lift off, and complete the flight and reentry to earth. Any scenario that leaves you with less than 23 per cent of your fuel at the point of insertion into earth orbit means you'll need to abort the mission."

"What do I do with the Ramsey boosters once I'm in orbit?"

"You can jettison them. You don't want the extra weight when you're making your lunar landing and takeoff."

"Sounds like you've covered all the bases, Max."

Max sighed and looked out his side of the canopy. "I hope so, Doc. I sure hope so."

After dropping Max off at his place, Josh set a course to Ashley's. The memories from adolescence of the knot in the stomach, the slight perspiring, the tightness in the throat, and the fear of long stretches of silence in conversation all came back as he flew through the scattered clouds. The feelings were exciting and depressing. The emotional rush of a budding romance painted Josh's perception of life with all kinds of vivid colors where there had been nothing but gray for a long time. He reprimanded himself. He had no business getting involved in a relationship now. The last thing he needed was an emotional attachment. It also wasn't fair to Ashley. He couldn't allow the relationship to develop very far, that was for certain. Her date for tonight was a man who would soon be

141

part machine with no guarantee that he would ever return to being fully human.

He arrived 10 minutes early and debated waiting in the PAV until time caught up with him, but decided to risk whether she was ready early. She was. The conversation in the PAV was good, the quiet moments inconspicuous enough not to be uncomfortable. The restaurant Josh had chosen offered good ambiance; the food was excellent and the service flawless. The restaurant was located on the edge of an old rock quarry, and after dinner he suggested they take the elevator to the gardens at the bottom of the man-made canyon. They slowly walked along a path that wound through landscaped areas with plants, rocks, and streams. Lights of various colors bathed the gardens in a kaleidoscope of greens, reds, blues, yellows, and purples. All of it was designed to heighten romance, and it seemed to be doing the job. Josh focused on the soft small hand he held in his.

They walked and talked. Her voice was soft, her words often punctuated with a giggle, a sound more pleasant to him than that of the bubbling stream nearby. It was a bad sign; he was thinking poetically, comparing her giggle to the sound of a stream? He was falling for her.

Josh brought himself back to a more stable mental condition with the reminder that he dare not share too much about Moon's Mercy. She was interested in his work, asking about what he was currently doing. He wanted badly to tell her, but thought better of it. He was careful to only give details of the Lunar Dolphdroid Project available to anyone with a little research.

The moon was bright as they flew back to Ashley's apartment. "That's their world," he said after a few moments of silence.

"Whose world, where?" Ashley asked.

Josh nodded toward the moon. "Up there, the moon. It's home to a life-form that I helped create. Now the politics and economics of the powers that be are set to end it all."

Ashley put her hand on his shoulder. "But you have a plan, don't you, Josh?" There was admiration in her voice.

Josh looked at her, smiled, and returned his gaze to the nighttime sky in which they flew. "Yes, I do." He then corrected himself. "We do. You'd be amazed at how many people are willing to come forward and be a part of the effort to rescue them."

"I'd love to hear more about it," she said softly.

Josh reached his hand across the space between their seats and took hold of Ashley's hand, squeezing it. "I want to, Ashley. It's been a long time since I've been able to share hopes, dreams, fears, those kinds of things with someone." He took a deep breath. "But this is not the time. Maybe later." He gave her hand an additional squeeze, then released his grip. They flew the rest of the way to Ashley's apartment in long stretches of silence punctuated with occasional small talk.

Josh hadn't wanted to leave Ashley when he said good-bye at her apartment, but he forced himself to return to his PAV. She made him feel alive. He was wise enough, however, to know that it was an adult version of puppy love. He wasn't in love with Ashley yet, but was loving the feelings of being infatuated with a woman.

He had to get a grip on himself. He knew very little about her. In fact, she knew far more about him than he did about her. The observation came as a surprise to him, because it had never been easy for him to be open and vulnerable with any woman since Anne died. He realized that he had done most of the talking on their date and that he had to continually resist telling her more about Moon's Mercy. The team was committed to secrecy about the project and he, of all people, should be most committed to keeping the project under wraps. As he brought the PAV in for a landing at home, he congratulated himself for having maintained enough mental and emotional equilibrium to resist telling her too much about Moon's Mercy.

It had been misting when Josh entered the Extraterrestrial Research and Resources Center. Now it was pouring rain with flashes of lightning and thunder as he left the center and ran to his PAV. Maybe the drenching rain would cool him down, he told himself. No, it would take a hurricane-driven wall of water to do that! The nerve of Imus to call him in for a meeting for no other reason than to repeat his determination to go through with the decommissioning of the Dolphdroids!

Reflecting on his meeting with Imus, Josh realized there had been something new in what Imus had said. Threads of lightly-concealed threats had been woven through his meandering words, and there was a sense of tension in Imus that was at a level he hadn't sensed in the man before. Clearly Imus was under great pressure from someone to get Josh to stop fighting the extermination of the Dolphdroids.

As Josh closed the canopy on his PAV, muffling the sound of the pouring rain, he recalled Imus' parting words: "Josh, you're pushing this way too far. Just remember that I'm not in control of everything. A lot of it's out of my hands. People can play hardball, as you've already found out. Give it up, Josh, while you still can, before it's too late for you or your family. Stick to your work on the Saltwater Reclamation Project, and I can get you a boost in classification. I'm giving you a final chance. This is the last exit before there is no exit."

Josh punched and adjusted the controls with more than ordinary force as he prepared to take off. The nerve of Imus, trying to threaten him, then bribe him with a promotion in classification! Then a thought made a chill go up and down his spine. He recalled Imus' words: "Give it up, Josh, while you still can, before it's too late for you or your family."

" ...you or your family." Why hadn't the full meaning of Imus' words hit him at the time? Was it an empty threat, or had he heard something from Emmerson or the Warwick Syndicate? He clenched his fist and hit the console beside his seat. They could threaten him, and even his team, but his family? They had never asked to be put at risk, never volunteered to be involved. Well, Rob – yes, but Heather and Randy – no!

Josh activated the televiewer and punched in a number.

The screen came alive. "Oh, hi, Dad!"

Heather was smiling as her image flickered into view.

"Hi, Heather. I need to talk to Rob. Is he there?"

"No. He left about five minutes ago. He went to get a few things from the store and run a couple of other errands for me. I could transfer you to his phone. You want me to do that?"

"Please. It's kind of important. I'll talk to you later. Say hi to Randy for me."

"Sure, Dad." A hint of concern appeared on her face before the screen flickered. She could tell something was wrong, but decided to say nothing.

Josh stared out at the ground far below but wasn't really focusing his eyes on anything particular while he waited for Rob to come on the line.

"Hi, Dad. What's up?"

"I just came from Imus' office, and among the coercive, threatening, and bribing statements he made were veiled threats against my family. I'm concerned for Heather and Randy, and you, too."

Rob's expression turned somber. "I don't know why it didn't occur to me, Dad. It's the oldest trick in the book; the most effective, too – get to you by getting to your family. Do you think he was serious or maybe it was just talk?"

Josh shrugged. "Hard to say. Imus seemed uncomfortable with what he was telling me. No, I don't think he was making it up on the spot. I'm thinking he was giving me a genuine warning. I think we ought to take it seriously."

"You have any ideas about what we should do, Dad?"

"I think you should take Heather and Randy to a safe place, a secret place. I know you'd have to take time off without pay. I'll cover whatever living expenses you incur; I might as well give you some of your inheritance now rather than later. I've got an idea where you could take the family. How about..." Josh broke off in mid-sentence. "I just remembered. This conversation might be monitored. I've said too much already. Can I stop by the house this evening?"

"Sure," Rob replied with concern. "See you then."

Josh had to inform the other team members that their families might also be at risk, though it was unlikely. They'd probably go after his own family first. Still, the rest of the team needed to be warned. He didn't want to give the opposition any ideas, however, and decided that he should make his calls from somewhere other than his PAV or home.

He plotted a flight path to Ashley's. He could think of nowhere more pleasant to make his calls on such a dreary, rainy morning.

He wasn't fooling himself. It was just an excuse to see her again. He knew his feelings for Ashley were growing. He had begun to reason that perhaps a serious relationship might actually help the mission, that it would give him a greater incentive to see it

145

come full circle, bringing him back to earth and into his own body again. Was he trying to talk himself into the legitimacy of a relationship with Ashley?

Was she having the same feelings for him that he had for her? If she was, she probably was thinking about a future with him. She had a right to know what his future held.

He was about to call Ashley and tell her of his intentions to stop by when it suddenly occurred to him that her life might also be in jeopardy. The opposition certainly realized by now that he was getting serious about her. He decided against making the call.

The rain had stopped and the children in the neighborhood were playing in the puddles, but they stopped and watched as Josh landed his PAV at the outer edge of the apartment complex. He waved at the children through the canopy. The landing of a PAV at the apartments was undoubtedly still unusual enough that it momentarily caught the attention of the children. Once the engine was shut down they went back to their play.

"Hi, Josh," Ashley said enthusiastically after opening her door. She gave him a hug and motioned for him to come in. "You're a bright spot in an otherwise very drab morning."

"My sentiments exactly," Josh replied.

"Have you had breakfast yet?" she asked as she closed the door behind him.

Josh paused. "I guess I haven't. Several concerns have taken priority over oatmeal this morning."

"Oatmeal?" She frowned. "I don't think I have oatmeal." Her face brightened. "How about pancakes?"

"That would be great."

As they made their way to the kitchen Josh explained his concern for the safety of everyone close to him, including her. He explained his concern about his communications being monitored and asked to use her televiewer.

"Sure, Josh. You make any calls you want while I make those pancakes," she said.

Josh made calls to Risner, Tony, and Bill and asked each of them to call the remaining members of the team. He felt better but still had a gnawing concern that wouldn't leave him. All three tried to reassure him that Imus was undoubtedly getting desperate and making veiled threats that probably weren't real. Josh wanted to believe them, but he knew Imus too well.

"Josh...... Josh."

The voice was soft and inquiring. Josh realized he was staring at the blank screen of the televiewer. He turned and looked at Ashley.

"You were staring into space, Josh. You're worried, aren't you?" She walked toward him. "Why would anyone want to hurt the people you know? Are you in some kind of trouble?" She put her hand gently on his shoulder. "Because if you are, I want to be there for you. After all, that's what a friend's for." She paused, took his hand and pulled him from his chair, leading him toward the kitchen. "The first pancakes are ready. Let's eat and you can tell me what this is all about."

While they ate he told her all about the Lunar Dolphdroid Project and the details of what had been unfolding. She listened in rapt attention as he talked. He left out many of the details so as not to bore her, but it felt good to share the biggest project of his lifetime. After sharing his plan to become Adam she looked shocked, then asked, "But how will your going to the Dolphdroid colony as a Dolphdroid yourself, as one of them, save them? Even if you can turn them around, make them behave, isn't the decommissioning a done deal?"

Josh thought for a moment. "That gets a little complicated, maybe I'll tell you about that another time." He sensed he had said too much already.

"Who in the world would want the Dolphdroids out of the way? I mean, they're on the moon, no longer a danger to anyone but themselves."

"Organized crime, Ashley, organized crime." Her face went ashen.

She paused and swallowed. "Are you sure?"

"As certain as I can be at this point. There really is no other explanation. It's obvious that Imus Hartung is in a serious bind, and that someone is pulling his strings and jerking him hard. He's someone's puppet, no doubt about that. I believe Emmerson's in the same predicament. He apparently borrowed heavily from this crime syndicate. The only way they can see their way to getting a return on their money is if the Dolphdroids are out of the way and

Emmerson's state-of-the-art replacements can take over and make everyone a tidy profit."

"What would happen to Emmerson if he didn't pay?" Ashley asked.

"They would send him swimming in a deep lake with a concrete block chained to his legs, but only after breaking both arms and legs. They don't like it when people fail to take care of their debts."

Ashley was shaking. He walked around behind her, placing his arms on her shoulders. She lowered her head and started to cry. After a few moments he took her hands and brought her to a standing position, then embraced her gently. She responded by hugging him tightly. They stood together, her tears wetting his shirt.

After a time she looked up and gave him a weak smile, wiping the tears from one eye and then the other. Josh told her he needed to be going; he had some things that had to be taken care of. She nodded. They embraced again at the open door to her apartment, then he kissed her lightly on the lips. He wanted to do it again, more firmly and with abandon, but resisted the urge. He looked her in the eyes and said softly, but with firmness, "Ashley, you might be in danger, too. It won't take them long to discover that you and I have spent some time together. I don't think it's very safe for you to stay here alone. Do you have some place you could go for, say, a week?"

"I... I don't know," she stammered, staring at the floor and brushing her hand through her hair, then biting her lip. "I can think about it." She looked at Josh intently. "Do you really think it's necessary? Do you think that I'm really in danger?"

Josh forced a smile and knew immediately that it looked artificial. "Probably not. I just tend to be on the cautious side, especially with people I care about."

As his PAV leveled off at the local cruising altitude Josh reflected on his growing relationship with Ashley, aware of his conflicting feelings. He wanted to get closer to her, she was such a caring, warm, and undeniably beautiful woman. And she possessed an uncanny resemblance to Anne. On the other hand, he felt like running from the relationship. He couldn't understand his concern, other than the fact that he had been single so long, and that he wanted to give full attention to Moon's Mercy. Perhaps he was simply uncomfortable with sharing his life with someone other than Anne. Or maybe he knew he didn't have a life to share. There was a good chance he would never be Joshua Christopher again. How could he have allowed himself to get romantically involved at this crucial juncture in his life?

The televiewer activated, interrupting his thoughts. "Hi, Dad."

"Hi, Rob. What's up?"

"I just got home a few minutes ago. Thanks for the package you sent Randy. Heather said it was delivered just before I got here. Randy's at the neighbor's. Heather called over there and he's coming home soon. She told him there was a surprise waiting for him. I thought if you were in the neighborhood you might want to swing by and see him open it. You're going to spoil him, you know."

"A package? I didn't send a package to Randy."

"But it's got your return address on it."

"Rob, get out of the house NOW! RIGHT NOW! It could be a bomb!"

Josh could see bewilderment on Rob's face, then concern. "Right," Rob said, and he disconnected.

Josh pushed the throttle on the PAV to its maximum.

Chapter 17

Josh breathed a sigh of relief when he saw three figures huddled at the end of the driveway. Randy waved with one hand; his mother had a firm grip on the other. Rob had his arm around Heather. Josh landed the PAV hard, bouncing it off the ground. He quickly shut down the engine. When he climbed out of the PAV Randy broke free from his mother and ran to Josh, giving him a big hug. "Grandpa, there's a bomb in a box in the house."

"Now, we aren't sure about that, Randy." Josh tried to sound calm, embracing Randy while looking at his parents. "I called the bomb squad," Josh said.

Within five minutes the bomb squad arrived. Two men immediately jumped from out of the cab of the truck, pulled open a side storage compartment, took out heavy protective clothing, and began to quickly put it on. The back of the truck opened, and a man jumped out. He lowered a ramp and began to activate the bomb retrieval robot.

As the two men dressed, Josh briefly explained that the package was not from him, though that's what the label indicated, and that there could be people who would want to harm him or his family.

"Let's just hope we were called out here to open a present for the kid," the mustached man in charge said.

Once suited in their gray bulky protective outfits, the two men staggered to the front door and propped it open. They looked at the box sitting in the living room, then backed out. The two men's voices were muffled by the face masks as they talked to each other, and to the third man, now seated at a control center in the back of the truck, via a com link.

Watching a monitor while manipulating hand and foot controls, the man in the back of the truck moved the four wheeled robot with two long arms slowly toward the front door. The mustached man asked Rob and the others to move across the street. Within a couple of minutes the robot backed out the front door, carrying the box, and slowly made his way around the house to the backyard. Josh and the family positioned themselves so that they could see into the backyard. The robot began to tug at the wrapping on the box.

Suddenly there was a blinding flash of light and a deafening blast; the sound hit the chests of Josh and the others. Grass, dirt, and parts of the robot went flying. The two bomb experts, watching from the corner of the house, were thrown backward like giant gray rag dolls tossed away by an angry child. Glass shattered as it fell to the ground from windows in the nearby houses.

As the dust settled, the robot operator, Josh, and Rob ran to the two men. Ripping off their protective face gear, they saw that they had apparently suffered no harm, other than having the wind knocked out of them. When the robot operator was assured by his two co-workers that they were fine, he walked over to where the robot had been opening the box. A large crater three feet across and two feet deep marked the spot. Josh noted that parts of the robot were scattered over the entire backyard. One of the robot's wheels was jammed between two large limbs of the oak tree in which Randy's swing now hung by one chain. More glass shattered as a remaining piece from a broken window in the house fell from its frame.

"Bill Zucker here." Bill's image came on Josh's televiewer in his PAV. Josh had the canopy up and the background noise from the police, the fire department, and media people made it necessary for Josh to turn up the volume.

"Hi, Bill. I'm at Rob's place. A bomb just went off. No one

was hurt, but it was addressed to Randy. They tried to kill my grandson, Bill!" Josh's voice was charged with emotion.

Bill didn't say anything for a moment; he glanced down and then made eye contact with Josh. "What are you going to do next?"

"I've told Rob to take the family someplace where no one can find them. He didn't hesitate in agreeing with me. I don't want their lives endangered any more than they already have been." Bill saw Josh shake his head. "I just can't believe they would stoop to these means to stop Moon's Mercy. My grandson, an innocent child!"

"Josh, I've got some other bad news. We need to talk on a secure line."

Josh struggled to turn his thoughts from Randy to what Bill was saying. A secure line? That's right, they were talking between televiewers, and the signals could potentially be intercepted. Had he said anything he shouldn't have? He knew the explosion had him badly rattled. "I'll get in touch with you as soon as I can. But I need to stay here for a while longer." Josh took a deep breath. "This is turning into a nightmare. I assumed there would be personal risk, but I never considered the risk to anyone else. Maybe the mission should be aborted. If the powers that be knew it was all over then maybe they'd leave my family, and all of you, alone."

"Josh, the only way they'd leave you, your family, or any of us alone is if you were dead. It's gone too far. They're assuming you'll stop at nothing. They won't believe it even if you'd make some kind of public announcement. It'll be OK, Josh. We'll see this thing through and no one's going to get hurt."

Josh looked at Bill. His friend's face betrayed the fact that he was worried in spite of his confidently spoken reassurance.

The police had further questions for Josh after they finished questioning Rob and Heather. Josh was grateful they had the sense to leave Randy alone. It was an hour before most of the authorities of one kind or another were gone.

Rob walked up to his dad. "Well, Randy's going to play over at one of the neighbors'." Rob glanced at his house. "There's so much glass in the house, and so little in the windows, that the place will take days to fix up. It's just as well that we'll be gone." He paused. "Randy has a thousand and one questions; he actually finds it rather exciting. Heather is petrified that they'll try it again."

"You know, Rob, I never figured that rescuing the Dolphdroids would threaten the lives of my family. I didn't anticipate the involvement of organized crime. They're the ones behind this, you know. That's a very scary thought. I wouldn't blame you if you wanted to pull out of the project."

Rob gave his dad a weak smile. "That did occur to me, for a fleeting moment. The truth is that they're not after Randy because of my involvement in the project; it's because of yours, Dad."

"I know. Should I drop the mission? I will, Rob; you just say the word, and I will."

Rob put his hand on his dad's shoulder. "I don't think that would do any good. The opposition, whoever did this and the sabotaging of your PAV, is going to assume you're not going to give up on the project, even if you said you were."

"That's what Bill said, too."

"There's no turning back, Dad. At any rate, I couldn't pull out now. It's kind of strange, but the longer I work on the project, the more determined I am to see it through."

"The risk is too great for you and your family, Rob, and for the rest of the team and their families. It's hard to guess what the syndicate will try next, who they'll try to get to. They're professionals. We were lucky to have stopped this bomb. We may not be so lucky next time. Maybe I should call off the project. It's worth a try; maybe they'll let everyone be."

"It wouldn't work, Dad. The only way they'll leave us alone now is if you're dead. That's what concerns me most, that they'll target you until they succeed."

"You're the second person to say that."

"To say what?"

"That the only way they'd be convinced they had the project stopped was if I were dead."

"Well, it's true. They know that as committed to the project as the rest of the team is, it wouldn't continue if you're no longer around. Dad, you ARE the Dolphdroid project, and Moon's Mercy is yours too. Without you it's all over, and they know that."

Within a few minutes Josh was airborne, heading to a nearby mall where he could use a public televiewer without fear of listening ears. The mall wasn't very busy and several of the viewer phones were open. He entered one of the booths, closed the door, and punched in Bill's secure number.

Bill's expression was serious. "Doc, one of Rob's west coast researchers contacted me after he was unable to connect with Rob."

"Communications must have been disrupted at the house because of the explosion," Josh said.

"Rob had given this man my number in case he couldn't be reached in an emergency." Bill paused again, pursed his lips, then said, "I'm afraid I have a bomb of my own to drop on you."

Bill paused, too long a pause for Josh. "Talk to me," Josh said.

Bill took another deep breath and said, "Doc, this investigator insists he has uncovered proof..." He paused again and then continued. "He claims that Ashley is an informant for the Warwick Syndicate; her assignment has been to get close to you and feed them information about Moon's Mercy."

Josh stared into his viewer, oblivious to the shoppers walking by and the background music of the shopping center. Everything faded away. His thoughts came to a standstill, his mind unable to process the information.

"I asked him if he was absolutely sure about this. He said he was; once he had her name, it didn't take long to contact another source to confirm what he had been told. I'm sorry, Josh."

With great effort Josh pushed aside the emotional debris Bill's news had created and tried to think what this meant for Moon's Mercy. He mumbled, "How much did I tell her? If I've jeopardized this mission..." His mind raced through the various times he had spent with Ashley. Bill stared silently into his monitor, allowing Josh time to process the information. Josh fast-forwarded through conversations he had had with Ashley. She would know some names and some of the plan. How much of the plan? He hadn't told her some of the key details. A momentary sense of relief came over him, but it soon was overshadowed by a profound sense of betrayal "I just can't believe this."

"I know," Bill said.

Josh tried to collect his thoughts. He had to put aside personal feelings and evaluate the degree to which the mission had been compromised. He looked into the televiewer, attempting to

155

focus on Bill. "I think we're still in business. She doesn't know about the location for the craft or the details of the timetable. I think we're going to be OK." He hoped he wasn't being overly optimistic.

"Good," Bill said in a subdued tone.

Josh was surprised by the next feeling that came over him: a sense of commitment to the mission that he had never felt before. Then he realized why. He now had one less reason to stay as Joshua Christopher. His relationship with Ashley had been eroding his resolve, he now realized. Another part of him was dead. Only Rob and his family had any claim on him now; they were the only ones that made the mission personally costly. He had his friends who he knew cared about him, and he certainly cared about them, but there was no one else really close. Still, he felt nauseous. He tried to ignore the turning in his stomach. "I have to make some other calls, Bill." Then, noting the concern on Bill's face, he added, "I'll be OK."

"You sure?"

"Yes, don't worry." With that Josh broke the connection. He stood in front of the televiewer, staring at nothing. A passing security guard paused, looked at him, and asked, "You OK, sir?" Josh nodded, then punched in a number.

A red haired, mustached, round faced man's image appeared on screen. "Henry, this is Josh Christopher."

A look of recognition and a broad smile came across Henry's face, even before Josh finished introducing himself. The smile stretched his red mustache wide over uneven teeth. "Helloooo, Josh!"

Some things never change, Josh thought. Henry's greeting was one of them. He always put a long last syllable on his greetings.

"I can't believe you're calling me, Josh! It's been ages. I've kept up with you through the news, though. I can't believe you called." Henry paused, looked intently into his monitor, the smile slipping from his face. "You need your old buddy Henry to help you, I can tell. Go ahead, shoot."

"I need to talk to you in person, Henry."

They agreed to a time and place; Josh cut the conversation short, before it could turn into reminiscing. Henry had been the first person that came to mind when the bizarre idea occurred to him. Henry, always the practical joker, had pulled off more amazing stunts while they were in high school than Josh could remember, and Henry rarely got caught. Now he was a private detective and had a reputation for getting the job done for his clients. Sometime his methods were unorthodox but they usually got results. Josh knew he was the man he needed. If anyone could pull it off, Henry could.

Josh then called Sam Courtney, a building demolition expert. He had been Josh's neighbor fifteen years ago. Sam was great at his work but never seemed to be very adept at making friends. Somehow he had latched onto Josh and had kept in touch all these years. Sometimes Sam could be annoying, but now Josh needed him. Sam wanted to hear the details over the viewer, but Josh insisted they get together. Another appointment was marked on Josh's electronic organizer.

Rick Hagerty was next on Josh's call list. He was a stunt pilot who made his living doing air shows. As a young boy, Rick had looked up to Josh and a few of the other local pilot heroes of the war. He had sent Josh an encouraging note after the Dolphdroid story broke. Now he needed Rick's help. After a brief conversation Josh had another meeting scheduled on his electronic organizer.

Josh's last call was to Emmerson Brunner. Josh was convinced that Brunner was a significant player in all that was happening and was probably a co-conspirator with the personal attacks against himself and his family. Emmerson was the last person Josh wanted to talk to. He coded in Emmerson's number. They talked for less than a minute and Josh ended the conversation.

After Josh broke the connection Emmerson stared for a few moments at the blank viewer, then punched in a number. The receptionist put him on hold. He waited. The soft hold music and slow-moving symbols on the televiewer were annoying him. The sounds and images were designed to sooth the impatience of the person put on hold, but they only served to do the opposite with Emmerson. His palms were sweaty, his heart was pounding, and his stomach felt like it had turned to stone.

"Mr. Brunner, to what do we owe the pleasure of your call?"

It made Emmerson nearly nauseous the way the mob could call you "Mr." and treat you with the utmost respect while they held your life in their hands and were willing to snuff it out on a whim.

"Good news, Mr. Williams! Joshua Christopher just called, and he's willing to negotiate." Had he come across sounding calm?

Had he projected the confidence that comes with having good news to share? Brunner hoped so.

Williams' immaculately trimmed narrow black mustache twitched slightly, the only indication that this news had come as a surprise to him. "I see. Perhaps I had better let you talk to Mr. Warwick."

Emmerson's nausea increased. He was sure he was going to be sick right in front of Williams or, horror of horrors, in front of Warwick! He had only met Warwick on one occasion, a brief greeting at a social event. He didn't want to talk to the man who, with a simple command, could end a life. The viewer went dark for what seemed an eternity as the call was transferred, with no calming music or video this time, just blackness and silence. Finally the screen flickered and Warwick, dressed in a Stersman double-lapel suit with a bright red tie, came on the screen.

Prompted by a severe case of the nerves, Emmerson spoke first. "Good news, Mr. Warwick. I was just talking to Joshua Christopher and he has agreed to meet so we can discuss a mutually beneficial settlement. I think we're back in business."

"Mr. Brunner, we have never been close to going out of business." Poor choice of words, Emmerson mentally castigated himself. "It has always been a question as to whether you, Mr. Brunner, would be going out of business."

Trying to ignore the veiled threat, Emmerson continued. "I've lined it up with Christopher to talk with him the day after tomorrow at the airport cargo quadrant." Emmerson paused, swallowing a lump that felt the size of a camel. "What should I offer him, Mr. Warwick?"

"First of all, I have serious doubts that Christopher will accept a buy-out. Principled people don't have a price, something you would know little about, Mr. Brunner." Warwick paused while someone placed a cup of tea in front of him. He grasped the tea bag's tag and methodically moved it up and down, assessing this new information. "It could be some kind of a trap," he finally said. "This move is not in character for someone like Joshua Christopher. Of course, I had hoped that our persuasive efforts would have this effect. Perhaps he feels we are mercenary enough to reject out of hand his willingness to drop the project without a demand from him for monetary compensation. I'm not at all convinced he is interested in dollars. Nevertheless, we've blundered the job of removing him to the point that the authorities are taking a serious look at us. I never like that kind of attention. Offer him two million. If we get the contract on lunar mining we can make that up in no time." Warwick took a sip of tea, then looked into the monitor and leaned forward. "Mr. Brunner, this is your last chance. Good day." The screen went dark. Emmerson, exhausted, slumped in his chair and put his head in his hands.

The next day blew in with strong winds that left the sky mouse-gray and spattered everything with occasional raindrops. The water ran up the canopy of Josh's PAV in rivulets as he flew across the state to a sky bike dealer. His purchase would have to remain a secret if his plan was to work. Even his team would have to be left in the dark on this switch of plans.

Later that day Josh flew to the airport to meet Rick Hagerty. With the sun shining for the first time that day, the mowed grass at the side of the landing pad glistened like millions of diamonds as Josh landed his PAV. He gave the craft a slight forward thrust after it touched down, then taxied toward the site of his rendezvous with Emmerson the next day: a small hangar a good quarter of a mile from where he had touched down. As he taxied, Josh noticed the placement of fences, buildings, fuel trucks, and planes. Some of the trucks and planes would be in a different location tomorrow, but he was counting on a routine that would put most things in the same general location it was today.

Hagerty was waiting at the hangar. It was obvious by his sheepish grin and sweaty-palmed handshake that Josh was still his hero. After initial pleasantries were exchanged, Josh steered the conversation to his purpose for meeting with Hagerty. Within 10 minutes the meeting was over and Josh was lifting the PAV into the air. He glanced down at the ridge of earth that bordered this side of the airport. Brush and small trees covered the side facing away from the airport where it sloped down to a small creek. Josh followed the creek with his eyes as he increased power to the PAV for a normal climb. It should work, he thought to himself.

The flight from the airport to Sam's took only 10 minutes. Josh was happy for Sam. He had been a brash young general contractor who had the winning bid to build the new Saltwater

Reclamation Project headquarters. Josh had privately warned him that his bid was too far below the others to be realistic. Sam was offended, and by the rules, Josh had to accept the low bid. The miscalculation almost put Sam under, and would have if Josh hadn't suggested a partnership with Sam in a small company he was purchasing. A sonic explosion technique was the big development for their newly formed business venture, and it was profitable from early on. The method proved incredibly effective at destroying buildings, a method that would one day be the preferred method for imploding old buildings. Josh had been behind Sam's decision to get out of the general contracting business to spend full time on their joint venture. Josh had been happy to have Sam buy him out and was glad things had gone well for the company since then. As he neared Sam's place he felt the pride of a father for a son who has done well. Sam had never forgotten what Josh had done for him and was anxious to help out his mentor.

Josh kept the meeting brief, and within an hour he was back in the air. As he gained altitude he felt a deepening conviction that what he was planning was the only way to get Emmerson and the Warwick people off their tail. It hurt Josh to think of the temporary pain it would cause his family and the even longer painful anguish his team would have to suffer. He couldn't afford to tell them beforehand; the risk of the wrong people discovering what he was about to do was too great.

This was the moment, Josh thought to himself as he approached the airport. The rising sun cast long shadows as he surveyed the area closely with the same critical eye for detail he had been trained to have during the war. There appeared to be a normal array of aircraft parked in the area, maybe a few more than average. Josh spotted the sports car with a man standing beside it. It was Emmerson. A man was washing a PAV near Emmerson, most likely one of Warwick's hired guns. Josh rehearsed the plan: Rob would get the one-hour time-delayed message on his televiewer. His biggest concern, next to the plan itself working, was that Rob would be informed at the right time about what he had done.

Josh lowered his PAV to the grass just off the pavement and on the other side of the low embankment that formed the airport's boundary, a good distance from where Emmerson stood. Josh shut down his PAV, exited, and climbed the embankment and descended on the other side. The walk to Emmerson was unnerving, not unlike what the gunslingers in the old west must have felt walking down the abandoned main street with their opponent standing there, waiting. The parallel brought another concern to Josh's mind: the possibility of an ambush from the side. He tried to put that fear to rest with the thought that Emmerson and the Warwick clan wouldn't be so stupid as to murder him in broad daylight.

As Josh approached, Emmerson broke into a smile that was like a mask. Emmerson extended his hand; Josh kept his in his pockets. Seemingly unaffected by Josh's coolness, Emmerson spoke with forced affection. "Josh, ol' buddy. It's been ages."

Emmerson looked haggard. Life for someone who sells his soul to another, as Emmerson had done to the Warwick clan, had to be hard on your health, Josh reasoned. "We may have been old buddies in the past, but the past is past, Emmerson. Recent events haven't exactly nurtured our relationship. You almost got my grandson killed with that bomb delivered to him. He'd be dead if your plan hadn't failed. That's changed things a whole lot, 'ol' buddy.'"

Emmerson glanced away for a moment, unable to maintain eye contact. He recovered his composure and looked at Josh again. "Listen, Josh, I had nothing to do with that, honest. It just goes to show what kind of a bind I'm in. I owe lots of money, I mean LOTS of money, and these people are going to protect their investment, unfortunately for you, at all costs."

"How in the world did you get mixed up with them in the first place, Emmerson?"

"It's a long story, Josh. I was desperate for funds to keep the project going. I knew I could come up with a humaniform robot with enough artificial intelligence to be capable of colonization and, therefore, of turning a big profit. I kept at it even after news broke about your deployment of the Dolphdroids. I was sure public reaction would kill the LDP, but obviously I was wrong. In the meantime, I was running out of funds. Someone put me in touch with Nielson and Associates." Emmerson suddenly stopped talking. He had said more than he had wanted to say. Then he went on as if it didn't matter. "They loaned me the money, but I found out too late they were just a cover for the Warwick Syndicate."

"But why did the Warwick Syndicate lend you money for your project when it wasn't a sure thing that the Dolphdroid project would fail?"

"Because the lunar surface represented an entire new market for them, one with virtually unlimited possibilities. If the only thing standing in the way was a small colony of Dolphdroids, that could easily be taken care of. That's what they figured."

Josh's face flushed with anger. "Do you mean to tell me that the Warwick Syndicate initiated the problems between the Dolphdroids?"

Emmerson knew he was doing too much talking, just digging himself a deeper hole. "Let's just say that they're bound and determined to win at all costs. There's just too much at stake in this. They won't stop, Josh. It's out of my hands. I'm just warning you, people will die if you don't do something." Emmerson paused, then continued, "But I guess that's why you wanted to see me and make some kind of deal, right?"

"Keep talking."

"I'll admit, you caught me off guard on this. I didn't think you were the type to make a deal." He quickly added, "Though I can't blame you." He paused. "You aren't trying to pull some kind of trick, are you?"

"Trick?"

"Yeah, trick. Because if you are, give it up, Josh. These people are playing for high stakes and they play for keeps. I wish I'd never gotten involved. Man, how I wish I'd never gotten involved! I wish I'd stayed a million miles from their money. But I didn't, so I have to play the game through the best I can. My life's on the line, Josh. You hold my life in your hands."

"Now you're pleading, Emmerson."

"I know," Emmerson replied with a lame smile. "So do you have an offer, Josh?"

"Five million."

Emmerson looked dumbfounded. "Five million? You've got to be crazy! There's no way they're going to give you five million. They're prepared to give you two million. I know it's going to be their only offer. These people aren't into counteroffers."

"Then I'm afraid we can't do business."

"Are you serious? I mean, first of all I found it hard to

believe you'd negotiate any kind of a price. Now this, a ridiculous price that you gotta know they won't accept. You're up to something, aren't you? This is some kind of game, isn't it? Don't fool around like this, Josh. Please don't, or we're both history."

Josh smiled, saying nothing for a moment, enjoying watching Emmerson squirm. "The lunar surface represents the last available real estate, Emmerson. It ought to be worth billions in their eyes. Five million is my offer."

Emmerson looked shaken. He lowered his head, his shoulder drooped. "I don't know, Josh. I guess I'll see what they have to say." Then he lifted his head and looked Josh in the eyes. "But I don't think you'll be alive to hear any counteroffer. It'll be cheaper to kill you."

"Just check with them and get in touch," Josh said. He turned and walked back to his PAV.

Emmerson watched the retreating figure as he climbed the embankment to his PAV on the other side. His head was throbbing, his mind swirling with thoughts about what would happen now. Would they give in to his offer or give a counteroffer? Fat chance!

Emmerson walked to his car, started the engine, and glanced at the embankment. He watched for a moment, then saw Josh's PAV come into view as it rose into the air from behind the berm of earth. Emmerson shook his head, bitterly disappointed that Josh hadn't accepted the offer. He watched the PAV as it cleared the embankment and turned sharply toward the trees. Momentarily hidden by the trees, the PAV came into view again and began a steep climb. Suddenly the PAV was replaced by a bright fireball. A loud explosion quickly followed that shook Emmerson's car. He watched in shock as the fireball fell to earth behind some trees. A moment later billowing black smoke poured from the impact point, then there was another explosion and more black smoke.

"He's dead. They killed him," Emmerson said under his breath.

Chapter 18

    Emmerson sped up the entrance ramp from the airport onto the freeway. He breathed a sigh of relief when he entered the flow of traffic. He knew the airport would quickly be shut down after the crash of Josh's PAV. That would mean tight security at the airport, including the exits. He had no desire to be questioned about why he was at the airport. He hadn't done anything wrong, but he was the last one to speak with the dead man. What about security cameras? Would there be any record of his being at the airport? What would he tell the authorities if they wanted to interview him? Why would the Warwick Syndicate blow Josh away in full view of the airport? And how did they do it? Did they have a bomb on board his PAV? Had they fired some kind of a missile? He hadn't seen one. His thoughts were interrupted by his phone beeping. The ID screen showed it was a call from Williams. How he hated the man. Williams, as Warwick's top aide, was almost always the person he had to talk to. The conversation was brief and to the point. They had a camera hidden somewhere and had watched the whole encounter. Williams accused him of blowing up Christopher's PAV and Emmerson's vehement denial fell on deaf ears. They actually thought *he* had blown up the PAV! Emmerson fired back, "You guys did it. You had to have done it – I sure didn't!"

    Williams laughed mockingly, "Now why would we draw

attention to a clandestine meeting at such a public place by blowing someone up?" Then Williams broke the connection.

As Emmerson drove, he considered what Williams had said. The man made sense. It didn't add up for the Warwick family to dispense with Christopher in such a public way. But what really bothered him as he took a cloverleaf onto another freeway was that they thought he had done it. Then a sense of relief came over him as he realized that the one person who threatened the removal of the Dolphdroids was gone. It didn't matter who had done it, the fact was that it was done. It served the man right. He should have realized he was playing with some big, bad bullies in the Warwick family. It was a good thing Christopher was dead, right? Then Emmerson's mouth went dry and a lump formed in his throat as he realized that he still had to deal with the Warwicks. He tried to reassure himself that with Christopher out of the way things would get better. The Dolphdroids would soon be history, and he'd have his own humaniforms ready to replace them within a year. Soon the lunar surface would be populated with his creatures and he'd be a very wealthy man. His line of logic was only partly successful at calming his fears.

Bill Zucker was the first of the team to hear about the crash on a local newscast. "A personal air vehicle has crashed at Cargo Express Airport. We have just received confirmation that the pilot was the award-winning scientist Dr. Joshua Christopher, former head of the now threatened Lunar Dolphdroid Project. Witnesses say the craft exploded soon after taking off from the airport. The craft was completely destroyed and the body burned beyond recognition." As Bill stared at his viewer the image switched from the reporter to the crash site.

Numbness and shock overwhelmed Bill. Disbelief put up a valiant fight against the harsh truth that glared at him from the viewer. The reporter's voice faded to the background as Bill intently watched the screen showing scattered debris with only a part of the canopy giving any hint that it had been a PAV. The distant voice on the newscast was talking about the certainty of an investigation, saying there had been previous attempts on Dr. Christopher's life and that of his family. Foul play was suspected. The reporter finished and the news anchor went on with the next story, but Bill was no longer listening. He sat numbly for a few moments, then turned off the viewer.

His world had spun off its axis. Josh was gone. Waves of anger flooded over his grief. This was no accident, he knew that much. It was the Warwick Syndicate, it had to be. They had done this. What would happen to Moon's Mercy? It was what Josh was living for, but what was Moon's Mercy without Josh? Josh, gone? It was so hard to imagine. Rob, what about Rob? Had he heard yet, had they notified him as next of kin? His viewer announced that he had a call from Risner.

Risner's image came on screen. He looked ashen, speaking without giving any kind of a greeting, "What in tarnation has happened?" He knew. Another call came in, and Bill put Risner on hold. It was Phil Kirkpatrick. A friend had told him. Bill put both of them on the screen and they shared all the things friends share when they've lost someone close.

Bill's viewer indicated another call coming in. It was Rob. Bill decided to leave his two friends on. Rob could use all the support he could get. Maybe he didn't know? It occurred to Bill that if this was the case, he'd really appreciate his friends being in on the difficult conversation.

The three were silent, their eyes glued to their screens, when Rob flickered into view. He knew about his father, they could see it on his face. Bill swallowed hard, searched for the right words, and found himself making what seemed to him a lame attempt at expressing his condolences. The other two nodded in agreement. Rob listened expressionless. When he spoke his voice was as expressionless as his face. He asked if any other of the team members had been contacted. He was told by Risner that they had not. The three said they'd get on that right away.

Another call was coming in. Bill put everyone on hold, allowing them their own conversation while he took the incoming call from Tony. Tony knew, too. He added Tony to the conversation and all of their viewers were now dotted with five images.

Rob said, "I know that you and the rest of the team have been behind Dad on this project from the very beginning. I know you're wondering what to do next. We won't worry about a memorial service at this time. Bill, I believe Dad gave you some instructions about what to do if something like this happened. I'd suggest you carry them through to the letter. Remember, it's likely our conversations are being monitored. I'm going to disconnect before this call can be traced. I'd still rather not have anyone know where my family and I are staying. Goodbye for now." Rob's image left their screens.

"So, exactly what were these instructions from Josh?" Risner asked.

Bill paused, then shook his head and said, "I don't think I'd better say over the viewer."

The four stayed on their viewers together for another 15 minutes. No plans were made, just feelings shared. Finally Risner said, "This is sounding too much like the conversations I've heard around caskets in funeral homes. I've had enough." With that, his image disappeared from the screens of the remaining three. They decided to end the conversation too.

Bill sat back in his chair and tried to recall one of the last conversations he had with Josh, the one in which Josh had given him the instructions for this worst-case scenario. Josh had been insistent that he take what he was about to say seriously. Bill remembered trying to blow off the whole idea that something so terrible might happen that Josh would no longer be part of the plan, but Josh had been insistent. The whole team was to meet at Josh's uncle's and aunt's farm in Iowa as soon as possible if something like this happened.

Rob's warning about the monitored conversations led him to decide that he would have to make contact with the team members without using televiewers. Rob was undoubtedly right that their viewers were being monitored.

Bill found it difficult and time-consuming to set up a meeting at the Iowa farm without using the televiewer. Secure computer links turned out to be the best option with most of the team. With a couple of the team members it required a face-to-face invitation.

His efforts had paid off, and the farmhouse was crowded. The last of the team had just arrived in a rental car from the Des Moines airport. It was one of those two story plus an attic farmhouses from an era long gone. Josh's uncle and aunt, in their late 70s, were in the kitchen, having made certain all the guests had coffee or tea and a generous helping of dessert bars.

Quiet slowly settled on the room, and Risner took advantage of it. Sitting in a chair, leaning forward and holding a cup of coffee in his hands, he exclaimed, "I just can't believe this has happened. I'll tell you, some heads are going to roll over this; justice has gotta be done. They've gotta pay."

"Now just calm down, Risner," Tony said in a soft tone, hoping Risner would emulate him. "We need to do some serious thinking before we let our grief and anger run away with the situation."

"Tony's right," Phil said. "We have to respond, not react. Bill, when Rob came on his televiewer the other day he referred to following his father's orders. There's a lot of buzz among the team here as to what that's all about. Obviously you know something we don't."

Bill glanced around the room filled with people in every chair, some sitting on the floor, a few standing in corners and doorways. All eyes were on him. "Actually, I don't know anything more than any of you do. All I know is that a day or so before…" he paused for the right word, "…the tragedy, Josh told me that no matter what happened, the team was to meet here as soon as possible. I thought it was rather strange at the time and still do." Bill glanced around the room again. "I really don't understand why he would want us all together."

Risner spoke, shaking his head and raising his arms, "What for? What's the sense of meeting like this? It's all over. It's done. We're done!"

Nancy Saunders spoke up, her voice soft but controlled. "You mentioned to me a few minutes ago, Bill, that Rob told you the preliminary results of the Air and Space Investigation Board."

"Yes, he got in touch with me just before this meeting. The results are mostly what you would expect. The board determined that there had been a significant amount of explosives aboard Josh's PAV. So far they haven't identified the specific method of detonation." Bill hesitated in an effort to compose himself, because his voice was beginning to sound shaky with emotion. "The body was beyond recognition, pretty much incinerated. An investigation is centering on the possible involvement of organized crime."

"Well, maybe now they'll put some real heat on the Warwick

Syndicate," Risner interjected. "I can't believe they were stupid enough to take Doc Chris out like that, right there in public view, at an airport of all places! They should have known they'd be the prime suspects in the investigation."

"That's what has me bewildered," Tony responded. "It really wasn't a wise move on their part, not at all their style, from what I've been told."

"Maybe they didn't do it," Nancy said.

"Who else?" Risner replied, anger obvious in his voice.

"Just a thought," Nancy said under her breath.

"So, what's going to happen next?" Risner asked.

"Good question," Tony replied.

"I know," Risner snapped back.

"Bill, Josh gave no indication as to what we ought to do once we got together?" Phil asked.

"The project's dead in the water without Doc," Risner said, ignoring Phil's question. "I mean, who wants to get his brain transplanted into a robot? What would it accomplish? Doc never made clear just exactly how his becoming the second Adam was going to save the Dolphdroids."

The squeak of the back door drew everyone's attention. All the team members were present and accounted for; no one had left the meeting. Josh's uncle and aunt were still in the kitchen. Everyone knew no one else should be coming. Great effort had been made to conceal the location of the meeting. Hearts were pounding.

Footsteps came slowly down the hallway, echoing on the hundred year old oak floor. The steps grew louder, and then a figure appeared in the short hallway leading to the living room.

Risner, seated across the room from the hallway, identified the figure first, and shouted, "Doc Chris! What in tarnation!"

Chapter 19

"Am I late?" Josh said, glancing around the room at their astonished faces. His eyes locked on Ashley, sitting in a high-backed wooden chair in the far corner. She bit her lower lip in relief and joy, but the fear of what Josh thought of her kept her in the chair. Josh shot a glance at Bill.

Bill saw a combination of hurt, concern, and bewilderment on his face and said, "It's OK, Josh, she's really with us now. She can be trusted. But how can you... I mean, you're supposed to be..."

Josh looked around the room again, letting his eyes fall on each person as he spoke. "I owe all of you a really good explanation for what's happened and a huge apology for what I've put you through." He noted how the shock of his walking into the room had sent three of them to their feet. "Risner, Dr. Mesner, Tony, you might as well sit back down and get comfortable. This will take a lot of explaining."

The men sat down while Josh moved to a more central location along the wall near the kitchen; his uncle and aunt had now joined the group, his aunt holding a dish towel to her mouth in amazement.

Josh took a deep breath and began. "As you know all too

well, the pressures to drop the LDP have been intense, to say the least. I had no idea when we began this project that organized crime would enter the picture. It became obvious the mob would stop at nothing to keep us from saving the LDP. The sky bike attack, the sabotage of my PAV, and the package bomb intended for my grandson Randy certainly hadn't exhausted their repertoire of intimidation." Josh paused and looked at the woman to whom he had given his heart. "I also discovered that my relationship with Ashley was orchestrated from the very beginning by the Warwicks so they could have access to information about the project. Because of that relationship I compromised the mission, and for that I apologize. Her presence here is about as big a surprise to me as my presence must be to you. I trust you all enough to know there's a good explanation, but first let me do the explaining. After all I've put you through, I owe you that much."

Risner, driven by a need to always be saying or doing something, had gotten up, gone into the kitchen and brought back a cup of coffee for Josh. "Thanks, Risner," Josh said as he took the cup, though he didn't take a sip.

"Several days ago someone on the team made the statement that the only way we would get rid of the opposition was if I were dead. The Warwick family would think that the end of me would be the end of the project, and that would be that. I decided that it wasn't a bad idea for me to be dead so, with some help, I staged it."

"But what about the fragments of a body they found at the crash site?" Bill asked.

Josh smiled slightly and nodded. "I know you've got a zillion questions. I'll start from the beginning. I needed to get myself killed, and the opposition had to see it happen. I lined up a meeting with Emmerson under the guise of asking for a payoff to quit fighting the termination. That was really the most risky part; I knew they'd consider it out of character for me to make an offer like that. I counted, though, on their innate sense of greed to get them to at least agree to meet with me. I wasn't disappointed. My greatest concern at the meeting was that they might help me do for real what I planned on faking: my being killed."

Josh paused and took a sip of coffee, then continued. "I had installed a significant amount of explosives in my PAV to blow it into small pieces. An explosives expert named Sam Courtney owed me a favor and offered the help I needed to make it happen. I also need a quick-release parachute to break my fall when I jumped from the craft during the brief moments it was obscured from Emmerson and his friends by the berm of earth and some trees just after I lifted off. It partially opened in the short drop to the ground and that, along with the soft muck in the swamp on that side of the airport, kept me from breaking any bones and I was able to slip into the marsh and get away."

The group was silent, focusing on every word. He didn't like the next part of his story, but he knew he owed them the full explanation. "About the body parts that were found. I had contacted a long-lost college buddy, Henry Brigster, who's a private detective and more. He eventually found a cadaver at some morgue, don't ask me where, that matched my basic size. The deceased was a transient who had been on ice for several months. The cadaver took a ride with me that day."

Nancy Saunders inhaled sharply and then exclaimed, "You mean there was a corpse in the PAV with you when you landed at the airport? Wasn't it difficult..." she paused and started again. "Didn't you..." She decided to take a different approach and stated, "Some people might consider it misuse of a body."

"I certainly didn't relish the idea and I was confronted with the issue full force, believe me, while traveling with the thawed body in the PAV. I reminded myself, however, that a dead body is no longer a person. Some people donate their bodies to scientific research and the body I carried with me in the PAV would be serving as great a purpose. Bodies are cremated all the time, and his fiery cremation would allow Moon's Mercy to move ahead unhindered, at least for awhile; that's how I looked at it."

"The poor soul may have made a greater contribution in death than while he lived," Dr. Mesner reflected, sadness in his voice.

"They won't discover that the tissue fragments don't match your medical records?" Bill asked.

"In a case like this, where there's no reasonable doubt as to the identity of the crash victim, they most likely wouldn't follow through with that kind of lab work. Law enforcement agencies have overworked labs, and a job like this would certainly be placed on the bottom of the 'to do' list," Dr. Mesner observed.

"You blew up your new PAV," Risner interjected. Spontaneous laughter from most of those in the room broke the tension.

"Rob! What about Rob? Does he know you're still alive?" asked Nancy.

"Yes, he was the only one who knew about my up-and-coming tragic death. It's one reason he's stayed in isolation and didn't join the rest of you. He didn't think he could impersonate a mourning son convincingly enough. A brief stint on the televiewer talking with Bill was all he felt he could handle. That, of course, is the reason I couldn't let the rest of you in on my plan. The Warwicks and authorities might have had second thoughts about what happened with the PAV explosion, and if the acting of just one of you hadn't been up to academy award standards it would have blown the whole scheme. Now that a little time has passed they're not as likely to be watching you so closely. Still, a mournful demeanor in public would be appropriate for all of you," Josh said with a smile.

Bill shook his head slowly. "Rob's acting on the televiewer was good enough to fool me."

"Again, I know what I did was very cruel. Knowing how shocked you would be and how you would grieve was the worst part of the plan, even worse than riding with a cadaver. My only comfort has been that we'll have the Warwick Family off our backs for, hopefully, a significant length of time."

Josh explained more of the details of his faked death: walking through a large drainage culvert near the crash site to a location a quarter of a mile away where it emptied into a small stream, changing to clean clothes he had stashed in an old abandoned shed, and walking to a nearby restaurant where he had parked a sky bike.

After regaining their emotional equilibrium following the shock of seeing Josh alive, and re-energized by a spirit of hope that permeated the group, the discussion turned to developing further details of Moon's Mercy. Although Bill wanted Josh to take over leadership of the meeting, Josh insisted that Bill continue in the role. The acquisition of Adam from the Smithsonian West became a primary subject of discussion and planning. Bobo wanted only himself, Josh and one other person involved in the mission. Josh decided on Risner, and the group agreed. Risner knew Adam as well or better than anyone.

With a final warning to keep away from the press and to suppress their euphoria over Josh's being alive, Bill closed the meeting. The sun had set and it was beginning to grow dark. Everyone remained for a time, filling the farmhouse with conversation and laughter. Slowly, the group grew smaller as people left, each person having a personal word with Josh before departing. Ashley moved to the kitchen and began helping Josh's uncle and aunt do some dishes. She would wait until Josh could see her alone. They had to talk.

Risner was the last to leave, checking the final details of the acquisition of Adam with Josh. In two days they would meet Bobo McClarin in California for the "midnight requisition," as Bobo called it. They would travel separately, minimizing the chance of someone discovering that Josh was alive.

Josh closed the screen door as Risner stepped off the porch and walked to his car.

"You go ahead and chat with Josh, dearie," Josh's aunt encouraged. "I'll just tidy up a bit more."

"Thanks," Ashley replied.

She draped the dish towel over the drying rack by the sink and walked over to Josh who was still standing by the screen door. He turned and looked at her. The distance seemed an infinity to both of them.

"I was surprised to see you here," Josh began, his words empty of emotion.

"And I was surprised to see you here." She had a hint of a smile that tried to break through her worried expression.

"Let's take a walk," Josh suggested, opening the screen door.

"OK."

Both were silent as they walked, until they passed the old barn and started up the lane that ran along the edge of the field. Without looking at her, he asked, "How is it that Bill allowed you to be with the team?" He thought it a non-judgmental way to give her the opportunity to explain herself, though he was still questioning Bill's judgment.

"He believes that I've fallen in love with you."

"I believed that, too, and it almost cost us the mission."

Ashley stopped, and so did Josh. She touched his sleeve, but then thought the better of it and pulled back her hand, crossing her arms and looking up into the sky. "Look, Josh. I know this is incredibly difficult for you to believe, but please hear me out." He started to walk, and she did, too. "I had no idea who hired me to get close enough to you to get the information they wanted. I assumed it was the usual corporate intrigue."

"OK, I can give you that much, maybe. But why would a nice girl get mixed up in what you thought was corporate cloak and dagger stuff?"

"It seemed innocent enough, Josh. I was..." She paused, then corrected herself. "I'm a struggling actress, and I needed some money. A friend told me about how she had done some of this kind of work: go out on a few dates with a lonely company executive, get him to have a few too many drinks so he tells you everything the competition wants to know."

"And you didn't have a problem with this? Just how much of yourself would you be willing to exchange for this information?"

She shook her head. "I would never go to bed with anyone, if that's what you mean. I made that promise to myself, and I meant it."

"That's not the impression I got."

She sighed. "That's because I was falling in love with you. I can't act that well."

"You acted just like my wife in so many ways it was uncanny. You even fixed yourself up to look like her. How did you know how she looked and acted?"

"I watched some home videos. I didn't ask, but I assumed they took them from your home. They spent a lot of time working with me so I could get her mannerisms down. I can't believe I did it, and I hate myself for it."

"Well, that explains why my videos appeared to have been out of order. It's amazing what lengths they went to in order to get to me. And you were part of it."

She ignored his last comment. "She was beautiful, Josh, and so graceful. I studied and studied the videos, but was afraid I'd never be able to imitate her."

"Obviously you did a pretty good job. You pulled me right into your trap."

"My job was to get you to fall in love with me, or at least be infatuated enough that you'd let your guard down. Something happened that no one expected, least of all me. I started to care about you. I started to fall in love with you."

"And how many others of your stooges did you 'fall in love' with?" Josh asked, holding up both hands in a quotation marks gesture.

She shook her head. "This was my first job. I realized partway through that I could never do this kind of thing again."

"And you had no idea you had been hired by organized crime?"

"Of course not!" She burst into tears. Josh glanced at her. Was it still part of the act? The thought crossed his mind. She continued, "I thought it was a legitimate company, I told you that. I'm scared, Josh. I know now what these people do to anyone who doesn't play things their way. I've turned on them, and they're now going to want me dead! They know by now that I've defected. Even before your fake death they knew I was weakening, that I might be a problem for them. 'A liability instead of an asset' is how they put it. This has turned into a nightmare, an absolute nightmare." Then she glanced at him, wiping a tear away. "The only bright spot, and it's made all the difference, is that you're alive. I thought maybe I had inadvertently been an accomplice of your death. That was the worst part of this whole thing."

Josh wanted very badly to believe her. Bill had whispered to him before leaving, "She's OK, Josh. We can trust her. She needs our help now."

"How much did you tell them about Moon's Mercy?"

She wiped away another tear. "I pieced together your plan to take a robot from the Smithsonian West and somehow use it. I gave them the names of most of the team." She broke into tears again. "Now they're going to be targets too. They'll want to kill them all, the very people who are protecting me now."

"Not necessarily." Josh found himself reassuring her, "They want to continue in business, so they won't do any unnecessary killing just to get even; it would draw too much attention. I'm no expert on organized crime, but from what I gather they'll go after one of their own who tries to quit on them, sort of their version of enforcing life long commitment, but I don't think you fit into that category."

"So you don't think I'm in danger?"

"I don't think so, though the safe approach is to keep you out of sight until they move on to other more important concerns."

She nodded. "That's what Bill thought." She looked at Josh. "He finally believed my story after I came to him out of desperation, afraid for my life. That's why I was here at the meeting. He figured the safest place for me was with the team. I wanted to be here, too. Somehow I felt close to you among all your friends. I can't believe that you're alive! It's like a dream. I feel I have a second chance with you, to make it right with you, to do what's right."

Josh could sense she was resisting the urge to embrace him. He felt the same urge, and reached out his hand. She hesitated only a moment, then extended hers. They walked hand in hand in silence; the only sound was an owl hooting in the nearby woods. They stopped, turned toward each other, and embraced. Josh touched her chin gently with his hand, tilting her face upward. Their eyes met, hers with a glint of moonlight, and they kissed.

Arm in arm, they walked to the lake, where they sat on a fallen log. Picking up a small stone, Josh tossed it into the water. The dark ripples moved, in ever-widening circles. Ashley took a stone and did the same, sending out fresh ripples.

She leaned against his shoulder and spoke softly. "I want our lives to overlap, just like those ripples. I was happy beyond words when you walked into the room back there in the house. I had all sorts of feelings well up within me at the same time: disbelief, bewilderment, joy, and fear. I was afraid of what you'd think of me. Actually, I knew; I could see it in your eyes when you first spotted me." She hugged his arm tight. "I'm so glad I have a second chance with you, but now I'm afraid I'm going to lose you again. I know you have to become Adam. I don't understand all of the details, but I understand enough to know that it has to be. I'd never try to talk you out of this plan of yours, but I'm afraid I'll never get you back as Josh."

He wanted to say something to reassure her, but he knew he couldn't. There were no guarantees with this plan. He certainly wanted to come full circle with the project by coming back to being Joshua Christopher. He had reasons now that he hadn't had before: being reconciled to his son, which also gave him access to his grandson, and now Ashley.

"Everyone is going to do their best to bring this project full circle. I'm planning on being me again, Ashley."

"Your confidence is contagious, dear Josh. Keep talking like this. It makes me feel better." He took her request seriously and shared with her the status of the project and told her about each of the team members, about his connection with each one and the confidence he had in them. They talked until clouds moved in and obscured the moon, then walked back to the farmhouse. His uncle and aunt had gone to bed, so he left them a note asking if Ashley could stay with them for a few days. He laid the note on the counter by the sink and held it down with a glass from the cupboard.

Ashley followed him outside and walked him to the sky bike; he had parked it near the edge of the small woods a hundred or so yards from the house. The clouds broke, and the moon's light cascaded over the landscape with a soft glow. They both looked up at the moon as he held her. Would it really work, he wondered? Could he rescue the Dolphdroids from the judgement that would doom them? Getting there, as much trouble as it was turning out to be, would seem easy compared to the formidable task he faced when he got there. They stood beside the sky bike, looking at the moon, for a long time.

"I'd better be going," he finally said. They kissed, and he climbed on to the sky bike. Moments later he found himself flying above the low-hung clouds to have an unobstructed view of the moon. He felt good about being even a few hundred feet closer to the lunar surface. His destiny was there, he knew. He had to become one of them. They had no other hope; there was no other way to save them. He had to become the second Adam.

Chapter 20

The flight to California was uneventful for Josh and Risner. The Loadstar he piloted was a rental plane, small enough that Josh could fly it under his current license. His only concern was that someone would spot his name on the rental forms or flight plan. The chances were small with the thousands of flights of private craft each day, but it gave Josh some concern.

Bobo met them at the nearly abandoned rural airport that had a runway just long enough to qualify as a landing site for a Loadstar. "Welcome back from the dead," Bobo said tersely as Josh and Risner climbed into Bobo's car. "You know, I almost took another assignment when I heard you had bit the dust."

"Sorry to cause you such confusion," Josh replied, tightening his seat belt.

Ignoring Josh's sarcastic reply, Bobo said, "Let me go over the details," as he pushed the accelerator to the floor, making the tires squeal. "We can't afford any slip-ups. I don't much like the idea of messing with the Smithsonian West; we're in for some pretty nasty punishment if we get caught. Then there's the fact that I usually work alone, and if I do work with someone it's always a professional like myself. Theft is an art. But, seeing as how that hunk of bolts won't move without the right words from you, Doc, we'll have to make the best of it."

"We'll do our best not to mess things up, Bobo," Risner said, glancing back at Josh and rolling his eyes. Josh knew Risner didn't appreciate the reference to Adam as a hunk of bolts, so Josh shook his head warning Risner to resist saying anything that might upset the cantankerous Bobo. The burglar was a critical figure in this part of the plan, and Josh didn't want him to walk away from the project in a huff.

Josh, however, couldn't resist correcting Bobo. "This isn't exactly a theft, Bobo. I've explained before that Adam is my property and that he's only on loan to the Smithsonian West. The fact is, the paperwork it would take to get him out would delay the project for months, and would give the Warwick Syndicate all of the time in the world to stop the project one way or another. And since I'm supposed to be dead, it's essential that Adam's disappearance be seen as a theft by some unknown crook." Bobo glanced back at Josh and frowned. Josh quickly added, "Sorry about the reference to someone in your profession as a crook."

"Call it what you want, Doc," Bobo replied. "The fact is, you've hired me to get this mechanical wanna-be-a-man out of cold storage. It's time we talk details on what we're gonna do to make it happen."

Bobo explained the specifics as he drove, frequently pausing to take a deep breath, an event that expanded his stomach, seeming to stretch his seat belt to the breaking point. He dropped them off at a park about 10 minutes by car from the Smithsonian West and instructed them to wait an hour and then take a cab to the museum. They'd be arriving an hour before the Smithsonian closed. He would already be in the museum. Not waiting for a response from the two men who were now standing beside the car, Bobo roared off.

"And good-by to you, too, Mr. Bobo," Risner said as the car disappeared.

"Definitely not one for social niceties," Josh observed.

Risner looked around. "So, what do you do in a park while you bide your time before removing a display item from the Smithsonian West?" Risner asked.

They started to walk to a playground area where three children and their mother were enjoying some late evening playtime. A jogger went by; then a policeman on an electric bike purred past them, glancing their way. Josh saw Risner's face turn red as he picked up his pace, walking ahead of Josh.

When the officer was out of hearing range Josh said, "If you look any more guilty we're going to be picked up for questioning, and Bobo will be one unhappy man when we miss the rendezvous, to say nothing of me being identified and found to be alive, not dead."

"Sorry about that," Risner said, slowing his pace.

The hour stretched long, but eventually it was time to hail a cab. The cabby turned out to be the world's expert on everything. After a few minutes of pontificating on how to solve the world's problems he asked if they were from out of town. When they said they were, he proceeded to give them a short history on the mega city. The ride to the Smithsonian took almost 20 minutes. After paying the cabby and seeing him drive off, Risner said, "That's the trouble with a cabby knowing you're from out of town. It always takes longer than it should for you to be taken to your destination."

"Sorry, gentlemen, the museum closes in slightly less than one hour and the policy is that no new visitors be admitted within an hour of closing. We invite you to come back tomorrow," the guard stated in a matter-of-fact way. His statement bordered on the mechanical, but it was unmistakably firm.

Josh and Risner glanced at each other. Risner had a panicked look on his face that reflected what Josh felt in his stomach. "Look," Risner said, "we don't want an invitation to come back tomorrow." Josh observed the guard giving Risner a determined look and knew he had to do something before Risner pushed the guard into a corner from where he would never budge.

Reaching into his pocket, Josh produced as much money as the guard would earn in a week. Smiling, he said, "My friend is right; we can't come back tomorrow, and there really is only one display we're interested in. We'd be extremely grateful if you'd just pretend we arrived five minutes earlier."

The guard glanced at the money. His eyes widened, and then he glanced around, took the money, and said, "I guess my watch might be off a few minutes. Enjoy your visit to the Smithsonian West."

"That was close," Risner said in a voice loud enough that Josh was concerned the guard might have heard.

"At least we're in," Josh replied in a whisper, hoping Risner would take the hint to turn down his volume.

The building, though mammoth in size, was of simple design. There were four large pyramids that contained the display areas, with two balconies ringing each pyramid for additional display space. The four pyramids came together, forming a square common area that provided more display area and housed the large lobby, restaurant, gift shop, and offices. The main entrance where Josh and Risner had encountered the guard was located at the point where pyramids one and four came together.

They made their way past the information center and fought the flow of people leaving for the day, walking along the glass wall between the lobby and the fourth pyramid. They passed the original giant mechanical Nuberskinto used in John Hodge's blockbuster movie *From the Edge of Time*.

"The nation's attic," Risner commented.

"What did you say?"

"The nation's attic. That's what I've heard the two Smithsonian Institutes called: the nation's attics. It does remind you of an attic: things hanging from the ceiling, objects propped in a corner. Most of it useless, except for nostalgic and I suppose historical purposes."

"You talk a lot when you're nervous, don't you?" Josh said under his breath.

"Excuse me?"

"Never mind."

Glancing through the glass wall into the fourth pyramid, they could see displays with backdrops that gave a sense of realism to the scenes.

Having passed pyramid four, they entered pyramid three, where Adam was on display. Josh recalled the only time he had been in the museum, when they dedicated the display. The sadness of deactivating Adam had been tempered by the optimism surrounding the settlement of the Dolphdroid colony on the lunar surface. Risner had been back about two years ago, to do a check on Adam and make certain that the systems were still operational. Josh glanced around as they walked. The theme was agriculture and industry. Displays of prehistoric people were first. They made their way back and forth through several aisles of displays.

"He's down this aisle," Risner said, pointing to the right. As they made their way around the Mars display, they slowed their pace. The could see Adam straight ahead. The black and gray seven-foot figure stood motionless on a lunar display. Small rocks and craters were scattered around him. In his right hand he held a pick-blaster, in his left, a large piece of rock. There was a slight bluish glow on his face, the equivalent of a human's relaxed expression during sleep. His video imagery receptors – eyes to those who insisted on anthropomorphic terminology – seemed to stare blankly past them.

He stood there, a motionless figure in a pretend lunar world. Josh was surprised by his deep feelings of sadness. Memories danced through his head, like the time they were training Adam at home and he clumsily made his way around furniture and people. He pushed the recollections from his mind, forcing himself to think in the present. A sense of excitement came over him as he anticipated activating Adam in just a few short hours. Then a sense of sadness returned. Things wouldn't be the same as they had been when Adam was alive. Adam's dolphin brain had died and been removed, so he would act much like a basic robot: mechanical in response and movement, no personality, a non-conscious computer running a robotic body.

Then a different feeling came over Josh, one of awe and wonder. His own future was staring him in the face! He was looking at himself as he would be in a matter of days. He was looking at himself without benefit of a mirror, face to face with his future self. This was to be his body, this mechanical form that was now little more than a statue. Flesh would be replaced by metal alloys, muscles with servomechanisms, nerves with wires and fiber optics. The enormity of what was to happen crystallized in his thinking as never before. He struggled to put his thoughts around it all. But there was no other way. He had to do this if the race of creatures he had created was to be saved.

Risner's whispered words to Adam, "Hi, old friend," brought Josh back to the present.

"I knew this would be a bittersweet moment," Josh said "I've always resisted thinking about Adam standing here on display. He looks so… lifeless."

"Well, it won't be long until he'll be walking out of here under his own power," Risner said.

"I hope so. Do you think all of his systems are going to be

operational?"

Risner glanced at Josh. "It's a little late to be asking that question, don't you think?" Then Risner looked at Adam, leaning over the railing and letting his eyes roam up and down the motionless form, taking particular note of a small red diode under Adam's left wrist that was blinking in what most would view as an erratic sequence but to Risner was a code that was reporting data. "He's in good shape, good enough to walk out of here under his own steam."

Just then Josh noticed, among all the photos on display, one of him and Adam. He glanced around. A young boy was looking intently at the Dolphdroid display. An older couple, apparently his grandparents, was nearby. Suddenly Josh became self-conscious, concerned that the boy might identify him.

"Let's go find Bobo," Josh said in a soft voice. Nodding to the photograph, he added, "I don't want to be recognized, and I'm asking for it if we keep standing here."

"True," Risner agreed, glancing at the picture, "though you've aged considerably since then, my friend. There's not all that much of a resemblance."

"Thanks a lot, and don't call me your friend."

Risner allowed himself a slight smile. His eyes darted over Josh's shoulder. "There's Bobo," he said. They made their way toward him.

Bobo gave no indication he saw them until they were next to him, pretending to look at an old wooden plow. He mumbled, "See you guys made it. We'll make our way back to that Allis Chalmers harvesting machine in a few minutes. Meanwhile, let's keep our distance from each other."

Time moved slowly for Josh as he pretended to view the displays around him with great interest when in reality his thoughts were swirling around everything they were about to do. His stomach was turning as well. He decided that people who made their living as thieves must have a short lifespan, considering the stress they must have to deal with as an occupational hazard.

After viewing countless displays, about which Josh couldn't recall a single meaningful detail, he heard the announcement that the museum would be closing in 20 minutes. The next 15 minutes passed even more slowly as he made an effort to remain inconspicuous. A security guard with a butch haircut that came close to baldness walked up behind Josh and stated it was time to head toward the front entrance. The guard then moved on to a young family where a boy was enamored by an old-fashioned hand water pump and told them the same.

Josh moved toward Risner, and the two of them made their way to the farm display with the Allis Chalmers harvesting machine. Bobo came from the other direction.

The machine was orange, the color of all Allis Chalmers machinery of the last half of the twentieth century. Josh knew a lot about farm machinery, having spent many summers on his uncle's farm as a child, though this particular brand and style of harvester had long been obsolete when he was a little boy. It had a header made up of a cutting bar and reel that pushed the grain over the cutting bar when it was in operation. A wide piece of canvas ran from the cutting bar up into the machine. Running at 90 degrees to the header was the main part of the machine: a large rectangular box-shaped structure that contained a set of mechanisms which separated the grain from the chaff.

Risner looked intently at the machine. "How are we supposed to fit all three of us in there?"

"We'll fit," Bobo replied.

Josh had his doubts about the rotund Bobo fulfilling that prediction.

Risner pointed to a nearby silo. "Why not hide in there?"

"Because the security guard often looks in there at closing time. I've checked the security recordings. Take my word for it. The safest place to hide is inside this machine."

They waited until the last of the museum visitors in the vicinity had made their way around the corner toward the exit.

"OK, let's do it," Bobo said. "Here, give me a lift."

Risner glanced around. "Security recordings? That means there are security cameras watching. I see one up there." Risner directed his eyes, without moving his head, to the location of the camera. "Aren't we being watched?"

Bobo shook his head. "If I hadn't thought of that by now, you've hired the wrong guy. No, they're not watching the cameras now. All the security people are on the floor at closing time. The camera monitors in the security center are on, but nobody's home.

187

Besides, I had an acquaintance do some remote programming to the computer system that stores the cameras' data. Part of the big bucks you've paid for my services is for the connections I have to get done what needs getting done. There'll be an inconvenient gap of missing images for the entire time we've been in the building, so quit being paranoid and hoist me up into this contraption."

Josh and Risner complied, and with Bobo climbing, grunting, and grasping, the two of them managed to heft Bobo into the machine, shoving him in like a cork in a bottle. Josh assisted Risner next. It was clear there would be no room for him. He glanced around. The harvesting machine had a bin that temporarily held the harvested grain. He informed them that he would be hiding in the grain bin. He heard Bobo's muffled approval, then climbed onto the machine and down into the bin, settling into a crouched position.

The grain bin grew increasingly uncomfortable as the minutes slowly passed, and Josh developed a cramp in his right leg. The bottom of the bin was sloped to the center from both sides so the grain could flow downward and into the auger. The auger was covered with a small tent-shaped piece of metal across the bottom, so there was no comfortable place for his feet. Josh kept trying to shift his weight without making a noise. Risner and Bobo were no better off, squirming uncomfortably in the tight confines of the machine. The wooden slats upon which they lay were uncomfortable enough, but additional boards set on edge and cut to angled points jabbed into the bodies of both men. Risner's proximity to Bobo made him realize the man didn't believe in frequent showers.

The sounds of people slowly faded. Eventually, after what seemed an eternity to the three, the lights in the large room were dimmed. They heard a guard walk slowly by, then more silence. Josh could hear Risner whisper to Bobo, "When?"

"Shhhh," was the only response.

Josh's legs became numb, and he wondered if they would move at his command when it was time to climb from the bin. The footsteps of a guard drew near, then receded. More silence. Josh wondered what he had gotten himself into. If someone had told him six months ago that he would be hiding in a piece of farm equipment at the Smithsonian West, he would have thought the person was crazy. Would Adam really activate at his command? He had to.

The whole plan depended on it. Then it occurred to him as he reviewed the various stages of the plan that each stage had to work if the plan was to work. The odds of success created a sense of overwhelming futility which he fought to resist.

"OK," Bobo whispered.

Josh extracted himself from the storage bin, flexing both legs a couple of times when he climbed back down to the floor. He helped extract Risner, who was already halfway out of the machine. They both helped Bobo squirm out of the tight compartment. Pulling his pants back up to the bottom of his bulging stomach, Bobo said, "Let's get over to that pile of bolts and get him out of here."

As they walked, Josh whispered a concern. "It's so quiet here. I need to activate Adam with an audible command; the guard might hear."

Bobo shook his head, "Don't worry about it. You'll see."

In a few moments they were standing in front of Adam. "He looks even more forlorn in the dim lighting than he did earlier," Risner observed.

They heard voices and all three quickly turned their heads; then Bobo smiled. Josh and Risner listened more carefully, and relief came over their faces. The voices were coming from a media player; a distant guard was listening to a talk show.

"I told you not to worry about giving your bucket of bolts a command."

"Would you stop referring to Adam as a bucket of bolts?" Risner whispered with a force that made the words almost sound like a wheeze.

"Whatever," Bobo said.

"How did you know he'd turn on a media player?" Josh asked.

"Just did my homework. I had a friend plant a bug a few days ago. Just wanted to know what the sounds of the night were in here. I don't like to have any more surprises on a job than I need to have. The guard should stay put and we'll be going the opposite direction, through the freight dock over there." Bobo pointed his stubby index finger toward a display of stuffed farm animals across the aisle.

"Sounds like you thought of everything. I just hope you did," Risner said.

"You're paying me to think of everything," Bobo replied. "OK, Doc, the guard's media player has a commercial running now. Commercials always run louder. This is the moment. Tell your metal friend to wake up."

Josh's heart was pounding. He cleared his throat, took a deep breath, and said, "Adam!"

The facial glow brightened quickly from the usual blue to a pink, to an orange, bright red, and back to a light orange.

"It's the normal start-up color change," Risner said. "He's coming around!"

The diaphragms of both optical units dilated to full open position.

Josh spoke in a low voice, "How are you, Adam?"

"Just a moment, Dr. Christopher," Adam said in a voice whose familiarity cut deep into Josh's heart and filled him with warmth and joy he hadn't anticipated. How he had missed Adam! The robot continued after a pause of just seconds. "I did a complete diagnostics of my systems. It appears I am doing fine."

"I'm fine, you're fine, we're all fine. Let's get moving," Bobo said. "Wasting time is a security risk."

"Put the pick and rock down and follow us, Adam," Josh commanded.

Adam bent over, placed the two items on the floor, straightened up, and stepped out of the display.

Bobo pulled a small electronic device from his pocket and waved it at Josh. "This will deactivate the High Tech Beehive that has surveillance over this area."

They rounded the corner and Bobo pointed to an upside-down cone that hung from a ceiling beam. The cone was covered with small holes, each holding a High Tech bee. A red light flashed on at the point of the hive. Bobo swore, spun around and looked at Josh and Risner. Alarm flashed from his eyes. "I was too late; I didn't think it would detect anything at this distance. The bees are going to come after us; we've got to run!"

No sooner had Bobo finished speaking than they heard the drone of mechanical wings. "Oh, great! We've had it now. Thanks for nothing, Bobo!" Risner exclaimed.

"This way," Bobo nearly shouted. He had made a right turn that would still take them in the general direction of the exit at the docks but at a nearly ninety-degree angle to the bees.

"We'll never outrun them," Risner declared as they rushed down the aisle with Adam in close pursuit.

Chapter 21

The High Tech Bees swarmed in the air below the hive for a brief moment, their heat-sensing devices searching the area for the warm-bodied intruders they were programmed to attack. One of the bees got a lock on the three men and an inter-bee link communicated the information to the others, causing them to move in a swarm toward the fleeing men.

"Heat! They're attracted to heat," Bobo puffed as they ran.

Josh's mind raced as he probed his short-term memory of the displays around him. An image flashed into his mind. "The cattle tank! There's a tank with water. We've got to get to it."

"A cattle tank?" Risner asked as he ran beside Josh, with Bobo lumbering right behind.

"We have to dive into it," Josh said.

"Dive into it?" Risner asked in bewilderment as he and Bobo changed direction to keep up with Josh.

"He's right," Bobo gasped. "The bees... will lose us... if we're in... the cool water... can't read our body temp."

"There!" Josh exclaimed, staring at a large circular wooden tank brimming with water next to an old wooden windmill. The hum of the bees grew louder.

Risner stole a glance over his shoulder past Bobo, who was now a few feet behind him. "They're almost on us!" he exclaimed.

It seemed to Josh that the remaining distance to the tank was a journey in slow motion. He took a flying leap and pierced the mirror-like surface, disappearing in a swirl of bubbles. Following right behind him, Risner was in mid-air when he heard Bobo yelp. Josh felt the push of water against his body as Risner dove in. He waited for another splash as he held his breath. The third splash never came.

Bobo stumbled, the pain of the first bee sting having thrown off his stride. He hit the floor with an expulsion of breath and recovered enough to roll over and over in a futile attempt to escape the attack. Bee after bee flew onto his body, thrusting their injectors deep, releasing their incapacitating drug.

Josh surfaced first, having realized that the cold drenching would temporarily mask his body's warmth to the bees' sensors. Having felt only Risner enter the water after him, it was no surprise to see Bobo roll slowly over on the floor, moan and become silent and still. Spent High Tech Bees were making clattering noises as they lost power and flipped around on the floor like a bucket of minnows dumped on the ground.

Risner broke the surface of the water gasping, then stood up in the tank. He wiped his eyes and saw the unconscious Bobo. "Oh, great! Now what are we going to do?" He quickly glanced around, climbing out of the tank. "The guards'll be coming soon. We gotta get out of here!"

"I know, I know," Josh fired back with irritation. "The activation of that hive had to have set off alarms. We don't have much time." Josh ran his fingers through his wet hair as he tried to think of what to do. "And what do we do with Bobo?" he asked as he climbed out of the tank.

"I can carry the man you call Bobo," Adam responded.

Josh and Risner looked at each other. "Why didn't we think of that?" Risner said.

Josh and Risner turned their attention back to Adam, who was standing near the tank, then at the unconscious Bobo. "Good idea, Adam. Pick him up and follow us."

Adam quickly walked over to Bobo, his large metal feet making crunching sounds as he stepped on the spent High Tech Bees. Bending over, he gently picked up the heavy Bobo with seemingly no effort.

"Rest well, you're in the arms of the 'bucket of bolts,'"

Risner said as they headed toward the loading docks.

"An irrelevant comment, and why do you refer to me as a bucket of bolts?" Adam asked.

"It's a long story," Risner replied. "I hear a guard coming!"

Josh heard it too, and exclaimed, "We can't outrun him." He glanced around, and saw a men's room entrance. "In here."

As Adam made his way through the door carrying Bobo, the unconscious man's head hit the frame with a resounding crack. "Sorry about that," Adam exclaimed with no emotion.

Glancing at the limp Bobo in Adam's arms, Josh remembered that he carried a weapon. "Put him down," Josh ordered Adam. Adam quickly complied.

Josh found the weapon tucked into Bobo's belt, underneath his shirt. "Here it is!" Josh exclaimed, holding it up for Risner to see. "It's just a pocket stun gun, single shot."

"You've got just one chance; make it count," Risner said.

"I plan to," Josh replied.

The small pistol was different from the laser pistols that were deadly. This weapon had an extra large barrel out of which a single discharge of an electrified clay-like glob was fired. Flattening on its target, the glob could discharge a large enough jolt of current to upset the nervous system and paralyze the victim for a minute or two. In law enforcement it had replaced the taser. Josh had never fired one, but he quickly found what he was sure was the activation switch to charge the clay inside.

"You ever fire one of those before?" Risner asked.

Josh looked at Risner, said nothing, and turned his attention back to the weapon.

"Oh, great!" Risner exclaimed, and nodded toward Adam. "Why not give it to him?"

Josh looked at Adam, back at Risner, then back at Adam. "Adam, take this weapon and when the guard approaches, fire it at him. It will stun him so we can get away."

"No problem," Adam said, taking the weapon and stepping back out into the corridor.

Josh watched from the doorway of the bathroom, crouched, his form hidden behind an artificial plant near its entrance. The guard came around the corner with his gun drawn and abruptly stopped at the sight of Adam. "What? What in the world are you doing out of your display? I knew it would happen sooner or later. They say they've deactivated you robots, but look what's happened now." The guard paused, then asked, "Can you understand me?"

"Perfectly well."

Josh noticed the guard glancing down at Adam's right hand. "I hope you get a charge out of this," Adam said, and fired the weapon. There was a muffled "pop" as the weapon discharged. The guard staggered, then slumped to the floor.

Risner looked at Josh. "'I hope you get a charge out of this'? Where did that come from?"

Ignoring Risner's comment, Josh said, "Good job, Adam."

Seeing the gun lying near the guard's hand, Risner said, "We could've been shot!"

"We still could," Josh reminded him, "unless we get going. The other guards have been alerted, so we don't have much time. I hope the transportation Bobo lined up is waiting. Adam, pick up Bobo. We've got to get to the loading dock."

Adam picked up Bobo and they quickly made their way down the hallway, Risner's shoes squeaking as he and Josh left wet tracks on the floor.

"We're sitting ducks," Risner whispered as they walked across an open area.

"I know," was all Josh said.

Both men breathed a sigh of relief when they were in an area more crowded with displays. Josh made a right turn.

"This isn't the way to the loading dock," Adam stated.

"How do you know?" asked Risner.

"Because I walked into the museum under my own power. It is one of my last memories before the long sleep."

Risner said, glancing at Josh, "I always did underestimate his abilities." Looking at Adam, he asked, "Which way do we go?"

"Straight ahead to the next corner and then turn to the left."

Josh and Risner looked at each other. Risner shrugged. They started walking at a brisk pace in the direction Adam had indicated, with Adam and his sleeping cargo right behind. After the turn to the left, the large loading door came into view.

"There it is!" Risner exclaimed.

"Did you doubt the accuracy of my instructions?" Adam asked.

Risner glanced at the robot. "You know, Adam, I remember this side of your personality before you were given the dolphin brain. The transplant made you far less irritating and arrogant. I hope the coming transfer will give you a chip off the old block. Josh I've been able to live with."

"What are you talking about?" Adam asked, as they continued toward the door.

"It's a long story we can't go into now, Adam," Josh replied.

They were at the large overhead door. Risner rushed over to the control and pushed the "open" button, but both men already knew it wouldn't work. They had spotted the numeric pad next to the controls.

"Oh, great! That's what I was afraid of. It won't work without punching in a code, which only Bobo knows," Risner exclaimed as he glanced at Bobo, limp in Adam's arms.

"Let's try to wake Bobo," Josh said. "Put the man down." Adam complied.

Both men knelt beside Bobo on the floor at Adam's feet, then looked at each other. They heard someone coming.

"We've got to get through that door right now!" Risner exclaimed. Looking at Bobo, he added, "He's not going to be any help."

"You want the door opened?" Adam asked.

Josh and Risner looked at each other, turned to look at Adam, and said together, "Yes!"

Adam said, "Then you should have said something before you spoke." He walked over to the door, grasped part of the frame with one hand, and began lifting. The door creaked, and something on each side snapped. Adam lifted the door up to the full height of his arm's reach. Darkness and the night's breeze greeted them.

"Great, Adam!" Risner exclaimed.

Josh gave a backward glance at Adam as he and Risner hurried out. "Pick up the man and come quickly," he ordered.

A lone light cast an eerie yellow glow on the dock area. Josh and Risner glanced around, searching for the vehicle Bobo had arranged to pick them up. No vehicle was in sight. Josh felt panic well up within him.

Bobo moaned in Adam's arms.

Risner turned to where Adam now stood behind them,

holding Bobo. Risner grabbed one of Bobo's arms, shaking it and shouting in the man's ear. "Where's our getaway truck?"

Bobo slowly opened his eyes, looked at Risner, and groaned.

Risner repeated the question, but Bobo's eyes slowly closed again.

Josh glanced into the museum through the open cargo door and saw a guard come into view from a side aisle about 50 feet from where they stood. He glanced back out into the inky darkness and felt profound relief at the sight of a panel truck pulling around the corner with its engine roaring. "Here's our ride!" he exclaimed.

Josh and Risner ran down the ramp as the van skidded to a stop. Josh turned toward the building and shouted, "Adam, close the big door, quick!" Adam responded instantaneously, tossing Bobo over his right shoulder so he could use his left arm to pull down the door.

"Stop!" the guard shouted, firing a warning shot over their heads. The laser shot hit the door frame, punching a hole in it and sending sparks flying. The door came down, locking the guard inside.

With Bobo still over his shoulder, Adam walked quickly with long strides to the van. He let Bobo fall off his shoulder into the van, where Josh and Risner grabbed hold of him and with great effort dragged him toward the front of the cargo area to make room for Adam. Adam climbed into the back of the van on his hands and knees. The back door began to close, activated by the driver, who didn't wait for it to latch before leaving the loading dock area with a squeal of the tires.

Josh looked through the window in the back of the van just in time to see the dock door slowly go up, silhouetting two pairs of legs. There were now two guards. One of them threw himself to the ground, rolled under the door, quickly got back onto his feet and took aim. "The guard's going to shoot!" Josh shouted.

The driver of the van began weaving the vehicle as an evasive move, but the guard's aim was good and the laser shot pierced through the back window, shattering it and going past Josh's head, narrowly missing him, and shattering the windshield into thousands of pieces of shrapnel. Undaunted, the driver kept going, forgoing the evasive maneuvering for a straight escape route across the parking lot.

The vehicle roared up an entrance ramp to the freeway, merging with the traffic.

"You OK?" Josh shouted to the driver, trying to make his voice audible over the wind blowing in where the windshield used to be.

"Yep," was the driver's only reply.

Risner brushed the shattered glass off his clothes. Josh kept his eyes focused out the broken rear window, fearful of spotting someone in pursuit. Bobo moaned, moved his legs, and turned his head, looking up and back, trying to focus on the blurry image of Risner.

"Have a nice nap?" Risner asked.

"Oh, shut up," Bobo said under his breath, then moaned again.

"How are you feeling?" Josh asked.

"A little tense," Risner replied.

"I didn't mean you."

"Oh."

"Bobo, you OK?" Josh asked.

"I'll make it," he replied.

"Dr. Christopher, I'm down to twenty percent charge. I won't be able to duplicate my recent heroic efforts with this little energy reserve."

Josh looked at Adam, whose face had a blue tint. It was good to see him and hear his familiar voice again, a voice and face he would soon hopefully call his own. The whole project at that moment seemed unreal and outlandish. He pushed those thoughts from his mind. "Don't worry, Adam. You shouldn't have to use that level of energy again. Hopefully, the worst is over."

As they drove, Adam expressed curiosity concerning his reactivation and his being taken from the museum. Josh gave him a brief description of what was going to happen. Adam nodded approval when Josh concluded. His processing unit didn't allow him any feelings. Josh looked at Adam and reflected that without a sentient mind attached to his processing unit, as the Dolphdroids had, Adam's response could only be logical. That's why he had created the Dolphdroids, that's why they were now conscious, sentient beings, and that's why they needed to be saved. Josh was brought back to reality by Risner's voice.

199

"Well, Bobo, is your plan still going to work, since we'll soon have a citywide search under way for us?"

Bobo, rubbing his face, replied, "In this business you always plan for the outside chance that things will get fouled up. Don't worry. In a minute we'll be changing trucks and everything will be back on track."

The driver soon pulled the van into an abandoned building where a small freight truck was parked. He told them to make the transfer quickly. Bobo staggered to the truck, the effects of the H.T. Bees still not worn off. Risner noted the writing on the side of their new transportation: AL'S WHOLESALE SEAFOOD. When the driver closed the door, there was darkness and a strong fish smell.

"Oh, great. I hope we don't have to ride long in this sardine can," Risner exclaimed

The glow from Adam's face was the only light. "His face makes a great nightlight," Bobo said, nodding to Adam.

Adam looked at Bobo and said, "I detect that your statement was not meant as a compliment but as a derogatory statement with the intent of providing an element of humor. No one is laughing. Perhaps a statement that Josh's mother always told him would be appropriate here: 'If you can't say something nice, don't say anything at all.'"

"Well put, well put!" Risner interjected.

The trip to the airport was bumpy and seemed to take forever. Josh spent the time asking Adam questions to determine how his physical and mental systems were operating.

The driver eventually pulled to a stop, and a few moments later he opened the back door, letting in some much-appreciated fresh air into the cargo compartment. He pointed to a small freight plane as they piled out of the truck; its two jet engines were already warming up. The aircraft had the logo ROSSAU FISH FREIGHT painted on the tail.

"Oh, great! More fish ambiance. What's the deal with the fixation with fish?" Risner asked.

"I know somebody in the fish wholesale business who has connections, OK?" Bobo said.

As they climbed aboard, Risner said, "Well, at least the smell isn't as strong as in the truck."

Josh paid Bobo, who left the cargo bay of the small plane as slowly and carefully as he had entered, holding on to both railings of the fold-up stairs. Standing on the concrete floor of the hangar and still grasping one of the railings of the stairs, he looked up at Josh in the doorway of the plane. "It's all yours from here on out. I'm going home to bed." With that, Bobo turned and slowly made his way toward a car parked in the hangar.

The pilot Bobo had provided looked of questionable character, but Josh was comforted by the expert way he went through the pre-flight check. Air traffic was reasonably light and the plane was airborne within a few minutes.

"Well, I'm glad that's over," Risner said as the plane gained altitude. "I don't enjoy playing cops and robbers, especially when we're the robbers."

"First of all, we weren't robbing, only taking back what's rightfully ours," Josh corrected. "Second, it's not over." He looked at Adam sitting beside him on a freight box. "It's just beginning."

Chapter 22

The office building was one story, of vintage early 21st century architectural style. The landscaping consisted of a row of short evergreen bushes, several of which were barren of any needles. The security lights in front were competing with the first faint light of morning. It had been a long, exhausting night. The tension of the escape with Adam had left Josh's nerves jangled, allowing only a light and fitful sleep on the flight back from the west coast to Florida. He had envied Adam, able to shut himself down at will in order to conserve his electrical energy.

Jim Roeper, who had met them at the airport in a van, suggested that they stop for breakfast sandwiches and coffee to go. The 10 minute trip from the restaurant to Roeper Robotics allowed them just enough time to finish eating. Josh felt refreshed after finishing his sandwich, and he savored the last of his coffee.

"What did you do with your staff?" Josh asked as he put his empty coffee cup into the crumpled fast food bag.

"I gave them a two week bonus vacation," Jim replied. "I told them they had worked hard on our last big contract and deserved the extra time off."

"It'll cost you dearly to have production stopped and still pay salaries," Risner commented.

"I know."

Before letting Adam leave the van, they put a raincoat with a hood over him. It was the largest Jim could find. Although the hour was early and there was no activity in the area around Roeper Robotics, Josh had instructed Jim to find something that would conceal Adam's identity.

"He looks like the hunchback of Notre Dame," Risner said as Adam climbed out of the van in his new attire.

Walking up the sidewalk to the front entrance, Josh put a hand on Jim's shoulder. "I appreciate it, Jim. Your facilities are just what we need to test Adam." Josh paused. "To run tests on Adam and me." It was another one of those moments when the full impact of what he was planning to do hit him. "At any rate, I appreciate the sacrifice you're making."

Jim looked at Josh. "It's not near the sacrifice you're making." He unlocked the front door and held it open for the others. Jim grabbed Josh's arm as he was about to enter. "You really think this can work, don't you?"

Josh paused a moment. "It will work. It has to work."

The plan was for Josh and Adam to stay at Roeper Robotics out of sight for two days, do some preliminary testing on both of them, then fly to the surgery site. The surgery itself would take 8 to 12 hours. After a day to stabilize Josh/Adam, he would be brought back to Roeper Robotics. Josh's human body would be placed in suspended animation at the surgery site with the expectation that the procedure would be reversed when the mission was accomplished. Josh couldn't keep from going over and over the schedule in his mind. He thought about how much effort everyone was putting into this and the great risk he was taking in order to save the Dolphdroids. It just had to work.

They walked past the secretarial station, a collection of three desks, and a small waiting area with a couch and chairs. Josh realized that he hadn't been here since the first run of Dolphdroids had been brought to life. Jim explained that his facility had lacked a couple of pieces of the rehabilitation equipment they would need for the project, but Risner had helped locate the items. Josh noted the familiar set of heavy-duty parallel bars used by the Dolphdroids during therapy after their creation. There was the balance beam, wider than normally used for humans. The specialized equipment brought back a flood of memories of an exciting era in his life when dreams, innovative solutions to problems, and a team of enthusiastic people all came together to achieve something never done before.

Jim led them into another room where cots had been set up. Josh surprised himself with a strange and frightening thought: he wouldn't be sleeping in his own bed in his own home again for a very long time, maybe never. The finality of it all struck him as never before – prompted by a lowly cot. The mind works in strange ways, he thought.

The next two days passed quickly, with various members of the transition team meeting with Josh and each other. Josh had taken Dr. McKay's advice and instructed the team not to bother him with details he didn't need to know. In his first session Dr. McKay sat across from Josh on a swivel, backless stool on wheels, rolling inches one way, then the other. He said, "Josh, try to imagine what it will be like to look in the mirror for the first time after waking from the procedure." The doctor paused. "You'll be staring a Dolphdroid in the face, and that Dolphdroid will be you!" The session lasted about an hour and fifteen minutes, then Josh said he thought they had gone long enough.

Jim Roeper also spent some time with Josh, going over the physical rehabilitation equipment and reviewing how, as Adam, Josh would be doing a variety of exercises to familiarize himself with his new body. Nancy Saunders arrived that first evening and worked with Josh on the challenge of the social ramifications of his new identity. "You'll be relating to people from inside a body made of metal, hydraulics, and wires instead of flesh, blood and bone," she told him. "It will be difficult for you and your friends and family, including me," she added with emotion in her voice, "to adjust to that change." Josh nodded, gazing out the window, watching a rabbit eat on the grounds of Roeper Robotics. Then he turned his attention back to Nancy. "My primary concern is that I relate to the Dolphdroids successfully, that they accept me as one of them and that the mission can be accomplished. That's what I've got to focus on."

"I understand," Nancy said.

The next day Josh spent several hours in session with Tracy Mason, with Dr. McKay and Nancy Saunders sitting in. Their focus was the integration of Josh's social behavior as Adam with the Dolphdroids, a subject of far greater interest to Josh than what

Nancy had attempted to focus on the day before.

"You'll be like the Dolphdroids, yet different," Tracy explained. "As Adam you'll be an android but also human, while the Dolphdroids are android but also dolphin. We don't know to what degree that will make a difference, but it might be significant," she cautioned Josh.

Josh slept fitfully during his last night at Roeper Robotics, tossing and turning on the narrow cot. Tomorrow he would fly to the surgery site, spend a day in pre-surgery tests, and have the surgery the next morning. Many thoughts went through his mind. Images of Rob and Randy seemed to be ever present, like large oversized paintings. Then there was Ashley. He tried but couldn't keep thoughts of her from intruding into all of his other thoughts. She seemed to rule his emotions as well. He tried to distance himself emotionally from her by reminding himself that she had played him for a fool, but he had to admit that she had been brave in walking away from her connection to the Warwick Syndicate, something that most people would say spelled almost certain death. He believed her when she explained that she thought she was involved in espionage, not a crime syndicate that often used murder as a solution. He believed her, and he wished that he could see her again before the surgery.

It was obvious to him that there were emotional strings holding him back that weren't there when he conceived the mission. He now had a good relationship with Rob, and that gave him greater access to Randy. How he enjoyed being a grandfather! Then there was Ashley. He had much more to live for as Joshua Christopher than he had before this all began. A recurring question that seemed to play itself more frequently than ever was whether the procedure could be successfully reversed. Before, he hadn't cared that much. Now he did.

The mission offered no guarantee of success. Would he be able to relate with those he created but who had fallen so far from what they were intended to be? Would they listen to him, accept him, and would events unfold as he had planned so that he could save them? Would everyone play into his plan, even those against him? His mind reeled with thoughts and feelings, concerns and doubts. Sound sleep eluded him until it was nearly morning.

Everyone was up early. The day was overcast with a slight drizzle. Empty coffee cups and doughnut crumbs were scattered about, evidence of a hurried breakfast before they were to leave for the surgery site. A truck with no identifiable markings, different from the one used to bring Josh, Adam, and Risner to the center, was waiting outside the back entrance to the Roeper complex. Most of the team would be traveling to the off-shore site in several PAVs and a Skipcat helicopter. Only Josh, Adam, Dr. McKay and Bill Zucker climbed into the back of the truck for the ride to the airport where they would board the Aeon for the trip out to sea.

The ride to the airport seemed to take forever in Josh's estimation, but they eventually pulled up to the helicopter. The tri-prop Aeon was a large flying machine that had been decommissioned by the military a dozen years earlier. Industry had bought most of them for transport purposes. Within 15 minutes the giant three blades pulled the craft and its occupants into the air.

The Aeon seemed to crawl its way through the sky, its blades beating the air loudly, reverberating through the cargo bay. Hours later, after two refueling stops, the ship finally came into view.

"There it is," Bill shouted over the roar of the engines. Josh squinted through the scratched side window, focusing on where Bill was pointing. The ship was just a dot on the horizon. As they flew closer, it appeared to be a smaller vessel than Josh had imagined it would be, but he reminded himself they were still a good distance from the ship. He knew he was getting anxious, even feeling concern over whether their tri-prop might be too large to land on the vessel. He rejected the thought as illogical. Bill certainly wouldn't have lined up the Aeon only for them to discover that they were too large to land. Bill had told him it was a cargo vessel with several holds, one of which had a prefabricated operating room unit on loan from the Red Cross. As the vessel loomed larger, Josh recalled Bill's explaining that the units were used in emergency situations around the world and that most of the space stations also had them. Someone at the Red Cross owed Bill a favor, so he was able to rent one of the units that were in standby storage.

Josh felt the vibration and heard the sound of the Aeon's landing gear being extended. They were above the ship. Some seagulls that had been resting on the ship took flight. Team members stood on the deck of the ship, holding their hats and embracing their midsections to keep their open jackets from flapping wildly as the Aeon's blades beat the air around them to hurricane levels. It gratified Josh to see them waiting: Risner, Nancy Saunders, Dr. Kippler, Phil Kirkpatrick, Tony Williams, and some who were unidentifiable because their heads were tilted down in the face of the Aeon's blast. Suddenly Josh's heart leaped in his chest. She stood separate from the others, head turned from the gale-force wind yet trying to look at the descending craft. Ashley! No one had told him. His mind tried to tell him that it wasn't advisable to have her here, but his heart was calling the shots and all he could think of was how glad he was to see her standing on the deck.

The Aeon settled onto the landing pad and the pilot cut power to the three engines. While the blades were still taking their final turns before going still, Josh disembarked from the copter, taking the metal fold-down steps of the craft two at a time. He greeted the team members one by one. The last to greet Josh, other than Ashley, was Dr. Kippler. After a brief greeting and several short instructions, he reminded Josh to get a good night's sleep, then walked away.

Josh glanced over at Ashley, who was leaning against the ship's railing, arms folded across her chest, hair blowing in the sea breeze. Josh smiled, and she smiled back. He walked toward her. She hesitated only a moment, then ran to him.

Embracing Josh and leaning her head against his chest, she whispered, "I just couldn't stay away. I had to be here. I hope you understand."

"I do." He put his hand beneath her chin and gently tilted her head back. They looked deeply into each other's eyes and then kissed. Embracing each other, they stood on the deck, looking out to the horizon. Finally Josh said, "You're making this project a great deal more difficult for me. You understand that, don't you?"

She glanced up at him, then put her head back on his chest. "I know. And I'm glad to hear that, in a way. I mean, I want you to want me here, but I also feel badly that I've complicated the mission for you, that I've made it more difficult for you. I didn't intend to fall in love with you."

"Nor I with you," Josh said.

She hugged him tightly. "I'm just so happy you believed me and were willing to forgive me."

"Love covers a multitude of sins," Josh replied.

She sighed. "I just can't believe that I've finally found a man I truly love, and now I'm going to lose you."

"And I can't believe that I've finally found a woman who can help me move beyond the loss in my past – and now I have to walk away from her."

"It's almost like death separating two people, what you're about to do, Josh."

It would be very similar to death, her words reminded him. He would no longer inhabit his body; he might never live in it again. The suspended animation might not keep his body alive and he would come back to his own corpse and be stuck as Adam until his brain died. The initial process might not even work and he'd die in the transfer to Adam. He was staring at death on a couple of fronts.

They remained silent for a long time. Ashley broke the silence. "We could still have tonight."

Her words and what they meant sent his heart pounding and made his face flush. He was quiet for a moment, then said softly, "Oh, Ashley, I would love nothing more, you have to believe that." He paused again. This had been a subject he had thought about more often than he would ever want to admit to her. He squeezed her, then said, "What we both want is what should be part of an ongoing relationship where two people are so committed to each other that they're married. I really believe that, I always have. It's the sacrament of marriage, that's the way I look at it. Experiencing the sacrament without the marriage just wouldn't be right."

"I sort of thought you might say something like that. It's just that I want to be as close to you as I can be, to give you myself completely."

"Me too."

"What are the chances of your coming back into this handsome body so I can marry you and spend my nights and my days with you?"

"Odds are impossible to compute in a first-time scenario like this. There are too many variables. I hold out hope, though – lots of hope. A few months ago hope didn't factor into this plan, at least not hope for myself. Hope for the Dolphdroids, yes – that's what this is all about – but I had no personal hope beyond wanting to save them. Then things improved with Rob and his family, and we're reconciled." He looked down at her. "Then you came along. You've given me hope that life could be good again and now that hope is making this final step so difficult."

"You're sure there's no other way to save your friends?" she asked, returning his gaze.

He shook his head. "No, I'm afraid not." He raised his hands, gently holding her face. "Look, there's still room for lots of hope. Many good people are involved in this project. It can work."

She sighed and hugged him tight. "I hope so."

"See, now you've got it." Josh said.

"What do you mean?"

"You said, 'I hope so,' and what we need is hope."

"Oh, Josh."

She kissed his cheek, and they held each other tight.

One of the five cargo compartments had been designated as a meeting room. It contained two folding tables placed side by side, and seven folding chairs that occupied one end of the huge hold. Several meetings convened around the table throughout the day and into the night. The compartment had been designed for cargo, not committees, so voices echoed annoyingly off the steel floor, sides, and ceiling of the compartment. Cold seemed to emanate from all directions.

The surgery team busied themselves getting the surgery module prepped, with Dr. Kippler grumbling about the inadequacies of the facility. Phil Kirkpatrick, Risner Billingston, and Roger Masters ran a battery of tests on Adam, who was lying on a heavy metal table.

Josh was relieved when they assured him that Adam was in good shape, though his relief was tempered with concern when he saw the three men replacing Adam's left knee super magna joint. Risner reassured Josh that Adam was in top condition with only this one knee being marginal and that they thought it best to replace it. The only work yet to be done on Adam, they informed Josh, was Adam's cranial cradle, the new home for Josh's brain, and it would be prepped just before the surgery.

Josh walked around the ship between meetings. He found sitting difficult. He knew himself well enough to realize that this was a symptom of anxiety. Walking toward the hold that had been designated the cafeteria, he overheard Phil and Bill discussing the inrobation. To the average person on the street the word would be just another technical-sounding term, but to Josh it was a familiar term, one he had invented when he first began work on the Dolphdroid project. It brought to mind the afternoon when Rob, who was probably no older than five at the time, asked, "What does inrobation mean?" Josh knew his reflecting on such nostalgic themes was another symptom of his being anxious, but he allowed his thoughts to go where they wanted. He recalled getting down on one knee and explaining to Rob, "It means putting a living brain into a robot." Rob had accepted the definition without further questions. He reflected on the word. It had now taken on a whole new, profound level of meaning. It meant putting his own brain into a robot. Suddenly the entire plan seemed bizarre.

Josh decided not to enter the cafeteria hold after all and moved on down the access hallway, passing a smaller hold the size of a room in a house. It had been designated the lab. Tony was working at a table, stooped over a square glass container with wires and tubes coming out of it. Josh knew what it contained: the interface that would connect his own brain to Adam's processor. Weeks ago Tony had taken a sample of Josh's tissue from the inside of his mouth and began a culture. He glanced up at Josh.

Josh stepped into the room and walked over to Tony. He looked at the container. Faintly visible in the cloudy, bubbling fluid was a cylindrical plastic object that was covered with a slimy-looking pinkish substance: a culture of his own flesh. One end would be connected to the base of Adam's cranial cradle and the other end to his own brain stem. Staring at the contents of the container, Josh reflected on a harsh reality: after the inrobation he would lose temporary contact with the outside world through his five senses, afloat in a dark, endless sea of consciousness with nothing but his thoughts. The sensory deprivation would plunge him into a world of his mind's making, likely to be a nightmare of hallucinations. His hope was that it wouldn't last long, that the interface would start working within a couple of days. Tony had warned him that the Dolphdroids had the advantage of a longer period of incubation in which to coat the interface adequately. In his case the time frame was so short that the tissue coating on the interface would be marginal at best.

"How's the tissue growth, Tony?" Josh asked.

"Actually, very good. I'm pleased. I decided to test a new set of growth hormones." Tony smiled. "You don't want to know where I harvested these hormones."

Josh looked at him, expressionless. "Humor me. Where?"

"From a chicken embryo."

"It's a very fast growing little creature; think about it. You start out with a single-celled embryo, put it in an incubator, and in three weeks you have a chirping, scratching little yellow ball of fuzz. I've been working on it for some time, extracting the growth hormones. I was able to alter them enough so that they work on human tissue. It sped up the process considerably on your tissue here."

"Maybe that'll keep the length of sensory deprivation to a minimum," Josh replied.

"That's my hope," Tony said as he glanced at his computer monitor, hitting a few keys to pull up another screen that made no sense to Josh.

"Thanks, Tony, for trying to keep me sane through this," Josh said as he patted his friend on the back and turned to leave.

"No problem," Tony said. He leaned toward the monitor, already deep in thought.

Josh made his way back into the cafeteria and found Nancy Saunders sipping a cola and eating chips at one of the small tables with Stuart McKay, who was sipping a cup of tea. Nancy's short blond hair seemed to glow in the bright industrial lights used to illuminate the hold. She greeted Josh, offering him a chair. Josh knew they wanted to talk, probably about his relationship with Ashley. He would try to be patient with them, realizing it was their job to make certain the transition went well. He realized that they saw his falling in love as a potential problem. He had to admit that he did too, but their concern annoyed him. He declined the offer, saying he had some things to check out. He poured himself a cup of coffee, gave each of them a pat on the shoulder, and walked back out of the hold, sipping the steaming brew.

One of the ship's crew members informed Josh that another PAV had landed. Just then Rob came around the corner.

"Rob!" Josh exclaimed. They embraced.

"I flew to Mobile, Alabama, rented a car, and drove to a PAV rental facility. I'm hoping the effort covered my tracks well enough," he explained.

"Sounds like it did," Josh replied. Putting his hand on his son's shoulder, he added, "Let me show you around." Josh enjoyed the diversion of walking around the ship with Rob. When the tour was finished Rob said he'd like to get a snack in the cafeteria. Rob gave him a pat on the back, turned, and headed to the stairs. Josh watched his son. It felt good to be close to him again.

Josh had anticipated another meeting of the entire team that night, but Bill informed him that there was no need for such a meeting. Everyone gathered in the cafeteria for the evening meal, allowing Josh the opportunity to make a little speech of appreciation. With all eyes on him, he stood and began to share how important each of them was to him. His speech was short. He concluded, "Each of you is playing a strategic role in saving the Dolphdroids. As a team you'll make it happen. If the mission fails, I want to thank you now for giving it your all. The old saying is true that it's better to have tried and failed than never to have tried at all, but I don't think that's going to be the case. I believe *Moon's Mercy* will achieve the goal we've established for it! I know it's a strange thing I'm doing but it's the only way to save them." Josh paused to gain a better hold on his emotions. The group was silent and no one moved. Josh took a deep breath and concluded, "I love them, will become one of them, and will give myself for them. I'm going to save them. This will succeed!" After he finished, everyone applauded and, one by one, came up to Josh to shake his hand, give him a slap on the back, or a hug. Standing off to the side, feeling awkward about her unique relationship with Josh, stood Ashley.

As he walked toward her he said, "I've been wondering where you've been keeping yourself all afternoon," he said.

Ashley put her arms around him and looked up into his eyes. "I don't want to make a nuisance of myself. You have a lot on your mind, and each of these people has a right, a need, to take up your time. They've all contributed a great deal to this mission, while I…" She hesitated. "While I almost destroyed the mission…and you. I'm just glad they've even allowed me on board the ship. The least I can do is stay out of the way."

"You're now an asset to the mission, not a liability, Ashley."

"How can you say that?"

"Well, before you came along my only concern was to get to the lunar surface and complete the mission. Looking back, I think I saw it as a one-way mission, almost a suicide mission, because I'd probably never be fully human again. It's different now. I want to be Joshua Christopher again and spend the rest of my life with you. You've given me something I didn't have before, and that's hope for a life beyond the mission."

"But you've also reestablished a relationship with your son and his family. That's a big reason to come back. You had that reason before I came into the picture."

Josh was quiet a moment before he spoke. "You're right. They mean the world to me. But you're now part of my reason for wanting to come back, a big part of the reason. And the team here knows that. Your presence here is certainly a strange turn of events, but they're getting used to what's happened. They know it's important, given our relationship, for you to be here. I need everything that's possible going in my favor, and they know that your being here is a big plus for me."

She squeezed him tight. "I'm glad to hear that, Josh, I really am."

"I love you very much, Ashley. What you've given me is hope, and hope is essential for this mission to succeed. You've become a real asset to the mission. You don't have to do anything to help make it a success except be here, and be waiting for me when I come back."

He kissed her, and then they walked around the deck several times. "Look, Josh!" She stopped and pointed to the horizon. There was a full moon rising, a giant orange ball seeming to emerge from the distant edge of the sea. They both stood in silence. "You can almost see it move. I never realized that before. See? The bottom edge of the moon is suddenly not touching the horizon."

As they watched in silence, the water near the moon's location began to shimmer, reflecting the color of the moon just above it. "Look to the right of the moon! Dolphins!" Josh said.

At first, all Ashley could see was an increase in waves on the nearly smooth sea. Then a dolphin broke the surface of the water, leaping partially into the air. Another one followed, then a third. The last of the three left the water completely, its body arched in the air, a perfect silhouette in front of the moon. The scene lasted only a moment before the sea had reclaimed the dolphin, but the image was indelibly imprinted in Josh's mind. He sighed. Tomorrow was the day.

Chapter 23

Josh stared at himself in the mirror. He had slept fitfully and his face showed it. This face, the familiar face that always looked back at him from countless mirrors, wouldn't be the face staring back at him after today. He would have a face like those he had created. This face, along with the body to which it was attached, would soon lie in suspended animation in a life-support system pod. The pod could end up being a casket; there was no guarantee.

Of course, as he had argued with himself on several occasions, most people put into suspended animation were very ill and waiting for a transplant organ or a medical procedure that wasn't available yet – quite a lucrative rip-off, he had always thought. His, however, was a healthy middle-aged body, and that fact increased the odds in his favor. On the other hand, all the automatic functions controlled by his brain would have to be maintained by an electronic interface run by Tony William's newly designed computer program. Tony himself admitted that it was crude in comparison to a brain. All in all, Josh's chances of having a warm body to come back to were not reassuringly high.

The mirror started to fog up again with the moisture from the shower he had just taken. Washing and drying his body, something he had done daily his whole life, had been different this morning. With new clarity he understood that he was giving up his humanity to become the second Adam. Wiping the mirror and seeing his reflection clearly, he realized that he was experiencing feelings that could only be interpreted as grief. Dr. McKay had warned him this would happen.

As he towel-dried his hair, he forced his mind to shift subjects. He visualized the Dolphdroids on the lunar surface. He reminded himself of how they needed him, their creator. He didn't have to do this, but love compelled him. He must give up the goodness he wanted to cling to in this life in order to bring the good back into their existence.

The slow rocking of the ship prompted his thinking to go in an entirely different direction. The fact that they were doing the procedure on a ship in international waters, because it was illegal in most countries, brought a lump to his throat and tightness to his stomach. There was a reason this was true; the procedure was untested on humans. The thought wasn't new; it had occurred to him countless times, but this morning it took on meaning as never before.

Josh had a small measure of comfort when he thought about Kippler doing the surgery. Kippler was one of the world's leading neurosurgeons. In fact, many people considered him to be the best. He was also a renegade, a man who didn't mind taking risks, who was willing to do the unusual, to risk failure. OK, Josh reprimanded himself, he couldn't let his thinking go there. Kippler had almost lost his license to practice medicine after a couple of incidents over the years where he had pushed the envelope. Now it didn't matter to the good doctor, because he was retired. Kippler really had little to risk and much to gain, Josh realized. If the procedure failed and he died, the world would never know because the world believed Dr. Joshua Christopher to be already dead. If the mission succeeded, the doctor would go down in the annals of medicine as having done the first human brain transplant.

The only participant who stood to lose everything was, of course, himself. No, Josh corrected himself. That wasn't true. If Moon's Mercy failed the Dolphdroids stood to lose everything. A new resolve came over Josh as he put on his robe and left his room.

Amidst the busyness of all the team members the atmosphere was subdued, everyone dealing with a combination of feelings that ranged from concern for Josh to excitement that the project was finally unfolding. Dr. McKay was the first to greet him.

"How are you doing, Josh?"

Josh knew the question wasn't the usual insincere question people used to greet each other where the answer wasn't going to be taken seriously. The doctor really wanted an answer. "I'm coping. I'd be lying if I didn't admit to some apprehension and some doubts. In your experience with brain transplant patients, is that normal?" Josh asked, forcing a smile.

McKay smiled back, a genuine smile, realizing that humor could be a good coping mechanism. Then again, it could also be a bad one. He'd suspend judgment on that for the moment. "Actually, you're writing the book on this kind of experience. You'll be happy to know that however you're feeling we can consider it the norm. With a database of one person, you call the shots." The two started walking together. McKay turned serious. "Do you feel good about proceeding with the mission?"

"I'd feel worse if we canceled it."

"What did you say to yourself in the mirror this morning?"

Josh stopped and looked at McKay. "Very perceptive, doctor. It was an interesting moment. A very reflective moment, pun intended. Seriously, I had to say good-by to myself."

"There's a very good chance, Josh, that you'll be coming back and be able to look at that same face in the mirror again. Maybe 'See you later' would have been more appropriate than 'Good by.'"

"I hope you're right. At this point I'm trying to keep my focus on the mission. I have to go, but I don't have to come back."

"We'll work at making both a reality," McKay replied.

Rob and Ashley approached. "Two of my favorite people," Josh said.

"How you doing, Dad?"

"Fine." He took Ashley in his arms. She snuggled close, turned her head up and whispered in his ear, "I love you."

Josh looked over her shoulder at Rob. "Tell Randy..." The words caught in his throat. He cleared his throat and swallowed. "Try to explain to him what I had to do. Be sure to tell him that I love him. Tell him to take care of the ant farm, because those little creatures depend on him."

"Will do, Dad." Rob's voice was also filled with emotion, and he blinked several times in an effort to clear his vision through the brimming tears.

They arrived at the entrance to the surgery unit. It had been closed for several hours to purify the air. A large blue tent-like structure had been assembled next to it as a surgery prep area. McKay held the curtain open for Josh.

Josh turned. Most of the team had quietly followed them to this point, and now they stood in silence. Faces were somber; a few worked at brave smiles. Absent from the group were Drs. Mesner and Kippler and their surgery support people who were already getting prepped for the surgery. His eyes paused on Ashley's face, now wet with tears.

Josh cleared his throat. "All of you have worked hard and risked much to get us to this point. I'm very proud of you and deeply indebted to you. Without you *Moon's Mercy* wouldn't be happening. I appreciate your dedication to the lunar colony and to *Moon's Mercy*. You've made it possible for the Dolphdroids to have a second chance at life." Josh paused, then continued, "This is one of those decisive moments. I've had moments of doubt about continuing this mission; perhaps you've had them too. But the Dolphdroids need to be saved. We will accomplish that." Josh said no more, allowing his eyes to drift across the faces of the team.

Risner broke the silence. "We're with you all the way, Doc Chris." The small crowd broke into applause. Josh nodded appreciatively, turned, and stepped into the tent.

Everything had a blue hue from the tent's color. "Hi, Cathy," Josh said to the nurse who was standing by a gurney.

"Hi, Dr. Christopher." He noticed hair clippers on a small table next to her.

She glanced at the clippers. "My first job is to give you a haircut, Dr. Christopher."

Josh almost laughed. "You know, of all the things I thought about this morning, getting a haircut wasn't one of them. How about the bald look? I think I'd like that," he said as he lay down on the gurney, allowing his head to extend over the end where there was a bowl to catch the clipped hair.

"That's the exact style I had in mind for you, sir." Both seemed to feel that light banter was best under the circumstances.

Josh could feel the loss of the weight of his gray hair and the cool air of the room wafting across the top of his quickly balding head. Cathy applied lather, which felt cool on his scalp, and shaved him.

"Oh great!" Josh heard the familiar expression coming from Risner.

Josh was out of sight to those outside the prep tent but the tent provided no sound barrier. He debated whether to ask what had upset his friend. Curiosity won out. "What seems to be the problem, Risner?" Josh asked.

There was silence, then some whispered tense conversation.

"You there too, Bill?" Josh asked.

"Yes, Josh."

Lying still as Cathy finished shaving around his ear, Josh called out, "Talk to me, gentlemen, talk to me."

The flap entry of the tent parted and both men entered. Their expressions were a mixture of little-boy embarrassment at being caught in a private conversation they shouldn't have been having along with a look of concern. They walked over to the gurney.

"Thanks, Cathy," Josh said as he took a towel from her, sat up on the edge of the gurney and began drying his bald head. "Now fill me in on what has you guys so concerned."

The two glanced at each other. Bill spoke. "We just received word that Imus Hartung held an early morning news conference."

"And?" Josh asked.

Risner jumped in when Bill hesitated. "He's announced the official termination of the lunar project."

Bill added, "In 120 days." He cleared his throat. "I didn't know if you should be told before the procedure or after. I was going to check with Dr. McKay and Dr. Kippler as to what they would advise, but Risner's loud mouth has now made that a moot point." Risner gave Bill a stern look.

"It's OK, " Josh reassured them. "It only deepens my resolve to go through with this. If anything, Imus' timetable should be a great motivation. If I can complete the therapy in a month's time, that will give me approximately three months with the Dolphdroids. It's not a lot of time, but it'll have to do."

The curtain of the prep room parted again, and in walked Gunnard Kippler. "We're ready to go, Josh."

"Let's do it," Josh said softly.

Kippler called for one of the surgery assistants, a short, slightly-built man in his thirties with a goatee, who wheeled in the operating table. Kippler told Cathy she could leave the room and she did, giving Josh a pat on the shoulder as she left. Kippler asked Josh to remove his robe and lie down on the table. The surgery assistant covered Josh's naked body with a sheet up to his shoulders and wheeled him out of the prep tent while Risner held the curtain open. Ashley and Rob were waiting.

The surgery assistant stopped the gurney by Rob. Josh pulled his arms from beneath the sheet, sat up, and embraced his son.

"I'm glad we've squared things away between us, Dad."

With a voice threatening to break with emotion, Josh gave his son several sound pats on the back and said, "So am I, Rob, so am I."

Josh glanced at Ashley. Her eyes revealed her feelings, and a stream of tears ran in erratic patterns down each cheek. She leaned forward and they embraced.

"I love you so much, Joshua Christopher." He felt her body shudder with emotion as she began to sob.

"And I love you, Ashley. I love you more than you can know," he whispered. He kissed her gently on her lips, now salty with tears, and lay back down. Reaching up to wipe off her tear-smeared cheek, he added, "I'll be back."

Ashley and Rob nodded in agreement, both attempting to smile, as she wiped her cheek with the back of her hand.

"It's really time to go," Josh heard Kippler say softly. Josh turned toward the doctor. Standing next to Kippler was Dr. Mesner.

"You two gentlemen are about to make history. I hope it works so you can go down in the annals of medical science. You deserve that much. Of course, that's only a secondary reason for why I'd like you to succeed," Josh said, attempting a smile.

"It's always better to be known as a doctor who succeeded at a new procedure," Kippler replied, "than to be known as a doctor who attempted one and failed. I can assure you I plan on being listed in the annals of medicine under the first category."

The gurney was rolled into the operating room sanitizing area – a space hardly big enough for the two doctors, the surgery assistant, and Josh. Once the outer door closed, a fine mist filled the air, sterilizing all surfaces. The surgery assistant removed the sheet covering Josh and replaced it with a metallic sheet that was uncomfortably cool to the touch. The assistant opened the lid of a small metal locker on the floor and handed a surgical gown to each of the doctors, then removed a third and put it on, all three changing positions several times so as not to bump each other in the tight-fitting quarters. Masks and gloves were retrieved from the locker and put on. A door then opened at the side opposite from where they had entered, and the assistant wheeled Josh into the operating room where two more masked and gowned assistants waited with Dr. Gray.

Josh's attention was immediately drawn to Adam, lying motionless on a gurney. The assistant positioned Josh's gurney next to Adam's. Glancing to his right, Josh noted the life-support system pod that would be the home for his body. Could this mechanical/electrical cocoon keep his body alive? If it didn't, he'd be Adam for the remaining lifespan of his brain.

The scenario that was beginning to unfold was too much to put his thoughts around, so Josh shifted his gaze from the life-support pod to a bag of his own blood that was hanging from a pole. It would be delivered with an IV to Adam's cranial cradle, from where it would provide his brain with the oxygen and nutrition it needed to survive. His new mechanical/electrical body would be home to his brain, and his brain needed his own blood to survive. It would be his one physical connection to the man he had been.

This had been a brick wall that stretched on for weeks during the development of the Dolphdroid project: how to renew this needed blood supply in a closed system without bone marrow. Eventually a method had been developed whereby the blood cells could be stimulated to multiply on their own. The process was now being studied by the larger medical community as a possible solution to the ever-present problem of the blood supply shortage. The bag of blood seemed small to Josh, but he had to remind himself that it would be enough.

One of the surgery assistants immediately started a disinfecting process on his skull using a wash that was as cold as the metallic sheet covering his body. While the wash was being applied Josh focused his attention on the bubbling sound coming from the container on a shelf that held the interface. Hanging above it on the wall was the laser saw that would be used to cut his skull open so

223

they could remove the top of it like a cap, exposing his brain for removal. He had already noted that the top of Adam's head had been removed. His stomach muscles tightened at the prospect of what was about to happen.

Now two assistants were positioning another small machine on a cart between him and Adam. It was a temporary life-support device with its own supply of his blood to keep his brain alive during the short time of transfer to Adam.

Josh's thoughts were interrupted by the pain of the IV being placed in his right hand. Once Dr. Gray saw that the assistant had fastened the IV to Josh's hand with tape he grasped Josh's shaved head gently with both hands, moving his hands softly and slowly, deciding where to mark the skin for the placement of the guides of the laser saw. Drs. Gray and Mesner began talking, using medical terms, some of which Josh understood but much of which he didn't. It would begin soon now. He closed his eyes.

Moments later Dr. Kippler put his hand on Josh's shoulder. Josh opened his eyes, turned his head, and looked at the doctor. "We can begin anytime now, Josh. Are you ready?"

Josh took a deep breath, nodded, and said, "Let's do it."

Josh watched as one of the surgery assistants punched in a code on the IV unit that began a drip which he knew would render him unconscious in a matter of seconds. Was it a death sentence or would he come back to that eerie kind of consciousness which the Dolphdroids had described after their own inrobation? Would his be the same experience or would it be different? He wouldn't have to wait long to find out. Josh flexed his hands, and he realized that it would be the last time for a long time, if ever, that he would be able to do that. He quickly forced himself to focus his thoughts on the Dolphdroids, the ones for whom he was doing this. They were his creation and they needed him to save them. He loved them. That was what he kept thinking until the IV drip had him thinking no more.

Chapter 24

Can't get out! Can't get out! The PAV is exploding!

Anne is thirty feet tall and trying to grab the disintegrating PAV and screaming, "You can't marry that mobster Ashley. Never, never, never!"

Ants from Randy's room, as big as people, are trashing the room while tiny Dolphdroids the size of ants try to stop them. The ceiling lifts off the room. The ants and Dolphdroids stop fighting, look up into the nighttime sky, and see Imus flying his pyramid-shaped building into the man in the moon.

Bill laughs and his mouth is full of snakes. They slither out of his mouth and he just keeps laughing. He stops laughing and says, "Josh, ol' boy, I tricked you. I work for the Warwicks. You fool!"

"No brain! I'm walking around with no brain! How can it be? My head feels so empty with no brain! Don't put anything else in my head but my brain."

Bill, Rob, and Ashley look on, deeply concerned. Adam jerks convulsively, his arms and legs making a resounding clang when they hit the metal framing of the gurney.

"Do you think it'll last any longer than it did with the

Dolphdroid's inrobation?" Bill asked, glancing at Tony.

"I just don't know," Tony responded. "There wasn't quite the quality of cellular growth on the interface as I would have liked, but it should have been adequate. He's just coming out of the anesthetic, so these involuntary bodily reactions are actually a good sign. It means that at least some messages are making it through the interface from Josh's brain to Adam's body."

"I hate to see this," Ashley said, covering her mouth and closing her eyes.

Tony put his hand on her shoulder. "He's hallucinating." Glancing at Ashley, he realized that she hadn't been briefed much on this aspect of the inrobation. "You see, Josh is experiencing sensory deprivation. That means his brain is getting little input from the world outside. The interface is like a bridge between Josh's brain and Adam's body. At this point the interface is still inefficient and few signals are crossing that bridge. The brain is designed for sensory input and will make up its own experiences if it doesn't get it. Plus, there's the likelihood that we don't have the chemistry of Josh's brain quite on the money. All of this is causing hallucinations."

"I hope it doesn't last much longer," Ashley said in a whisper.

"It should begin to subside shortly," Tony comforted.

The moon crumbles into pieces and falls to earth. A giant Dolphdroid, twenty feet tall and spewing fire from his eyes, angrily burns everything and everyone within his fiery sight.

Voices are coming from far away. Now they're getting closer. Light flashes brightly, light of all colors; out of focus forms hover above him. They're looking at him.

"Josh, can you hear me? This is Tony. I'm right here. You're going to be OK. Just relax. Can you do that for me, Josh? Try to relax. Don't fight it. We're all here."

Voices! Pleasant voices, friends…relax, they say. Calm, be calm. It's OK. Lights, colors, a person's silhouette in the light… Not alone… It's OK… Just relax.

"He's quieting down," Ashley murmured with a note of optimism in her voice.

"I think he can hear us," Tony added.

"His response to your reassurances indicates that the interface is working much better than it did twenty-four hours ago," Kippler said.

Tony glanced at Kippler, amazed that such a brilliant man would find it necessary to state the obvious. Kippler didn't notice Tony's annoyed look; he kept his eyes on Adam.

Ashley leaned over Adam. It was difficult for her to imagine that the Josh she knew was inside the cold, metal body. She hesitated a moment and then said softly, "Josh, this is Ashley. I'm right here. Don't worry, OK? You'll be fine. I know you'll be fine." Her voice wavered and she turned away.

Rob stepped forward, putting a hand on Ashley's, then bent over Adam. "Dad, this is Rob. Can you hear me? We're right here. Things are looking good right now. Just hang in there. You can do it!"

Kippler, Mesner, Risner, Tony, and Phil were studying the bank of screens. Kippler and Mesner were in front of the half dozen displays showing the biological readings, while Risner, Phil, and Tony were crowded around several monitors that scrolled and flashed computer data.

"I wish I could pick up a human arm and get a pulse reading," Kippler said he glanced from one monitor to another.

"So true," Mesner replied. "But in his case we at least have a human who's been inrobated. With the Dolphdroids we were attempting to communicate with the minds of dolphins, creatures that were largely strangers to us. At least Josh is no stranger."

Kippler shook his head. "You have my utmost respect for having worked with the dolphin mind. This seems more than challenging enough."

Bill was annoyed with the two doctors' emotional detachment and couldn't keep quiet. "Part of the extra tension in all this, doctors, is that we are not dealing with a dolphin trying to wake up in a robotic body. We're dealing with a human being, but more than a human being, a human being who happens to be a very close friend." Bill paused. "That makes all the difference in the world."

Bill turned from the group hovering around Adam and walked to the other end of the room, where a three-man medical team was attending to the life-support system pod that housed Josh's body. Raska Symour was asking for data readouts and jotted down the information on a compuclipboard. He glanced at Bill, then returned his gaze to the clipboard.

Peering through the curved glass, Bill looked at the lifeless form. A silver sheet covered Josh from shoulders to toes. The pod, and Josh's motionless body lying in it, created the macabre image of a body on view in a casket, and made Bill's stomach turn. Josh's head was completely bandaged, with a pair of tubes emerging from the bandages. They kept a special fluid flowing through Josh's empty cranial cavity, hopefully keeping it fit for the eventual return of Josh's brain. Tubes came from his nose, mouth, and arms. Bill couldn't help but think that this high-tech container might very well end up being Josh's casket.

Bill felt someone lightly nudge his side. He turned to look. It was Ashley. She gave him a weak smile and said softly, "Seeing you stand here gave me the courage to come over and take a look." She turned her gaze slowly from Bill to Josh's body, moaned with grief, put her hand to her mouth, closed her eyes, and leaned into Bill. Bill put his arm around her and hugged her tight.

Raska said, "He's doing very well. All the vitals are looking good." He nodded toward a readout screen that displayed several numbers changing by the second. "Those indicate that the AAFD, the artificial autonomic function device, is working fine." He knew that Bill understood, though he was showing no response to his efforts at reassuring them. He explained for Ashley's benefit, "The AAFD does the work of the brain's running of what we call the autonomic functions, all those involuntary and unconscious actions our bodies do, such as making the heart beat, prompting the secretion of hormones and digestive juices – those kinds of things. Our brain sends constant signals, prompting our bodies to carry out these functions. The AAFD is a marvel of medicine. We've used it as a temporary backup many times in emergency medical situations with humans, but never to provide all of those functions until now. That's only been done with animals, including the inrobation process to create the Dolphdroids." Raska's voice trailed off as he realized that Ashley wasn't listening.

Bill, recognizing Raska's effort to be helpful, said, "Thanks, Raska. Looks like you're doing a good job."

Ashley took hold of Bill's arm. Josh's face appeared peaceful, and that gave her a measure of comfort. Then she reminded herself that Josh was really a few feet away, encased in the hard, cold body of a machine. The sense of peace evaporated. She let go of Bill's arm and touched the glass dome of the life-support pod. "Do you really think Josh will be able to come back?" she asked, caressing the glass slowly.

Bill took a deep breath. "Well, I'm counting on it, and so is everyone else. I know that originally Josh didn't care a whole lot either way. He had very little to live for. That changed, though. Rob came back into his life, and that brought his grandson back into his life, too." Bill turned his gaze from the pod to Ashley. "Then you came into his life. He'll be back." Bill tried to sound confident, though he struggled with his own doubts.

Someone spoke from behind them. "Ashley, let's get something to eat, OK? Things look under control. We can come back later." It was Nancy Saunders. At this stage of the operation she had little to do and decided that Ashley could use some attention. Ashley nodded, gave a forced smile, and followed Nancy.

Voices, they sound familiar…
Can't seem to move…
It's Bill, Bill's talking…
Lights. There are lights. Colors, shapes, things moving…
I want to move, can't move. What's wrong with my body? It happened! I wanted this to happen. I have a different body. I have Adam's body. I'm Adam!

"We've seen a great deal of improvement in the last few hours," Risner said to Bill. "I suspect that he's aware of his environment, that he knows we're here." Turning to Adam, he added, "Don't you, Josh?"

"At least the convulsive movements have stopped," Bill said, relief evident in his voice.

"It does appear that everything is nominal," Les Mesner added.

"So things seem to be progressing satisfactorily, in your estimation?" Gunnard asked Mesner, wanting further assurance.

Mesner shrugged, "As best as I can tell. Obviously this is different than the Dolphdroid inrobations, but I have a sense about it," he said, nodding.

Bill decided to try to get a specific response from Josh. Leaning over the quiet metallic form he said quietly, "Josh, this is Bill. You're doing well." He paused. "Josh, could you move your arm? Try moving your arm, Josh."

Bill straightened and watched Adam's arms. There was no movement. He turned to Kippler and Mesner. "I guess it's still too soon to expect…"

Kippler was pointing to Adam's right arm. "It's moving!" he exclaimed. Trying to regain his professional demeanor, he added with forced calmness, "Good, Josh. That's excellent!"

The third day after inrobation, the ship tossed back and forth in the rough seas. The supply of motion sickness pills was exhausted within hours. The epidemic of nausea, though, hardly dampened the cheers and applause when Adam sat up at Rob's request. Even more reassuring to those familiar with Dolphdroid behavior was the facial change of color from a light blue to soft yellow, the Dolphdroid's version of a smile. Though he couldn't communicate verbally, it was obvious that Josh was pleased with his accomplishment of sitting up.

It had been a jerky movement with a few pauses. Unlike a human body, which would need one or both arms to pull one's self into a sitting position after a time of incapacitation, Adam's body had the strength in his muscle-like mechanisms to sit up without using his arms.

The cheering and clapping subsided, replaced with silence as everyone waited to see what, if anything, Adam would do next. Adam sat on the gurney, legs out straight, staring ahead, motionless. Finally, soft but deep guttural sounds emerged from Adam's voice chamber, like some unknown language being played at a slow speed.

Ashley gasped, "Josh! Can you hear us, see us? Can you say something? Oh, Josh, try to speak, please."

There were a few more garbled sounds, then nothing more. Adam's face turned back to a blue hue and he slowly laid down again.

"I think he's frustrated," Kippler said. "He needs some time alone without further stimulation, and some rest."

They moved away from Adam, staggering like drunken sailors trying to compensate for the rocking vessel. They made their way to the dining area, Kippler and Mesner trying to reassure Ashley and Rob that the interface was becoming more effective by the hour in transmitting messages from Josh's brain to his Adamic body.

Ashley found it difficult to find encouragement in their words. "But the jerky movements of his body and the slurred speech, he's acting like he had a stroke."

"Don't worry, my dear," Mesner said as he put a hand gently on her shoulder, trying again to reassure her, "He's doing just fine. That interface is doing its job better every time we observe him. We'll begin to see some significant improvement very soon."

"I hope so, doctor, I really hope so," Ashley said.

Kippler added, "In fact, we feel he's doing so well that we're planning to take him back to Roeper's facility tomorrow. Jim's company has the therapy equipment that we need for Josh – for Adam – to work with. He's stable enough for transport, so it's time we get off this motion sickness machine. I, for one, have had enough of being at sea."

The next morning brought calm seas and a glorious sunrise that bathed the ship in a pink and purple glow. The Aeon helicopter's three sets of blades were a blur as it warmed up on the deck. Down below, in the hold of the ship, a small cluster of people were transferring Adam from the cot he had been lying on for three days to a stretcher that 10 of the men would carry out to the Aeon.

They had difficulty hefting Adam up the several sets of stairs that took them out of the hold and onto the deck. As soon as they made it to the deck Ashley ran up the few remaining stairs and came alongside the men carrying the stretcher, getting a glance now and then of Adam between the men straining to carry their heavy cargo. She had felt encouraged when she visited Adam before breakfast. He had held out his hand toward her; his face had taken on the yellow glow of a smile. The cold but gentle grasp of his metallic hand had felt good to her. Then he had given Rob a thumbs up sign. He had tried to speak, but it came out as jumbled nonsense. The failed effort prompted him to move his head slowly back and forth, and his face changed from yellow to blue with flickers of red. They knew that Josh was frustrated, still feeling a captive in his new body, but they couldn't help but be encouraged.

After the men secured Adam in the Aeon for the flight, they

returned to the hold and brought the pod and life-support system on board. Although Josh's body was considerably lighter than Adam's, the weight of the pod itself made the task no easier than hefting Adam on board. Bill, Rob, Ashley, and Drs. Kippler, Gray, and Mesner stood on the deck near the Aeon's steps and watched Josh's body and Adam being loaded. Ashley saw the rising sun momentarily shine on Josh's expressionless face, the green glow of the lights on the monitor the only reassurance that his body was alive and well. The scene looked like a casket being loaded into the aircraft, and it sent a wave of nausea over her that had nothing to do with the rocking ship. She glanced at Rob. It was obvious that he was dealing with the same emotional vertigo.

After determining that both of his incapacitated passengers were secure for travel, Bill took a seat between them and harnessed himself in for the ride. Once his harness was tight he glanced at Adam, then at the pod containing Josh's body. Josh's body was quiet, deep in suspended animation; Adam's was jerking involuntarily every few seconds. Bill stared straight ahead, toward the cockpit. "Let's go," he shouted to the pilot.

It was early afternoon by the time they had Adam and the pod containing Josh's body settled in at Roeper's Robotics. An analysis of the data from the pod showed no irregularities. Dr. Gray and Phil Kirkpatrick did a systems check on Adam and found him to be operating normally. Both precious cargoes had weathered the trip well.

Kirkpatrick began some basic physical therapy of leg raises and knee bends with Adam. He brought in Janice Lasper, the speech therapist who worked on the last half of the Dolphdroid project and she began working with Adam after dinner. She was in her early thirties, with short blond hair and a full figure. She had never indicated any interest in men other than a professional relationship. She had done extraordinary work with the Dolphdroids, and Kirkpatrick had convinced her to come back to work on Moon's Mercy.

The room where Adam was located had been the accounting office for Roeper Robotics just days earlier, until its emergency make-over. When Ashley walked in she was struck by the amount of electronic wizardry on display. It reminded her of the time Josh had said that with the Dolphdroid project the line between medicine and mechanics was a fine one. Ashley could see that Janice was preparing to leave. She smiled at Ashley and said, "He's coming along fine. He didn't form any intelligible words yet, but he's getting close. I'll be back tomorrow morning for another session, after Phil has his physical therapy session."

Ashley smiled weakly and nodded. Janice paused a moment, but said no more and left, feeling sorry for Ashley. Bill had confided in Janice that he had considered sending Ashley home for a few days, at least until Adam was functioning and able to communicate, but he had decided against it. There was a distinct possibility that the Warwick family had a contract out to find her. They would have many questions for her and they would get the answers using any means necessary. For Ashley's own safety, and for the security of the mission, Bill had decided that it was best to have her with the team. Though Janice herself had little interest in the romance department, she knew that Ashley's presence not only was keeping her safe but might also contribute to Adam's progress with the various therapies, including speech. He certainly would be anxious to talk to Ashley, to reassure her that he was fine.

Ashley watched Janice leave, then moved toward the huge metal form that she still found difficult to believe housed her new-found love. The large head turned toward her and glowed yellow. She smiled and touched his hand, then attempted to hold it in her own. It felt like a giant metal glove. She felt the hand slightly move, twisting at the wrist, then Adam slowly began raising his arm! Ashley gasped.

"Oh, Josh!" she exclaimed, then leaned down and attempted to hug the large iron torso. She talked to him, frequently requesting that he attempt to move his arm again, or at least move his fingers, but there was nothing. She continued stroking his arm and talking to him. Finally, one of the men attending to Adam said to her in a soft, concerned voice, "Why don't you get something to eat? We'll call for you if something changes." Ashley didn't respond for a moment, and just kept staring at Adam. Finally she nodded, gave Adam a pat on the arm, and slowly walked from the room, glancing back for a look from the doorway.

The rest of the day and into the night two or three team members checked on Josh's body and Adam. By two in the morning there were two attendants remaining, one assigned to monitor Josh's body and the other to monitor Adam.

The team had rooms reserved at a nearby mom and pop motel that offered no eating facilities other than a vending machine with snacks and another with beverages. What made it attractive for the mission was its proximity to Roeper Robotics. Everyone seemed to gather in the small cafeteria of the Roeper Robotics dining room at about the same time early the next morning. It was a simple breakfast of bagels, cereal, juice, and coffee, and it didn't take long for most of the team to finish and walk to the old accounting office.

Ashley waited until the others had made their observations of Adam and Josh's body. All appeared nominal, she thought. She had been with the small group crowded around Josh's still form, and she lingered while the main part of the team worked with Adam. When they seemed to have finished their observations and the discussion among them had quieted, Ashley made her way over to Adam. She tried without any success to get him to squeeze her hand or raise an arm.

"Don't get discouraged. These things take time," Phil assured her.

"It did with the Dolphdroids, too," Risner added. "Actually, I think Josh, Adam, or whatever you want to call him, is making better progress than any of the Dolphdroids did." Risner paused. "What are we supposed to call him? Josh or Adam?"

Suddenly deep sounds came from the form lying on the gurney. The sounds stopped, started again, then stopped. Then more deep sounds came from Adam.

"I think he's trying to talk," Risner said.

Adam turned his head toward Risner. He made a few more inarticulate sounds, paused, and then said in unmistakably clear words, "Call me Adam."

Chapter 25

Roeper Robotics was not a small facility, but as the team neared the end of their second week of seclusion familiarity made the rooms seem smaller and the halls shorter. Everyone had memorized where every crack was located in the ceiling and walls of their motel rooms.

Rob had been gone for three days, his boss insisting that he cover a gathering of CEOs of the Fortune Five Hundred companies. The team had agreed that they should maintain a communications black-out with Rob, not being sure they would be able to arrange secure communications. He had taken the first available flight to get back to Roeper Robotics, but he had taken the extra precaution of booking a flight to a different city, then to another one, and finally, a flight to the small urban airport near Roeper Robotics. He considered the extra precautions to be necessary to avoid being tracked back to the facility. Upon his arrival Rob walked toward the old accounting office when he saw Adam walking toward him, with Ashley at his side. Ashley smiled and glanced proudly at Adam.

"Hello, Rob," Adam said.

Rob stopped, his jaw dropping and his eyes widening. The voice wasn't the deep bass voice Adam had possessed in his early years up till he awakened as Josh – it was his dad's own voice!

"You're walking, and you have your own voice!" Rob exclaimed.

Ashley said, nodding to Phil who was standing nearby, "Phil took a recording of Josh's voice and tuned Adam's voice to it."

Phil said, "That's the simple explanation, but I guess it'll do."

"In all of our planning we never gave any discussion to something so minor as what kind of voice the new Adam should have," Rob said.

"I thought you'd like the added touch," Phil said.

Ashley and Adam had stopped now, standing in front of Rob. "It is a nice touch," Rob replied, smiling and looking at Adam. He knew he shouldn't have been surprised. Each Dolphdroid had been assigned a unique voice print as well as a face print. It had been part of the plan to maintain individuality among them. In the early stages of the project, on Josh's birthday, Phil and his associates had assigned the voice prints of public figures to three of the Dolphdroids they were activating. They thought it would add a light moment to a special day for Josh, but he didn't find the humor in it. The three Dolphdroids were re-programmed with nondescript but unique voice prints before lunchtime.

Ashley leaned against the massive metal hulk standing beside her. "It really helps me remember that it's Josh inside here," she said, as she patted Adam's chest with her hand.

Adam looked down at her and his face turned an even brighter yellow, indicating a broad smile. He gently put his large metal arm around her shoulders and pulled her close. Adam turned his gaze back to Rob. "It sure is good having you back here, Rob. It concerned me that the Warwick family might try something."

"You really are OK, aren't you, Dad?" Relief was obvious in his voice. He cleared his throat and said, "I took every precaution, Dad." It was still difficult for him to look at Adam and think of him as his father. However, the change in voice and the significant progress that Adam had made during his absence was making it easier. "I stayed in a different hotel each night, and during the meetings I hung with the press crowd. When it was time to come back here I made sure I covered my tracks several different ways."

"Good," Adam said. "The last thing we need is for the Warwick Family to identify our location. There's little doubt that a major disaster would hit this facility within a few hours of their discovering where we are. I'm glad it won't be long before we're out of here."

Risner had joined them. "Your Dad..." He started again. "Adam is doing great. The interface is operating at nearly 100 percent. The physical therapy is virtually completed, and you can hear for yourself that he has no trouble talking, so speech therapy is no longer needed."

While they were walking toward the dining hall Bill came up, welcomed Rob with a handshake, and joined them. Tony and Nancy were already in the dining hall and stood to greet Rob – Tony with a handshake and Nancy with a hug. Adam stood while the others found seats. Noticing that he was the only one standing, Adam moved to the unoccupied bench by the wall and slowly sat down.

"I don't get tired of standing, so I sometimes forget that I can use the option of sitting down," he said.

Adam's observation prompted a question from Rob. "How does it feel, Dad? For instance, how's your sense of touch? Do you see and hear like you did when you were still in your own body?"

Adam had responded to similar questions from the team but, because of his unplanned trip, this was Rob's first opportunity for a genuine conversation with his father since inrobation. Before he left on his reporting assignment it had still been difficult for Adam to communicate.

"It's amazing," Adam began. "The sense of touch through the sensors is good, though not as good as with human hands; it's more like wearing thin gloves with thousands of little holes in them that would allow the skin to touch a surface. The hearing is like a good televiewer link, not quite like human hearing, but close. How I see, my sense of sight, well, that's taking a little longer to get used to. It's a great deal like the face-viewers you wear for virtual reality. I see everything in detail. It's just different somehow. All in all, I'm feeling comfortable in this new body. I thought it would be more like wearing full body armor, but it's better than that. It feels like a body to me, though not the same as my human body. It's difficult to explain."

"It's amazing, truly amazing," Nancy said, shaking her head.

"Your Dad's done so well, Rob," Ashley said.

"He sure has," interjected Bill. "He's done so well that we're finished with the therapies. Tomorrow we're leaving here. It's time to implement the next phase of Moon's Mercy."

Two weeks after settling in at Roeper Robotics, the team was vacating the facility. The longer they stayed, the greater their risk of being discovered by the Warwick Family. Adam said that Roeper Robotics also had to get back to the business of being Roeper Robotics.

On the morning of the move everyone was busy packing equipment and erasing any trace of the unusual operation. Several people who had been part of the project for the last two weeks were no longer needed and would have to be content with hearing about developments via a tightly controlled grapevine or waiting until parts of the mission became public and made the news.

Adam shook their hands, a gesture he had refrained from using until he had mastered the art of picking up an egg without crushing it. Drs. Kippler, Mesner, and Gray stood clustered together. They had grown to appreciate each other and had established a rapport, the result of sharing the risks and the achievements of the first human inrobation. Each took his turn saying good-by to Adam. By noon everyone was gone except for those who would be traveling to Iowa, where the mission would be launched. Gathered around the table in the dining hall were Bill Zucker, Nancy Saunders, Risner Billingston, Phil Kirkpatrick, Tony Williams, Rob, and Ashley. Adam stood behind Rob and Ashley. Conversation was subdued as they discussed the details of getting Adam to Iowa.

After dark, Adam, unable to fit in a normal-sized car or PAV, was transferred to a remote area of the city by panel truck, where an old medic-transport helicopter was waiting for him. Rob, Ashley, and Bill would make the trip with Adam; Nancy, Phil, Risner, and Tony would catch a commercial flight later that night.

The smell of bacon, eggs, coffee, and fresh breakfast rolls wafted up the stairs into the bedrooms on the second floor of the old farmhouse. Cots had been brought in to accommodate the extra guests and were put beside the existing beds in the two guest rooms and in the hallway. Even with a bathroom upstairs and another one downstairs, it still took some time before everyone had made their way to the kitchen to enjoy Aunt Henrietta's breakfast feast. Uncle Ben dutifully did whatever she told him to do as she busied herself with several tasks at once.

Henrietta glanced at Adam, who stood to the side of the refrigerator, having tried his best to stay out of her way. She said, "I wish you could try one of these, Josh. They're my new and improved version." She had been shocked when Adam walked into the house late the night before. Although she adjusted quickly to her nephew's new persona, she made it clear that she wouldn't refer to him as Adam but would continue to call him Josh.

"I know, Aunt Henrietta, I'd love to try one, too. I still have vivid memories of how good your rolls taste," Adam replied.

"Oh, great," Risner chimed in. "Now we have a robot calling a dear old lady 'aunt.' Aren't we all one big happy family!" The lack of sleep had put him in a foul mood.

"Don't you want to try one of my rolls to see if this old lady can still bake?" she teased.

Risner rolled his eyes and said, "OK, you talked me into it," and took one.

The sun was already above the barn and was casting its warm rays into the kitchen, giving it a golden glow. Risner glanced out the window. From where he sat he could see a rooster scratching for breakfast in the farmyard. The large brown bird paused long enough to flap his wings, stretch as tall as he could, and crow. Having announced the arrival of another morning for what seemed to be the umpteenth time to Risner, he resumed scratching for breakfast. Risner returned his gaze to the table, shook his head in disgust, and continued chewing his roll.

When Uncle Ben determined that his wife was through giving him orders, he sat down, reached for a roll, and said, "Max Henderson called just a few minutes ago. He'll be arriving shortly with the craft." Ben paused, his eyes drifting upward as he pondered. "I can't recall the name of the craft."

"The McCord 983 Defender, Uncle Ben," Adam interjected.

"Yeah, that was it!" Ben exclaimed, pointing to Adam with his index finger while the other fingers continued to grasp his roll.

"Do you think your wiring can handle all of our electronic equipment?" Bill asked.

Uncle Ben laughed. "You could run the entire nation's

highway network control system from up in that attic! Yep, it'll handle anything you plug in, I guarantee it."

After breakfast the team lugged the equipment up the two flights of steps to the attic. Ben and Henrietta had shoved their fifty-plus years of accumulated memories to one half of the attic to make room for the team. Soft light filtered through four windows, each draped with sun-faded, fly-specked, dusty curtains.

The telemetry equipment that the team moved into place would allow them to keep in touch with Adam, monitoring his functions and communicating with him until he left earth orbit for the moon. It also would allow them to code in the crucial request to the National Airspace Control, authorizing the craft to enter earth orbit.

While Bill, Risner, Nancy, and Rob were seated around the kitchen table making additional plans, a call came in on the televiewer and Uncle Ben hurried to answer it.

"Slow down, Ben," Aunt Henrietta mildly scolded. She slowly shook her head. "He always hurries to answer that thing. I've told him a thousand times that they'll wait until you answer it."

"Max will be here in about five minutes," Uncle Ben announced. "I love it when a plan comes together," he added, making a fist with his one hand and punching it into the open palm of the other.

Adam and Ashley were in the living room looking though a family album that Aunt Henrietta had dug out of the closet at Ashley's request. Aunt Henrietta glanced at the two while clearing the table. She smiled. It looked humorous seeing the large metallic figure of Adam seated on the couch, his weight crushing the cushion down and out of sight into the framing of the couch. As they looked at the pictures Adam reminisced about the time he had set the hay field on fire when he was five years old and was playing with a laser lighter that he had taken from the kitchen. Ashley laughed when he described how he had poured water on himself while trying to lift a pail over a fence to feed the horses. Her attentiveness encouraged Adam to keep the stories coming.

Bill stood on the porch with Uncle Ben, waiting for the arrival of Max with the pilot and the McCord. Uncle Ben filled the time with a review for Bill of how all the different crops were doing and the prices they were bringing. "I see him!" Ben exclaimed, interrupting himself while commenting on the current price of corn. He pointed a bent and bony arthritic index finger toward the east. Apparently Max had instructed the pilot to come in from a high altitude on a glide. Bill was pleased; it was a good tactic, keeping the noise of the craft to a minimum by bringing it in on a steep glide. A normal long approach near ground level would have taken the craft over several farms, and that would have drawn unnecessary attention; it wasn't every day that people saw a McCord 983 Defender land at a farm.

Bill and Uncle Ben stepped off the porch and walked toward the hayfield that Ben had just harvested the day before. By the time they reached the edge of the field, the craft was making its final approach, pulling out of its steep descent at treetop level. The nose of the craft came up as the landing gear lowered just feet above the hayfield. The engines thundered as the thrusters were reversed and the pilot added a momentary burst of power. Bill winced, thinking how everyone within a two-mile area probably had heard the noise. Suddenly the noise stopped as the pilot cut the engines and the craft dropped the last two or three feet to the ground, bouncing back into the air once before settling down on the landing gear.

The canopy slid back a moment after the craft rolled a short distance to a stop. Max was in the back seat behind the pilot, and already had his helmet off.

"You got something to pull this thing back to the barn?" Max called out as he climbed from the craft.

"I'll get my tractor," Uncle Ben said. He turned and walked as quickly as he could to the storage shed.

The pilot removed his helmet, laid it on the control panel in front of him, and climbed down after Max. Bill eyed the pilot carefully. He had been growing more cautious around strangers over the past few weeks, worried that someone might be infiltrating the project. The pilot appeared to be in his early thirties, had dark, thinning black hair and a closely shaven face that still showed the outline of where the man could easily grow a thick beard. He ran his hands through the wisps of black hair as he approached Bill, extending his hand. "The name's Elliot, Elliot Hale." Glancing back at the craft, he said, "It's in good shape." Turning to Bill again, he said, "Max did some essential repairs, changes, and upgrades. I understand he's going to make some more modifications. I've had some experience in maintenance as well as being a pilot, so he's asked me to lend a hand." Elliot glanced around, taking in the farm scene before him. "You have anything to drink in the house? I'm really thirsty."

"Sure," Bill replied, "Aunt Henrietta's probably in the kitchen. She can help you find something to drink and will certainly offer you something to eat. That's her way, you never leave her presence hungry."

"Sounds good. Now that you mention it, I'm sort of hungry too." Elliot gave Bill a friendly pat on the shoulder and started toward the house with a cocky stride.

Max came up and stood alongside Bill. Nodding toward Elliot, Max said, "He's a friendly cuss, that's for sure. Drove me nuts with all of his jabbering on the flight here."

"Can he be trusted?" Bill asked, his eyes still fixed on Elliot, who was now climbing the steps onto the porch of the house.

Max turned his gaze back to Bill as Elliot entered the farmhouse. "Wish I could give you 100 percent assurance on that, but I can't. Course I wouldn't have got him to pilot the craft if I didn't think he was OK. You know," Max added, nodding toward the house, "it's hard to find pilots of former military craft that don't hold at least a cat's spit of allegiance to the government. After all, that's who's signed the paycheck for them over the years. And what we're doing here certainly doesn't have the unqualified endorsement of our government; just ask Dr. Hartung about that."

"I'd rather not, Max. Hopefully, he knows nothing about all of this."

"I'm with you there. Have no fear, as far as Elliot goes. I think he's safe. It's great that he's not only a pilot but also a mechanic. I can use all the help I can get to make the modifications we need."

"Where'd you find him?" Bill asked.

"Actually, he found me," Max replied, turning to look at the craft Elliot had just piloted. Bill turned his attention in the same direction as Max continued. "When I went back to do the final paperwork on the engines, they said a man had been in since Josh and I were there and got to reminiscing about flying some of the different air-space craft. He said he was particularly fond of the

McCord 983 Defender, and that if they knew of anyone flying one privately, or even someone who was restoring a 983, to let him know. He left his number with them, they called me, and I called Elliot. I know he's a good pilot, I saw that from our flight out here, but I can't, as of yet, vouch for his mechanic's skills. Time will tell."

Bill took a deep breath, turning his attention back to the farmhouse. "Well, it still might be a good idea to ask for his wrist communicator during his stay with us. We could tell him it's a normal precaution. Actually, that's not a bad idea for all of us. Any one of us might make a friendly call to a family member or friend. Someone doing a search for any of us might get lucky and trace the call to here, compromising the secrecy of the mission."

Within an hour Bill had collected all of the wrist communicators, though most of the team members insisted they wouldn't have made a call anyway. Elliot seemed to hesitate only a moment, then handed his over. Bill also asked Uncle Ben and Aunt Henrietta to put an access security code on their televiewer. He then made his way to the attic and inputted a similar code to the communications equipment being installed there.

The boosters arrived at the Des Moines airport the next morning and were delivered by truck around 3 p.m. Max and Elliot had already begun some of the retrofitting work on the McCord 983 Defender in anticipation of the arrival of the boosters. It became obvious to Max that Elliot had greatly exaggerated his abilities as a mechanic. He was eager and willing, but that didn't compensate for his lack of experience and limited knowledge. "All he does is talk. He's driving me crazy," Max complained to Bill when they stepped outside after breakfast. "He definitely gets more talking done than work."

Watching a crow land on a fence post by the barn, Bill said, "I know."

Max continued his tirade. "Why, he even had the audacity to put in his suggestions for Aunt Henrietta's grocery list before she goes to the store later this morning. I can't believe he doesn't have a belly on him, the way he wolfs down food."

"Like you?" Bill added, glancing at Max, as they started walking toward the barn.

A hint of a smile came across Max's face. "Yeah, like me."

"Start jogging every morning like Elliot does before breakfast, and maybe you can be fit and trim like Elliot and still eat as much as he does."

Max frowned and shook his head. "It's not worth it," he grumbled. "When I see my first smiling jogger I'll think seriously about giving it a try, but not before."

Adam spent most of his days in the attic, where Tony was downloading information on the Dolphdroid colony for him. With the late afternoon sun streaming in through the dusty west window, Adam told Tony, "It's astonishing! I have memories I've never lived! I feel like I've been to the colony and back." Nancy sat next to Adam, her notes in front of her, helping Adam process the new information.

Phil and Risner spent the days running tests and making adjustments on Adam's body. Much to Phil's growing annoyance, those days were frequently punctuated with "Oh, great!" as Risner discovered functions that failed to measure up to his strict standards. Phil found it exhausting to keep the excitable robotics expert calm enough to be efficient. The greatest hurdle was Adam's right wrist, which continually failed to function within parameters. Uncle Bill, in one of his daily visits to the attic, leaned over, his hands on his knees and his eyes scrutinizing the problematic wrist. "I think a quarter inch washer put right there would do the trick." He moved his hand from his knee and pointed a crooked index finger. Much to the credit of Phil and Risner, they tried his suggestion – and much to their chagrin, it worked.

What time Adam didn't spend in the attic was spent training on the McCord Defender flight simulator that had been purchased from a re-seller of military surplus equipment. Josh, though an accomplished pilot, had never flown a McCord Defender before – and he had never flown any aircraft as Adam. Tony Williams found it challenging to adjust the simulator for Adam's purposes. The visual data was normally fed to a 360 degree 3-D screen, the audio data to speakers, and the "feel" data to lifts and pumps in the simulator in which the trainee sat. All the data had to be reconfigured into a format that could be inputted through Adam's external interface so that the controls could be run by his thoughts and his on-board processor. The team members stood silently by, finding it strange watching Adam seated in the simulator, his arms and legs motionless, flying the simulator through complex maneuvers simply by thinking the commands.

Adam looked forward to the late evenings when the teams called it a day and he could spend time taking walks with Ashley under the stars and in the moonlight. It was the only time that Adam ventured outdoors other than the short trips between the house and the simulator in the chicken coop. Adam's disappearance from the Smithsonian West had made the news, and it was feared that the locals might get a glimpse of him. A sighting of a Dolphdroid in Iowa would be big news, and it would have disastrous results for the mission.

The time passed quickly for everyone. A growing sense of anticipation was palpable.

"Tomorrow morning?" Bill asked Adam.

"Tomorrow morning," Adam replied.

They were standing in the kitchen watching Uncle Ben put away the last of the breakfast dishes. "Excuse me," Uncle Ben said, looking up at Adam. The top of Adam's head was a mere inch or two from touching the ceiling. "I need to put this pan away in the cupboard behind you. You take up half the kitchen, you know."

"I know," Adam replied. "Sorry about that."

"No need to apologize. I was just stating a fact. Tomorrow morning?"

They both nodded. The team had started an informal countdown three days earlier. The Defender was ready to go, Max had assured them. Adam had finished his flight training with the simulator. Risner said Adam's systems had been tuned and tweaked and were ready to go.

"Why are you doing the dishes alone, Uncle Ben? Where's Aunt Henrietta?" Bill asked.

"She went to town to get some groceries and took Elliot with her. He said he wanted to pick up a couple of things. You people are eating us out of house and home."

Bill laughed. He knew not to take Uncle Ben's complaining seriously. It had been obvious that Ben and Henrietta were thoroughly enjoying the company and the distraction of all that was going on.

Max came through the kitchen door, puffing hard. Sweat soaked his shirt, causing it to stick to his protruding belly.

"What happened to you?" Adam asked.

"I've started to..." He paused to take a couple of deep breaths. "... to exercise. If it keeps Elliot in shape, maybe..." He took another couple of breaths, leaning over, putting his hands on his knees, then glancing from Bill to Adam. "... maybe it'll do the same for me."

He straightened and wiped the sweat from his forehead with the back of his forearm as he staggered to the refrigerator. "I need some iced tea," he gasped. He opened the refrigerator and lifted out a large pitcher, then glanced back inside before closing the door. "Who puts potato chips in the refrigerator?" he asked as he took the pitcher over to the counter and reached into the cupboard for a glass.

Bill glanced at Adam. Adam looked at Bill. They both looked at Max.

"What did you say?" Bill asked.

"Someone put potato chips in the refrigerator. Kind of strange, if you ask me."

"Mr. Chips!" Adam exclaimed.

"Uncle Ben, who put the chips in the refrigerator?" Bill asked.

The urgency in Bill's voice caused Ben to stop drying a glass. "That Hale fellow, Elliot. He's been putting chips in the refrigerator ever since he's been here. Says he likes to eat cold potato chips. Why? What's wrong?"

"What's wrong is that there's a space pirate who reportedly hires himself out to crime syndicates and anyone else who can use his services. He hits on spacecraft, bombs facilities, does all kinds of destruction for hire. He's an ace pilot. He's called Mr. Chips by the intelligence agencies because of his strange taste in snack food."

"How do you know that for sure?" Uncle Ben asked.

Adam replied, "Elliot – Mr. Chips – is probably the best air/space fighter pilot alive. He flew in the last conflict and took out a dozen craft by himself."

"Elliot?" Uncle Ben asked with disbelief. "I can't believe it. He seems like such a nice fellow."

"Believe it," Bill said.

"He's with Henrietta!" Ben exclaimed. "Will she be safe?"

"I think so, Uncle Ben. He has a different evil in mind than hurting Aunt Henrietta," Adam reassured him. "But we need to keep him from communicating with the Warwick Family."

Bill took a deep breath, "I know. We also need to keep him from getting to an air-space craft. Maybe he's supposed to blow this whole operation off the map of Iowa."

Bill and Adam looked at each other, trying to figure out what to do next.

Bill broke the silence. "We need to get hold of Henrietta."

Uncle Ben lifted his arm and paused, glancing at Bill and Adam. "I don't have my communicator. You took it, remember? Henrietta doesn't have hers, either."

"Where does she shop?" Bill asked.

"There's only one grocery store in town, Michaelson's. She'd be there."

Bill rushed over to the televiewer by the pantry door, quickly inputted a few key strokes to unlock the device, and asked, "Uncle Ben, what's the number for the store?"

"I don't know, I'll have to do a search for it. Here let me at that," Uncle Ben said.

Within a minute Aunt Henrietta was on the viewer. Shelves of groceries were behind her. "OK, what did you guys forget to put on the list?"

"Where's Elliot?" Bill asked.

Aunt Henrietta seemed taken aback by the question. "He asked me to drop him off at the airstrip on the other side of town. He said he had to ask the mechanic some questions. I told him that I didn't think there would be anyone there this early in the morning, but he insisted on being dropped off anyway."

Bill looked at Adam and said, "He must have a craft at the airstrip."

Adam nodded. "It would seem so. He'll want to finish this job himself. Just being an informant wouldn't be enough action."

"You think he's going to hit the farm?" Bill asked.

Adam was already heading toward the door. "I'm certain of it. We need to launch right now. He's probably already in the air."

Chapter 26

"Tell Aunt Henrietta to stay in town!" Bill shouted over his shoulder to Uncle Ben as he followed Adam out the door. Bill jumped the last porch step, which had been crushed by Adam's weight making a hasty exit off the porch. Max paused before the broken step, then jumped as Bill had done.

"I need to get into the air. He'll fire on me instead of the farm and the team. That should keep everyone else safe. I can defend the McCord from destruction when it's airborne," Adam said as he moved swiftly toward the barn, searching the horizon for any sign of the aircraft.

Pushing his viewer lenses into extreme telephoto mode, Adam saw a black speck above the horizon. It flickered with light, reflecting the morning sun. "He's coming!"

Adam reached the small side door of the barn and fumbled with the latch. Exasperated, he gave up and walked through the closed door sending splintered wood flying in all directions.

Adam pushed the external control to open the canopy and lower the steps. "It better be ready to fly," he said.

"It should be, I guess; I think so," Max replied.

Adam looked at Max while the canopy retracted and the steps unfolded and lowered, producing a whirring sound.

Max raised his arms, spreading them wide, glancing from the nose to the tail of the craft. "This is just such short notice. I mean, I was figuring on an extended pre-flight check in the morning."

"Me, too," Adam said as he climbed up, his metal feet clanking on each step. Grasping the side of the open cockpit with both hands, he lifted his torso and legs, swinging his body in one quick motion into the seat of the craft.

He quickly began flipping switches. The cabin lights came on and the strobe lights began flashing on the top of the craft and at the ends of the wings. There was the sound of the fuel pumps starting up. When they reached full pressurization they fell silent. He was ready for ignition. There had been no time to do a last full-systems check, no time for goodbyes. There was no time for anything but getting away from the farm so no one else would be injured or killed by Elliot. Adam was the target, and he had to become a moving target. He had to get out now!

Adam saw Uncle Ben struggling to open the large door at the end of the barn where, according to the plan, they were to pull the McCord out with Ben's antique Farmall "M" tractor.

With the volume of his voice at maximum, Adam shouted in a thunderous voice that rattled a loose board on the rafters. "Forget the door! Get out of the way, Uncle Ben! I'm flying it out!"

"But you can't do that, Josh!" Bill shouted, failing to notice that he had used his friend's human name.

"I have to, Bill," Adam said in a voice closer to normal volume, but with determination that left no doubt there would be no further discussion. In a softer voice he said, "Tell Rob and Randy that I love them, and Ashley, too." He activated the canopy and it began to slide forward. Simultaneously the ladder folded up into the fuselage. Just before the canopy closed Adam turned to Bill and said, "Thanks for everything, Bill. Get out of the barn." Looking at Max, he said, "You too, Max, go, now!"

Uncle Ben had managed to move the large door only a couple of feet when, at Adam's command, he abandoned his efforts, slipping through the opening and out of the barn. Bill and Max fled through the splintered door.

Seeing that no one remained in the barn, Adam set the

throttle in the start position and hit the ignition. The engines of the Defender roared to life. He pulled the control stick all the way back, causing the engine nozzles to shift so they spewed flames high up against the back wall of the barn, instantly igniting the dry siding. The thrust from the engines shoved the rear of the craft down on the rear wheels' shocks while lifting the nose slightly.

Adam glanced at the small control panel Max had installed for the extra Heidstar engines. They were intended to give the extra thrust needed to achieve escape velocity from earth's orbit. He needed their thrust now; there was no time to taxi out and use the makeshift runway that had been prepared. He flipped back the protective cover and punched the square recessed button that armed the Heidstars, then hit their ignition switch. The Heidstars came instantly to life, spewing an inferno of flames that filled the barn behind the Defender in brilliant orange light.

Adam shoved the throttle all the way forward. Instantly he was slammed into his seat as if he had been rear ended by a large object at high speed.

Bill, Max, and Uncle Ben had joined each other about 50 feet from the barn when they heard the roar of the Defender's engines, then a deafening increase in sound from within the barn as the Heidstars ignited. Every crack in the aged, warped siding of the barn glowed orange. The sound visibly shook the old building.

The combined hot blast of the exhaust from the engines instantly turned the half of the barn behind the Defender into an inferno, the flames bouncing off the wall behind the Defender and quickly rolling forward back toward the craft. The Defender, however, had already hit the large barn doors, with boards and braces flying in all directions.

The moment the Defender cleared the barn, Adam nudged the stick forward to prevent the craft from doing a backward flip. He reached for the control that retracted the landing gear. He'd need the advantage of slick aerodynamics. With regret, he shut down the Heidstars to conserve their fuel. Without their extra punch he'd never achieve escape velocity, leaving him in the grip of the earth's gravitational pull and ending the mission.

The McCord Defender was climbing at a 45 degree angle. When Adam turned his attention from the Heidstars' controls and looked out the front of the canopy, he immediately identified a craft dead ahead at less than a thousand feet. It was a Tessmore XL craft, undoubtedly piloted by Elliot. Adam knew he was an easy target for the Tessmore's laser gun, heat-seeking missiles, and the dreaded energy ball. Jerking the control stick hard right, Adam moved away from a head-on confrontation.

Glancing at his heads-up rear monitor view displayed on the left side of the canopy, he saw that Elliot had altered his course and was on his tail. Instinctively, Adam knew that this was the moment when Elliot would fire. Adam made a hard left turn, pitching his weight to the right, his head clanking against the canopy. In the rear monitor he saw a bright light coming from the Tessmore and then saw a ball of flame sail past him. He had never seen the eneredo in action before. It was a fearsome display of deadly force, a flickering ball of fire as bright as a welder's torch. A direct hit by its magnetic plasma energy would blow a craft apart, while a near miss would take out all electronics and freeze the inboard computer. The Defender didn't have a warning system for an eneredo; the weapon was too new. Adam realized that if he hadn't guessed when Elliot would release the fireball he would have been history. The sobering reality was that the Tessmore carried two more eneredos if it was fully loaded, and it probably was. Then there were the two heat-seeking missiles the Tessmore could carry.

"Warning, laser fire!" the Defender's computer shouted. Adam knew it would take no more than a couple of seconds for the laser cannon to power up before it could fire its streak of death. Adam hesitated for only a fraction of a second, attempting to time his move, then did a hard right. His instincts proved accurate again. Elliot fired a burst, but the Defender was no longer at the target point and the laser disappeared into thin air. Adam knew his timing couldn't always be so good. One of these times Elliot would score a hit. If only he had weapons! He had been in many a dogfight in his early years, but never without weapons. Here he was in a fighter craft with its weapons removed because the team had decided to save the weight. An encounter with a hostile force had never been a serious concern.

"Adam!" It was Bill. He must be back in the house, in the attic with the communications equipment.

"I copy." Adam said. "I have myself in a nasty situation at the moment."

"We understand. Wish we could do something," Bill said.

Adam glanced at the rear monitor. Elliot was coming up on his tail. He had to try to put some distance between him and Elliot. "I'm going vertical," he said as he pulled back the stick, sending the Defender into a vertical climb. The rear monitor showed the Tessmore doing the same, though since it was a heavier craft it was climbing more slowly. Adam allowed himself a sense of relief, but only for a moment. He had to remember that he was like a helpless rabbit trying to outrun a predator. He needed a place to hide. He noticed a storm front in the distance with huge, bellowing cumulus clouds. He jerked the stick in the direction of the clouds, leaving his vertical ascent and rolling over, flying upside down for a moment, then righting the craft as he flew straight toward the cloud formation. He knew he had to escape from this engagement or he'd be killed. A rabbit can only run in an open field for so long, he thought. It had been a favorite analogy of his trainer in his early days of flight school. A slower predator can always catch a faster rabbit if the rabbit remains in the open. The rabbit's only hope is to find cover. It was also Adam's only hope.

Elliot was at a greater distance than before the vertical maneuver, but Adam knew he was far from safe, even at his current distance. If the man fired a heat-seeking missile it would be over. Normal response time was usually too slow to alter course from a fast approaching missile. Elliot would certainly use one any second.

"You're not going to win this way," the voice came into the Defender's cockpit. It was Tony. "Interface with the craft. Do it now!"

Adam hesitated for only a moment. He knew what Tony was suggesting: if he could run the controls of the craft directly from thought commands, the response of the craft would be almost instantaneous, as if it were an extension of his body. Quickly he reached behind his neck, found the connecting cable coming from his headrest, and fumbled at getting it placed over the receptor in the back of his neck. When he felt it in place, he pushed it in the rest of the way. He heard it click.

Without hesitation, and while glancing at the rear view that showed Elliot within a couple of hundred yards, he threw the switch that transferred all controls from manual to thought. A strange sense came over him, much like he had felt in the simulator – but this felt stronger, more real. It gave him a sense of confidence. He knew that he had to concentrate all his thoughts on controlling the craft. The plane was an extension of his new metal body, a metal body housing his metal body, with even more metal, mechanics, electronics, and processors – and wings and engines, too! He thought of dipping the right wing. It dipped. Good! It was going to work!

    The interface allowed him to see ahead with his eyes and to the rear with the Defender's rearview camera at the same time. Unlike a human pilot, the input from his eyes and the camera was digital and he processed them both the same, and very quickly – the ultimate peripheral vision.

    The voice of Tony shouted into the cockpit, "Fly by your thoughts, Adam! You and the McCord are one!"

    There was a flash: a heat-seeking missile had been fired. Adam felt at one with his craft. Time seem to stand still as he divided the couple of seconds between launch and impact into seemingly hundreds of small increments of time. He calibrated the shortening distance between missile and the Defender. He knew it was drifting to the right of dead center. Then, at the right millisecond, he jerked to the left, and the missile streaked by the right side of his craft. Adam's visual reception was extraordinary, and he identified the missile as it flew by. This particular model of missile he knew well. It was called the Heat Hound. It had traveled a considerable distance to get from the Tessmore to his Defender and had spent most of its fuel, too much fuel to alter its course and come around again to seek out its target. If the Heat Hound missile had the fuel to make a u-turn, there was a 50/50 chance that it would lock onto the craft that had fired it, instead of the enemy craft. This was one of the quirks of the Heat Hound. It had happened on at least three occasions that he was aware of since the missile had been put into service. They had built in a nine-second self-destruct delay so it couldn't come back and bite its master, as fighter pilots were fond of saying. His personal processor interfaced with his brain fed him the countdown from the nine-second mark of launch. Adam watched it disappear into the horizon, leaving behind a hazy trail of exhaust. It would be of no further danger. Adam saw a flash of light in the distance. It self-destructed at exactly the nine-second mark.

    Adam looked at the thunderheads. They were looming large.

He was getting close. There was another flash of light from the Tessmore; Elliot had fired an eneredo. Elliot loved the new weapon and was trigger-happy about using it. He should have waited; the distance was too great for any kind of accuracy. Adam waited until the bright ball of light was almost on him. He had an idea, and his face glowed with a smile. The eneredo was almost close enough. Adam waited a few milliseconds longer, then jerked to the right and the eneredo went sailing past, close enough that its light illuminated the cockpit.

Adam took note that the Defender's systems were still operating; the eneredo had not gotten quite close enough. Instantly he gave a thought command and shut down the Defender's engines. A warning voice from the craft's computer shouted the alarm, "Engines shutdown in flight! Warning! This is not a recommended procedure!" "Of course it's not," Adam mumbled to himself. Adam gave another thought command and the computer was quiet. He had put it into stand-by mode. The rear view screen remained lit with the communication system status lights. Silence filled the cabin; the wind whistling at the edges of the canopy was the only sound. The Defender's nose quickly dipped down, and the craft began to plummet toward earth.

In the Tessmore there was a chuckle. Elliot was grinning. He could see that the eneredo had knocked out all the Defender's systems. He watched the craft drop toward earth. Then the smile disappeared. "Now you're a sitting duck," he whispered. He armed the other missile.

"What happened to your power, Adam?" It was Bill.

"Dad, you copy? Are you OK?" Rob asked.

Adam could picture all of the most important people in his life hovering together in the attic of the farmhouse watching the telemetry readings.

"I'm trying a little maneuver to see if the Heat Hound will bite its master," Adam replied.

"So your systems haven't failed?" Tony asked.

"No, but that's what I want Elliot to think."

The Tessmore had begun a steep dive in an attempt to stay close to the plummeting Defender and was closing in fast.

"I didn't think Elliot would be happy with seeing me just drop out of the sky. He wants an explosion, and wants to experience it from a front row seat," Adam added.

Adam saw the flash from the Tessmore in his rear viewer. The missile was heading toward him. It was difficult for Adam to determine whether the missile had locked on to his shut-down engine or if it was still in search mode, but it seemed as though the missile's path was slightly off a trajectory for a direct hit on the Defender. It would be too late to do anything about it; the computer would take at least five seconds to go active again. The Heat Hound went by in a blur with a roar, within twenty feet of the Defender. It had failed to read the residual heat from his shut down engines. It had used little fuel with the close distance between the crafts and the help of gravity. Adam watched as the missile came out of its dive ahead of him and began to circle right and climb again, going back to the general area of engagement. It appeared to be heading back toward him. He was still plummeting toward it, as was Elliot, who was now only a couple of hundred feet behind him.

"Adam! It's coming back! Boot up and use evasive maneuvers!" Bill shouted.

"I don't think so," Adam replied.

The smile on Elliot's face had given way to a look of anger, then bewilderment, when the missile sailed by the Defender. It occurred to Elliot, too late, that the missile had failed to lock on to the Defender as a target because it wasn't spewing heat – but he was! Some minds freeze, but not his. Instincts prompted him to react faster than conscious thought could. He fired another eneredo. The Heat Hound instantly locked on to the biggest heat source, the eneredo, not the Tessmore's exhaust. The missile's explosion rocked the Tessmore, it was so close. At least one piece of the exploded missile slammed into the fuselage of the Tessmore; Elliot felt it and heard it. He did a quick check of his systems as he continued plummeting earthward behind the Defender. He was still in one piece, and all systems seemed to be nominal. Adam was a worthy adversary, Elliot thought, but he had never failed to terminate a target, and he wouldn't fail this time.

Adam saw the flash behind him, and relief flooded over him. He reactivated the Defender's systems as he said to his ground crew, "Elliot met his end by a boomerang missile. The Heat Hound came back to bite him. I'm re-booting the computer."

"We copy," came Bill's reply.

"I'll need new orbit insertion data. What we loaded into the Defender is of no use to me now, I've been jumping all around the sky up here."

"We'll get on it," Bill replied.

"Oh, great!" Risner exclaimed.

"What's the problem?" Adam asked.

"Your problem is Elliot. He's still with you," Risner said. "According to our sky map he's right behind you."

Adam focused his attention on the rear view of the craft. How could he have not noticed? The Tessmore was a dot in the distance, but a large dot! Elliot would not go away! Adam focused his attention on the high cumulus clouds ahead of him. The Defender's systems had re-booted to full operation, so he pulled the craft out of its dive and headed toward the largest of the cloud formations that billowed in the shape of a giant mushroom. The Tessmore's radar, like the Defender's, wouldn't work at extremely close range. This was a close range dog-fight so maybe the cloud cover could be an advantage. Hiding can be a good defense, Adam reasoned.

As the first moisture of the cloud whipped past his canopy, Adam took a last glance through the rearview camera. The Tessmore was still coming, and quickly gaining. Adam had his craft at maximum speed without the benefit of the afterburners or the Ramsey boosters. He needed to save them for the extra push he'd need to gain escape velocity from earth orbit and put him on the trajectory for the moon.

It would take precious fuel, but Adam saw no recourse other than going nearly vertical. Perhaps the Tessmore wouldn't be able to keep up. He went vertical and had climbed for several seconds when the cloud thinned. Elliot was right on his tail! He had no choice – he kicked in the afterburners. "Warning! Aircraft approaching!" his computer announced. Elliot was invisible in the clouds but close enough for the computer to warn him, which meant that he was too close. Again, Adam had no choice. He reached for the control that activated the Ramsey boosters; they weren't integrated through the interface for Adam to activate them by thought control. The moment he activated the boosters he felt a slight jolt, but nothing more; then the computer announced, "Failure of starboard auxiliary power!" The right Ramsey booster had failed to ignite, so the left one had shut down immediately after ignition. The engines had to work as a team; with only one functioning the Defender would careen out of control.

Adam quickly retried the ignition sequence. There was the same jolt and the same warning. The Ramsey boosters were dead weight. All Adam saw behind him through his rearview camera were the clouds.

"Warning, laser fire!" the computer stated. The streak of laser light was to his left; he could see it out the canopy. It was a close call. Adam became conscious again of the rear camera view. He could see the faint image of the Tessmore through the thick cloud. Elliot was very close and getting closer. Adam knew he had to do something, and quickly.

Chapter 27

Josh had always been amazed by the ability of the human brain to unconsciously process all of the input about a given situation and come up with a burst of insight, sometimes without any conscious thought involved. No artificial intelligence program had ever been able to come close to such creativity. Such a burst of insight had come to him now, as Adam, and he was already acting on it without any conscious thought, reaching for the manual jettison control for the worthless Ramsey boosters. He pulled the lever firmly. Small explosive-release charges jolted the Defender even though it was at full throttle with afterburners.

Elliot smiled again when he saw the Defender appear through the cloud's fog right in front of him. He was within range for the laser cannon and fired. He waited to see the bright streak hit the Defender, destroying it. The Defender was still there. He had missed, but in another five seconds he would be so close as to not miss. Then he saw two bright flashes and two dark forms coming toward him. The boosters! What happened next took less than a second. The detachment of the boosters was so strange that his mind couldn't process what was happening quickly enough. The one booster would miss him on the left; the other was dead on. His eyes were transfixed on the second booster hurtling toward him. It seemed as if he could see every detail of the nose cone of the booster. It was the last thing he saw.

Adam had little time to wonder whether the move had worked. Almost immediately after he felt the release of the boosters he saw a bright flash in his rear view that illuminated the fog of the cloud around him.

Within moments the Defender broke through the top of the cumulus cloud at 25,000 feet. Adam shut down the afterburners as he took in the scene in the rearview camera. The huge cloud was already growing smaller beneath him as he climbed upward, though gravity was slowing his speed without the afterburners.

"Are you there, Adam? Talk to me!" It was Bill.

"I'm here."

"What happened to Elliot?" Rob asked.

"Well, let's just say I had to jettison the boosters and he happened to be in the way."

"Good!" exclaimed Bill.

"Good and bad," Adam replied. "Can you download the data to get me into orbit? I've wasted a lot of fuel."

"And you've lost the Ramsey boosters," Bill added.

"Tell me something I don't know," Adam replied. "Tell me if we still have bingo."

"Bingo? What's bingo?" asked Phil Kirkpatrick.

"Bingo refers to having enough fuel to complete the mission with a comfortable margin to spare," Max answered.

"Do we?" asked Risner.

"No way," Max said.

"Why not?" Risner asked.

Max pointed to some figures on a monitor. "Because he used up too much fuel in dealing with Elliot. If he had the Ramseys there might still be a chance, but he doesn't. This mission is doomed."

Bill was ignoring the discussion, punching computer keys, watching the screen's response, then punching more keys. After about a half minute he leaned back in his chair. "Max is right. We can't achieve escape velocity from earth's orbit, let alone have enough fuel left for a liftoff from the lunar surface and the trip back."

Everyone was silent. Then Bill asked, "You copy, Adam?"

"I copy," Adam replied.

"I don't think you have much choice, Josh – I mean Adam," Bill shook his head in frustration. This dual identity wasn't getting any easier to deal with. "You might as well bring the Defender back to the farm."

"Bill's right, Adam; we need to abort the mission," Max added.

There was silence. "You copy, Adam?" Bill asked.

"I'm going for orbit," Adam replied.

"Oh, great!" Risner exclaimed in a voice barely above a whisper, glancing around the attic. "What will that prove?"

"I heard that, Risner," Adam said.

"There's no way we can make this work, Adam," Bill said in a soft but firm voice.

"I'm going for orbit," Adam replied. "We'll make things up as we go. We're not canceling this mission now. By going for orbit we keep our options open. Who knows, we might come up with a brilliant plan. Get me into orbit and start working on that plan."

Bill looked at the others, nodded, and said, "We read you, Adam. We'll go for orbit." Bill began punching his keyboard again. Within a few moments he sat back and glanced at several of the monitors to reassure himself that they were displaying what he wanted to see. "OK, Adam," he said. "The data you need has been uploaded to you. Go for orbit at your discretion."

"Do you have the slightest idea what you're going to do once you achieve orbit?" Max asked.

"Negative," Adam replied. The data had been received by the on-board computer, and he manually punched in the necessary commands, his large metal fingers making the task awkward. The Defender abruptly changed direction and attitude, the engines throttling up; then the afterburners kicked in. "I have max power," he said.

The gradual shift in the sky's color from blue to black never ceased to amaze him. Even through his new eyes, he was in awe. It had been years since he had been in space, and he had missed it.

Finally the engines went silent and he heard the positioning thrusters give short bursts that put the Defender into an upside-down position in relation to the earth, keeping the canopy away from the sun's rays. He slowly bent back his metal head and gazed out the top of the canopy with his electronic eyes focusing upon the earth. He had checked his instruments and he was where he was supposed to be: at an altitude of 120 miles traveling at the orbital velocity of 17,500 miles an hour.

Over the next hour the conversation between Adam and the team in the farmhouse attic covered several topics. Adam asked about the barn. It was burning to the ground. The fire department had arrived, but the firefighters were only watching. They had told Uncle Ben they couldn't save the barn.

After some discussion they decided that Elliot probably had not informed his employer of Adam's location or about the farmhouse control center, waiting until he could report that Adam had been destroyed.

The conversation in the attic came back to the fundamental problem. Risner had settled into an old overstuffed living room chair. He mumbled, "Looks like this chair's been up here since before dust was invented." He crossed his legs, looked at the bank of monitors, and glanced around. "How can we continue the mission? He's going to need more fuel. Could we find him an orbiting tanker, pull some strings, and get him a fill-up?"

"Won't work," Max responded.

"Why not?" asked Risner.

"Because the Defender isn't set up for space fueling," Max said.

"That was shortsighted, wasn't it?" Risner shot back.

Max sighed. "Look, I didn't factor in a dogfight or having to ditch the Ramseys. This didn't turn out like we planned."

Adam interrupted their exchange. "Do we know anyone up here that could give me a proper send off?"

"What do you mean?" Phil asked.

"Is there anyone who could give me a piggy back ride to escape velocity?"

"I don't think that's ever been attempted before," Risner mumbled.

The others entered into a discussion about the feasibility of Adam's idea.

"It just might work," Max said to Adam. Then he summarized what they had been discussing. "Orbital traffic is reasonably heavy right now, with various colonies in orbit. I think they said recently there are about 300 people up there. Then there are the life cylinders. They're always being supplied by various craft from earth. And what about the scientific space stations? What are there, maybe a dozen or so? Let's see, I can think of at least two zero-gravity manufacturing plants up there. Oh yeah, the orbital warehouses, I forgot about them. I think there are three, if I'm not mistaken. There's gotta be help available from some..." Max interrupted himself, holding up an index finger, then wagging it in the air. "There is someone," he continued. "There's my nephew, Harry Messburg."

"Why is your nephew in orbit?" Phil asked.

"He runs a cargo transport vessel between the colonies, life cylinders, scientific stations, factories, storage stations, wherever. The kid gets around."

"Would he cooperate?" It was Adam's voice over the com link.

Adam couldn't see Max's smile. Max leaned forward. "Normally he wouldn't care a lick about helping someone solve their problem. He pretty much figures everybody should take care of themselves. But I happen to know he's always been intrigued by the Dolphdroids, ever since he was a teenager. I just talked to him last Christmas, and he asked about you, Josh – I mean, Adam. He's always admired you."

"Can his craft do the job?" Bill asked, running his fingers through his hair.

"Good question," Max replied. "It's one of the first station-to-station cargo transport vessels put into service. It's not much to look at. He got it at a good price, it being as old as it is. It may be old and sometimes not all that reliable, but it's big."

"One of those Troy Haulers?" Adam asked.

"You got it," Max replied.

"Can you find him, quickly?" Risner asked.

"Yeah, if he's not passed out at some bar."

"Oh, great!" Risner responded. "All we need is for Adam to be pushed to 25,000 miles an hour with a kid who's hung over and piloting a bucket of bolts."

"Hey, it's an imperfect world, OK?" Max snapped back.

"How do you plan to explain to this guy, your nephew..."

Uncle Ben couldn't think of his name.

"His name's Harry," Max interjected.

"How do you explain the situation to Harry without someone eavesdropping on the conversation, including this Imus guy?"

"We can get his vessel code and instruct our communications system to send a command to tune his system to the frequency we want. It'll be as secure as the conversation we're having with Adam," Max responded. Uncle Ben nodded.

"Let's do it," Adam said.

It had been two hours since Max had begun the effort to locate Harry. He had been right; Harry was at a bar on one of the warehouse vessels. Fortunately, he had just begun his social time with some long-time drinking buddies, so he was still sober. Max had a difficult time convincing him to return to his ship so they could have a secure conversation. He eventually gave in and returned to his ship. Once on a secure line with those in the attic he listened as they explained the situation. It was hard for him to believe all that he was hearing. When he had been fully debriefed he was asked if he would be willing to contact Adam. He quickly agreed, stating he'd do anything to help Dr. Christopher. He broke connection with those in the attic and adjusted his communications systems.

"Adam, this is Harry Messburg. Do you copy?"

Adam abruptly came to full consciousness. His new physical body needed no rest, but his brain still needed sleep. The boredom of waiting had put him in slumberland.

"Adam here. I copy. Thanks for responding to your uncle's request."

"Are you really Adam, Dr. Christopher?"

"One and the same," Adam replied. "Actually two and the same."

"Wow! This is great! I heard all about the theft of Adam. I figured some prankster stole him for the fun of it."

"It actually wasn't a theft. I technically own Adam. He was just on loan to the museum."

"Wow! That's wild! You know, Dr. Christopher, I have a scrapbook at home filled with printouts of stories about the Dolphdroids. I started it when I was a teenager. I always thought inrobation was the most amazing thing!"

Harry kept on talking excitedly. Adam waited for him to take a long enough breath for him to break in. At this rate, they could make another orbit before Harry would stop talking, and there wasn't time for that. Adam finally was able to say, "Yes, well, the Dolphdroids are in serious trouble. We've initiated this plan to save them. And, as you already know, we've run into a serious glitch."

"I know, you need me to give you a kick in the posterior and send you off to the moon at 25,000 miles an hour."

Adam's face glowed with a smile. "That, in essence, is exactly what I need you to do. Can you do it?"

"I have no idea, Dr. Christopher..." he paused. "Or should I be calling you Adam? Wow! This is crazy!" He gave a nervous chuckle.

"At this stage of the project it would be best to call me Adam. How soon can you rendezvous?"

"Ah, let's see." Adam and the crew in the attic heard Harry mumbling to himself as he looked at his instruments and did some calculating. "Two hours and fifteen minutes."

"Good," Max said. "We'll just take this one step at a time. Get fully fueled. We'll pay the bill. See you in two hours and fifteen minutes."

"Yep. Signing off," Harry said.

"Bill, did you copy?" Adam asked.

"I certainly did, Adam. Sounds like you have a big fan in Harry."

"I hope he's a fan that can make this happen," Adam said. "Max, you still there?"

"Where else? Of course I'm here."

"I need you to track down the schematics and specifications for a Troy Hauler. Could you do that pronto and upload them to me? I need to figure out where exactly I need to set the Defender on Harry's Troy Hauler."

Max took a breath and leaned forward. "Adam, you need to know that I've never heard of a Troy Hauler breaking orbit and going to escape velocity. That's done by the newer freight haulers, but I don't think it's ever been done by an old Troy Hauler."

"I figured as much, Max. But there's always a first time. Now, get me those schematics."

"Will do," Max said.

Within half an hour Max had located and uploaded the schematics. The freighter looked familiar to Adam. He recalled hiding his fighter craft under the belly of one during an intense battle. It had given him the element of surprise, just enough of an advantage for him to take out the enemy craft.

Adam rotated the image of the Troy Hauler on his viewing screen. It was a large ugly craft, just as he had remembered it, designed with practicality in mind, not aesthetics. It was rectangular, with two large engines in outboard formation on the back, one in each rear corner. A box-shaped cockpit sat on the top near the front, giving the impression that it was an afterthought in the design process. It did, however, give the pilot a 360 degree view. There was a loading dock in the square front of the craft, and two docks on each side. The top and bottom surfaces were irregular in several places where various pieces of operating equipment were housed, allowing easy access for maintenance. The craft was in stark contrast to the aerodynamic look of the new freighters that flew in atmosphere and space. The Troy Hauler had been built in space, operated solely in space, and would never see atmospheric flight. The craft's far-from-aerodynamic surface should make it possible to get a toe-hold with his craft so Harry could take the Defender to escape velocity.

The wait for Harry's arrival might have been nearly unbearable save for the fact that Adam was able to have an extended conversation with Ashley. The rest of the team had left the attic, giving them the privacy they needed.

After about a half hour, their conversation was interrupted. "This is Harry. Do you copy, Adam?"

"I copy, Harry. Ashley, find the others and get them back up to the attic. We're ready to rock 'n roll."

"I should be coming into visual range within 15 minutes or so. I had to wait in line to get fueled up, and this beast takes a heap of fuel when it's full. I don't usually fill it up because I don't always want to tie up so much money that way. But I'm going to need a full tank to get you on your way to the moon."

"Don't worry, Harry, you'll be reimbursed for the fuel," Max said, having just returned to the attic.

As Adam waited for the rendezvous he went over the details

of the plan. It would have been much easier if there had been a compatible docking mechanism, but there wasn't much of a need for a freighter and fighter to dock. Improvisation was the game plan.

Finally the cumbersome freighter drifted into view from the darkness of space. Harry began counting down the distance between the two craft. Adam fired his bottom-side controllers to move the Defender slightly above the Troy. Harry was trying to adjust the Troy's trajectory, but the freighter's controllers didn't seem to lend themselves to fine-tuned adjustments. One of the controllers didn't appear to be working at all.

"Leave the last minute adjustments to me, Harry."

"Glad to. I assume you have an idea how we can do this."

"I always have an idea," Adam said. "Whether it's always a good idea is another issue."

"Now that's comforting. Thanks for instilling such confidence in one of your biggest fans. You're making this plan up as you go, aren't you?" Harry was tilting his head up and looking over his right shoulder. Adam was firing one controller after another, moving the Defender into a position just above the Troy and toward the back of the freighter.

"You ever try to cross a stream of water by jumping onto a rock a couple of feet from shore?" Adam asked.

Watching the Defender move closer to the top-side of his freighter, Harry said, "Yeah."

"Well, Harry, I suspect you hadn't exactly figured out every step you were going to take, hadn't identified every rock you would need, to cross the stream. You just had at it. That's sort of what we're doing here. We're doing what seems the right thing to do and then we'll figure out what the next step is after that."

Adam was scanning the top side of the Troy and found the location he had identified on the schematics as the best place to set down. He briefly fired the top-side controllers as he lowered his landing gear. The Defender drifted down toward the Troy. Adam gave a quick burst on the rear controllers and the Defender inched forward. Harry felt the Defender make contact with the Troy and saw the craft's landing gear give a little; then the suspension on the gear pushed the craft back up. Adam countered the slight bounce by giving a short burst on the top-side controllers, and the Defender stayed in position, settling on the back of the Troy. Then Adam fired the forward controllers and the Defender rolled back a couple of feet until the two rear wheels bumped against a protruding cover that housed the OPS, the Orbital Positioning System, giving the landing gear the firm bracing the craft would need when Harry began firing his engines to take them to escape velocity.

"I'm in position, Harry."

"Welcome aboard, Dr... I mean, Adam. Just one concern, a biggy in my estimation. When I fire my engines there's going to be a sizable jolt, seeing as how I'm light with no cargo on board. I'll try to be gentle, but this ol' girl isn't always exact in her response to my controls. You could go flipping off the Troy's back."

"I've considered that possibility, Harry. I'm planning to fire my top-side controllers while you do your major burn. I'm hoping that keeps me hugging the Troy."

"Do you think you'll have enough thrust to hold you in place?" It was Bill from Attic Control.

"We won't know until we try," Adam replied.

"I'll do my best to power up slowly," Harry said. "By the way, what am I supposed to say to the authorities when they ask why I've broken orbit and I'm on a lunar trajectory?"

"Tell them the truth," Adam said.

"Are you sure that's advisable?" asked Risner from Attic Control.

"I'm not going to ask anyone to lie for me," Adam said. "Technically there's nothing illegal about Harry taking the Troy to a lunar trajectory, but lying to the authorities could get him in a lot of trouble. I'll already be on my way. Let them try and catch me."

"Harry, this is Bill Zucker. I've got the coordinates for you. If we're going to do this we'd better do it soon, before some orbit patrol gets interested in what's going on up there. Looks like your next window for leaving earth orbit is in 35 minutes and 20 seconds at my mark. Five, four, three, two, one, mark!"

"Mark! Let's do it," Harry said. "No sense taking another spin around the world first. Just download the data. This Troy Hauler may be old, but she's got a new brain. Just had the latest processor put in a month ago. She's as smart as I am."

"I assume that was meant to be reassuring," Max said.

"Uncle, uncle! Have some faith in your nephew! We'll make this happen. We'll find that next stepping stone across the creek, don't you worry."

"Well, I'm ready to go if you are, Adam," Harry said after the 35 minutes had passed, a time that seemed to have stretched to several hours for Adam. Harry had spent most of the time studying the telemetry from Attic Control and checking out his systems with an uncharacteristic attention to details. "Don't worry, I'm not going to mess this up," he had told his uncle half way through the 35 minute wait.

"You have enough fuel to do a reverse burn and get yourself back into earth orbit, right?" Adam asked, knowing the answer but wanting the reassurance.

"Yep. Says here I should be just fine. These old engines have never burned as long as they're going to have to for this whole thing to happen. It should clean them out real good."

"Then let's do it," Adam said. "Give me a countdown and I'll start firing my top-sides at the count of two so I'm snuggled down good on the back of the Troy."

"Implementing engine ignition on the count," came Harry's response. "Five, four three, two…"

Adam fired his top-side controllers. He felt the Defender push down on its landing gear's shock absorbers.

"…one, firing!"

Adam's internal gyros allowed him to feel the jolt as the Troy's engines came to life. His controllers seemed to be holding him onto the Troy. He felt the Troy's engines go up to full thrust, and the nose of the Defender began to lift. Adam quickly diverted more of the thrust to the front top controllers. The nose settled down lightly on the Troy again.

"According to the info on my screen, we'll be doing a five-minute seven-second burn," Harry informed Adam and Attic Control.

"Looks good from here," Adam said.

"And here," Bill added.

The five-minute seven-second burn seemed to go fast for Adam as he kept a close watch on the burn of his controllers.

"Engine shutdown," Harry announced. The Troy's engines went silent. "We're zipping along at 25,000 miles per hour. Wow! This old bucket of bolts has never seen this speed before!"

Adam shut down the top-side thrusters that had held him secure to the back of the Troy. "Thanks for the ride, Harry. You've done your part in rescuing this mission."

"You're welcome, Adam. Dr. Christopher, I've considered it an honor to be a part of what's happening. Just think, I did my bit to help rescue the Dolphdroids! Incredible!"

"We hope so, Harry, we hope so."

"How are you going to do that, anyway?" Harry asked.

"It's rather complicated, Harry."

"Sure. I understand. Ah, you can leave anytime you wish, sir."

"Thanks again, Harry." Adam fired the bottom-side thrusters and the Defender lifted off the back of the Troy Hauler. "Clear," Adam said.

"I'll give you some more distance," Harry said, and fired his thrusters that moved the Troy down and to the right of the Defender, turning the big craft 180 degrees until his main engines faced in the direction they were both hurtling at 25,000 miles per hour. Adam watched in his monitor as the huge engines on the Troy fired, lighting up the darkness like torches. Quickly the Troy receded, growing smaller in his monitor, as it slowed its speed forward while the Defender continued at escape velocity. Soon the light from the Troy's engines were the size of stars; then the dots of light disappeared as Harry shut them down again.

Space was silent, Adam noted. It wasn't so much an observation of physics as it was an emotional reality. He was alone in a strange body in a small craft heading toward a mission that was a long shot at succeeding at best. He might never see Rob, Randy, Ashley, or the earth again. His human body lay in suspended animation, perhaps never to be inhabited by him again. The earth already looked like a blue, brown, and white ball suspended in blackness. The moon loomed in the distance some 200,000 miles away. Its brilliant beauty was soon to be eclipsed by death to its inhabitants. He was their only hope. He was finally on his way to rescue them.

Chapter 28

Adam found the journey from earth to the moon to be surprisingly boring. There was little for him to do. Communication with those in the farmhouse attic was kept to a minimum, certainly very little chit-chat. They were reasonably confident that they had a secure communication link, but there was no sense taking a chance. As the moon loomed large and amazingly beautiful, Adam welcomed the preparation required to put the Defender into lunar orbit. It took hours of inputting data, rechecking the data, and then committing it to the on-board computer's flight plan program. The craft had been turned 180 degrees to put it into an engine-forward position for the final burn and rotated, putting it into a heads-up position in reference to the moon. While he waited for the moment, Adam checked and re-checked all the data and systems.

"Firing the main engines," Adam said. His anticipation suddenly built as he felt the shudder of the engines that would slow the Defender, allowing the moon to capture it and put it into lunar orbit.

Then the engines went silent. He checked his readings, as did those in attic control. "You're in lunar orbit!" Bill exclaimed.

Adam put the Defender into a heads-down position, tilted his head back, and watched as the lunar landscape slowly moved under him. After what seemed forever, he finally spotted Copernicus, the crater that was home to the Dolphdroid community. It looked beautiful, 56 miles in diameter and over 12,000 feet high from floor to rim. He knew the statistics well; he had been involved in the selection of the site.

With the Defender still flying rear-forward, Adam fired the main engines again, slowing the craft so that the lunar gravity could begin pulling him to the moon's surface. The plan was to land outside the rim of Copernicus. The terrain was flat, but it would still be a challenge landing the Defender. The craft had been designed to fly in atmosphere or space; landing on the surface of the moon, where there was gravity but no air, would be a new challenge. Max had helped set up the procedures and the computer was programmed to do most of the work, but it still would be touch and go.

The Defender's engines gimballed back and forth slightly, making the small corrections needed to keep the craft backward and downward at the right angle and speed. The engines were at 35 percent thrust. Adam trusted their calculations that they should have bingo, enough fuel left for a return flight to earth when the time came, but knowing the engines were consuming precious fuel prompted a tinge of concern.

"You're looking good from here," Bill encouraged.

"Everything appears to be nominal from here too," Adam responded.

"I wonder if the Dolphdroids are observing the descent and, if they are, how they're reacting," Rob said softly.

"Fifty feet to touchdown," the computer announced.

There was only the blackness of space straight ahead. Adam had his primary attention on the rear viewer, watching the lunar surface grow closer and closer.

"Make sure you identify a specific touchdown point before those engines start obscuring your view with the dust they'll be kicking up," Max warned.

"Max, I know. We've been over this a thousand times in simulation."

"Sorry, Adam. It's just that this is for real."

"I'm aware of the reality of the situation, Max." Adam was

watching through his rearview monitor. There were many small craters, and he wanted to stay away from every one of them. The Defender was descending backward at the right speed, a foot per second, and at the right angle, 75 degrees.

"Thirty feet to touchdown," the computer said. Adam activated the landing gear, hoping the small wheels wouldn't get buried in the lunar dust, assuming the craft landed right-side up as it was supposed to do.

"Twenty feet to touchdown," came the computer's update.

Adam gazed intently at the rearview monitor. The engines were beginning to kick up dust, blurring his view. He had to quickly identity a landing spot, take over manually from the computer, and try to hit the spot. There was a small crater to the right of the craft, about 10 feet across and maybe five feet deep. He had to stay away from there. To the left of the craft there was a large boulder; that was no place to go either. Straight back were two smaller craters next to each other, maybe eight feet across and three feet deep. He'd have to fly over them. Just beyond the two craters the surface appeared to be level.

"Ten feet to touchdown," the computer announced.

Adam's view was obscured by the dust kicked up by the engines. He'd be flying the craft blind for the final seconds. Guessing he was just passing over the two small craters, he gimballed the engines, leveling the craft to a position parallel with the surface.

"Five feet to touchdown," the computer stated.

Adam shut down the main engines and fired the bottom-side thrusters to ease the final feet of the fall to the surface. "Three feet, two feet, one foot, touchdown," the computer announced. Adam didn't need to be told. The craft hit the surface with the rear landing gear, bounced up again, and then came down with the nose gear landing first. He cut the bottom-side thrusters. The rear landing gear quickly followed the nose gear, hitting the surface. He burned the top-side thrusters. The shock absorbers of the front and rear landing gear caused the craft to bounce slightly again, but it felt as though both stayed on the surface. Adam cut the thrusters. Silence filled the cabin.

"The Defender has landed," he said.

Adam spent the next hour checking the Defender's systems, going over details of the mission with attic control, and having a final conversation with Rob and then with Ashley. Once he left the Defender he would be out of communication with anyone on Earth. It was a difficult sign off, but an hour and five minutes after touchdown Adam concluded the conversations with everyone. "Love ya, Rob; I love you, Ashley." He paused for a moment, turned off the communications system, and then shut down the Defender's operational systems. He had thought space was silent, but there had always been the soft sounds of the Defender's systems. Now there was complete silence.

His sat there for a few moments in the silence, considering his next move. He was about to climb down to the lunar surface. As Josh he would have needed a spacesuit. As Adam, he needed no such protection. He, like the other Dolphdroids, had been designed for the vacuum of space and the environment of the harsh lunar surface. A funny thought occurred to him: he could have flown the entire mission to the moon with the canopy open, like a ride in a convertible with the top down! His face glowed with the colors of a broad smile. He leaned forward and hit the egress button. The cabin hissed, releasing its air pressure, and the canopy slid open.

Adam looked up into the star-studded sky. It suddenly occurred to him that what was about to happen to him was like a birth. He was a mechanical object coming out of a larger mechanical object, not all that different from a child coming forth from its womb. He was leaving the womb that had brought him from the other world to this one. His leaving was a birth into a different world, where he was to join those he had become like, joining those who faced a death sentence to save them from that death sentence.

Adam slowly extracted his bulky frame from the seat, climbed out of the cockpit, and knowing he was dealing with much less gravity than on earth, jumped to the lunar surface. Dust billowed around his feet and drifted upward and outward in all directions.

His first concern was the landing gear of the Defender. The craft would have to do a rather complex bounce maneuver to lift off the lunar surface, and if the wheels were buried in the dust too deeply that could be a problem. With relief, he saw that the rear wheels were only up to their axles in dust, and the front gear sat even higher on the surface.

Adam looked at the open canopy, imagined it closing, and it did. Once again he was relieved; the thought command had worked. He didn't want to leave an unlocked vehicle. If a Dolphdroid happened upon the Defender he could easily cause unintentional or intentional harm. As always, it was best to lock your vehicle before leaving it – another humorous thought Adam realized – and his face glowed with the colors of a smile.

He turned from the Defender and began walking toward the outer ridge of Copernicus. It appeared to be about a mile away, but it loomed high, even from this distance.

He realized that he had to perfect the technique of walking on the moon. He experimented with hopping; he had seen vintage video clips of the first Apollo lunar astronauts getting around like that. He settled on taking long, bounding strides, just as the Dolphdroids had learned to do. At one-sixth the weight he had in his new body on earth, he felt a sense of freedom here on the moon's surface.

Shadows were sharp at their edges. A lack of atmosphere and moisture meant no diffusion of light. It was a world of stark contrast.

Climbing the 12,000 foot ridge of Copernicus proved daunting, even at one-sixth the gravity of earth. Several times he paused to find the route of least resistance. In some places the ridge was so steep that his feet slid backwards. Piles of rock, debris from the meteor impact that created the crater thousands of years ago, blocked him in several places and he had to pick a different route. He stopped occasionally to allow his power cells to catch up in their production of energy for his leg flexers.

Ten and a half hours after leaving the Defender, he reached the summit of the ridge. He paused to take in the vista. The ridge stretched to his left and right, growing smaller in the distance in both directions before nearly being obscured by the curve of the moon's surface. Ahead of him lay a great plain. It was difficult to imagine that the mountain range to his left and right was actually a full circle that was the rim of the Copernicus crater.

The journey down the ridge to the crater's plain was less difficult, but not without its challenges. There were still piles of rocks he had to navigate. Sometimes he was able to bound down steep inclines in long strides, like a delighted child running down a steep sand dune, but the trip to the base of the ridge still took several hours.

Starting across the plain, Adam realized that he wasn't thinking very clearly. His mechanical body wasn't tired but he was mentally exhausted. He would need to sleep. Finding a large rock, he positioned himself so that half of his body was in its shadow while the other half was in the light, the most energy efficient way for his brain to maintain a proper temperature in the cranial cradle. He locked his body into a standing position with a thought command, did the same to shut down all his sensual receptors by 75 percent, and was soon sound asleep.

It was a deep sleep, so Adam never saw, through his 25 percent sleep vision, the lunar car coming toward him. Metal hitting metal on his right shoulder woke Adam with a start. His visual receptors instantly came to 100 percent function as he jumped back. He saw a Dolphdroid lowering his right arm to his side, apparently having given him a tap on the shoulder that woke him.

Another Dolphdroid stood beside the first, the activated laser pick in his hand aimed directly at Adam. Both of them wore robes.

It was Adam's first opportunity to receive communication through the low level FM signal he had designed for the Dolphdroids to use. Communicating via the FM frequency had been part of his therapy using a communications simulator. Apparently the simulations had been accurate; he had no trouble understanding what the Dolphdroid said: "Come with us."

The Dolphdroid with the laser pick ordered him to sit in the second bench of the lunar buggy with him, while the other Dolphdroid climbed into the first bench behind the controls. As they bounced along the lunar landscape at top speed, he recalled how they had sent three of the lunar buggies in the third year of the colonization. He remembered the first time he had seen one of the vehicles. It had been in a warehouse in Detroit, the location of their manufacture. He would never have guessed then that he would someday ride one of them on the lunar surface under these conditions. At least he didn't have to walk the remaining miles to the colony. He tried communicating with his new companions, but they remained silent.

276

To calm his fears and to pass the time, Adam rehearsed the history of the development of the lunar buggy. Trucks to haul the excavated lunar materials had been sent up the first year because they were needed for the work the Dolphdroids were required to do. In the second year of colonization the Dolphdroids had requested a smaller vehicle that could be used for their own transportation; that had prompted the design and manufacture of the buggies. Adam glanced at the Dolphdroid seated next to him, his hand firmly grasping his laser pick. The Dolphdroid stared straight ahead. The driver focused on his driving. "What are your names?" Adam asked. "My name is Adam." Both remained non-responsive. Obviously they had been instructed not to talk to this strange visitor. He yearned to connect with his creation, but they would have nothing of it.

Adam couldn't help but be fixated by the robes they wore. The Dolphdroid next to him was clad in an all-gray robe while the driver's was gray and maroon. Adam had the distinct sense that these two had been sent to retrieve him, and that they weren't acting on their own initiative. He found their silence unsettling. The bottom line, he realized, was that he was in custody.

It was a long ride to the colony. At one point he could stand the silence no longer. He turned to the gray clad Dolphdroid next to him and asked, "Are we going to the colony?" The Dolphdroid gave no response, continuing to stare straight ahead. With nothing else to do, Adam watched the landscape. As they drew nearer to the colony he observed that the frequency of tracks left by vehicles and Dolphdroids increased. On earth the wind and rain worked constantly to erase the telltale signs of people, but here in the windless, rainless environment of the atmosphere-free moon every mark of activity remained unless it was obscured by more recent activity. The lunar surface had a long memory.

Eventually the colony came into view as they crested a small hill. The low structures were moon-tone in color, their appearance like that of smooth-surfaced adobe, made out of a composite of lunar dust and what was called Level III Bonder. Adam knew that the visible structures were only a small part of the colony's habitat; much of it was subterranean.

Adam was experiencing mixed feelings as he rode through the colony in the back of the car. The street surface was solid, made of the same mix as the structures. It kept the dust level down. Adam remembered a long discussion about a solution for the dusty streets when the colony was first built, and the decision to use the same composite for the streets and the structures. This was all here – the Dolphdroids and their colony – because it had been his vision for it to be here. Now they were in trouble and he was here to help them, but his reception up to this point was anything but warm. A few Dolphdroids, all robed, were walking around and glanced their way as they drove by, probably noticing the "naked" Dolphdroid in the back seat.

They pulled up to one of the larger structures, a building with two triangular windows, point down, and a large clear dome that capped the structure.

With the first words spoken to him since being apprehended, the Dolphdroid who had been guarding him said, "Get out and follow me." The driver joined them.

Three Dolphdroids, one wearing a green cape, another in a red, and the third in a two-tone blue and green cape, were leaving the building. They kept glancing at Adam and his two escorts as they made their way down the street.

The access/egress door opened, and Adam was led into the building. He immediately picked up on his FM receptor a cacophony of conversations. With the guard staying closely by his side, the driver led them down a set of stone steps. As they descended the stairs, a large round room some thirty feet in diameter came into view; it was the source of most of the conversations Adam had been picking up. Twenty or more Dolphdroids gathered in small groups, some seated at tables, some at chairs arranged in a circle, and some standing. The room became silent; every face turned toward Adam as he took the last step of the stairs. When his two escorts came to a stop Adam decided it was wise for him to do the same. The atmosphere was thick with silence and stares.

"Bring our guest over here," came a firm and commanding voice from a Dolphdroid at one of the far tables. The Dolphdroid who had given the order was reclined on a large stone bench with one leg extended on the bench. A cape, brilliant red with silver lining, and considerably larger than those the others wore, cascaded from his shoulders and flowed over the bench. There was no mistaking that this Dolphdroid, with his commanding voice, large cape, and body language, was the leader.

With a firm grip on his right arm, the driver of the car pulled Adam toward the Dolphdroid in charge. Suddenly Adam felt, for the first time, a hint of shame at being naked. He and the team had discussed the advisability of bringing a robe on the mission, but with Elliot's attack imminent, there had been no time to pack a suitcase. It wasn't that clothing covered any private parts; the Dolphdroids had none. Yet the wearing of clothes, particularly a robe, had been one of the results of their fall from perfect performance. Their stares were not so much because he was a stranger in their midst, but because he was naked.

"May I have a robe?" Adam asked.

A Dolphdroid to Adam's left, wearing a multi-layered robe with a cape, took off the cape and placed it on Adam's shoulders. Adam glanced at the benevolent Dolphdroid and said, "Thank you." Then he glanced at the others, detecting a noticeable expression of relief in the color display of many of their faces, but not the leader's. It seemed to Adam that he was disappointed that someone had come to the aid of the stranger standing before him.

Adam was here on a mission. He had inrobated himself among them for a reason. With new resolve, he looked directly into the face of the red-robed leader. This Dolphdroid, whichever one he was, possessed power and authority that he hadn't been given from Earth above. Unit One was to be the leader, but by the molded shoulder number just partially visible under his robe, Adam could see that this was either unit three or unit thirty-something.

"What is your name?" the leader demanded.

"Adam. What is yours?"

The leader's facial color turned red, indicating that he was annoyed at the question being reflected back to him. He glanced at a Dolphdroid to his right, who was apparently a personal attendant of some kind. "Tell our guest."

The Dolphdroid paused a moment, gazing at the leader, then looked at Adam and said, "Agur. This is Agur. He leads us."

"Not all of us," came a soft but distinct reply from somewhere in the crowd by the stairs, obviously counting on the distance from the self-proclaimed leader and the crowd to provide anonymity.

"Enough!" Agur shouted, looking in the general direction of

the group by the stairs. Most of their faces faded to white, the color of intimidation and fear.

Agur turned his attention back to Adam. "You're not one of the units of the colony; you have no shoulder number. We saw the burn of a craft's engine as you dropped from orbit. You're from Earth, aren't you?" It was more of a demand than a question.

"Yes, I'm from Earth. I'm the first of your kind – of our kind," Adam said, taking his eyes off Agur and looking around the room, wanting the truth to be heard by all of them. "I'm the Dolphdroid prototype."

"I heard about him," one of them behind Adam whispered to another.

"Me, too," said another in a soft voice.

"Quiet!" Agur shouted. In a tone that tried to sound more controlled, he added, "I'm trying to carry on a conversation." No one spoke. Looking at Adam again he asked, "Why have you come to the colony? Are you running from the humans or are you here to help the humans?"

Adam glanced around the room. Every visual receptor was focused on him; he had to measure his words carefully. He realized how crucial his response would be. "I am neither pro-earth or pro-lunar. I am pro-Dolphdroid."

"But that means you have to be anti-human," a Dolphdroid seated at a nearby table interjected.

"True words," another responded. Others seem to mumble agreement.

"Why must being pro-Dolphdroid and pro-human be mutually exclusive?" Adam asked.

Agur gave a hearty laugh that had an edge of spite. He paused a moment, leaned forward and said, "Because the humans are against us, that's why. You should know that! They've made the decision to decommission us, as they call it. It's extermination, plain and simple. We won't stand for it. We will not die! The humans are a threat to us; they're our enemies. And you..." Agur paused, pointing a finger at Adam. "...And you have come from Earth. How do we know that you're not a spy?"

"Why would Earth send a spy now?" Adam asked. "There would be no purpose for it. As you've already said, they plan to do away with the colony. I'm not here to spy on you. I'm here as one of you, to be with you, to help you."

"Then you're a fool," Agur said. "The death sentence has been imposed on every Dolphdroid. Our life value rating is only three. From what we've been able to figure out, the decommissioning order demands that 450 life-value points be terminated, which means all 146 of us must die. You make it 147. You've walked into a death camp. Didn't you know this?"

"I was aware of the order," Adam said.

"Then my original assessment of you was right; you're a fool. We are not going to go without a fight – a fight we can win!" Once again his face turned red with rage. "You pose a threat to us, you who call yourself Adam."

"But, Agur, he came to join us. How could he hurt our plans?" The Dolphdroid who spoke was in the far corner of the room, his boldness encouraged by his safe distance from Agur.

"I'm not sure of the exact nature of the threat to the colony, but I'm certain he's a threat; that's all I need to know," Agur said. Turning his attention to one of the Dolphdroids who had apprehended Adam, he ordered, "Migbe, bring me my laser pick."

As Migbe dutifully turned to leave, a gasp went up from several Dolphdroids in the room.

"Are you going to kill him?" someone asked.

"We can't take any chances. He might be a spy. He might sabotage our plans. There's no other way," Agur replied.

Chapter 29

Migbe had left to find a laser pick. The other Dolphdroid who had apprehended Adam moved closer and firmly grasped Adam's upper arm. The Dolphdroid wanted to be sure that he wouldn't escape.

For the first time since landing, Adam feared for his life. Dying might be the only way to save the Dolphdroids, but the time wasn't right. He recalled having told his son on more than one occasion that timing often defines whether a deed is good or bad and that it's the difference between success and failure. This was not a good time to die.

Migbe was back within moments. Adam had seen a pile of mining tools outside the entry as he was escorted inside. Apparently one of the tools had been a laser pick, which Migbe was now carrying in his right hand. It had been designed as a tool for blasting rock into fragments in the mining process, and had obviously become the weapon of choice in the lunar colony. How easily a tool can become a weapon, Adam thought. Being philosophical in times of stress was a way to keep one's wits about him, and Adam knew he was doing that. He had come to be among the Dolphdroids, to

283

save them at great effort and expense, and he wasn't about to blow it now. His words and actions had to be measured.

"Are you so afraid of me that you have to kill me?" Adam asked Agur. "True courage allows a person to coexist with the unknown and unproven."

Agur was taken aback by Adam's statement. He had been ready for a simple but impassioned plea for mercy. Adam's boldness had thrown him off, causing him to pause before responding.

Agur's hesitation created a few moments of silence. A Dolphdroid standing behind and to the left of Adam, emboldened by Adam's statement, suggested, "What would it hurt to let him live?"

"He seems harmless enough to me," chimed in another. There was a mumble of agreement. Agur's leadership, though strong, apparently wasn't strong enough to give him complete control in the colony, Adam reflected.

Adam took advantage of the momentum being generated in his favor. "I've come to be a help to all of you," he said, glancing around the room. "I'm from Earth, and you feel betrayed by Earth, but there's conflict there just as there is here. There's a conflict beyond you that's about you. I've not come to fight against you but to fight for you."

"But they want to terminate us," Agur argued. "How do we know that you aren't here to make certain it happens? Can you prove that you're not pro-Earth?" Agur knew that it was a poor choice of words the moment he spoke them.

"Some of us are pro-Earth, Agur," a Dolphdroid from the crowd said. "That doesn't mean we want to give in to whatever evil forces there are and lie down and die. We all want to live. It's just that some of us don't believe that being militant is the way to solve our problems."

"Listen to Agur," demanded the Dolphdroid holding Adam's arm.

"No, we don't have to listen to Agur. He's not Unit One. He's just assumed that position," argued another Dolphdroid behind Adam. There were muted conversations that, as best as Adam could determine, were expressing both points of view. It was clear that Agur didn't have a clear mandate to lead.

"Perhaps this stranger among us can be more useful alive

than dead," Agur stated, trying to regain control. "If he's against us – and I suspect he is – perhaps he has friends who would like to see him stay alive. He might make a good hostage. I think we'll hold off killing him for now. Nastar, put a locator on him and secure it. If he attempts to leave the colony we'll know about it. If he tries, kill him on sight."

Adam was relieved. Agur had found a way to back down without appearing to do so. Some of the Dolphdroids probably saw through the charade, but at least he wouldn't be executed on the spot. As soon as Nastar returned with a locator and fastened it around Adam's ankle, Agur said, "Leave my presence. You have wasted enough of my time." With a wave of his arm that made his cape ripple, he added, "Be gone with you!"

Adam turned and started to make his exit. The crowd of Dolphdroids parted, clearing a path for him. Once outside in the lunar brightness he stopped and looked around. Where to now? he wondered.

Five Dolphdroids left after Adam did. One, wearing a short blue cape, spoke first. "You stood up to Agur. No one's done that for some time." Glancing around at the other four, he continued, "I don't know about the rest of you, but it's given me the courage to think thoughts about Agur I have not allowed myself to ponder for a long time. There's something about him that doesn't seem right to me, and never has."

"Me, either," chimed in the one standing across from Adam in the informal circle that had formed. "I know the future looks grim. Agur thinks he can fix it – he might be making things worse."

"What happened to Unit One?" Adam asked.

"Oh, he's around, but Agur has him so intimidated that he doesn't resist him," one of them replied.

"He doesn't care that Agur took his rightful position given him by the creator of the Dolphdroids?" Adam asked. It seemed strange to refer to himself in the third person, but it was important to keep his identity a secret at this stage of the mission.

"I guess he cares, but he figures that maybe Agur has more leadership abilities," said one of the other Dolphdroids.

"Agur's told him that he has no leadership skills so often that he believes it," added another of the Dolphdroids.

Adam glanced around the group. "You all have taken names. What is Unit One's name?"

"Prota," one of them replied.

Adam looked at him and asked, "What is your name?"

"Hasper."

Adam asked the remaining four to introduce themselves, and tried to commit them to memory as each took his turn: Ober, Cosber, Rimmer, and Lespin.

Adam began to walk down the street and the others followed. The basic layout was familiar to him. Although the Dolphdroids had been given total creative control in its construction, the team on earth had closely observed the colony's remarkable progress. Walking down the street, Adam thought about how the colony had drifted so far from the Contract of Life. They were a fallen race, a race of sentient beings he had created to live a life far better than the one they were living. It made him profoundly sad.

The five Dolphdroids were joined by two more near the resources conservation module when Ober introduced Adam to Nibin and Ferber. At Adam's request they entered the module, and he was given a brief tour. This was where water and oxygen were extracted from rock, both necessary for the maintenance of the dolphin brain each Dolphdroid possessed.

Leaving the conservation module, the Dolphdroids led Adam down the street to the module that controlled the solar disk array, a farm of approximately a thousand solar collectors that bordered one end of the colony. The energy was converted in this facility into broadcast form, sent to a receiver in earth orbit, and then relayed to the various life-cylinders.

The farm wasn't producing any energy for earth at the present time; that was obvious to Adam, because he knew something about how the system worked. This was a surprise to him; apparently it was a new development within the last few hours, since his arrival on the moon. "Why is no electricity being produced?" he asked.

"Agur ordered it shut down just before you appeared in the colony," Ober stated.

Adam wondered how the life-cylinders in earth orbit were doing without energy from the solar array, their main source of energy. They had reserve power and contingency plans, but this development certainly had everyone in the life-cylinders and on earth scurrying to compensate for the loss of lunar power. Why would Agur do such a thing? Out of spite for earth? Probably, but it only served to drive another nail in the coffin of the Dolphdroids' fate.

"Show me the duplex module," Adam said. The module, so named for being two modules connected by an enclosed walkway, housed the coordination of the mining operation.

"It's shut down, too," Rimmer said.

"By order of Agur," Lespin added.

As they walked, they came upon the module called the commissary. This module had intrigued Adam when he first heard about its construction six years ago. It was a place where Dolphdroids could buy, sell, and trade items that they made. He had also learned that it contained game rooms, including a large room for team games.

Stopping at the entrance, Adam looked at the others and said, "Let's go in." Without waiting for a response from his companions, he entered the module, turned right, and entered a gymnasium-sized room. "Hoop ball," Lespin explained. Adam nodded as he watched two teams of Dolphdroids in two different colors of loosely fitting jerseys, move with surprising agility up and down the court. It was the Dolphdroids' version of basketball. He had heard the ball was nearly solid rubber with a small center of compressed air to allow it to bounce in the one-sixth gravity like a basketball would on earth. When the ball changed teams, according to some rule Adam wasn't familiar with, most of the players looked in Adam's direction. Some did so surreptitiously, while others blatantly stared. Walking down the side of the hoop ball floor, Adam and the seven entered another play area. A half dozen Dolphdroids were taking large circular disks the size of serving trays and sliding them, with considerable force, along the floor to the other end of the room where they were attempting to knock over rock pillars about a half foot in circumference and two feet tall. It appeared to be a cross between bowling and shuffleboard. "Slide and Score is what it's called," Cosber volunteered as Adam watched them play. The action stopped for a few moments while they looked at Adam; then they continued their game.

Adam and his companions made their way into another room

where a half dozen Dolphdroids were playing computer games. What caught Adam's attention were three Dolphdroids, each standing motionless and connected by a line to three free standing data terminals with lights glowing and flashing. Two additional machines remained dark and unused. It was obvious that the three machines were doing some serious data processing. What intrigued Adam most were the faces of the Dolphdroids. They glowed a brighter yellow than he had ever seen on a Dolphdroid face before.

"What are they doing?" Adam asked no one in particular.

There was a long pause. Adam glanced at each of the seven around him. Finally Rimmer broke the silence. "Those are full-reality generators. When you're interfaced to one of those machines," he said, raising an arm and pointing, "you're detached from reality and are able to experience whatever you have programmed to experience."

"How long do the programs run?" Adam asked.

"Indefinitely, but forty-five hours is the maximum, because then they need to have oxygen and water restored," said Cosber.

"I assume that they go to the commissary for that?" Adam asked.

"They ought to, but someone usually retrieves the oxygen and water for them so they can stay with their programs," Rimmer said, looking at Hasper.

"Do you get the oxygen and water for them, Hasper?" Adam asked.

Hasper's face turned pink with embarrassment. "Yes, sometimes. Tader pleads with me to replenish his needs, so I do. Lately Bilgrade and Starsa have synchronized their schedules with Tader's so I bring all three their oxygen and water."

"We've argued with Hasper many times about this. He shouldn't help Tader, Bilgrade, and Starsa stay plugged in and tuned out," Rimmer said with annoyance as he stared at Hasper.

"This is what you call this pleasure addiction? Being 'plugged in and tuned out'?" Adam asked.

Cosber nodded. "They're called chip addicts and the full-reality generators are usually called pleasure machines." Cosber paused, shook his head, and added with sadness, "It's rendered the three of them useless. Others have tried the programs – I'll have to admit I have too – and some seem to get by using them recreationally, but they're addictive. You can live in a make-believe world where everything is good and nothing is bad, where there's always instant gratification and no delayed gratification, and where it's all pleasure and no pain, not even the pain of ending the pleasure, except for a momentary interruption for water and oxygen."

"When are they due to come out of the program for replenishment?" Adam asked.

Hasper checked his internal clock. "In two hours and fifteen minutes," he said.

"We'll come back then," Adam stated in a tone that indicated that his decision was not open to discussion.

They visited the maintenance module next, where a Dolphdroid was working on a vehicle. He didn't look up to see who had entered until Hasper said, "Adam, this is Prota. Prota, this is Adam."

"So you're Unit One," Adam said.

Prota turned to look at Adam, his face turning orange, indicating shame. "I heard about your coming. Glad to meet you. Yes, I was Unit One, but it hasn't worked out for me to stay as Unit One. Agur felt he could do a better job. I resisted for a while, but I eventually gave in. I don't like what he does, but I couldn't match him when it came to being a leader. I'm not as good at leading as he is, so I'm not really Unit One."

"It sounds as if Agur's convinced you of that, but it's not true," Adam said.

"Prota would make a far better leader, but he's let Agur intimidate him," Lespin added.

"You know, Prota, that you have been made equal to any other Dolphdroid by the creator," Adam said, "but you have allowed Agur to create a difference that doesn't exist. You weren't called to be the leader because you're better. You're the leader simply because that's what you were called to be. All of you are equal to each other but different from each other – and you, Prota, are different in that you were appointed to be the leader."

"I know that's what the Contract of Life says, but it's sometimes difficult to believe, especially when I come face to face with Agur."

Adam glanced around the group and then back at Prota. "Agur is a legend in his own mind. He isn't better than you; he isn't better than any of you. He has gained the upper hand because you've allowed him to do so. His greatest strength comes from your own weakness. Be strong and he can't be stronger than you."

Prota shook his head. "That's difficult to believe."

"Belief is often difficult," Adam said, glancing around the group. Then he changed the subject. "Prota, what were you working on when we came in?"

Prota glanced behind him at a medium-sized personal transport vehicle. "Agur has me fixing up this old Nexter 3000."

Adam nodded. "It was used until recently to transport up to 15 people between earth orbit and the lunar surface. Why are you repairing it?"

Prota took a moment to answer. "I'm not sure. It was the next maintenance assignment I got from one of his assistants, the one named Migbe."

"We've met," was all Adam said, remembering his wake-up call from the nap he was taking during his hike to the colony.

"I asked Prota the same question," Ferber said. "It seems to me that Agur must have something in mind for the craft, and it isn't going to be good."

"No doubt," Ober chimed in.

When it was time for the three chip addicts to come out of their programs, Adam and his new friends were standing nearby, waiting. Bilgrade was the first to stir. Small spasms jerked his arms, he began to raise his head, and his body became more erect. He looked at them, glancing back and forth. He was awake. By now Tader and Starsa were coming around, too.

"Where's the water and oxygen, Hasper?" Bilgrade asked.

"We don't have any," Hasper replied.

"Why not? You know that's what we need!" Bilgrade was angry.

By now Tader was fully in touch with reality. He looked at Adam. "Who are you?"

Starsa was now fully awake, too. All three chip addicts stared at Adam; then Bilgrade spoke. "I've never seen you before."

"It surprises me that you remember anything about the real world, Bilgrade. You three have been plugged in and tuned out for so long that I can't imagine you know anything about anything,"

Lespin said.

"And I really don't care," replied Starsa.

"Neither do I," said Bilgrade.

"So get us the oxygen and water!" Tader demanded, staring at Hasper.

Hasper hesitantly started to move, his face turning pink.

"No, Hasper," Adam said in a soft voice, putting a hand on Hasper's shoulder. "Let them get their own supplies. By helping them you're only hurting them. You become a contributor to their addiction."

"It seems to me that you're nothing but trouble," Tader said, disconnecting his line from the full-reality generator and taking a step toward Adam. Following Tader's lead, the other two addicts disconnected their lines and stepped forward.

"If my recollections are right, you have approximately twenty minutes left on your oxygen and about thirty minutes left on your water supply," Adam said calmly. "You can stay here and talk until your time runs out or you can get going. I suggest the latter."

Tader was giving serious consideration to what Adam had said, unable to escape the logic. Glancing at Bilgrade and Starsa, he said, "Let's go." With his face blooming red with rage, Tader gave a final glance at Hasper and stomped out of the game room with Bilgrade and Starsa in tow.

Adam walked to the doorway and stopped, watching the three hastily make their way through the middle of the hoopball game, forcing the game to stop. The players' faces momentarily flashed with annoyance, then they continued their play. Adam turned his attention to the game. Ober saw the curious look on Adam's face and approached him and began to explain the game to him, more out of a desire to distract everyone from the tense confrontation that had just happened than out of any deep urge to explain the game.

The game soon came to an end, with the winning players making it obvious they were glad about the win. Before the celebrating was over, the three chip addicts returned.

Adam glanced their way as they headed back to their machines and said, "How about a game of hoopball? You'll probably be able to teach me a few things."

The three laughed. "Hoopball is a silly game with little

291

gratification. Why would we trade the machines for that?" Tader said with disdain.

"There are ways of experiencing pleasure without escaping from your world. The best pleasures are enjoyed in a world that isn't all pleasure. Easy pleasure can be your enemy," Adam replied, focusing his attention on Starsa. Adam sensed that he was less attached to his addiction.

"But the pleasure machines are harmless," Bilgrade argued.

"No, they're not," Adam retorted. "I know very little about these machines, but I suspect that you've had to increase the output on the machine on a regular basis to keep the pleasure level up to where you want it. Am I right?"

They seemed surprised at Adam's insight. "What's wrong with that?" asked Tader.

"What's wrong is that you'll finally get to the point where it will over-stimulate both the biological tissue and the assisted thought processor. You'll probably go into a long-term shutdown mode and die from lack of oxygen or water."

"That might be better than this world," Tader argued.

"You were created for more than the pursuit of pleasure," Adam continued. "In fact, true pleasure isn't something to be sought. It's the by-product of being and doing what you were created to be and do. Pleasure is a surprise you find as you live out your intended purpose. That kind of pleasure – the pleasure of living out your purpose for being – isn't addicting; it's freeing. On the other hand, in trying to find ultimate freedom in the pursuit of pure pleasure you've made yourselves captives." Adam glanced back and forth among the three. "Let's play a game," he added.

Tader shook his head. "It's totally out of the question." He turned and strode toward the pleasure machines. Bilgrade and Starsa hesitated, looking at each other.

"One game," Adam said quietly.

There was a pause. "One game," Starsa replied.

"Just one game," Bilgrade added.

They chose sides and began to play. It didn't take long for Adam to realize that his therapy to help him adjust to life in his android body wasn't the same as physical training for a sport. His mind, processor, and body didn't always coordinate as they should, and it inspired laughter from those who watched, and even from a few of the players of both teams. The game was soon over.

Adam tried to convince Bilgrade and Starsa not to return to the pleasure machines. "There's real life here, not with the machines," he concluded.

"The hoopgame was fun, but I'd miss the pleasure machine too much. I know some think we're throwing away our lives on them. OK, maybe I need to broaden my horizons. I'll try to cut back, but I don't see any harm in going to the machine for entertainment," Bilgrade said.

"You won't be able to cut back a little," Adam said.

"I think I can," Bilgrade said, and with that he headed back to the machine.

"I'd like to give real living a try again," said Starsa. "I have to admit that on occasion I've felt like life's passing me by while I keep myself entertained. The pleasure of the hoopball game wasn't pure pleasure like the machine delivers, but it was fun playing all of you – especially laughing at you, Adam. It may not have been pure pleasure, but it was real pleasure." Starsa paused. "It's not easy walking away from the pleasure machine."

"We know it isn't, Starsa," Lespin said, "but we'll help you."

"Come with us," Adam said.

Starsa turned and looked at Tader and Bilgrade standing motionless by their machines, already deep into their programs. They looked like statues, he thought – inanimate, lifeless statues. He turned his back to them and walked quickly to catch up with Adam and the others.

As they exited the commissary module, Adam noted that the shadows were lengthening. In a matter of hours the sunset terminator would be past and Copernicus would be in darkness. It was a strange way to exist, he thought, where light and dark go through a 29 day cycle instead of a 24 hour cycle. With personal illumination from a high-powered beam on their foreheads and another on their chests, the Dolphdroids managed to live and work during the dark cycle of the moon. Their Dolphin brains still needed a regular shorter cycle of sleep, like his human brain did, but over the years they had adjusted well to the 29 day lunar cycle.

Nibin interrupted Adam's thoughts. "Do you really think the ERR Center will terminate us?"

"Call it for what it is, Nibin; it's murder, out-and-out murder.

Termination is too soft a word," Rimmer corrected.

"I'm afraid so," Adam said. "The head of the ERR Center, Imus Hartung, seems determined to do it. That's why I came."

"What do you think you can do for us?" asked Ober.

"I think I can save the colony," Adam replied.

"How?" Lespin asked.

"Sometimes it's best not to say too much too soon. You'll know what you need to know when you need to know it."

Ober shook his head, "You're speaking in riddles, and not making sense."

Adam didn't respond, but his face glowed yellow with a smile. He looked from Ober to Rimmer as they walked. "You have something on your mind, Rimmer. Speak freely."

Rimmer didn't say anything for a few steps. "I don't mean to sound disrespectful, Adam, but we hardly know you. The sky blazes with the light of a craft from Earth with you on board. You stand up to Agur, something no one was willing to do. Somehow you inspire hope, but you also inspire questions, and I guess that's what makes me uncomfortable. I want to believe you and to trust you, but it's not easy."

"Doubts are OK, Rimmer. Faith and doubt always coexist. If something is for certain it doesn't take faith to believe in it, because it's a known fact. Faith can only exist where doubt is possible. I'll give you reasons enough to have faith, as more faith is required of you. My job is to inspire faith in you. Your job is to let yourself be inspired to have faith. At this point it might be good to remember that you have little to lose but much to gain by trusting me."

Their faces glowed yellow with smiles. Just then Nastar came stomping toward them and came up to Adam. "Agur wants to see you right away." He put his arm on Adam's arm to emphasize the fact that he didn't have a choice in the matter. Migbe, who had been a few steps behind Nastar, came up to Adam and took a position on his other side.

Adam's followers started to tighten into a circle around Adam and the two. Adam was glad to see their courage and commitment, but knew this wasn't the time to stir up trouble. "It's OK, I'll go with them," he said. Then, glancing from Nastar to Migbe, he said, "Let's go."

Chapter 30

Agur was seated at the far end of the large room, surrounded by his followers, just as he had been when Adam first met him. Agur had posed himself in the same kingly way as before, slightly leaning back in a chair with one foot extended and his cape flowing over his bent knee. He was engaged in giving extended instructions to one of the Dolphdroids, demeaning Adam by making him wait like a subject before a king. Adam was flanked by Migbe and Nastar, while Adam's friends remained at a distance, near the base of the entrance stairway.

Finally Agur finished his orders for the attentive Dolphdroid, who nodded dutifully, took a couple of steps back, turned, and left hurriedly. Agur turned his head slightly to look at Adam.

"I understand you've been interfering with the Dolphdroids' right to have a little rest and relaxation at the pleasure machines." Adam saw Agur shift his gaze slightly, looking beyond Adam toward the Dolphdroids near the stairway. Adam resisted turning to look, certain Agur was looking at Starsa. Agur wasn't happy that

Starsa had gone from an inanimate chip addict to being a friend of the newcomer.

"I didn't force Starsa to stop using the pleasure machine. I encouraged him and helped him, as did some of the Dolphdroids with me, but Starsa made the decision to forsake the machine. If you force someone to break a habit, you've done him no good, because the habit still has the person enslaved. Freedom only comes with exercising personal choice. We simply gave Starsa the help he needed to make that choice. Two of his friends were given the same help, but they used their freedom of choice to remain enslaved to their machines." Adam glanced at Starsa, turned back to Agur, and added, "Ask him yourself."

"My problem is not Starsa but you, stranger. Ever since you've appeared among us you've been nothing but trouble."

"That's quite a compliment coming from you, Agur. Trouble for you, perhaps, but not necessarily trouble for some of the others." Adam's face glowed yellow with a smile.

Agur leaned forward, striking another kingly pose, his face turning red. Extending an arm and pointing a finger at Adam, he said softly and slowly, "I'm warning you, stranger; I have had all I want of you. I have the ways and means of removing you permanently, and I don't mean sending you back where you came from. Death has already come to this colony, and one more certainly won't matter, particularly if it's yours."

Agur anticipated a response from Adam, but Adam stood before him, unmoving and silent. It was making Agur uncomfortable. Finally Agur broke the silence. With a wave of his arm he exclaimed, "Be gone with you!"

Adam remained motionless for a few more seconds, then slowly turned and left, his friends falling in behind him.

"That was not good," Rimmer said as they walked out into the dusty lunar street.

Adam glanced at him, "Why not?"

Rimmer shook his head, his gaze focused on the ground as they walked. "Because Agur feels threatened by you and may do something desperate."

"I agree," added Cosber. "He had things going his way until you came along. He won't tolerate your interference."

Adam replied, "My main concern right now is to get some

rest. I'm getting groggy. Where do you suggest I sleep?"

Caught off guard by the shift in subject, there was silence for a moment. Finally Ober spoke up, pointing ahead. "That module over there. It's where most of us take rest."

As they walked in the direction of the module Lespin asked, "Are there other Dolphdroids on earth that you lived with?"

"No," Adam said. "I guess you could say I'm the first and last."

"First and last?" Ober asked. "I don't understand."

"I don't think now's the time to try to explain," Adam replied. "Let's just say I had a life beyond that of being Adam."

"As a dolphin, you mean?" Ober asked.

"No, not as a dolphin," Adam replied. He saw their faces glow gray with confusion. "I don't expect you to understand," he added.

"Try us," Ober said.

"I think I should answer that question at a later time."

"Were you sent by our creator?" Hasper asked.

Adam just looked at Hasper. Hasper nodded and said, "You'll answer that at a later time, right?"

"Right," Adam replied.

They arrived at the dormer module. Nibin, Ferber, and Hasper said they also needed to rest. The others bid them goodbye and continued walking down the street. Entering the dormer, Adam found four other Dolphdroids in sleep mode, standing silently in the small room. Adam and his three friends each found a place to stand. Adam's face was the first to glow blue with sleep.

"We want to show you something," Rimmer said when Adam and the three joined the others at the commissary. Prota was there, apparently willing to risk Agur's wrath.

"It will take some time," added Cosber. "What we want to show you is about 300 miles from here."

"I hope we're not going to walk there. I don't have my lunar legs yet." Adam was half jesting, but also was recalling the long trek from his landing site to where he was apprehended.

Rimmer said, "We can use one of the low-level transport vehicles." Looking around at the group, he said, "There's only room for four. I suspect we'd all like to go, so why don't we draw lots?

Adam, please hold a hand behind your back with either one or two digits extended. We'll all do the same. Whoever agrees with you moves on to the next round, and the next, until only three remain. If too many guess wrong in the last round, we'll do it over again until there are three that agree with you."

"Interesting," Adam said. "But I would like Prota to go. Let's draw lots for the two remaining positions." On the fifth effort the selection was complete. Cosber and Lespin would join Prota in escorting Adam to the site.

Prota remained motionless as Adam, Cosber, and Lespin began walking. Cosber was the first to notice Prota's hesitancy; he stopped and looked at Prota. Adam and Lespin stopped too, looking at Prota.

Prota glanced from one to the other and said, "I know you want me to go, Adam, but I'm not sure I should leave my work that long. Agur might find out about my absence."

"Haven't you been pulling your share of work around here?" Adam asked.

"Yes, he has," said Cosber.

Adam continued looking to Prota for a reply.

Prota nodded, "Yes, I have."

"He's been working far more hours than he should be," Lespin added.

Adam walked over to Prota and put his hand on his right shoulder. "Prota, I think you need to go. It's important that you begin to exercise your independence. You'll never be strong unless you stand up for what's right. This is just a small step you can take in that direction."

"You want me to start fulfilling my role as Unit One, don't you, Adam?"

Adam's face glowed yellow. "Yes, I do, Prota. It's your rightful position, and you have the potential to carry out what your creator assigned you to be."

Prota shook his head slowly. "I don't know, Adam. I think I've reached whatever potential I have; perhaps I've even exceeded it and am operating at the level of ineptness."

Adam placed his other hand on Prota's left shoulder. He looked him in the face. "If you think you've reached your potential, then you have. If, on the other hand, you can find it within yourself to consider the possibility that you might not yet be all you can be, there's a chance that you can be more than you are now."

Prota stood motionless, staring at Adam. Finally he nodded. "I'll go."

The low-level transport vehicle was in a large module near the maintenance module. The four of them rolled it out of the module and onto the launch pad, then climbed aboard, Prota taking the controls. He glanced at Adam, who sat beside him. "I might as well start acting like a leader if that's what I'm supposed to be, right?" he said with a yellow glow on his face.

Prota activated the hydrogen-powered craft and the thin layer of dust on the launch pad swirled around them as the craft hovered, spun one way, then another, and slowly drifted off the pad before rising enough to clear the module.

"Maybe leadership doesn't necessarily have to include the ability to pilot a craft," Lespin said from a back seat.

"My sentiments exactly," Cosber chimed in.

"Have no fear, we're on our way," Prota cheerily replied.

Flying at a couple of hundred feet, the landscape whisked by in a gray blur as they flew at speeds close to 200 miles per hour. Adam used the opportunity to ask questions about life at the base. It was a mix of good times and bad times, they told him, but it was obvious to Adam that the bad times were dramatically increasing. In about an hour and a half Prota slowed the craft and descended.

Settling on the lunar surface in a swirl of dust, Prota cut the engine. Cosber explained to Adam, "We have to walk about a hundred yards. We don't like to kick up any dust that might settle on the LEM."

"The LEM?" Adam asked.

"We'll explain after we get there," Lespin said.

Adam could see an object in the distance, parts of it reflecting the last of the sun that was low in the black sky.

When they drew close the three Dolphdroids bowed their heads in respect that verged on worship, Adam thought.

"This is LEM," Prota said.

Adam immediately identified the machine that stood on four gangly legs. It was short in height and flat on top, like a giant metal bug. It had been the part of the craft that had brought the original lunar explorers to the moon. This was the bottom portion of the

Lunar Excursion Module, which remained on the lunar surface when the astronauts returned to orbit in the top portion. Gold foil covered part of the structure, though it had a coating of dust that dulled the golden shine. Human tracks were still visible after all these years, though the ones nearest the craft were obscured by the blast when the upper portion lifted off. A United States flag, with the old fifty star configuration was nearby. It had been here a long time, preserved well on the airless landscape.

Adam looked at the three Dolphdroids, heads slightly bowed, clasping their hands together. "Do you know what this is? It's an old spacecraft, used by the original human visitors here."

Prota nodded. "We know. It's a machine made by the humans who made us."

"It's like an ancestor of ours," Cosber said.

Lespin added, "There's just something about LEM. It connects us to something beyond ourselves. It's hard to explain."

"I think it helps us realize that there's more to life than who we are and where we are," Prota said.

They were all silent as they stared at the LEM. Finally Adam asked, "When did you discover the LEM?"

"We went in search of it two lunar cycles ago," Cosber said.

"Why did you suddenly decide to search for it after all these years?" Adam asked.

"I suppose it does seem strange," responded Lespin. "When things started to go wrong here with the colony, and with the increasing alienation from Earth, some of us began to sense a need to relate to our origins. I suppose you could say it became a fixation. The LEM was discovered by accident when two Dolphdroids were on an excursion."

"But you're honoring something created, not your creator," Adam said.

"Perhaps so," responded Cosber, "but we can't be in touch with our creator or anything to do with Earth. I guess the LEM is our best connection to what was, to who we are."

"Do you know there are other craft from the early years of lunar exploration scattered on the lunar surface?" Adam asked.

"Yes, we know," responded Prota. "One is over there." He pointed to the edge of a nearby crater. They skirted the LEM landing area, Adam following them, so as not to disturb the human footprints, Cosber explained. After walking several hundred yards they climbed over the edge of the crater. The craft came into view, an ancient vehicle standing on three legs, each with thick metal pads. A set of solar collectors crowned the top. A small shovel on a mechanical arm came from the midsection. There were human footprints all around the craft. Souvenir hunters had been at work, as evidenced by bare wires where something – probably a TV camera – had been removed. Searching his memory, Adam recognized the craft as a Surveyor spacecraft sent to explore the lunar surface before manned landings. Because of its location he thought it was Surveyor 3. The souvenir hunters had been the two astronauts who piloted the LEM they had just visited. He couldn't recall any other details of the mission.

"Both of these machines represent part of our past, a connection with Earth and with the one who made us," Cosber said.

"But you've had contact with humans all along," Adam responded. "Until recently they visited the colony. You may not have met your actual creator, but you've met others from Earth."

"We don't remember encountering humans," Prota said.

Adam was shocked. "You mean you have no recollections of humans visiting your colony or of any conversation with humans on Earth?" he asked.

They shook their heads. "It must be Agur's doing," Adam said. They stood silent. "Somehow Agur must have accessed your assisted thought processors and erased that portion of your memory." Apparently without the memory assist of the thought processors, they had little or no recollection of their human encounters on Earth. It shouldn't surprise him, Adam reflected. Forgetfulness is often a symptom of rebellion.

"Why do you worship these two objects but not the other pieces of equipment that have come from Earth? Those objects are all over your colony, equipment of all kinds."

Prota shook his head, "Humans didn't make any of those things. They were developed and made here on the moon, by us."

Adam was shocked again. Agur not only had wiped part of their memories, but had somehow also changed memories, creating an alternate reality of the past.

They started to walk back toward the LEM. Pointing to the LEM, Adam said, "You shouldn't worship an object. It's a created thing, like you are, except far more crude. You are the pinnacle of human creation."

"But these are terrible times," Cosber said. "More than ever some of us yearn to know the one who made us. I guess when there's a threat of no longer existing, you wonder why you've come into existence in the first place. We want – at least some of us want – a connection with our beginning. These machines provide that."

"There's a better way, and I'm that way," Adam said. They looked at Adam, bewilderment coloring their faces. "Let's go back to the colony," he suggested. "There's really nothing here for you."

Adam spent the next several days touring the rest of the colony and visiting with the Dolphdroids. Frequently he could be seen with nine Dolphdroids in tow, the nine he had met the first day: Hasper, Ober, Cosber, Rimmer, Lespin, Nibin, Ferber, Starsa, and Prota. Prota was sometimes absent, feeling obligated to continue work on the craft for Agur in the maintenance module. Adam eventually invited two other Dolphdroids, Yeester and Mibeeton, both miners, to join him and the others.

While Adam was talking with Yeester and Mibeeton, Kabro came up to him. He wore a short cape that barely came to his waist and was a swirl of bright colors. "Can I join you?" he asked.

Adam looked at Kabro, at the others, and back at Kabro. "Are you aware that associating with me will put you in conflict with the powers that be?"

Kabro nodded. "I know. I figure you have the best thing going right now, and I want to be part of it."

"Specifically, Agur's not going to be happy with you hanging around me."

Kabro's face turned yellow with a smile. "Yes, I know that."

Adam paused. "Welcome to our little group."

Adam knew that even if his mission was a success, there would be work to do after he was gone. He needed a core group that could be an ongoing influence on the Dolphdroid colony. He would need them as they now needed him. Adam was also aware that Agur was feeling increasingly threatened by the growing number of followers he was attracting.

"When will you do something to keep the evil Earth powers from destroying us?" Mibeeton asked him.

"I wish I could tell you more, but I can't right now. Your ultimate enemies on Earth need to be as surprised as you will be when things happen. If they know too much before it happens, they'll keep it from happening."

"There's talk that Agur has a plan to save us," Yeester said.

"I'm sure he's doing just as you say," replied Adam. "He may very well be working on a plan to save the colony, or a portion of the colony. He certainly has a plan to save himself. Each of you has to make a decision as to whether you trust Agur enough to put your life into his care."

"Can't you give us some kind of proof that you can really save us from destruction? You've said you haven't told us all you know. Maybe if you did, we'd have more confidence that things will work out," Ferber said.

"What you need now more than facts is faith. Facts can hinder faith. I can't do my best for you unless you believe in me," Adam said, glancing around the group.

There were nods of understanding, but also gray faces of bewilderment.

Adam continued. "It's true that I've come to save your lives, but I've also come to help you live better lives once you've been delivered from death. After all, there's more to life than trying to stay alive. I want to help you fulfill your potential."

"How?" Prota asked.

"You'll be fulfilled when you put your effort into the things of this world which can be used on Earth. You'll be fulfilled when you resist competing with each other. You'll be fulfilled when you recognize your need for each other. You'll be fulfilled when you show the same tolerance for the weaknesses and shortcomings of others that you want them to show you in your weakness and shortcomings. You'll be fulfilled when you enjoy being alone with yourself. You'll be fulfilled when others enjoy being with you and you with them. You'll be fulfilled when your greatest desire is to please your creator."

There was silence when Adam finished. Finally Rimmer raised his hand, sensing this was a serious moment that required permission to speak. Adam nodded at Rimmer. "Should we be working? After all, the mining products and electrical output we're called upon to produce for Earth seem to be feeding the hand that wants to kill us."

Several of the Dolphdroids looked at Rimmer, annoyed at the abrupt change of subject. Adam answered Rimmer's question. "You must remember that reality beyond your world also has powers of both good and evil. The battle between good and evil that you experience in your world is simply a spillover of a larger battle between good and evil beyond your world."

"Will going back to work save us?" Cosber asked.

"I'm afraid that no amount of doing good can save you. The plan to terminate you is irrevocably in place," Adam said.

"How are you going to save us?" Lespin asked. "Knowing your plan of action might calm our fears."

"It's too early to tell," Adam replied.

"Too early to tell us what you have in mind?" Rimmer asked incredulously. "Termination is in just a few weeks; then it'll be all over for all of us, including you. We'll just slump to the ground, or maybe even die standing in our tracks. In one second we'll be no more."

"You don't have to trust me if you don't want to," Adam said softly.

"What choice do we have?" Yeester said.

"So we should get back to work, is that what you're suggesting?" Ober asked.

"Yes, as best you can. I know that many aren't going to want to work," Adam responded. "This work stoppage is supposedly a result of the conflict with Earth, but in all truthfulness the lack of work around here is also a result of laziness. Some of the Dolphdroids love work so much they could stand and look at it all day!" Their faces glowed with smiles. "You're seeing work as an evil in and of itself, but you were created to work. Work was never designed as something negative, but as a positive. Work isn't what gives you your identity, but your identity can be expressed through work. You were created to be somebody, but you also were created to do something."

"It's difficult to have the inspiration to work when more than half the colony won't work," Rimmer argued.

"So what do you think you and your friends should do, Prota?" Adam asked.

Startled, Prota's face turned pink with embarrassment, then

to gray in bewilderment as he tried to think of an appropriate answer. He knew that Adam was singling him out, giving him a chance to express his calling as the leader. He shrugged his shoulders and said, "I suppose we should do what we can. We can't make others do what we want, but we can make ourselves do what we should."

Adam's face turned bright yellow. "Very good, Prota! Very good." Prota's face glowed yellow from Adam's approval.

Looking at his little band of followers Adam felt compassion for them. They not only needed to be rescued from death, they needed to be taught how to live again. He would have to provide many opportunities for such teachable moments over the remaining weeks.

The number of Dolphdroids who were sympathetic to Adam slowly grew, much to Agur's frustration. He called for Adam twice before the next sunrise terminator appeared. Agur had been told that a majority of the Dolphdroids who ran the solar power collector array were back at work and that the array was again exporting energy to Earth. His only comfort was that the mining of helium-3 was still shut down because several key Dolphdroids involved in the process were anti-Earth, still under his control, not that it would have done any good to produce helium-3 anyway. The transporting of all products between the moon and earth had been halted by Imus.

Two days before the next sunrise terminator, Prota came up to Adam as he took a walk outside the perimeter of the colony. Adam still found the lunar surface to be an amazing place of stark beauty. Without an atmosphere, the hills on the horizon looked as clear and vivid as the rocks and boulders nearby. He had just watched an earthrise, and it had been a spectacular scene. He missed Earth. He missed his son and grandson, and Ashley, too. How he yearned to hold her in his arms. It would be nice to have human arms again, arms of flesh and bone, arms that could feel Ashley's embrace. He missed his human body. Glancing down at his mechanical feet that sent up puffs of dust as he took each step, he reflected that it seemed as if he had been in this metal body forever.

"Adam," Prota said, interrupting his thoughts.

"Oh, hello, Prota."

"I know what Agur's plan is," Prota said in a subdued voice, though no one was near. The Dolphdroids Agur had assigned to follow Adam had become slack in their duties, and Adam often wasn't under surveillance.

"What exactly does the illustrious Agur have in mind?" Adam asked.

"It has to do with the vehicle he's had me working on for what seems like forever." Prota paused, looked around to reassure himself that no one was within receiving distance of the conversation, and continued. "He's planning to take 10 of his most loyal Dolphdroids to one of the life cylinders in earth orbit, subdue it, hold the occupants hostage, and demand that the termination be canceled."

Adam's face glowed red with anger. "Is there anyone in the maintenance module now?"

"No, I don't think so. I'm usually the first one to go to work each shift, and I'm usually alone for about a half hour," Prota replied.

"Good," Adam said. "Where can we find a laser pick?"

Prota didn't have to ask what Adam had in mind. Fear welled up within him. "I think I saw some outside the entrance of the commissary module."

"Good, that's on the way. Let's go," Adam said as he started walking at a quick pace. Prota stood motionless for a moment, then made the effort to catch up with Adam.

Both remained silent as they made their way to the commissary module. Prota had a difficult time keeping up with Adam who was taking long strides, kicking up more than the usual amount of dust, his cape swaying first one way, then another. When they arrived at the commissary module Adam paused only a moment before picking up one of the three laser picks leaning against the structure. Grasping it in his right hand, he headed toward the maintenance module, Prota attempting to keep up.

Once inside, Adam paced back and forth in front of the craft, sizing it up. "I'm sorry to have to ruin your hours of work, Prota, but we can't allow Agur to carry out his plans." With that, Adam raised the laser pick, pointed it just ahead of the cockpit, and fired. The stream of bright light made the skin of the aircraft glow red for a moment; then there were sparks, smoke, and a small explosion that was silent in the airless environment. Prota knew that Adam was targeting the craft so as to do the most damage, taking out the computer and electronic control and guidance systems. He walked toward the back of the craft and took aim again. After another silent explosion, Adam had taken out the secondary computer system.

"What have you done?" a voice shouted behind them. Adam and Prota turned toward the entrance of the module, where Agur stood.

Agur turned his gaze from Adam to the smoldering craft and back to Adam again. With his face crimson, he screamed, "I'll kill you! I swear I'll kill you!"

Chapter 31

"You can't win by taking over a life cylinder," Adam answered angrily.

Agur stared at Adam for what Prota thought was an eternity. Then Agur spoke. "And you have a better plan? I keep hearing about the Dolphdroids trusting in you, but they don't have a clue as to how you're going to save us. You know what I think? I think you don't have a plan! And now you've destroyed the one chance we had to save ourselves. You're insane!"

Several of Agur's supporters had appeared in the doorway; two carried laser picks. Taking their cue from Agur, they started to move into the module, picks positioned to fire at Adam. Adam threw his laser pick down. "I'm not going to fight you. Fighting is no way to solve this."

"No, maybe not. Maybe the best way to solve this is to have you stand there while we blast you out of existence," Agur said as he and his followers moved closer to Adam and Prota.

"Adam's right; a confrontation won't solve anything." The direction sensors of Agur's and his followers' audio systems told

309

them that the voice came from the entrance to the module. They turned to see Cosber, Ober, Mibeeton, Ferber, Rimmer, and Kabro standing at the entrance. His facial color showed Agur that Rimmer had spoken.

Taking advantage of the distraction, Prota quickly bent down and picked up the laser pick that Adam had dropped. Adam put his hand on Prota's forearm in protest, but Prota jerked his arm back and took a step away from Adam while he aimed the weapon at Agur.

One of Agur's followers had noticed Prota's move and called his master's attention back to Adam and Prota.

"I don't want to hurt anyone, but I'm not going to let you kill Adam," Prota said. The armed Dolphdroid near Agur slowly moved his aim from Adam to Prota.

Adam's followers moved further into the module. Only Rimmer carried a laser pick. Prota realized it was an even match, two against two, and he felt a measure of confidence. Agur glanced again at the smoldering craft, then looked at Adam. "I don't want to see you again until the day of termination. You're the prototype, the one with the lowest serial number. They're going to terminate in numerical order. You'll die first. That's the next time I want to see you. I want to see you die." With that, Agur turned and strode from the module, his Dolphdroids following.

There was silence for a few moments. Adam's followers moved toward Adam and Prota, and a couple of them took a closer look at the destroyed craft.

"Do you think Agur's plan would have worked?" Ober asked.

Mibeeton jumped in with a reply before Adam had a chance to speak. "I suspect they'd have terminated Agur and his Dolphdroids in their tracks as they held the people in the life cylinder hostage."

"And then probably those of us left here," Cosber added.

"No," Adam corrected. "The termination process is set for two weeks and three days from now by an act of the Commissioners. It can't be moved ahead, back, or stopped. It's all locked into the master computer. Unfortunately Agur doesn't understand that, and I don't expect him to believe me even if I explained it to him."

Rimmer looked at Adam with his face colored with amazement. "How do you know that?" he asked.

"Let's just say I've been involved in the whole Dolphdroid project from the beginning," Adam said.

"Well, you are the prototype," Ober observed.

Adam didn't reply; he started to walk from the hangar. Agur and his followers were nowhere to be seen. Adam headed toward the commissary module, with the others following.

Rimmer broke the silence. "Well, Prota, it appears you've really annoyed Agur."

"I was just thinking about that," Prota replied. "Until now I was in the middle on the whole pro-Earth, pro-lunar issue. I always thought it was difficult to take a stand, but now it's more difficult not to take one. I feel relieved about having made a once-and-for-all decision. I did that when I pointed the laser pick at Agur."

"The only one he hates more is Adam," Ober added.

"Agur still might try to kill you or have you killed before the termination date, Adam," Cosber said.

"It doesn't really matter, does it?" Kabro asked. "I mean, we're all going to die anyway. Maybe Agur's idea was the best chance we're going to have."

"Didn't you hear Adam say that it wouldn't have worked anyway, taking over a life cylinder and holding humans hostage?" Prota asked. Kabro said nothing.

Looking at Adam, who was walking to his left, Rimmer said, "We know you're the prototype and that you've been a part of the Dolphdroid project from the beginning, but you know so much. Just because you're a prototype doesn't explain why you know so much."

Adam's face glowed yellow. "You need some questions answered, Rimmer. But I want all of you together when I tell you more. Let's meet by the big mound of refuse rock near the entrance to the mining control module in two hours. Tell the others." With that, Adam veered off to the left, taking a small path that followed a rill, a valley between two strings of low hills. It was obvious that he wanted to be alone.

When the two hours had elapsed, everyone was at the refuse rock pile. Adam chose a large rock to sit on while his followers gathered around him, standing in a semi-circle. Adam had adjusted to his new body's lack of need to sit in order to rest. The normal posture for the Dolphdroids during inactivity was standing. Sitting seemed to be an intentional choice on their part, a posture for commanding attention. Adam wanted their attention.

He looked from one of his followers to another until his video sensors had panned the group. Their faces glowed with the brown of curiosity. Adam rested his left forearm on his knee and spoke. "I'm more than the prototype of our kind," Adam said. He paused before adding, "I'm also your creator."

Their faces glowed with the green of surprise, then transitioned to the gray of bewilderment. "But how can you be the creator? You're one of us! Besides, a human designed and created us, didn't he?" Cosber asked.

"Being both creator and created is a contradiction," Rimmer added.

Adam held up his hand to forestall the onslaught of any more questions. "I'm not only Adam; I'm also Joshua Christopher, the human who created you."

"But how can that be?" Ober asked.

Adam took several minutes to explain the basic steps that led him to where he was now. He tried to be brief in summarizing what had happened until his arrival on the lunar surface.

When he finished Lespin exclaimed, "This is incredible!"

Adam nodded. "That's why I've decided to tell you, but not everyone. To some it wouldn't seem credible. No sense wasting the truth on those who won't accept it."

"It could also be dangerous letting the wrong ones hear it," Rimmer observed.

"It could get you killed," Ober added. Adam's face glowed in a smile.

Prota raised his arm, asking to speak. Adam nodded at him. "Isn't this a suicide mission for you? Wouldn't it have been better if you had stayed on earth as Dr. Christopher? Does your being here really change anything? Won't we all die anyway, including you? None of this is making sense."

Adam looked from one Dolphdroid to another. "I'd like to tell you all about the plan, but if word got back to Agur he could find a way to keep it from happening."

"But he's going to die with the rest of us. Wouldn't he want you to succeed?" Rimmer asked.

Adam shook his head. "Hatred is a strange thing. It can

keep you from seeing the truth. It's also possible that Agur will devise another plan. I think it would be advisable for me to keep out of sight until the time is right, near the time of termination. For your sakes I need to stay alive until then."

They stood motionless before Adam, considering what he had said. Finally, Prota nodded in agreement.

"There's the abandoned mining shafts," Lespin suggested.

Adam decided that Lespin had a good idea. He soon concluded their meeting and insisted they disperse. They watched him as he made his way to the area where the entrance to the oldest mine shafts were located.

His friends made individual, surreptitious, and short visits to the abandoned mine shaft so as not to expose Adam's location. There were still long hours when he was alone, giving him plenty of time to reflect on his life. The location and the loneliness were, at times, claustrophobic. He wanted to spend more time with his friends, but that wasn't wise. He had to stay out of sight for now. Timing was everything.

Forty-six hours before termination, Ober and Cosber came bounding into the shaft. "Adam! You've got to leave, now! Agur knows you're here! He's sending some of his followers with laser picks to get you, or kill you," Cosber exclaimed.

Adam quickly followed the two into the starkly lit lunarscape. The sun was about 10 degrees above the horizon. Adam realized that the dark cycle had come and gone while he had been in the mining shaft.

"How did Agur find out about my location?" Adam asked as they bounded along.

Ober and Cosber looked at each other, then Cosber spoke. "Kabro told him."

"Kabro?" Adam asked, finding it hard to believe.

"He's not really on our side, it turns out. He was planted by Agur to keep track of you and report any plans you had."

"Traitor!" Ober exclaimed, his face red with anger.

"I still can't believe it. He seemed so sincere," Cosber said.

At Prota's suggestion they took Adam to the maintenance module and hid him in a storage room. When the door was closed,

Adam felt like a set of clothes that had been hung in a closet, the room was so small. Standing still in the dark, he was glad that he hadn't slept in hours. Sleep would help pass the time, but was he only hours away from never awakening, as either Adam or Josh? Sometimes sleeping seemed a waste of time, and with the termination time drawing near it seemed even more so. Sleep took a while to come, but when it did Adam slept deeply.

Suddenly Adam was jerked back to wakefulness. It was Prota. Adam saw several of the other Dolphdroids standing outside the open door of the small storage room, Prota having squeezed in to wake him.

"Agur's gone, Adam. He left a couple of hours ago with three or four of his followers," Prota said.

"Gone? Gone where?" Adam asked.

"We think they've headed to the far side," Prota replied.

"In what vehicle?" Adam asked.

"They took one of the two drilling vehicles," Prota said.

Rimmer spoke from just beyond the door. "Kabro, who was left behind and is really angry at Agur, says they're planning to dig a tunnel. They hope to get out of range of the termination signal from earth."

Adam realized that Agur's order to retrieve him from the mines was a distraction created for the remaining Dolphdroids, pro-Earth and pro-lunar, so that Agur and his select few could get away.

"But what will they come back to? It'll be a dead colony. They probably won't be able to do all the tasks necessary to survive for long," Nibin said. By now Adam and Prota had left the small storage room and were standing with the others.

"That's true," added Ferber. "I doubt that any of them can run the oxygen reclamation project, or even the waste reclamation equipment."

"I suspect they'll just wait things out," Prota said. "They might have enough supplies stored away for a long time. Eventually humans will arrive and start production again. They could commandeer a craft and head to earth orbit as Agur originally planned, and then maybe to Earth itself. Who knows? All I know for sure is that they're gone."

"You might be right, Prota," Adam said. "Agur certainly has a plan of action. He's out to save himself, and he took a minimum of Dolphdroids with him to ensure his survival. Taking too many would have been cumbersome, and too few would have left him shorthanded."

"Maybe the followers he left behind will finally realize the truth about him, the kind of unit he was," Ober said.

"We'll have to see," Adam replied.

"Maybe they won't have long to think their nasty thoughts about Agur. The termination time is almost here," Rimmer said with a note of resignation. Then, realizing that his statement showed a sense of hopelessness, he quickly added, "That is, if your idea doesn't work, Adam."

Adam's face glowed a pale yellow. "I can appreciate your doubts, Rimmer. I haven't told you much about my plans for saving you."

"Now might be a good time," Prota said.

Adam nodded. "Meet me back here in three hours. Mibecton and Yeester, could you two bring a supply of oxygen and nutrient/water tubes? Prota, I need to see you alone, please."

After the others had filed out into the lunar brightness, Adam said, "Prota, I need to do an interface with you. I must give you a security dated file. When you need to know what I'm about to tell you, the information will be accessible."

Prota hesitated. Interfacing information between two Dolphdroids wasn't an uncommon experience, but he had never heard of a security dated file before.

Adam smiled, sensing Prota's confusion. "It's an upgrade developed after you were made. There's not much use for it, so we never bothered sending the software upgrade to the colony. It'll allow me to tell you something now that you don't need to know, and shouldn't know, until later."

"How will I know when I can access it?" Prota asked.

"That's part of the program. You'll know," Adam said as he began unscrewing the tip of his right index finger. Prota watched him for a moment, then began doing the same.

"The left one, Prota," Adam said with a slight smile. The pink of embarrassment came over Prota. He had forgotten for a moment that the transmitter and receiver in an interface were on opposite hands.

Adam extended his right hand, pointing with his index finger.

Prota did the same with his left hand, his index finger extended. They touched fingers; Adam gave his hand a slight twist and they were locked. A few moments later he reversed the twist, they disconnected, and each returned the cap to his index finger.

"Didn't feel a thing, and not any wiser either, as far as I can tell." Prota tried to joke, feeling uncomfortable with Adam's serious demeanor.

"Just make certain you carry out the instructions I gave you, Prota. OK?"

Prota nodded. "Certainly, to the letter."

"I need to see Kabro. Do you know where he is?" Adam asked.

Prota looked surprised at Adam's question, but he quickly recovered and said, "I think he and some of Agur's other followers – former followers – are in the commissary module. I understand they're having what could be called a hate party with the guest of honor, Agur, in absentia."

"Thanks, Prota," Adam said.

"You're not thinking of going to the commissary module, are you? That could be dangerous," Prota said.

"Perhaps it could be dangerous, but I suspect the former followers of Agur are so angry, confused, and fearful that they don't know what to think or do. I really must see Kabro before I can fulfill my purpose here." Without waiting for a reply, Adam headed out the door and took the path to the commissary module.

Heads turned as Adam took the last few steps down into the module. He scanned the room, searching for Kabro among the couple of dozen or so Dolphdroids clustered in groups of various sizes. He spotted Kabro standing with two other Dolphdroids at the far end of the room. Kabro's face was a swirling mixture of emotions.

Approaching Kabro, Adam asked, "May I see you privately, Kabro?"

Kabro glanced down in embarrassment, then at the two he had been talking to. He looked at Adam, paused a moment, nodded, and then walked past Adam, across the room, and up the steps to the outside.

"I make no apologies for what I did," Kabro said as soon as Adam cleared the door and was outside.

"How long were you on Agur's side?"

Kabro glanced toward the horizon, then at the ground, and focused back on the horizon again. "From the beginning," he replied.

"And when was the beginning?"

"When Jake Stawson came to us."

"And?"

"And Jake Stawson set us on a new course. He was against human control."

"But he killed one of you; he was a human who killed a Dolphdroid, and you welcomed him?"

"He had to kill him. The Dolphdroid had become a problem, even threatening Jake."

"How did he threaten him?"

"I can't remember exactly. All I know is that Jake was against human control of the colony. He was pro-lunar."

"But he was sent by Imus Hartung, who's in charge of all extraterrestrial projects. Surely you must have known that," Adam said incredulously.

"Yes, we knew that, but Jake Stawson made it clear that Hartung and all humans were out to terminate us; they saw us as a threat."

"He was supposed to investigate and, if possible, bring some resolution to whatever issues he found," Adam replied.

Kabro shook his head vigorously. "Jake Stawson realized that our real problem was the human connection; if we severed that connection we could solve our own problems."

Adam knew it was no use to argue. "So you, Agur, and the others decided that the connection with Earth was the fundamental problem."

"Yes. Agur felt we had to be very aggressive in resisting human control. That became obvious when we heard that we were being terminated."

"How did you find that out?"

"Jake Stawson told us."

"Why do you think he did that?"

Kabro paused, as if the question had never occurred to him before. "I guess he wanted us to know what we were up against."

"Perhaps he wanted to create as much negativity against Earth as he could," Adam suggested.

"Well, the humans deserve it, don't they? They decided to terminate us. It looks like they're going to succeed. Maybe Agur and his clique will survive, but not the rest of us. I hope Agur doesn't either, the double-crosser."

"Look who's calling the kettle black," Adam said softly.

"What?" Kabro asked.

"Never mind. You need to know, Kabro, that not all humans are against the Dolphdroids. In fact, those involved in your creation have been fighting to save the colony."

"Including you?" asked Kabro.

"Including me. The battle in your world is only a small manifestation of the much larger battle that's going on beyond your world."

"And we would have had a chance of winning if you hadn't destroyed the ship," Kabro said. "Agur was going to hold a life cylinder hostage and force the humans to capitulate. Now we're doomed. It's your fault. If you thought you were helping, you were badly mistaken. So, where's your brilliant next plan? You don't have one, do you?"

"Yes, in fact I do."

Kabro looked at Adam disbelievingly. "You know, Adam, I almost started to believe you; I really did. I found you to be very convincing. In all honesty, you're a better unit than Agur, but I also believe you're naïve and misguided. I'm not sure why you came. I know you think you came to save us, but it's obvious that you don't have the means to do that. In fact, by your coming you've ruined the chance for all of us to survive. It's your fault! You've managed to guarantee our destruction, not save us. Can't you see that?" Kabro quickly turned and entered the large room where a group of Dolphdroids were playing hoop ball. Adam stood there for a moment, watching him. He realized that Kabro was a lost cause; he had been against Adam from the beginning, a traitor in their midst. Adam turned and headed back to the maintenance module.

The three hours had not yet passed when Mibeeton walked in, completing the group of, now, 11. They gathered around Adam in a loose circle. Adam saw strain and concern on all their faces.

"Mibeeton and Yeester, can I have the oxygen and nutrient/water tubes?" Adam asked.

They handed him 12 sets, including one for Adam. Mibeeton said, "I wish we would need 13 sets. How could Kabro have done what he did?"

"What is, is," Prota replied.

Adam laid 11 of them on Prota's workbench. "We'll share one among us," he said as he turned toward them with the remaining set.

Adam placed the oxygen tube on his connector and opened the valve on the tube for a moment, allowing a small portion of the oxygen to enter his system. Then he closed it again, detached it, and handed it to Prota. "Take some as I did and pass it on," he said to Prota. The gray hue of bewilderment came over Prota. His first thought was that this wouldn't be nearly enough oxygen for all 12 of them. Then he realized that he was supposed to take just a small portion, so there would be enough left to go around. He complied, taking the tube, attaching it to his connector, opening the valve, and allowing a small portion of the oxygen to enter him before turning the valve off again. He then detached it and passed it to Ober on his right. Ober followed Prota's example. By now Adam had done the same with the nutrient/water tube, then handing it to Prota. Again, Prota followed Adam's example. One by one the others did the same with both tubes, all remaining silent, aware that this was in some way an important symbolic act.

"I'm oxygen and water to you," Adam said. "Because I'm here with you, you'll be able to live. Because I'll die, you'll live."

The colors of green and gray, surprise and confusion, swirled on their faces. Rimmer was bold enough to speak. "How can you die in our place? We all have to die. It's going to take all of us to satisfy the life-value points. You're just one unit."

"It'll be OK," Adam replied. "Just trust me. It'll be OK for you." Then Adam turned to Prota and nodded. "I have interfaced with Prota and have given him some instructions and explanations under a secure file in his assisted thought processor. At the appropriate time this information will be available to him. Please follow his instructions to the letter. He's to be your leader."

The remaining 15 hours before termination had proved too much to take for three of the Dolphdroid colonists, who committed suicide by opening their oxygen vents to the vacuum of space. Several others watched in disbelief, but did nothing to stop them.

The three bodies lay in the dust near the entry to the commissary module, one with his black face of death looking up blankly, the other two face down. Adam and the eleven walked past without saying a word. Once inside the commissary module, they pieced together that several others had wandered off together to the nearby hills to live out their final hours, or perhaps to commit suicide as well – no one knew for sure. It was reported that two additional Dolphdroids had plugged in and tuned out on the pleasure machines, joining the regular addicts, preferring to spend their remaining hours distracted by the imaginary. Those gathered in the commissary module were finding some semblance of comfort in numbers.

It was understood that the termination would take place in numerical order in five-second intervals, moving from the lower numbered units to the higher. Adam, being the prototype, would be the first unit terminated. "We should all go at the same time," someone near the middle of the group said. "It's cruel for us to have to watch each other drop dead one by one."

Watching the Dolphdroids huddled in the room, Adam questioned the wisdom of having built the Dolphdroids with internal clocks in their assisted living processors. It certainly was a curse for them now. Some became hysterical, thrashing around, punching holes in the walls, shaking their fists toward the ceiling and Earth beyond. Most remained quiet; several sat slumped against the wall, a position of defeat that Adam had never see them take before.

Adam's attention faded from the drama of coming death in the room to vividly picturing Rob and Randy. Would he ever see them again? He was surprised by the new wave of sorrow for Anne's absence. How he missed his beloved wife! Then images of Ashley rushed in, prompting momentary guilt for the place she now held in his heart when he was still missing Anne. There was regret that he hadn't had a chance to say a proper goodbye to Ashley, though he had had no choice but to make the quick exit that he did. Now the moment was at hand. The whole mission had as its goal what he hoped would happen in just a few seconds. It had to work; it had to!

Everyone's eyes were on Adam. Prota stood next to him. With 30 seconds remaining, Rimmer said, "Adam, no matter what happens, thanks."

Adam turned, his face glowing yellow for Rimmer.

There was silence. Fifteen seconds. Every Dolphdroid was acutely aware of time, of each precious second of life that ticked by. Ten, nine, eight…

Prota put his hand on Adam's arm. They all expected to die, but it would begin with Adam. They would watch him die to see how they would die.

Prota looked at Adam and said, "I'm not sure what's going to happen, but I believe you have a plan. I hope it works."

Five seconds.

Adam glanced at the eleven near him, then at the others in the room, and said, "I love all of you. It's done."

One, zero.

Chapter 32

Adam's face went gray; his arms jerked slightly, then went limp. His face turned darker gray, then black, his knees buckled, and he collapsed to the floor, onto his knees. He swayed for a moment, then fell forward onto his face.

Several Dolphdroids had stepped back to avoid being hit by him. Silence filled the room. Then Lespin exclaimed, "Prota, you're still alive!"

"It's been 10 seconds," said a Dolphdroid from the far corner of the room.

"I am! I'm alive!" Prota said, extending his arms and rotating his hands, glancing from one to the other.

"Now it's been 15 seconds and no one else has been terminated, either," someone else stated.

"Adam's the only one who's going to die," another Dolphdroid said, with hope and relief in his voice.

"I don't know what's happened, but we're all still alive!" another Dolphdroid added.

Everyone gazed at the still form lying face down on the floor. Relief was visible on the faces of most of the Dolphdroids, but the expression of the eleven and a few others slowly turned to a deepening purple of grief.

"Let's get him out of here," Prota said in a subdued voice.

Rimmer grasped one of Adam's arms and Ober took the other. Prota grasped one leg, and Lespin took the other.

"Turn him over first," suggested Lespin, and they did.

Stooped, ready to lift the body, Rimmer paused. He looked at the other three, then at the rest gathered around. "Where should we take him?"

Prota looked at Rimmer, then at the crowd of Dolphdroids, all of whom had moved closer, curious to see the death they had escaped. "I don't know. Let's just get him out of here," he said. They lifted Adam's body by the arms and legs, his midsection sagging as they carried him out of the module.

Once outside they paused, still holding the body. "The place where the others are buried?" Rimmer asked. The other three nodded. Through their group communications link they heard celebration erupt in the commissary module.

Without a word, the four started toward the makeshift cemetery containing the bodies of the four Dolphdroids, at the top of a small hill on the northern edge of the colony. The rest of the eleven and several others had left the commissary module and had caught up with them as they carried Adam.

The procession of Dolphdroids walked slowly, a gray cloud of dust in their wake. They began to talk – statements of amazement about being alive, questions about why only Adam had died, and words of grief over his death.

"'I love all of you. It's done.' Those were his last words," Rimmer said.

"What did he mean by 'It's done'?" Lespin asked.

"I guess he meant that the job of saving us was done when he died," Ober suggested.

"But how could that be?" asked Rimmer. "After all, it was supposed to take the life-value points of all of us, and more, to satisfy the judgment against us. How could the dying stop with Adam?"

"He was more than just one of us," Ober said.

"Yeah, he was the prototype," Lespin added.

"He was more than the prototype," said Ober. "He was Joshua Christopher, our creator; somehow that made the difference.

It's a mystery. The reality is that he died and we didn't."

They passed the last of the storage modules, turned, and climbed the small hill where four large stones marked the graves of the dead Dolphdroids. The four had been covered by a thin layer of soil, their forms still vaguely visible.

They laid Adam down slowly; his limp head swung to the left as they lowered him. The four who had acted as pallbearers stood and joined the others as they stared down at their beloved leader.

Starsa broke the silence. "I can't believe that he's dead." Deep purple colored all their faces.

Rimmer noticed first – and one by one the others did, too – that Prota's face had changed to gray bewilderment, then the tan of thoughtfulness, then the yellow of a smile.

"What?" Rimmer asked, looking at Prota with annoyance in his voice.

"It happened. It happened just like Adam said it would!" Prota exclaimed, glancing around the group.

"What happened like Adam said it would?" asked Ober.

"Not long before the termination time, Adam did an interface with me. I couldn't read any of the data he was feeding me. He said it was a security dated file and that I would automatically access it when the time was right. The file just opened!"

"And?" asked Rimmer.

"Don't just stand there, tell us!" demanded Cosber.

Prota glanced at Adam, then looked at the others gathered around his lifeless form. "We aren't supposed to bury Adam here. He wants us to take him to the craft he came in. We're supposed to put him into the cockpit and attach the interface to the one in the craft."

"He wants to be buried in his air/space vehicle?" Rimmer asked in disbelief.

"No," replied Prota, his face glowing the brightest yellow any of them had seen. "We're not burying him. He's told me, or is telling me now – the data's still downloading – that he's coming back. But first he needs to go to Earth before he can come back to us."

"That makes no sense," Cosber said.

The others stared at Prota in amazement and disbelief. "Are

you OK, Prota?" Rimmer asked.

"I'm more than OK! I'm telling you what Adam told me via the interface, nothing more, nothing less."

Rimmer asked, "Why did Adam interface with you and not someone else, or everyone else?"

"Are you jealous, Rimmer?" challenged Ober. Rimmer's face turned red with anger.

"Listen," interrupted Starsa. "Prota is the first unit, the rightful leader. Agur took that away from him, remember?"

"He let Agur take it away from him, and look at the mess it caused," Rimmer said.

"It seems to me that by interfacing with Prota and giving him this information, Adam has affirmed Prota's rightful position among us as leader," Starsa said.

Several conversations erupted among the small group until finally Prota interrupted. "Listen! I didn't choose to be the number one unit. I'll lead because I'm supposed to, not because I want to or need to. I believe that Adam is Dr. Christopher. I know he's dead, but he had a last wish. Let's honor that wish and get him to his craft."

There was silence. Then four of them picked up Adam's body, but they didn't move. "Where's his craft, and how do we get there? We're not going to walk, are we?" asked Starsa.

"Adam gave me the coordinates during the interface," Prota said. "As to how to get there, any ideas?"

A discussion ensued, with the group finally settling on a plan to use an old drilling rig that was parked behind one of the mineral storage modules.

The four Dolphdroids who had picked Adam up carried him, while Prota bounded ahead to activate the vehicle. Several had expressed concern that it might not power up, having not been used for some time, but it did. A couple of the units headed off to collect additional oxygen and nutrient/water tubes for the trip, a normal backup safety procedure that allowed for unforeseen delays. Prota told Mibeeton to take the controls. With all of the Dolphdroids and Adam's lifeless body aboard, Mibeeton slowly lifted the craft and gradually increased the speed so as not to dislodge anyone from their precarious perches.

Few in the colony observed their departure. A celebration of uninhibited relief and joy had broken out in the commissary module, with most of the Dolphdroids laughing, singing, or dancing.

Conversation and silence alternated on the journey as they grappled with all that had happened since Adam's arrival. Lespin was the first to spot Adam's air/space vehicle. Mibeeton slowed the drilling rig and brought it to a stop, slowly settling it on the lunar surface. After dismounting they all walked around the air/space vehicle, curious about its design. The wings looked strange to them; they had never seen wings on a vehicle before.

"There's a code bar. How do we open the cockpit without the code?" asked Ober.

"I don't know," Prota said. Then a look of surprise flushed his face and he quickly added, "Yes I do! I can open it! I know the code!" He saw the surprise on the faces of the others and added, "It was part of Adam's message from the interface. I didn't know I had it. It's strange having information that I didn't know I had." With that Prota walked up to the craft and entered a code into the five-button code bar. A light came on in the canopy, and it slowly slid back.

It took six of them to hoist Adam's body into the cockpit and get him situated in the seat. Prota found the interface coupling behind the seat and attached it to the receptacle in the back of Adam's neck. The mystery was solved. That receptacle had been the topic of more than a few conversations among the colonists, because none of them possessed it.

"How is he going to get back to Earth?" asked Ober.

"Maybe he's still alive inside, but won't his mind die because of lack of oxygen and water? It's a long way back to Earth," added Lespin. "We could pack some tubes with him, but he can't move. He won't be able to service himself."

"Why do you think he might still be alive? He was terminated. He's got to be dead," Starsa said.

"Listen," Prota said as he double-checked the interface coupling link, "I don't know all the answers. His body is dead, that's apparent. Anything more than that, I don't know. He only told me what I needed to know." Prota glanced down at the others. "I know I'm supposed to be taking leadership here, but don't expect miracles, OK?" Prota turned back toward the cockpit and took a last look at Adam, then climbed down the ladder to the ground.

"What happens now?" Rimmer asked.
"I don't know," Prota replied. "I really don't know."

Giant Dolphdroids chased him; others stood and laughed at him…

…The Earth above melted and dripped onto him in cold, wet globs of mud…

…Rob rose from the dust of the lunar surface, furious and screaming at him…

Every so often reason returned for a moment, and Josh knew he was hallucinating. The sensory deprivation was causing his mind to make up wild, crazy, scary nightmares. It was an experience he vividly recalled having in the initial hours after his mind had been transferred to Adam.

Then he remembered that his last image had been of the Dolphdroids in the commissary module at the zero count. After that everything had gone dark and silent. He knew that his mind lay isolated in its cranial cradle, his Adamic processor and body dead from the termination. He could only hope that the plan had worked and that the others were still alive.

He had no external stimuli by which to measure the passage of time. His internal clock had ceased functioning with the rest of his body.

Perhaps he should have told them more: that his cranial cradle had been modified to act as a lifeboat, with enough oxygen and water making it capable of sustaining his brain independently of his body until his return to earth. No, he knew it had been the right decision to limit what he shared with them. It was important that they have faith, and too many facts would have spoiled that. What if Prota chose not to share the information from the interface that was stored in the security dated file? If he did share the information, would they believe him, at least enough to help move his body to the air/space vehicle? He needed them to place him in the cockpit and connect the interface coupling. He couldn't do it himself. If all went well, he could use the interface to close the canopy and fly the craft back to Earth. If they failed to place him in the cockpit, for whatever reason, he was doomed to die.

Suddenly he sensed more to his existence than just his thoughts! Input! He was experiencing input!

It wasn't tactile input, but telemetry input from the air/space craft. He was back in his vehicle. He became aware that the cockpit was open and that the on-board computer was in stand-by mode. He could see, not through Adam's eyes but through the eye of the craft's rear view camera. First things first. He would think the cockpit closed.

They stood watching the vehicle in silence, the motionless top portion of Adam's body visible in the cockpit seat; it was a strange coffin for their friend. They waited because they had no compulsion to go. Suddenly the canopy began to slide forward, and several Dolphdroids jumped. The canopy closed completely and locked in position. A light came on somewhere on the control panel – they saw it reflected in the canopy – then another light, and another. Moments passed. They stood transfixed. With no atmosphere to transmit sound, there was no rumble when the main engine powered up, but they saw the vehicle shudder. A blast of flame came from the nozzle, the exhaust swirling dust into a huge gray cloud. The engine's nozzle gimballed up and down, to the right and to the left, spraying exhaust in a different direction with each movement; the controls were being tested.

The thrusters under the craft fired a short test blast. There were two in the nose, two in the middle and two at the rear of the craft. Then the two in the nose fired again, this time at full power. The front of the craft lifted, the landing gear's suspension extending fully as the nose's weight was carried by the thrusters' blast. When the nose wheel lifted from the lunar surface, the main engine exploded into full afterburner power. The craft shot forward, dragging its rear landing gear through the dust for a few feet. The thrusters at mid and aft position began firing at full power, and the craft cleared the lunar surface. Without the drag of the rear landing gear in the lunar soil, the vehicle gained speed quickly.

The Dolphdroids watched, transfixed. Then Rimmer exclaimed, "The hill!" They all watched as the craft streaked toward a tall hill. At its current trajectory, it wouldn't clear it.

"Oh no!" Lespin exclaimed.

Just when they thought Adam's craft would slam into the side of the hill, it banked sharply to the right. As it banked, the landing gear retracted, giving the craft another three feet of clearance. The hill sloped down slightly where the new heading was taking the craft. The nose of the craft pitched up sharply and it slipped over the top of the hill, its belly skimming the lunar surface, spewing up clouds of dust, for a moment obscured by the cloud of dust; then they saw it again, climbing steeply.

"It's assuming an orbital trajectory," Rimmer said.

"Somehow somebody is taking control of the craft and taking the body back to Earth," Ober conjectured.

"But how could they fly the craft that expertly from Earth?" asked Nibin.

"Maybe it was a computer-controlled liftoff," suggested Ferber.

"I don't think so," countered Prota. "I think Adam flew it himself."

They all turned and looked at Prota.

"But he's dead!" explained Rimmer.

Continuing to stare at the departing craft, Prota said, "Maybe, maybe not."

The others turned their gaze back to the diminishing light of the craft's engine until it looked like a giant star hovering high above the horizon.

"I'll be seeing you," Prota said softly.

"What did you say?" Lespin asked.

"'I'll be seeing you.' That's what Adam is saying to us. Seeing the craft disappear looking like a star stimulated the release of another file that Adam gave me. He's telling us, 'I'll be seeing you.'"

They all looked at Prota. He returned their gaze, glancing around the group. "'I'll be seeing you.' That's what he says."

It was a strange body, this air/space vehicle, and it was his only connection to the world outside his mind. The reality hit him: his Adamic body was dead. It had been planned that way, but it still seemed strange. He had flown this craft before with all of the tactile inputs as Adam. Now that body was dead, and he had only the input that came through the sensors of the McCord 983 Defender. It was limited input, such uninteresting data as fuel-to-oxidizer ratio, external surface temperature, and the last time a lube job had been done on the landing gear.

330

He concentrated on the visual image from the rear camera. The only forward image was the radar, a one-dimensional view. The image was blank as he cleared the hill after banking his craft and retracting the landing gear. There were nothing but stars ahead of him; they were infinitely beyond the range of radar.

Flying forward by looking backward was no easy task. He accessed the necessary information from the on-board computer to insert him into lunar orbit. The quickly receding rear image of the Dolphdroids would be indelibly imprinted on his mind. They looked so forlorn, so abandoned – but they were alive! The rescue mission had succeeded. It was finished! He could go home.

He spent the brief time in lunar orbit alternately plotting his burn to put him on a course back to earth and gazing at the lunar surface through the rear camera. Anxiety mounted as he made his final prep for the burn to take him from lunar orbit and send him back to Earth. It had to work, or the craft would be his casket and lunar orbit his graveyard. Much to his relief, the burn went successfully and he settled back for the long journey home.

As the flight progressed, he transitioned from thinking primarily about the Dolphdroids to focusing his thoughts on Ashley, Rob, Randy, Bill, and the others. He thought about sky, trees, wind, and the taste of apple pie. Then his thoughts focused back on the moon. He was leaving the Dolphdroids and the parting brought with it sorrow. The emotional pull between Earth and the moon seemed to coincide with the gravitational battle for his craft, a battle where the lunar pull weakened and Earth's pull grew stronger.

The flight would have seemed much shorter if he could have communicated with Attic Control back on Earth. They must all be anxious to know whether he was alive. Telemetry would have told them and the world that the colony of Dolphdroids was alive. It had to be big news on Earth. It had to be sheer agony for those who loved him, wondering if he was alive or not. His craft's locator had been disarmed after he had left Earth orbit. The only way they would know he was out here between moon and Earth would be if he broke silence, and that he wouldn't do.

It was difficult to predict how the powers-that-be would respond if they knew he was on his way back to Earth. He doubted that they would shoot him down, but the possibility was real enough that he and his team had decided that it wasn't worth taking a chance.

They might think – or use as a cover story – that he was a renegade Dolphdroid bent on revenge. He didn't want to do anything to jeopardize his return to Earth and his reunion with the others.

His heart went out to those waiting in Attic Control at the farm. By now the news sources around the world had surely reported that only one of the lunar colonists had been terminated, and his family and friends would know that the mission was successful. His life-value rating as a human in robotic form had more than covered for the life-value of all the Dolphdroids, who were dolphins in robotic forms. They would know that as Adam he had given his life for the Dolphdroids, but they had no way of knowing that the lifeboat support system had worked, that the Dolphdroids had placed him back aboard the McCord, and that he was flying home.

Living in a dead Dolphdroid body was even stranger than living in a live one. He was receiving all of his external input from the McCord, his only link with the world beyond his mind. The McCord was his new body. Strange, he pondered.

He thought of his other body, lying in suspended animation on earth. Was his human body still alive? Perhaps it had died and had already been buried. The thought was chilling.

Not counting his current incarnation as a spacecraft, he had inhabited two bodies in his lifetime and at this point his Adamic body was dead and he didn't know about his human body. The termination process had caused a complete annihilation of the main circuitry of the humaniform body that had been Adam. The transfer back to his human body had to work, or he would be a disembodied being for the rest of the natural life of his brain.

The days of the journey to earth were filled with such thoughts. Sometimes he slept, and for those times he was thankful, because they afforded him a natural form of suspended animation.

The actual piloting of the craft was controlled by the on-board computer and required little of his attention. Once in Earth orbit, a reentry flight plan that Max had programmed into the computer would bring the craft within several hundred feet of landing. The remaining few hundred feet to touchdown would have to be done by him, using images provided by the McCord's radar. Landing safely would be his big challenge.

Chapter 33

The journey from moon to Earth was a bittersweet transition. Adam already missed Prota, Rimmer, Lespin, Ober, Cosber, and the others. At the same time he was becoming increasingly anxious to see Rob, Randy, Bill, and the rest of the team. Then there was Ashley. He struggled to recall how she looked, talked, acted. He couldn't remember some of the details, and it frustrated him.

He knew the flight was near its end when the on-board computer signaled the McCord to turn around so that the engine faced Earth. Within a few minutes of the maneuver the big burn of the engine began, slowing the craft enough to allow it to be caught by Earth's gravity and pulled into orbit. It was a relief to know the burn had happened; otherwise he would have slingshotted around the Earth and sailed off into certain death in empty space. The canopy was filled with the colors from blue oceans and swirling white clouds as the McCord settled into its orbit with the canopy facing Earth, but Adam was oblivious to the sights as his Adamic body lay in the stillness of death, isolated from all sensations except the input of telemetry from the McCord via the interface.

Following the first orbit the computer fired the engine again, slowing the craft below orbital velocity. After the engine shut down the computer fired the thrusters in various configurations, turning the craft, putting it into a belly-down position and adjusting the attitude for reentry.

When the buffeting of the craft stopped, he knew that the transition from falling to flight was complete, always a welcome moment for a pilot returning from space. He was acutely aware that he was just a passenger, the computer doing all the work. All he could do was wait until the computer slowed the craft's speed by navigating through the normal reentry flight pattern of several large "S" curves. Finally the engine roared to life. The craft had made the transition from a glide to powered flight, and he knew he was near the Earth's surface and close to his destination of the farm.

Adam gave the command to aim the radar toward the ground sooner than he had to, but he couldn't help himself. Finally, telemetry revealing the first detail of what was below him came into his consciousness. It was a meandering line of variable thickness: a river. He had identified his first Earthly object! Straight lines that he quickly identified as roads began to appear. Hundreds of fuzzy items clustered together became visible and he knew they were trees. Scattered small squares and rectangles came into view too; buildings! They were buildings!

A sense of panic came over him. What if he wasn't able to recognize the farm? It was an illogical thought, he realized, because he had viewed a radar monitor and responded to it more times than he could remember. This was different, though. He didn't have the benefit of normal sight. He had to control his feeling of anxiety. Then he remembered the rearview camera, and commanded it to pitch downward, toward the ground. The telemetry gave him the image of the landscape quickly receding. He watched closely. There it was! There was Parkersburg! He had just flown over the town. The computer had him on target. He was in Iowa, and the farm was straight ahead!

He had to remember that the barn was no longer there, that he had left it an inferno with his unorthodox takeoff. He spotted the lake, then the house, the layout of the fields, the lane that was to be his runway!

Taking command of the craft with mind control, he powered down the engine. The McCord's altitude began to drop quickly. He turned 10 degrees to the right, then two back again. There: he was lined up. He gave a thought command to lower the wheels. Then came the confirmation that they were down. Twenty feet from the surface, he powered up the engine. The craft slowed to a safer rate of descent. On the radar he could see movement up ahead: people!

People were coming from the house! Ten feet, five feet, two feet, touchdown of the rear wheels. The wheels hit hard, and the craft bounced momentarily back into the air; then they touched down again and maintained contact with the farm lane. He cut power and the nose wheel touched down. Telemetry told him that the craft was vibrating fiercely. It was no surprise; he was, after all, landing in a cow pasture. The buffeting decreased as he braked. The outlines of the people were clear now; he could identify them by their size, shape, and walk. There was Rob! Yes, he was sure it was Rob. The form next to him looked like Bill. Another form had to be Max. There was a female figure. It was Ashley! They were here to greet him. He was home!

"Let me in there to open the canopy," Max commanded. The others made way for him as they gathered around the craft. He punched in a sequence on the code bar. The steps began to unfold while the canopy moved backward, each action with its unique whirring sound.

"Is he OK?" asked Ashley, clasping her hands tightly.

"Let me see," Risner said, as he lifted his heavy frame up the small ladder. Max grudgingly stepped aside to give him room. Peering into the cockpit, Risner quickly looked over the quiet form of Adam lying in the seat. Then he realized that it had been a silly move. There was no way he could tell anything with Adam still in the cockpit. Obviously his mind was alive, since he had landed the McCord.

A uniformed man marched up to the craft. He carried a pistol and was flanked by two additional officers of lower rank. Bill had informed the local authorities as soon as the McCord had activated its identification device upon reentry. He had also informed the press. There would be plenty of witnesses to Adam's return.

"Get down from there!" ordered the officer, as he drew his weapon.

"Oh, great!" Risner exclaimed as he slowly climbed down the ladder, glancing at Bill with annoyance. It had been Bill's idea to invite the "circus," as he had put it in an earlier discussion in Attic Control. Risner hadn't been in favor of it.

Climbing up for a look and satisfied that Adam was no threat, the officer holstered his weapon and climbed back down. Adjusting his belt, he looked at Risner and said, "We'll need to send out experts of some kind, I'm sure, to make certain this Dolphdroid is dead. And I'm sure they'll have lots of questions. We're trying to determine the right channels we have to go through." It was clear to Bill and the others that the officer was out of his league. He was biding time until the federal and military authorities showed up. Several times he glanced at the cockpit. Bill was certain that the officer was afraid that Adam might suddenly come to life and attack them.

Pandemonium reigned at the Extraterrestrial Research and Resources Center. It had started at the termination event when only one Dolphdroid was terminated instead of the entire colony. A small contingent of the press had been allowed into the control room for the event. All of the identification numbers still glowed green after the event, except for one unit, the prototype. Imus Hartung had explained that the first to "go red," as he put it, would be the prototype named Adam who had somehow managed to activate himself at the Smithsonian West and find his way to the moon. Imus had capitalized on people's fears of a possible lunar attack by the Dolphdroids after Adam's activation and escape. He hinted at a conspiracy, that Adam had human help. Imus fed these fears by inviting representatives from various fringe and extremist groups who, for a variety of reasons, had been against the Dolphdroid colonization. They were to have provided the cheers and other expressions of celebration that the media would broadcast to the world.

Adam's number had gone red, but no others followed. The computer first indicated that all life-value units slated for termination had been terminated. The failure of the termination of the colony other than Adam prompted Imus to ask for a complete analysis of all data from the Adam unit. He fully expected the data to indicate that there was no organic brain tissue, because the dolphin brain that had been interfaced with Adam had died and had been removed. A gasp went up from the crowd when the computer showed that Adam contained a human brain.

It would be months later, while under the influence of several drinks at a cocktail party, that Imus first talked about these events to a few close friends and admitted that it was then, at that very moment, that he had lost all control of the events that would unfold. The letter of the law had been carried out, leaving no process by which the remainder of the Dolphdroids could be terminated. The Christopher/Adam unit had paid the death penalty for all of the others because of its human-value rating of 500. Though he had given it some consideration, Imus quickly realized that it would be impossible for him to implement another termination plan for the colony. News of the heroic and sacrificial act by Dr. Christopher had swung the popular and political opinion in a direction that was clearly pro-Dolphdroid.

Bill Zucker had called a press conference at the farm for a select group of journalists just an hour before Adam's reentry. At Bill's insistence Josh's body, with its cumbersome and bulky suspended animation equipment, had been brought back to the farm. Recognizable images of Dr. Joshua Christopher beneath the slightly frosted glass cover would be splashed across newspapers, newsreaders, web sites and on video media by the end of the day. The reporters scrambled to explain the many facets of the story: Dr. Christopher faking his own death, the disappearance of Adam from the Smithsonian West, the surgery to transfer his brain to the body of Adam, the suspended animation of Dr. Christopher, Adam's trip to the lunar surface, and how his death covered for the death of the lunar colonists. Then there was the unfolding story of the attempt to transfer Josh's brain back into his body.

Two days after the party in which Imus said more than he wanted to say, he sat in his smoke-filled office watching a viewing screen. The reporter, Robert Manford, was trying his best to describe the process of Dr. Christopher's brain being transplanted into the prototype of the Dolphdroids: a unit called Adam, previously housed in the Smithsonian West. The images on the screen flipped back and forth between shots of Dr. Christopher lying in suspended animation, Adam being removed, lifeless, from the airspace vehicle, and the file footage of the Dolphdroid colony. Imus leaned forward, tapped his cigar in the ashtray, leaned back, and placed the cigar back in his mouth. He watched the reporter explain that, unknown to even Dr. Imus Hartung and the rest of the ERR staff, Adam's life-value rating was 500 instead of the three rating for the Dolphdroids. He commented on the intense debate that had been held over the years about the low rating given to the Dolphdroids.

Imus drew heavily on his cigar and exhaled slowly as he slouched in his chair watching the screen. He had argued for a high value for the Dolphdroids until pressure put on him by the Warwick Family forced him to back off. He had always felt guilty for having shifted his position, but what else could he have done? His face showed deeply etched lines of concern as he watched the screen. He was supposed to have been in control of the situation, yet he was little more than a spectator now, like the millions of others who were watching this story unfold. The Warwick Family was very unhappy about his inability to contain the story. They stood to lose in a big way, and he knew they didn't like to lose. For the first time in his 65 years Dr. Imus Hartung deeply feared for his life, and it made him nauseous.

The reporter on the screen, with sun-bleached, short-cropped hair and a beachcomber's tan, went on to explain how the low life-value quotient had actually worked in Dr. Christopher's and the Dolphdroids' favor. He detailed how the termination of Adam, with a human brain, paid the full penalty established months earlier in the termination order.

The newscast switched to another reporter: Jessica Rummer, a slim woman with full lips emphasized by red lipstick, and red hair that was always pulled up into a bun. Standing beside her was Bill Zucker, looking uncomfortable at having been placed in front of a camera. The interviewer asked a question Imus had wondered about since the story broke: how could the brain in Adam, Josh's brain, stay alive even though the body had been terminated? In as simple terms as possible, Bill explained about the small mechanism called a cranial lifeboat that had been installed in Adam's skull to provide life support until his return to Earth. It was fed by extra canisters of water and oxygen that had been positioned in his abdominal cavity.

When asked about the chances of successfully reversing the procedure, Bill became visibly concerned. True, it had never been done before, but, the original surgery had to be done outside the legal borders of the U. S., and that had been successful. There was no law against doing surgery to reverse the process of returning a human brain to its host body, so that procedure could be done in the U.S., where the best equipment and support team could be utilized.

Turning to the camera, Jessica Rummer introduced the next reporter: "And now to James Kurteel in Delta, Ohio. Jim, how does this all play in small town USA?"

Standing in front of a grocery store, the short, heavyset Kurteel, with his ever-present smile introduced his piece, then handed the microphone to various shoppers he had cornered just before going on the air. He was in his element: the upbeat, human interest side of the story was what endeared him to his audience. By the time he finished his report it was obvious that the rescue of the Dolphdroids was playing well with the average citizen, and that Dr. Christopher was something of a folk hero. Kurteel closed by suggesting that the Dolphdroids were no longer the ignored, despised or feared creatures that they had once been; they had gone from demons to darlings.

Imus watched the screen with growing anxiety. The political climate was rapidly changing in favor of the Dolphdroids, thanks to the unbelievable, highly risky rescue effort that Christopher had undertaken and succeeded at. It certainly was endearing him and the Dolphdroids to the general populace. People love a hero, Imus reflected as he snuffed out the stub of a cigar, leaned back in his chair, and closed his eyes. He thought about Emmerson Brunner and how deeply the man was indebted to the Warwick Family. His humaniform robots wouldn't be needed on the moon now, at least not in the foreseeable future. There was no other ready market for them, either. Imus knew that Brunner had no way to pay the large, high-interest loans he owed the Warwick Family. He would die. Imus had a deepening dread that he himself was also a good candidate for cement boots and an unwanted swim in deep water. The Warwicks had counted on him to get rid of the Dolphdroids, and he had failed. He leaned forward and put his elbows on his desk and his head in his hands. He was a condemned man.

Jessica Rummer came back on camera and reported that surgery would be performed within hours to attempt to transfer Dr. Christopher's brain back into his own body. She emphasized the many hurdles involved in the procedure, then introduced a professor from a medical college in the San Francisco area who was an expert in the science of suspended animation. Imus heard none of the details; he was lost in his own dark thoughts.

Kippler came through the swinging doors into the surgery waiting room. Risner jumped to his feet, followed quickly by Rob and Phil Kirkpatrick. Tony Williams, who had been sleeping on a couch, woke up, rubbed his hands through his hair, and stood, too. Ashley remained seated, clutching a wet tissue, her red eyes intent upon Kippler.

Kippler smiled as he glanced at their tense faces. "Don't you folks worry now. He came through the surgery just fine. His vitals are good. His temperature, blood pressure, and heart rate are near normal. We'll be gradually weaning him off the life-support that's running his autonomic systems."

"When will we be able to see him?" Ashley asked.

"In a couple of hours, I suspect. But don't expect to be able to talk to him for several days." Kippler saw their disappointment. "On the other hand, he might be able to understand and respond much sooner than that. These are uncharted waters, as you know."

"That's an understatement," Risner mumbled.

Kippler glanced at the door that led to the lobby. "I understand there's quite a gathering of the press out there. I suppose I'd better tell them what I've just told you. This is a medical first and the press always loves medical firsts." Kippler turned to leave, then looked at Rob. "Your dad is truly a remarkable man, Rob."

Rob nodded. "I know."

Risner and Bill walked toward Josh's room in the Regis Rehabilitation Center. While glancing back to get a second look at an attractive nurse whom they had just passed, Risner said, "So anyway, Ashley called me and said she couldn't get hold of you and that she had something to show us; probably good news about Josh's progress – hope so, anyway. Last time I saw him he was able to say a few simple words and had fair use of his hands, but wasn't able to stand or walk. That was a week ago."

"It's been almost two weeks since I saw him," Bill said. "Since Imus put me in charge of re-establishing a working relationship with the lunar colony, I've had little time to do anything else."

Risner, glancing at Bill, said, "I couldn't believe it when Imus put you in charge of the colony after firing you."

"He didn't have much choice. With public opinion doing a 180, he had to show good faith in the Dolphdroid colony. I suspect when Josh is well enough he'll be put in charge, as he should be. In the meantime, I'll do what needs to be done."

"Just like ol' times," Risner said.

"Just like ol' times," Bill echoed.

"Good grief! Look at that!" Risner exclaimed, stopping and pointing ahead.

Bill looked ahead to see Josh slowly making his way out of his room, leaning on Ashley's arm. She was beaming.

Josh looked at them and smiled broadly. As he continued to walk slowly toward them he said, "It's good to see you guys."

Josh looked weak, even fragile, as he took uneven steps toward them, leaning heavily on Ashley's arm. The three men embraced and Ashley stepped back, tears streaking down her cheeks even as she continued to smile.

During the next two months Josh underwent intensive therapy, with Ashley at his side every day. Between therapy sessions, over coffee in the cafeteria, and while taking walks around the facility's grounds, they discussed wedding plans, laughing like teenagers in love. At the end of three months of therapy Imus asked Josh to return to the pyramid as full-time administrator of lunar operations. Josh insisted that Bill stay on as his administrative assistant, and Imus agreed.

Imus was often the topic of water cooler conversation. He seemed to everyone to be withdrawn. Most days he came late to the pyramid and left early. Emmerson Brunner had been found in a city park, apparently having fallen out of a PAV at high altitude. His death weighed heavily on Imus. He knew the Warwick Family always collected their debts, one way or another. Imus was waiting for what he hoped wouldn't happen. He had escaped prosecution for the attempted termination of the Dolphdroids, his part having been done within the law. Still, he felt like a condemned man, incarcerated by the fear that the Warwick Family would carry out their revenge.

The lunar mining operation was running at about 60% of where it had been before the trouble had begun. Transmission of energy from the solar disk array farm on the lunar surface was back up to full production. Not all the Dolphdroids were enthused about a restored relationship with Earth, but they lacked the organized leadership to put up much resistance. Agur had alienated himself from the majority of his followers by his selfish act of fleeing to the other side of the moon, leaving most of them behind to face termination.

After a month at his new duties in the pyramid, Josh made plans to return to the lunar colony for a short visit. "I have some unfinished business there," he told Ashley. He hitched a ride with the second transport ship to bring back helium-3. He had wanted to be on board the first cargo vessel, but when he discovered that it included a reporter he decided to join the next vessel.

The trip seemed to take forever, but Josh knew it was his impatience at wanting to see the Dolphdroids that was stretching time and miles for him. The big, boxy Craygor cargo vessel was anything but a luxury ride, having been designed to haul cargo, not people.

Eventually the huge craft entered lunar orbit, did its burn, and settled slowly to the landing pad. Dust around the perimeter of the landing pad sprayed outward in streaks as the flames from the five engines licked the concrete. Landing pads touched, and the suspension systems on the craft sagged under the weight of the vessel once the engines shut off, no longer providing lift. Several Dolphdroids who had been standing behind a blast protector at the edge of the landing pad came bounding toward the Craygor, ready to open the cargo doors.

Once the large door lowered to the landing pad surface, forming a ramp, the Craygor crew appeared in the entryway in their environmental suits, their anxious faces hidden behind the reflective surface of their helmet shields. They paused a moment, then walked down the ramp toward the Dolphdroids who waited for them at the bottom. The first vessel had encountered no problems with the Dolphdroids. This crew expected things to go well, but you never knew for certain. There was relief among the crew when one of the three Dolphdroids extended his hand in greeting. The Dolphdroids and crew spent a few moments extending greetings by shaking hands; then they all began unloading the supplies from the cargo bay onto a lunar surface transport vehicle. Once loaded, the vehicle made its way to the storage facility where they would be unloaded. The Craygor's crew bounded along with the Dolphdroids on foot, following the transport vehicle.

When everyone was gone, a lone figure in an environmental suit appeared in the opening of the cargo bay. Josh had kept his trip to the moon quiet, with few on Earth knowing about it. The crew of the Craygor had been instructed to remain silent about his presence. He hoped his message had been received by Prota and that his friends were waiting to meet him.

Frustration glowed on Prota's face as he tried to explain. "All I know is that I received instructions from Earth that all of us were to gather here after the arrival of the second transport. I was also told to bring a supply of oxygen and nutrient/water." He pointed to the tray of tubes at his feet.

"And you don't know why?" asked Rimmer.

"I think he's made that clear," Ober said, looking at Rimmer.

"Listen," Cosber said, loudly enough to quiet the grumbling and complaining. "We've got to start getting along better. This is ridiculous. After all that Adam's done for us, the least we can do is get along. We have a second chance."

"Part of me wants to believe that Adam isn't dead, that he's alive." It was Nibin talking. "I want to believe that he and our creator, Dr. Christopher, are one and the same. Do you think it's true? The news reports, images of a dead Adam and of Dr. Christopher alive could have all been faked. How do we know the whole episode of Adam's getting back to Earth and the transfer of his mind back into Dr. Christopher isn't a hoax? I wish we had some proof."

"How can anyone prove it to us?" Prota responded. "They've done about all they can. We can either believe or not believe. The choice is up to us."

The attention of the Dolphdroids who faced the stairs was captivated by something. The others turned to look. A human figure in an environmental suit was coming down the stairs. It was a new suit, pristine white. The helmet, like those of every human who worked in space, had the gold protective tint that kept its human inhabitant from being blinded by the sun. A couple of the eleven had worked with the crew from the first vessel that had arrived several days earlier, but for the rest this was their first contact with a human since the problems with Earth had begun.

"Greetings," the figure said as he came toward them. "Good to see you, Prota," he said, extending his hand to the surprised Dolphdroid. He moved around the group, greeting each by name.

He glanced down at the tray of tubes near Prota, bent over – an awkward move in the stiff and bulky suit – and picked up a tube of oxygen and one of nutrient/water. He extended the oxygen tube to Prota and said, "Take some, just a little, and pass it on, so everyone can have some."

Prota's face turned darker gray, reflecting a momentary sense of confusion and bewilderment about why he should replenish himself with such a small portion so as to leave enough to go around. Suddenly Prota's face glowed green with surprise. "Adam?"

All the faces quickly glowed green with surprise, then to yellow with joy.

"Is it really you, Adam?" asked Cosber.

"Yes," the visitor replied, turning so his back was to the brilliant sun and reaching for a control on his chest pack that caused the gold tint to fade, leaving the helmet transparent. The face of a man appeared – a middle-aged man with slight wrinkles at the corners of his eyes and at the sides of his mouth. He had tousled gray hair and blue eyes. He was smiling. It was the familiar image they had seen broadcast from Earth in recent weeks on news reports: the image of the one who had created them.

"It's Joshua Christopher," whispered Rimmer. Josh smiled. Silence filled the room for a few moments as the Dolphdroids grappled with what they were seeing.

Finally Prota spoke. "Then it's true."

"I want you to finish sharing the tubes," Josh said.

Silence returned as first the oxygen tube and then the nutrient/water tube were passed from one Dolphdroid to another.

When Nibin, standing to Josh's left and the last to partake, had finished with the nutrient/water tube, he passed it to Josh.

Josh slowly looked around the group, then began to speak. "I'm the one who gave you life, and I'm the one who gave you life again. I became one of you so that in my dying you might live."

For the next three hours, until the cargo vessel was set to depart, Josh talked with the eleven. He answered as many of their questions as he could. Then they followed him from the commissary module to the landing pad where the crew of the Craygor was going through their preflight routine, preparing for the trip back to Earth. He had only a few minutes left.

"You have a new lease on life now," Josh said to the circle of eleven gathered around him. "This is still a fallen world, but you can make a difference. Follow the Contract of Life that was given to you at the beginning."

"Why don't you stay here with us, at least for a while longer?" asked Rimmer. "It's not going to be easy for us. It would save us a lot of grief if you'd stick around."

Josh smiled; he was in the shadow of the Craygor and had his helmet tint turned off. The internal illumination of the helmet allowed them to see his face clearly. "There are a few of the colonists who don't believe that Adam and I are one and the same."

"But who better to convince them than you?" argued Rimmer.

"You!" Josh said. "You can convince them. Facts can coerce, but they often don't convince. Convictions are built on faith as much as on fact. By your example, living the way you were designed to live, you'll show the others a better way. Having me around wouldn't be an advantage for you or the others."

"Then take us with you," Ober pleaded.

"No," Josh replied. "I'm not going to take you away from the struggles that are part of life here, but I'll make certain you have all you need to live with the struggles." Josh paused for a moment. "It's best for me to go and for you to stay. You need to be able to express your love and obedience for me in freedom. If I were always here to give you guidance, instant answers, and unmistakable assurance, you'd never grow as you should. I need to give you room to do your own thinking, struggling with choices, affirming faith in the face of doubts, and expressing hope when things look hopeless."

The commander of the Craygor stood at the entry to the cargo vessel. It was time to leave. Josh looked at the eleven. Their faces glowed purple with grief. "I'll keep in touch." With those words, Josh turned and walked up the ramp. He paused and turned toward them. The ramp was raised, slowly concealing Josh from their view: first his legs, then torso, then his head. A light beside the door flashed green. It was securely closed.

Within a minute the Craygor was only a bright set of exhaust plumes that looked like a pair of giant stars in the black sky. The eleven stood watching until the plumes were no brighter than the surrounding stars.

"Let's go," Prota said. "We have work to do." They turned and headed back toward the colony, their forms casting shadows that bent and moved to conform to the uneven surfaces of the small craters and rocks they passed.

"It was not because of any good deed that we ourselves had done, but because of his own mercy that he saved us..."
Titus 3:15
from *Today's English Version* of the Bible

Made in the USA
Charleston, SC
19 October 2012